ONTHEROCKS

ON the ROCKS

THE KGB BAR FICTION ANTHOLOGY

edited by rebecca donner | foreword by denis woychuk

ST. MARTIN'S GRIFFIN
NEW YORK

www.stmartins.com

Book design by Jonathan Bennett

See page 281 for individual story permissions.

ISBN 0-312-30152-9

First Edition: November 2002

10 9 8 7 6 5 4 3 2 1

CONTENTS

EDITOR'S ACKNOWLEDGMENTS

I would like to express my thanks to all of the authors who have appeared at KGB and provided me with the pleasure of hearing their work, and to Denis Woychuk and Melvin Jules Bukiet for giving me this rare opportunity. Over the past four years I've been lucky to work with two partners, Jonathan Wei and, more recently, Emily Chenoweth, whose impeccable judgment and camaraderie have made running the fiction series a rewarding experience.

I'd also like to acknowledge James Clarke, Neal Donner, Ken Foster, Erich Gleber, Gordon Haber, and Sean Rocha for their advice and guidance in the production of this book.

Thanks to St. Martin's Press, to Emily Kirsch and especially Julia Pastore, who made this book possible.

And finally, I owe a special debt of gratitude to Julie Barer for her tireless persistence and wise counsel.

FOREWORD
by
DENIS WOYCHUK
Founder of KGB

———————

I'VE BEEN ASKED BY THE PUBLISHER OF THIS ANTHOLOGY, KGB'S third and latest, to tell the story of the KGB Bar and how it came to be.

When I was a small boy growing up in Brooklyn, my father took me regularly to visit his haunts in Manhattan. We got off the D train at West Fourth Street and Sixth Avenue and walked east, past Washington Square Park and NYU, past Lafayette Street, past the two gas stations at Bowery and East Fourth, and into the heart of the most Ukrainian neighborhood in New York, the Lower East Side. In those days the neighborhood was seedy and tough. It would be years before the "East Village" was invented by enterprising real estate agents who convinced the world that everything north of Houston Street, south of Fourteenth Street, and east of the Bowery was a very special place, but I knew it already.

On Sundays we went to a place called the Ukrainian Labor Home, a social club for Ukrainian socialists, a little building at 85 East Fourth Street (to call it a townhouse would be pushing it). The single large room on the first floor was known as the "Great Hall" where they held their banquets, dances, and parties; and above that, hidden away on the second floor, was their own private speakeasy. There were no posters of the great Soviet revolution, no photos of the politburo, no propaganda whatsoever visible anywhere—all that was hidden away in a double-locked room on the fourth floor because these people had been subject to McCarthy's feverish persecutions and they didn't want to advertise their political sympathies.

On Sundays in the Great Hall there was a dance class for children just a little older than I—I was about five at this time—who dressed in folk costumes from the old country and pranced around to an accordion. Did I want to join them? No, I did not. The room was twenty-five feet wide and one hundred feet long, larger than any room I'd ever seen before, and the sheer size of it gave me vertigo. Rather than dance lessons, I preferred the company of my father's cronies in the intimacy of their private club one flight up. There, we drank. (Yes, *we* drank.) Formerly a Lucky Luciano joint called the Palm Casino, the bar was built during prohibition well before the membership of the Ukrainian Labor Home bought the place in 1948. This was the members' true domain, and my dad and his pals set themselves up with shots of whiskey, vodka, Four Roses, or whatever—with a little shot for me. I tried to drink it down without spitting it up while the men laughed. We had a good time.

Years later, my father moved to East Tenth Street. I stayed with my mother in Brooklyn, and for a while, I lost touch with my father's friends. It wasn't until much later, when I was teaching writing at Pratt Institute and putting myself through school at Fordham Law, that I began stopping by the old neighborhood again. The boom-boom 1980s were upon us; the East Village was a hotbed of artistic activity. Age had taken its toll, and the members of the Ukrainian Labor Home were past feasts and big parties. Now they needed money, so they offered me the Great Hall, where I'd watched the children dance, to use as an art gallery. Law was practical, a means to make it to the middle class, but the arts was where my heart lived. And so, the Kraine Gallery was born. We did exhibitions by day and soon thereafter theater at night to help with the cash flow. I ran operations by telephone from my law office on Park Avenue, and the old men kept the bar. They weren't *that* old—pushing eighty or so—and they could still drink. The bar had a little kitchen belonging to the old men's wives, and on Friday nights I dined with my artist friends on pierogi and three-bean salad, maybe a little pot roast or some kapusniak, served by these little old Ukrainian ladies who made everything by hand. All told, a four-course meal with a shot of vodka cost five dollars. Even artists could afford that. And if you left seventy-five cents or a dollar on the table one of these sweet old things would chase you down with a shout, "Hey Mister, you forgot your money on the table!"

In the early '90s, the membership of the Ukrainian Labor Home had grown too old to continue their little bar/restaurant and the operation closed. By then I'd established myself in the public interest area of psychiatric law and had an office at a maximum security hospital for the dangerously mentally ill where I represented patients' rights. My gallery was out of business, in large part due to the stock market crash in 1987 and the subsequent disappearance of most of the galleries in the East Village. The bar was available, and although my Ukrainian grandfather was a successful bootlegger back in the '20s, I myself knew nothing about the bar business. I asked for advice and one of the first bits I got was, "Don't open a bar on the second floor. They go bankrupt." I was never much for free advice, and with a little help from friends going back as far as junior high school (I sold them a 49 percent interest), I got ready to open the bar for business.

But what do you call a place that's almost impossible to find without special knowledge or a guide, a place with a history of left-wing radicalism, which I intended to establish as a legitimate counterculture venue? "KGB" seemed to be the obvious choice. I called the Department of State in Albany and told them I wanted to register a new corporation. "KGB!" the clerk on the line replied. "You can't call a corporation KGB, not in New York State. Not KGB, FBI, CIA, or even GAY. You can't just pick a name out of a hat. You have to justify, give a good reason for whatever name you choose." He was wrong as a matter of law, but you don't argue with clerks at the Department of State. "Okay," I said. "I want to call it Kraine Gallery Bar, after my gallery of the same name." "That you can do," he replied reluctantly. And so Kraine Gallery Bar, d/b/a KGB Bar, was legally born.

A business's first obligation is to survive, and the first year we were barely meeting that obligation. Potential patrons could not find the place—we had only the tiniest sign—the first manager was suspected of embezzling and revenues were low. When I hired Dan Christian, someone who actually understood the bar business, as bar manager, things began to run more smoothly, freeing me up to con-spire with my partner, Melvin Bukiet, about what to make of our diamond-in-the-rough. We were both writers. I had published a couple of books for little kids, and he a bunch of novels, and we looked at each other over our drinks and it was clear: we wanted writers. Writers who would come and read their work for no pay but a few free drinks. The readings would be free to the public. Drinking would be encouraged but not required.

We booked Frank Browning for our very first reading in the sum-mer of 1994. Somehow the *New York Times* heard about it, sent a reporter and photographer, and that week ran an article about the new reading series at KGB. Melvin posted signs at Columbia Uni-versity: CURATOR WANTED FOR NEW READING SERIES—NO PAY, BIG PRESTIGE.

We were barraged with offers, and KGB has been rocking along ever since. Its obscure location turned out to be more of an asset than a hindrance, operating as a kind of velvet rope for the unini-tiated. We didn't even bother to put up a real sign until 2000—seven years after we opened.

Rebecca Donner, our editor, has done a magnificent job of pulling together some of the best material we've had at the bar during her four-year tenure as curator, and I want to thank her. I also want to thank Em-ily Chenoweth, who has joined us more recently but shares with Re-becca the responsibilities for keeping the Sunday fiction series running hot. I want to thank my partner Melvin, who, despite his modest pecu-niary interest in the bar's activities, has loomed large in KGB's literary scene. I credit him as an equal in creating the literary venue at KGB when it was just a couple of guys sitting at a bar speculating over drinks. I also want to thank Carla Sarr and Ed Sukman, my remaining partners; my bar staff Dan Christian, Johnny De Mastri, Jennifer Price, and Kim Savage for offering drinks and bartender's therapy to our many patrons; Eriz Zev, who has done a fine job managing both the Kraine and Red Room Theaters; and our participating writers and patrons for making the community that has become the KGB Bar.

INTRODUCTION
by
REBECCA DONNER

COMMUNISM IS DEAD, BUT IF YOU ASCEND THE STAIRS OF A CERTAIN four-story red-brick tenement building in New York's East Village, you might think otherwise. Turn right at the second floor and enter KGB, a small bar whose crimson walls display a photograph of Brezhnev, a sculpture of Lenin, a red-and-white hammer-and-sickle flag, and yes, even a balalaika. Russian socialists held clandestine meetings here a half-century ago, back when a group of Ukrainian émigrés established the building as the Ukrainian Labor Home. But today, the comrades are gone, replaced by bibliophiles and musicians, aspiring and seasoned writers, editors and agents, East Village locals and Brooklynites, who assemble here every Sunday night for literary readings; all that remains of the room's erstwhile function is the Kremlin kitsch.

The advancements of fin de siècle capitalism, however, are not immediately apparent. The toilets are always breaking down. The author's podium is splintered and requires a matchbook underneath the left leg to stabilize it. The podium light is missing a few screws, causing it to swing upward into the author's face; as a remedy, three cardboard beer coasters have been scotch-taped to the brass rim to prevent glare and squinting. A window on the south wall is cracked open (the small room is stuffy and needs air), and the hubbub from the street below—police car sirens, a passing motorcycle, shouts and laughter issuing from the bar across the street—is distinctly audible. Now and then sound filters in from a play produced in the theaters on the first and third floors of the building, making for unanticipated and sometimes felicitous juxtapositions: one night, when an author reached the dramatic denouement in a scene from her novel involving a hippie mom and her resentful daughter, the muted chorus of "The Age of Aquarius" could be heard through the floorboards.

You cannot expect a grand entrance if you are an author who has been invited to read your work at KGB. Once introduced, amid the applause, you must poke and nudge your way through the crowd to the podium at the far end of the room; then, you must deftly step over an electric cord that extends from the podium light to the outlet behind the bar to avoid an embarrassing fall. If you are in the audience, you must sit on rickety wooden chairs crammed around little tables, or on the rusted metal folding chairs hauled out when the rickety wooden ones have all been occupied—or, as is often the case in the cramped room, you must stand in the hallway or even down the narrow staircase, posing a fire hazard. Notwithstanding these inconveniences, KGB's popularity has steadily risen, ever since the bar hosted its first reading in 1994. *New York* magazine named KGB "Best Reading Series," National Public Radio devoted a segment to KGB and its literary cachet, as have lengthy articles in the *New York Times*, the *Wall Street Journal*, and other publications.

True to the collectivist ideals of the building's former inhabitants, KGB readings are free—there is no admission charge, no minimum number of drinks one must consume in order to sit (or stand) and watch the authors read their work. The curator of the readings is not paid, nor are the authors. Still, some of the most celebrated authors of contemporary literature have ascended the narrow stair-case to the splintered podium. That KGB manages to attract them is all the more remarkable in a city where a good number of excel-lent literary venues do pay stipends and honoraria to notable au-thors. KGB also prides itself on its reputation for featuring talented newcomers, who appear with debut novels in hand or, on occasion, with unpublished novels or stories.

Soon after I became curator of the fiction series in 1998, a member of the audience—an author who happened to be visiting from Chicago—asked me why KGB was so popular. It was a question I have since been asked again and again, and my response then, I must confess, was just as inadequate as it has been on subsequent nights. I can't say I recall every word, but I do remember saying something about the "special" atmosphere at KGB, inwardly shuddering at my Hallmark-y choice of adjectives. On other nights, I've launched into a tedious, lengthy disquisition on the subject of live readings, claiming that their veritable renaissance in the past decade has given birth to or perhaps reinforced the notion of the "author-as-performer," and that the communal aspect of such events (ever apparent, ha ha, at a Commie theme bar) fosters a lively exchange between readers and writers, which has in subtle and not-so-subtle ways changed the very act of reading and indeed of writing. One night, in one of my most shamefully inarticulate moments, I responded to the question with a mystified shrug. Minutes later, after the music had shut off and a hush had fallen over the crowd, I stepped up to the podium to introduce the first author, who had flown in from California earlier that afternoon to read from his novel. He produced an airline "barf bag," upon which he had scribbled a short story, and the audience responded with hoots and applause, one woman shouting teasingly that she hoped the packaging didn't bear any relationship to its contents.

The incident was an apt illustration of KGB's appeal to authors and audience members alike. KGB punctures literary pretensions of bookish authenticity; it is no place for the stuffy and the staid, for aesthetes unreceptive to work that breaks from convention. Authors often try out new material and read from works-in-progress here, which can be a risky affair in some settings. The smoky, dimly lit room offers a safe haven to those who stand behind the splintered podium and to those who come to bear witness to the event; here is a celebration of all things unvarnished and rough-at-the-edges, of the audacious, new, and unrehearsed. As one author put it, scrawled in the signed copy of his novel that he'd given me after his reading:

"KGB is the only place I've read my work where I didn't feel like a fucking pariah!"

This anthology compiles stories from some of the authors who have read their work at KGB over the past few years—young newcomers seeking to break new ground in literary fiction, as well as renowned authors whose celebrated work continues to evolve. In featuring both categories I have attempted to capture a range of voices in contemporary fiction. Some have contributed stories previously published in literary magazines, from the well- to little-known; some present new, unpublished work. Two of the contributors, Max Ludington and Karen McKinnon, made their literary debuts at KGB with the stories in this anthology, and went on to sell their novels. There are many fine authors, I hasten to add, whose work I regretfully could not include in this book due to length limitations, contractual problems, and so on; such is the difficulty of assembling an anthology.

These stories, in one sense or another, embody the spirit of KGB, a place where risk is celebrated and boundaries are transcended. In "Mortality Check," Philip Gourevitch, best known for his award-winning nonfiction, crosses genres and demonstrates his considerable talent for fiction. Similarly, Thom Jones defies one's expectations for characters macho and pugilistic in "Thorazine Johnny Felsun Loves Me," inhabiting the point of view of a hapless teenage girl. Francine Prose's noir-cum-realist story "The Witch" toys with expectations inscribed in both genres, in what amounts to a sustained and suspenseful duck-and-feint maneuvering.

The stories are diverse, widely different in tone, content, and narrative strategy. The dense, hard-bitten prose of Karen McKinnon's "Kindred" exhibits the compressed precision of poetry. Judy Budnitz's whimsical gem, "Hook, Line and Sinker," is characterized by a pared-down, minimalist simplicity; while others, like Dale Peck's "Cities of the Plain" and Jason Brown's "She," have an expansive reach, evoking a rich and vivid sense of community. Stories firmly rooted in the realist tradition stand alongside stories so inventive they defy categorization: Sylvia Foley's "y's story," an imaginative tour-de-force, features a letter of the alphabet as its protagonist; and Ben Marcus's virtuosic "The Least You Need to Know About Radio," manages to invent meaning while simultaneously dismantling it.

In compiling this anthology of KGB authors I did not have any particular theme or exclusionary rubric in mind. These stories were selected on the basis of one simple criterion: they moved me. Nevertheless, certain thematic or contextual leitmotivs, entirely unanticipated, can be discerned (such is the delight in assembling an anthology). Motherhood, with its attendant tribulations, is explored in the sensuous, meticulously rendered prose of Victoria Redel's "He's Back"; in Aimee Bender's "Dearth," a fanciful magical-realist tale of a woman and her potato-brethren; and in "Plane Crash Theory," Dani Shapiro's graceful and poignant account of a mother and her injured infant son. The impact of a parent's death resonates, however elusively, in Mary Gaitskill's "Dream of Men" and Elizabeth Tippens's "Make a Wish," although the emotional terrain each story inhabits is starkly different. Two stories compellingly limn the effects of a childhood friendship gone awry, Jonathan Lethem's "Planet Big Zero" and Victor LaValle's "Getting Paid." One story's protagonist is a celebrated writer (Joyce Carol Oates's "In Hiding"), another is a lesser-known writer (Peter Ho Davies's "What You Know"), both of whom are forced by unforeseen circumstance to examine more closely their personal motivations. And two stories feature drifters: Max Ludington's "Thaw" is a penetrating portrait of a character seduced by competing desires, and David Gates's "George Lassos Moon" features a ne'er-do-well-who-means-well protagonist so winningly portrayed that he breaks your heart.

This anthology offers a glimpse of what I've experienced in the four years I've sat on the barstool adjacent to the podium and listened to authors read their work. Though it is impossible to replicate the experience of a live reading, I hope these stories will capture some of the vitality of a night at KGB. So take a seat, as it were, in the front row. The music has shut off, and a hush has fallen over the crowd. May you be moved by every one as I have.

ONtheROCKS

HE'S BACK
by
VICTORIA REDEL

HE FOUND HER WITH THE BOY, THE TUB WATER BLUED AROUND THEM, so that he knew just how long they had been there, soaping and soaping at each other, the boy wearing sudsy breasts and slipping over her arms or sloped against her while she turned the frilled pages of some wet book and the boy, skulling and fluttering, finned against her and said, "He's back."

Not for long.

Not for long would he stand for it, the shed in that tub: hair and skin in pages, the boy's boats, all of her soaps, a creamy gray outline that lapped over them when they moved. And all that movement, her leg lifting from the water, the boy's dunking head, pointed toes, the watery swash of tits—not for long—not for long—or the way sometimes they pretended to have been asleep, and did he have to be so noisy? she asked, winking up at him, walking in that way he walked in whenever he came back.

He could be quiet.

Wasn't that the truth, walking in on them, midday in that tub, the boy looking up from where he knelt over her, his fingers doing a lacy thing on her throat.

No, they were not asleep. Not in the midday light or not in the evenings when she posted candles about the room, so that he walked in to where they glowed up at him from in the tub.

That was not sleep.

He would not have the chance to waken them. Not ever. That was also for certain truth. Look at the boy. He could barely lie still, let alone drift to sleep, fishing about with her in that water, flipping and flipping, casting his leg over her leg, smearing her clay masks in jagged lines over his cheek. They could barely get the boy to sleep at any hour, walking, it seemed, all night to him with the one last waking thing he needed.

Quiet, he could be quiet. She should better, at the least, know that by now.

They did not even have to be in the water. It was everywhere. The water, the water, overflowed, left murky in the tub, drips, towels dropped in hallways, a trek of powder footprints to where he found her with the boy painting all those toenails some crazy shade of red.

"Look at my boy," he said, and they glanced up at him, the two of them looking as if they had never seen him before.

As if they had never seen him before!

What did they take him for?

Wherever they were, he knew, he just knew, they were lying in wait, the boy shouting before he had even gotten into the room, "You too! You too!! Take off your shoes!"

He had done that and he would not do it again, letting her paint him red or suffering the lip outliner and clip-on earrings. What kind of clown did they take him for, smeary smile and rouged-up cheeks, just what did they take him for?

He would take them. What would they think of that, taking them out of those rooms and onto the street where she would have to see how others went about with their boys—buttoned up, in coats, in hand?

Forget about her.

He would just take the boy, and to a dry place, sawdust on the floors, meat crisp on bones.

The boy said, "Yes, I'd like that."

The boy said he wanted it juicy, pink, cut off the bone, with a drink that bubbled. He ordered the boy a malted.

———

A frog's mouth, that's what the boy said the mother looked like when the hair parted.

Not to look—that is what he told the boy.

"At what?" she asked, coming in, stopping in front of an oval mirror to dot and blend something creamy and pink under her eyes.

He wanted to tell the boy how still worse was the gawk of those lips when the boy's own head had pushed out. Now that was a sight not to be seen. And he had almost done it, squinting down to the blur so as almost not to see anything. But still, it was all too much seen, the stretched-open wreck of her, pulled to tearing, the way her face stretched out, too, all red and ugly with effort and, after all of it—bloody water, bloody shit, bloody head—after all was too much seen, the doctor waving him over, saying, "Oh, I know your type. So come on. Come right here. Get ready to catch it."

But he had seen it, the boy had, and that was her doing, she was no doubt letting him look at the whole thing, holding nothing back from the boy, flaps and hood and clasp, no doubt going ahead and telling the boy what everything was called. Where else would the boy have learned? Not from him, God knows. God knows there was hardly a moment she would let him have alone with the boy, always her with some urgent need, calling the boy back to tuck a loose strand of hair behind his ear, having to have to give the boy another, extra, one last before-bed special kiss and then, no doubt, another three at least.

No he had found her with the boy in the plain light of day, the boy bobbing about in her scented water and the boy announcing with not the least fear that she had a *my giant,* and her laughing, winking up at him, saying wasn't the boy so smart about everything, learning everything faster than she could find what to teach him.

So smart?

He would show them smart.

He would teach them both a thing or two.

They were not anywhere.

There was water, of course, water everywhere, damn near a flood he had walked in on, coming home just in time, he thought, to save the goddamn house at least. A wreck, that's how it looked, everywhere water, and dirty damn water, too, the way she left all the rooms week by week to collect dust. Not a chance could he have to say anything about it, her throwing him such a goddamn look if he so much as mentioned cleaning.

"If you want a maid, get a maid," she said.

Thank God he had come when he had.

Just in time to save the goddamn house from drowning.

What was she thinking? What was she possibly thinking? What could she be thinking going out like that? Not some few drips. Not some leaky faucet. Nothing less than running the tub was. What was it with her? And couldn't he just see already how it would be, her coming home from who-knows-where, and without a word to say about anything. Hardly so much as a glance she'd have for him after all he had been through, buckets and buckets, wringing the mop not twenty, not one hundred times with her dust water, her dirt water, picking out bits of her hair, her strings and feathers—from what? feathers?—but, yes, picking feathers out from the mop. And those towels. Impossibly heavy, those towels of hers, clumped all in a wet, dirty clump—he had a mind to throw them out once and for all, those towels, better than break his back, heaving and wringing those towels. He was surprised at that, that she hadn't even the mind to think of those precious towels. God knows it seemed sometimes they were all she did have a mind about. Certainly they were all she managed to clean, with her particular way of folding them, snatching his towel out from him before he was halfway dry and folding it in threes as if he didn't know by now that threes was the way she wanted it done. Her way, oh yes, that she could be bothered by. But shutting off the faucet? She could not be bothered by that, could she? And hot water at that. His ankles scalded in her water. Let it drown, he thought. Might as well for all she'd notice. She'd just be there with a stack of new towels, walking around a new set of rooms.

The boy was not any better. What could you expect? Spending his days with her and her soaps and her towels.

The boy probably thought it was just fine, fishing about like some swishy thing. But what did she think, that it was okay for a kid to spend his days puckered and gilled and bloated with water?

Or did she think at all? Certainly not if this flooded-out house was any indication of her level of thought.

Thinking or not, she had better get ready.

He would tell her as soon as she walked in the door.

When was she walking in? And just where was she? Down to the store for new perfume or whatnot, certainly not for anything to eat. My God, she barely ate a thing if they couldn't eat it right in the tub with them. Soggy cardboard, he had picked up plenty of that shit in his day.

He was nobody's maid. Nobody's mop-it-up maid, he sure as hell wasn't. She had better know that by now. He would let her know that. He would let her have it as soon as she walked in. It would be soon, too. How could she survive out on those streets one minute, a regular fish out of water out there, her practically shredding her clothes before she had even gotten through the front door?

He would find the right kind of maid, all right.

Yes, he would.

He would find a sweet one. He would go out and find the boy a real sweet one. He would find one who scarcely needed all those lotions she was always smushing on herself. The boy would like that. He was no fool, that boy. He would see the difference soon enough. It might take a bit, time enough to dry out that water-logged brain of his, but he would see the difference soon enough.

He would let that froggy see some real lips.

Oh yes, she would be back soon. With that boy of hers.

She came back wet.

The boy, too.

She came back wet and without a towel or a lotion or any of the oily sweet smells he thought she had gone out to get. She came back wet and late and the boy pressed wetly to her. She peeled the boy from her, laid him down in the tub and ran the water.

He slept.

She stripped out of her wet dress and underthings without so much as giving him a nod, not to mention a decent hello, not to mention the flimsy explanation he had expected from her at the very least.

The boy stirred in the tub, lapping thinly from side to side like the too thin twig of a child she had made of him. Anyone could see that, that the boy had barely anything to him. He was all stick. She had made sure of that, hadn't she—never taking the boy out to a park where he might run a bit with other boys. No, there was not even the name of a single boy that he could name. There was not one single boy for the boy. She had made sure of that, hadn't she, keeping the child home without even the pretext of his having a cold.

She ran it hot, the tub.

Without so much as a nod, she had come back.

What was she thinking?

Wasn't it he that had come back just in time?

He had eyes. He could see everything right down to the pucker of skin that hung unevenly. Wasn't it his evening that had passed mopping up her mess? Wasn't he the one who had, in the end, eaten a dinner of toast and cereal and a glass of warm milk? Let alone the nod, how about a simple turn of her head to show him that she could feel him looking at her. Look at her, without even panties left on, bending over the tub, the seam of her ass curving down on where her legs opened. Without so much as a nod or a glance to say that any of it was for him, the way she bent down lower to finger the water and the pucker broken just a nibble open.

Come on! The house, the boy, the split of her legs, wasn't any of it his, too?

Imagine it, her bending over herself with a blade of some kind, getting at all of it, cutting it down to what she had cut it down to.

And where would the boy have been? Was that really even a question? No doubt right there, right beside her, where the boy always was, watching her shave or cut or whatever at it.

Or, imagine this—the boy down in the tub looking up at her cutting it. The boy was probably right there, down in the tub looking right up at it, her one leg lifted up on the tub lip so that she could get at it all with the blade. Just imagine the boy watching the hairs dropping and sticking on the sides of the tub.

What was she thinking, he would like to know. She was not thinking about him, he could bet on that. She had not so much as asked him if he would like it—her all shaved down to look like some kind of girl again. Who was she trying to fool?

She might be able to fool some fool of a kid, but please, that was about it.

Those old wrinkled lips.

Please! He had seen it all stretched out.

There was no forgetting that.

He would tell the boy.

He would just walk right up behind her and get what was properly his.

It was his.

He would take it properly, all right.

Isn't this what she was asking for?

For him to do his job. Tell the boy what and how it was. Then have her—the old way.

Yes sir, he was back.

MORTALITY CHECK
by
PHILIP GOUREVITCH

THEY GOT KRETZKY COMING OUT OF THE LIQUOR STORE. TWO MEN, one blade, a sunny crowded street—he walked right into it. Three steps down the sidewalk he realized he'd stopped moving. Someone behind him held his wrist and a hand appeared before him, flashing a glimpse of steel. A skinny little white guy stood there in a limp, powder-blue sweat suit, not a person whom Kretzky, a big white guy in a black leather jacket, would have thought to fear. The man had hair the color of a nicotine stain, cut like a terrier's, and his face was red and pinched. He told Kretzky to shut up. Kretzky hadn't said a word.

The man's weapon was no longer than four inches. It looked almost dainty, cradled in his folded hand, the blade flat between his third and fourth fingers. But retract the hand into a fist, punch and twist, and Kretzky considered the prospect of survival was not good.

The mugger's eyes were all pupil, ticking from side to side in minute increments. Kretzky felt them on his chest, his groin, his throat, the bridge of his nose.

The hand of someone he couldn't see squeezed suddenly between his legs. Kretzky's guts constricted. He stumbled a half-step forward and felt his wallet slip from his rear pocket, his sack of liquor lifted from his fingers. He straightened up. The man before him jerked his hand up in a sharp salute, and Kretsky saw that what he had there was, in fact, a comb. The mugger swept it back across his scalp, grinned, and ran.

There had been time enough for Kretzky to grab his mugger, but

Kretzky had never been able to count on his reflexes. He turned around. The comb-man's accomplice was also gone. The pedestrian traffic continued, as it had throughout the dozen or so seconds of the crime, jockeying along the sidewalk.

It was a splendid early April afternoon, cold and crackling with flashbulb fluorescence, that polar New York light that Kretzky loved, careening down around him—light that made even the trash look new and swift and full of promise.

"Hey," Kretzky said. He thought he saw the blue sweat suit crossing the street several blocks away. "Hey you." He pulled his wedding band off and held it up. "Hey," he said. "You forgot this."

He found himself standing in the path of an oncoming woman in a short black plastic coat and purple tights. He held the gold ring out to her and smiled. Her green eyes appeared to darken in annoyance. She steered wide of him, clutching her collar tight at her throat.

"Have heart," Kretzky said. "I'm the victim here."

It struck him that he did not sound credible. He turned after the woman and saw the backs of three short black plastic coats with purple tights.

His chest was wet with sweat, and his temples throbbed. He had his jacket halfway off his shoulders and was trying to determine how to sit down on the edge of the curb between two parked cars when darkness ascended like a film from beneath the limits of his vision. The curb came up to meet him, and as he fell, a car alarm detonated—inside his skull, it seemed.

Kretzky had fainted before. The previous summer, on his honeymoon, in Valence in the Provence, he had sat on a café terrace with his wife, Erika, and watched as an antique biplane returning from an air show crashed into a water tower. A shout came from inside the café, and a man hurried into the street, where he stumbled, lost his balance, and fell forward on his knees. Events began to appear to Kretzky as if in slow motion. The man's head smacked into a cement planter holding geraniums. He was a mean-looking, drunken man in a gray suit, carrying a plastic briefcase, and he took the corner of the planter in the center of his forehead. When he sat back up, blood lined his face and pooled behind his glasses, which had survived the fall in place and unbroken. Kretzky believed he saw a bristling eyebrow torn and dangling over the man's nose, and he felt the sweat start running down his chest.

In the distance, smoke poured into the sky. Kretzky told Erika to go pay, quickly, he wanted to get out of there. He didn't tell her that he might vomit. He pushed back from the table, held his head in his hands, and watched as a waiter grabbed the fallen man beneath his arms and attempted to haul him into a chair. Nobody else paid any attention. A woman at the next table plunged her fork into a plate of filet tartare, a sticky mass of raw meat arranged in a swirl beneath a raw egg. Kretzky, who had wanted to honeymoon in Maine, found himself hating Europe. His parents had fled the Continent as children in 1940, and it appeared to him that nothing had changed; death proliferated, and the good burghers got on with their lunch.

Kretzky realized that he did not present an inspiring alternative. He sat hyperventilating in a swirl of bitter thoughts—for instance, that his brother, a doctor, would not be such a helpless wreck. His brother had a purpose in the world of detached eyebrows. Kretzky could only be in the way. He thought he wanted to be a filmmaker, and he'd wound up working as an exhibition designer at the Museum of Natural History, a good job he would have to quit if he ever hoped to make a film, if he could ever decide on an idea for a film he believed in enough to leave his job, if he could ever be certain enough about his willingness to take on the uncertainty, if he could ever be as certain of anything as he was, at that moment, of his overwhelming uselessness.

Sweet, watery saliva flooded his mouth from the lining of his cheeks. Kretzky got up from the café, and the darkness rose with him. He heard Erika crying, "Eddie, Eddie," and opened his eyes to find her crouched over him on the sidewalk, stroking his damp forehead with both hands. The image that came to him was of Jackie

Kennedy, sprawled over the murdered president's body in Dallas. The foolish grandiosity of the association made him smile. Then he looked past Erika, straight up the black skirt of a waitress with thick, strong legs and white cotton underpants, and he was overcome with desire. He began to laugh. Erika told him to be calm, but he considered the phenomenon of a quaint Provençal sidewalk strewn with the prone bodies of witnesses to a biplane explosion inescapably funny.

In the end, the wounded drunk had walked away unaided, and Kretzky, too, rose to his feet, feeling cooled and refreshed in the aftermath of his collapse. He spent the afternoon assuring Erika that he was fine, and made love to her slowly and at length to prove it. They agreed that she, who had to watch uncomprehendingly as he fainted, had been more rattled by the episode than he. They dubbed the experience a "mortality check," and told each other that she had felt cut off from him at the very moment that he had felt restored to her. But Kretzky had his doubts.

"I feel restored," he told his therapist, when he was back in New York, "but not to her. Not really. Looking up at that waitress messed up my domestic focus."

Dr. Garafollo nodded and crossed her legs.

"I don't get it," Kretzky went on. "We lived together for three years, but marriage undermines me. I haven't been so susceptible to terror since childhood."

"You've been married three weeks," Dr. Garafollo reminded him. "Such intimacy with the unknown requires some getting used to. Julius Caesar, you know, was a fainter."

"Great," Kretzky said. "And his best friend bumped him off. Plus, what I'm trying to tell you is, I'm not a fainter."

"*Who,*" Dr. Garafollo had asked, "are you trying to tell?"

Entering his apartment, Kretzky found Erika surrounded by floury measuring cups and spoons—they were expecting company—and he began to laugh.

"Honey, I'm home," he declared.

"So I hear." Erika cracked an egg and held the upturned shell halves trembling over a bowl as the white spilled, curling from the yolk.

"And don't you want to know what happened to me today?"

"Tell me," she said.

"I got mugged," he said, and watched with pleasure as she dropped the egg.

"Eddie!" she said. "Shit. You didn't?"

"I most certainly did. A junkie with a cold steel blade neutralized me right out here on Jane Street, and his sidekick robbed me blind."

Erika stared at him. She did not, Kretzky thought, look overjoyed to see him. "You're in shock," she said. "Sit down."

"I think you're the one who needs a chair," he said. He had decided on the way home not to tell her that he'd fainted, but he couldn't resist an allusion. "Mortality check," he said. "I already had the shock. You're having the aftershock."

"It's not funny," Erika protested. "You think it's funny? Right now, right this minute, I could be a widow."

Kretzky was stung by the speed with which she imagined him dead. "Sure," he said. "And Vidia could comfort you."

Vidiadhar Gandhi (no relation to the Mahatma) was the overnight guest who was due at any minute. He had been Erika's live-in boyfriend when Kretzky met her, and he was now keeping house with a man, but Kretzky didn't believe that he was gay, not as far as Erika was concerned. Kretzky disliked Vidia, and his dislike was aggravated by the fact that Vidia was immensely likable, an easy and amiable bon vivant, who treated Kretzky warmly and without a hint of competition. Even when Vidia and Erika talked shop—they both worked for National Public Radio—he would take pains to find a way to keep Kretzky in the conversation. Kretzky thought himself something of a champ for acting just as friendly in return, but he doubted that Vidia was fooled, and he knew Erika wasn't.

"A widow," he said. "How romantic."

"Back off," Erika said. "Don't you mug me now, dammit. You get yourself held up at knifepoint and come in here smiling, I'm allowed to worry. Why the hell are you smiling?"

"To protect you," Kretzky told her. "It's a reflex." He got some paper towels and proceeded to wipe the egg up off the floor. Then he asked Erika for some money so he could go out and replace the stolen wine.

Retreating down the stairs, he imagined Dr. Garafollo asking him, *Who, exactly, are you trying to protect here?*

Kretzky, who often spoke out loud when he was alone, hurried along the sidewalk, saying: "Myself. All right? I'm protecting myself. What's the alternative? Attacking myself? I shouldn't have married her. I faint to escape. Okay? Does saying it make anything clearer? Jesus, lord, give me a break. They grabbed my balls, and it's a beautiful evening, and I'm going to buy wine. Okay? Is that okay with everybody?"

When Kretzky returned from the store, Vidia opened the door, embraced him, took the wine from him.

"I feel like the guest," Kretzky said.

Vidia laughed. "After what you've been through, you should. Two muggers, a knife—and you look marvelous." ·

Vidia's hair had grown; he wore it tucked in soft, sleek backward curls behind his ears. Kretzky thought he should return the compliment, but he resisted.

"I'd be a wreck," Vidia went on. "I've been burglarized, pickpocketed, had my baggage stolen. Always devastating, but always anonymous. Face-to-face with the bastards, I'm afraid I'd do something rash and wind up paying the consequences."

He launched into a story about an elderly uncle in Chicago who'd been surrounded by a pack of young punks demanding his gold watch. "He's a very tall man, but old, with a cane, and all these little bastards dancing around him."

Vidia paused to pop a cork, and Erika stood watching him with a hunk of cheese in her hands, apparently forgetting that she was going to put it on a plate. "What happened?" she said.

"The old goat puffed up to full size, waved his cane over his head, and bellowed, 'What would your mothers say if they could see you now?' They froze, the punks. They'd never seen anything like him. They scattered." He poured the wine and held up his glass. "Cheers," he said. "Here's to cool heads in a searing world."

"Cheers," Erika said.

Kretzky drank up.

"I've always called myself a happy existentialist," Vidia remarked. "But getting robbed kind of puts the kabosh on that. Getting robbed takes the fun out of existentialism."

Kretzky savored a familiar suspicion that Vidia's lines were rehearsed, possibly stolen. Back when Erika had still been willing to complain about her ex, she had been the first to say that spontaneity was not his strong suit. Now, she laughed and repeated his words— "Takes the fun out of existentialism, that's good."

"Actually," Kretzky said. "I feel weirdly happy. I felt liberated." It was true. Rising from his faint beside the shrieking car alarm, assisted by a middle-aged woman who'd seen him fall, he had experienced an exhilarating sense of buoyancy. Spotting his reflection in a store window, he had stopped to straighten out his jacket, but it was his eyes that held him there. They were clear and bright, free of the evasiveness he often encountered in mirrors. He could not remember the last time he thought he looked so good.

"I felt like bursting into song," he told Vidia. "I came home grinning like a hurdy-gurdy monkey."

"I can vouch for it," Erika said. "You'd have thought he'd won the lottery."

"Good for you," Vidia said. "After all, you're a lucky fellow. It *is* like a lottery. Your number's going to come up some time or other, and you got off without a scratch."

"It's more than that," Kretzky said. "I felt like I was the one who got away with something. Not just my life. The relief was overwhelming. Everything seemed dispensable."

"What do you mean, everything?" Erika asked.

"I mean everything. What a load off."

"I know exactly what you mean," Vidia said. "We're so concerned with protecting our stuff, and then—pow—it's gone, and there we are, same as ever. It's very affirming, really. I know the feeling exactly.

"No," Kretzky said. "I don't think you do."

"Why not?" Erika said. "Vidia just said he's been robbed up and down. He's lost much more than you, and burglary, you know—it's like there's no home to go to after that."

"I'm not talking about loss," Kretzky said. "I'm talking about feeling like you were given something."

"Exactly," Vidia said.

"Right," Kretzky said. "Exactly."

It was during dessert that Erika noticed Kretzky's wedding ring was gone. She let out a small cry—"You didn't tell me"—and clutched his naked finger.

Kretzky bowed his head. Erika lifted his hand and stared at it. "I can't believe I didn't notice before."

"Absences," Vidia explained, "can be very difficult to recognize. When someone's just shaved off a beard, you can stare for some time before you figure it out."

For once Kretzky felt grateful for Vidia's ever ready commentary. Two bottles of wine had been drunk, Vidia had broken out a bottle of cognac, and Kretzky did not wish to account for the ring. He had long ago made his peace with the awkward necessity of keeping certain thoughts and information to himself to preserve relationships—all kinds of relationships—but he could not endure outright lying.

"They pulled it off your finger," Erika said. "What a thing. It's unspeakable."

"I was mugged," Kretzky said. "I was attacked and I didn't resist. I adopted a policy of appeasement."

He didn't know what happened to his ring. He had waved it at the fleeing mugger, and at the purple-legged woman in black, and then it was gone. When he came out of his faint, he had forgotten about it. As Kretzky understood the event, he had taken the ring off and thrown it away.

"You must feel so violated without it," Erika said. She held his finger to her lips as if it was injured. "I'm going to get you a new one tomorrow."

"No," Vidia said. "I want to get it for him. Will you allow me? I still haven't given you two a wedding present, and replacing this ring would be perfect. It would delight me." He raised his glass. "Sometimes, as the old hags said, foul is fair. Your ill fortune, Eddie, presents an ideal opportunity for me to express my love for you both."

Kretzky watched in horror as Erika raised her glass, and leaned over the table to kiss Vidia's cheek. "What a beautiful thought," she said. "I'm incredibly touched."

What did it mean? Kretzky didn't want Vidia's love, never mind his ring. He felt like he was only now truly getting mugged.

"Maybe there's insurance," he said. He felt a light sweat rise on his forehead and chest, and got up to open the window.

"I think Eddie's drunk," Erika said. "Are you drunk, Eddie?"

"Most likely," he said.

"I don't have to give you a ring if you feel uncomfortable about it," Vidia announced. "I could understand that. I never know the right thing for weddings. I just follow my feelings, and my offer is entirely heartfelt."

"Maybe we should sleep on it," Erika said.

"Yeah," Kretzky said. "Let's give it a rest."

In the night, the crash and grind of garbage trucks emptying dumpsters woke Kretzky from a dream of flying. He had to piss. He grabbed a towel, wrapped himself, and worked the bedroom door open silently. Vidia lay on his back on the sofa bed. He didn't stir as Kretzky tiptoed past.

On his return, Kretzky stopped to look at his wife's friend. He stood in the dim streetlight glow, with his knees against the mattress's edge, and leaned over the sleeping body until his head hovered a few feet above Vidia's upturned face. Kretzky didn't know what he was looking for. He felt excited and powerful, gazing down on the peaceful, and—yes—beautiful face, which looked as clear and unconcerned as his own face had appeared earlier in the shop window. Kretzky had always felt jealous of Vidia, but only now, seeing him alone in the bed, did it occur to him that what he envied was not Vidia's closeness to Erika but his freedom from her.

Kretzky loved Erika, and although he was not always happy, he assumed—and Dr. Garafollo had encouraged him in the assumption—that the reasons for his unhappiness would go with him wherever he went. But he had never, before his wedding, felt toward married people the furious jealousy with which he eyed Vidia's solitude on the couch. He had never before felt that he was in the wrong bed, and that the only way out of that bed was a violence— not physical, though it might feel physical—for which he wasn't sure he had the strength. He had married Erika to guard against that violence. Now, leaning over Vidia, the "happy existentialist," he wondered whether perhaps separation was not a failure so much as a triumph of correction over a previous error.

Kretzky stood there for two, maybe three minutes, before he noticed with alarm that Vidia's eyes were open. He couldn't recall whether they had ever been closed. He had heard of people who slept with their eyes open, but he thought it was just an idiomatic expression. He stared at Vidia, and Vidia stared back. Kretzky had no idea if he was being seen.

He was flying again when the alarm went off. He sat up elated, still possessed of the swift, tight-limbed sensation of soaring over open fields and treetops. He rarely had such dreams, and twice in one night he had taken off and been born aloft without any effort.

"So," Erika said. "What do we tell Vidia about the ring?"

Kretzky sagged back into the pillows. He recalled the man's eyes staring in the night, and imagined Vidia telling Erika, "Your husband's a psychopath." He would not protest; he'd be relieved to be found out.

"You don't want it," Erika said. "You think the whole idea's kinky or something."

"It is kinky," he said. "Wedding rings are kinky. They're a fetish."

Erika laughed and moved over him in a crouch. "Do they turn you on?" she asked, holding her ring finger in front of his face.

"They do not," Kretzky said. "To tell you the truth, I'd rather you got rid of yours than I get a new one."

"What do you mean?" Erika said. She sat back on his thighs and gave his stomach a little backhand punch.

"What I said," Kretzky said. "Who needs rings? A ring can't seal a hole."

Erika left the bed and began to dress in quick, angry movements. "What are you talking about?" she said. "I don't understand you." She moved to the door, letting her hand linger on the knob, apparently waiting for him to call her back, to explain himself, to apologize, to make up.

"I think," Kretzky said, "that you do understand me."

There, he thought, he had done it.

But what had he done? Vidia and Erika were chatting cheerfully in the next room, and he was still lying there cozily—in the wrong bed. Nobody was going to take it out from under him.

No, he had to get up, report his credit cards stolen, and go see Dr. Garafollo. He would tell her that he'd been mugged by a man with a comb and molested by an invisible assailant; that he'd thrown away his wedding band, fainted, stood like a stalker at two in the morning over his wife's ex, and tried to derail his marriage. There was only one thing Kretzky couldn't account for. The problem, he thought, was that he was in an excellent mood.

THAW

by

MAX LUDINGTON

THERE WERE ABOUT TEN PEOPLE IN THE PLACE, ALL MEN. JERRY
went to the bartender.

"Someone call a cab?" he asked.

"Yeah," the bartender pointed over at the pool table. "Billy! Your
cab's here."

A big Indian with hair as long as Jerry's looked up from the shot
he was about to take. "Already?" he said. "Hang on till I finish this
game."

Jerry walked around the bar. His lungs were still cold from the
negative temperature outside. "Where you headed to?" He wouldn't
mind waiting if the guy was going into Minneapolis, but he wouldn't
wait long for a fare going around the corner.

"Here and there. Don't worry about it." The man was about thirty,
Jerry's age, wearing a Harley-Davidson T-shirt, a leather biker vest,
jeans and cowboy boots. His black hair fell freely around his face
and shoulders.

"Well I wouldn't mind knowing what direction we're headed,"
said Jerry.

The Indian's drifting eyes took in Jerry's black jeans and sweater,
leather jacket, biker boots, blond ponytail and goatee. He gave Jerry
an approving grin. "Name's Billy." He offered his hand. His hand-
shake was respectfully firm. He leaned back down to take his shot
and missed.

"Is it the money you're worried about?" Billy burrowed a hand
into his jeans and pulled out a roll of cash. He peeled off a hundred-

dollar bill. "I'm going to keep you tied up for a while," he said, handing it to Jerry. "I need a driver. That right there's got to buy me at least a couple hours. You in?"

Jerry looked down at the bill. "You got me, brother. Hell yes."

Billy laughed. "All right then. Rack 'em up. I'm sick of playing against myself."

"Tell you what," said Jerry, "you rack 'em, and I'll call my girl-friend and tell her I'm not coming home now so she doesn't make dinner for me."

"You do that," said Billy.

When Betsy answered, Jerry said, "Baby, I know we had a date for tonight, but I just picked up a fare down here in Chaska, a chauffeur job. He laid a hundred bucks on me for starters."

"How long will you be?" she asked.

"I don't know. As long as he keeps laying C-notes on me I'll stay with him. Do you still want me to come over if it's late?"

"I want you here now."

"I know. I'll try not to be too late. Okay?"

"Okay."

Billy wanted to put twenty on a game of eight-ball, but Jerry declined. Billy broke the rack and nothing dropped. Jerry sank three balls on his first turn, Billy sank one—an easy tap-in—before missing again, then Jerry ran the rest of the table.

"You should have made that bet," said Billy.

"Yeah, I guess."

"Fuck it. Let's go. I want to go down to the rez, swing by my house and then into the casino for a bit."

At the car Billy said, "I don't like riding in back. Bad memories." Jerry moved the maps and newspapers he kept on the passenger side, and Billy slid in next to him. They headed east and the road hugged the frozen coils of the river for a few miles out of Chaska. They crossed the arched, gently down-sloping Ferry Bridge south-bound; the iced river below was blown clean of snow, flat and white-veined like cut quartz. They followed County 83 onto the Sioux reservation. On both sides of the road, fields were lit by the setting

sun and hay was mounded evenly through them. The snow had par-
tially melted a few days earlier in a warm snap, and with their bare
tops and snow-skirted sides the haystacks looked like primitive huts.
They threw a pattern of long overlapping shadows and the tops of
the stacks to the west shone moist and bright with refraction. Jerry
didn't know anything about farming, but it struck him as strange
that hay was sitting stacked in the fields in midwinter. The symmetry
of the mounds reminded him of parts of his hometown—Daly City,
California—seen from the highway, with small, single-level white
and cream houses laid out in endless rows. Jerry was saving for his
first visit home since he had gone into rehab in Minneapolis two
years earlier.

Billy directed Jerry to his house, which was set back in some
pine woods on an unpaved dead-end road in a cluster of dwellings
ranging from trailers to brand-new family homes. Billy's place was
a small white ranch house flanked by a satellite dish—which was
half as big as the house—and a new red Chevy four-by-four pickup
jacked up on knobby tires and a custom suspension, yellow racing
stripe down the side. Jerry pulled alongside the truck.

"She's a beaut, ain't she?" said Billy. "And I can't even drive
her except around the property. I got my Harley in the garage too,
and when spring comes I'm going out of state for a ride where the
cops don't know me. You ride, don't you?"

"Yeah, I used to, but I don't have a bike right now." Jerry admired
the truck's tires, the tops of which came to his window. "What happened? You lose your license?"

Billy laughed. "Yeah, they said if they catch me behind the wheel
again, drunk *or* sober, they'll put me away for a long time."

"Lucky you got me," said Jerry.

Billy went inside and Jerry waited in the car, engine running in
the sub-zero cold. The sky would soon give up the last of its light.
Jerry sat and watched his exhaust blow slowly down over the windshield and spiral off into the pine trees. He lit a cigarette and
cracked his window. He thought about his trip home in a couple of
months. His parents weren't there anymore—his father had driven

off a highway overpass a year before Jerry cleaned up. The accident had been spectacular enough to make the local news. Jerry had seen it on a stolen TV with tinfoil rabbit-ears in an Oakland squat. The news copter got a perfect shot with the demolished guardrail in the foreground and the flattened smoking Cadillac below it, flipped sunny-side-down. Jerry remembered saying, "Check that shit out," to a roomful of junkies who weren't listening. He didn't find out until the next day whose car it was.

His mother had married a guy who owned a discount department store and moved to Palm Springs. But Jerry's sister and her family were still in Daly City, and he wouldn't mind seeing his one real friend, Miguel, so long as Miguel had his shit somewhat together. Jerry would go in April when the winter business slacked off. By then he would have plenty of money saved for a plane ticket, a rental car, and presents for his sister's kids. He was thinking he might take Betsy if it worked out between them.

Mystic Lake Casino was a short drive from Billy's house. For miles around at night, the spotlights were visible, set in a ring on the roof so the beams formed a giant teepee in the sky. "Biggest Indian casino in the Midwest," said Billy as they pulled into the huge parking lot. "The only one bigger is that one in Connecticut." His voice dropped low and became mock serious, "You want to know how much we make off this thing?"

"Sure," said Jerry.

"Well, total, I don't know. But let's just say I get a very big check every month. Very big," he said, his voice reverential.

"Every month, huh? That must be nice."

"Fucking right, long as you live on the rez. I ain't rich, though."

"How do you figure?"

"Because rich people got a certain attitude. I ain't that. I'm just a regular guy with a shitload of money. It don't mean shit to me. It don't make me think I'm better than you. But I'm glad I have it anyway, know what I mean?" Billy slapped Jerry's shoulder and laughed. The sweet tang of booze wafted Jerry's way.

"I guess I do," Jerry said, laughing with him.

Inside, they walked through the maze of slot machines and black-jack tables. Billy nodded to all the drink girls and a few of them smiled as if they knew him. He raised his hand to a tall Indian pit boss with a waist-length black ponytail, dressed in the blue blazer and gray slacks of management-level employees. "Hey, Julius," Billy said. Julius gave him a grim stare and a small nod. "That's my cousin," Billy said to Jerry. He broke a hundred at the change booth and handed Jerry twenty to play with.

Billy went to a nearby bank of dollar slots and Jerry started playing five-dollar hands of blackjack. The last time he had been in the casino, a month and a half earlier, he had brought Betsy with him. She put twenty dollars into the slots while he won over a hundred at blackjack. She got all worked up—said it made her feel queasy—and vowed never to gamble again.

They had met two weeks before that, when her car was in the shop and she called a cab to take her home from the school where she taught kindergarten. She had moved fast that first night, and now that made him wonder. Jerry had never had any trouble attracting women, but he wasn't used to women of her type. He wondered what this petite blond teacher, who had gone to graduate school, saw in him. He wanted to think it was something he hadn't known he possessed, or hadn't been willing to acknowledge in himself. She seemed crazy about him, but sometimes he thought he was a fling for her, a walk on the wild side before she settled down with Mr. Right. Since he had gotten clean Jerry's wild side didn't go much past his clothes and hair.

On the way to her place in his cab, her blond curls bouncing in the rearview, Betsy chatted him up about what it was like to be a cab driver. Near the end of the trip she leaned forward and put her thin forearm over the back of his seat. "Well," she said, "another lonely Friday night. I'm just going to curl up with my cat and watch some movies, I guess."

"That sounds nice," said Jerry.

"What about you?" she asked. "Got big plans for tonight?"

"No, not really. I'll probably just hang at home, too."

"You want to maybe get a couple of movies and watch them together?"

Jerry played it cool, like he had been expecting it. In the video store she made plain, innocent suggestions for movies, and he agreed with them.

Partway through the first movie he made a pass at her and they spent half an hour fooling around on the couch. When she started taking off her shirt, Jerry had an unfamiliar impulse to stop her. He pulled his hand from under the shirt. He kissed her again and said, "I want to take you out."

"Right now?"

"No," he sat back and pulled her shirt down, "tomorrow night."

She looked confused. "You mean you don't want to do anything now?"

"Let me take my statement a little further." Her narrow body was across his lap and his hand was around the back of her neck. "I want to come over here and pick you up at seven tomorrow night and take you out to a nice restaurant." He kissed her. "From there we'll go to a movie." He kissed her again, harder. "Then we'll come back here and I'll rip your clothes off."

She stayed silent, staring at him.

"Hey," he said, "if that's not what you want it's all right. If you just want the one night, we can rip our clothes off right now."

She stared at him a second longer and then turned loose a crooked smile he knew he could get hooked on. "No, you just surprised me," she said. "Tomorrow night sounds lovely."

That was the last time he saw that smile. He hadn't managed to surprise her in quite the same way since. Her everyday smile was generic—it pulled the corners of her mouth straight back and thinned her already straight lips—and he imagined it was the smile she gave her students when they completed a pretty collage, or cleaned their play areas nicely. It didn't do much for him. She did have some things he loved, though: freckles spattered all over, dense in the vee of her neck, thinning onto her breasts, and petering out in her shaved white armpits; and she had quirky little hips—even if she didn't really know how to use them. She would learn, he kept telling himself. She was smart without using it against him. And she probably would never lie to him, an idea he was still trying to get used to.

Jerry was fifteen dollars ahead when Billy tapped him on the shoulder.

"Check it out." Billy was holding two large plastic cups filled with silver dollars. "Now we go downtown. Have some real fun."

On the way off the reservation, Billy told Jerry to go to Sultan's, an upscale strip club where his ex-girlfriend worked. He hadn't seen her in a while, he told Jerry. It had ended badly. He wasn't even sure she still worked there.

Jerry eased the car into a turn at fifty and the power steering hummed. It needed some fluid. It was night now, and Jerry thought of the frozen haystacks on both sides of the dark road. He wondered; if he let go of the wheel halfway through the long turn and let the car take its own course into the field, would it thump safely into one of the big mounds of hay, or thread them and slam into the forest on the other side?

"If she's there, I think she'll be glad to see me," said Billy. He paused. "It's probably better if she's not there anyway. We'll have more fun. You're coming in with me, right?"

Jerry thought of Betsy. "I don't know if I want to pay the cover."

"No, no, no, no. Fuck that, man. Everything's on me, food, drinks, cover, everything."

"In that case."

Sultan's was dark and high-ceilinged. Lights flashed around the stage, where a tall brunette was dancing to Aerosmith's "Crazy," slowly liberating herself from a gray business suit. Billy paid their cover charge, then slipped the hulking Scandinavian doorman an extra twenty and said, "Get us a corner table, will you, Sven?"

"Sure Billy," said the man. His name tag said Ron.

Jerry had been in the club once before, with a skinny junkie named Annie. He had met her in rehab and fucked her for about a month after they got out. It had been her idea to come to the strip club. She said she liked looking at the dancers, and looking at her man staring at them. They went to her place afterward and had sex with the lights off, and in the middle of it she asked him if he was imagining that she was one of the dancers. Jerry thought it was what she wanted, so he told the truth, he said Yes. That turned out to be the wrong answer, and she pushed him off and said she wanted to talk "about us." He got up, got dressed and went home. He didn't call her after that. He saw her at an NA meeting a few weeks later and she didn't seem to hold it against him.

A hostess in a mini tuxedo shirt and black garters led them to their table. Billy tipped her twenty dollars and ordered a bottle of champagne.

"I'll just have a coke," said Jerry.

"Come on," said Billy. "Have a little nip with me."

"No thanks. Strict policy, never when I'm driving." Jerry didn't see any point in talking about sobriety.

When the waitress brought the drinks, Billy tipped her ten dollars and said, "Is Diana here tonight?"

"I don't think I know her."

"Tall blond. Her stage name is Cheyenne."

"Oh, Cheyenne. No, she's not here tonight. I haven't seen her around in a while."

They watched the stage dancers, and Billy drank the champagne before starting in on mixed drinks. Dancers crowded around their table wanting to give them private dances, and every so often Billy paid for one. "Private" dances, done on a pedestal placed in front of the customer, cost ten dollars. Billy paid twenty or fifty for each one. Jerry shook his head politely when they asked him. He kept his eyes mainly on the stage, not wanting to stare at Billy's private dances. At one point all the dancers in the club paraded in a chorus line onstage, meant to entice reluctant customers to take their pick.

"Which one do you think is the hottest?" Billy asked.

Jerry was munching on a plate of fried cheese sticks with tomato sauce. He studied the dancers on the stage and picked out a thin, lithe woman with small breasts and perfect legs. She was shaped like Betsy. "That little redhead there is pretty nice looking."

"Her?" said Billy. "Come on. What about all those big titties up there?"

"I got nothing against them. But there's something about that girl I like." Jerry let his eyes stray down the line of dancers and they landed on the only other small-breasted woman there. She had grown her hair and dyed it blond, and put on just enough weight to make her ass worth shaking, but there was no mistaking Annie.

"Okay. I guess I see it," said Billy, and raised his hand to call the waitress over. Billy said to her, "Tell that little redhead there to come over here and bring a friend when she's done onstage."

"On second thought, make it the blond fourth from the end in the white outfit," Jerry said.

The waitress followed Jerry's eyes. "Okay, that's Nina," she said.

"You heard the man." Billy handed her a ten while searching the stage for Jerry's choice. "Jesus, you like them small titties, don't you?" Billy slipped Jerry a fifty. "Here, this is for her to dance for you."

"You don't need to do that," said Jerry.

"Hey, just take it. But make sure you get at least two songs and some conversation for it. Don't let her short you."

"Hi there." Their table was on a slightly raised area against the wall, and Annie was speaking from the lower level, right next to him, smiling and holding onto the round brass railing. Her see-through teddy was trimmed with fake white fur.

"How are you, Annie?" Jerry smiled.

"I'm good. It's good to see you, Jerry," she said, beaming at him.

She came around the railing and up two steps. Before she sat down she leaned over and kissed his cheek. He put his hand on her shoulder, and she pushed it away gently and said, "No hands in here. It's really strict. The security guys get pissed. And in here I'm Nina." Her face had gained color and a little healthy flesh. Her lips were thin and shapely, forming a shallow M, like a compound bow. She let her solid slender thigh lie along his and touched his forearm when she spoke. She looked over at Billy, who was engrossed in his own dancer. "Hey there, Billy. Long time."

Billy turned toward her and brightened with half-recognition. "Hey. What's up?"

"Not too much. Seen Diana lately?"

"No. She still work here?"

"Off and on," said Annie. Billy's dancer put two fingers on his cheek and turned his head back to her. Annie faced Jerry. "How do you know Billy?" she asked.

Without turning his head, Billy answered for him, "Oh, we go way back, me and Jerry. Ain't that right, buddy?"

"That's right," Jerry said.

"I know Billy's old girlfriend," said Annie. "She's great. She's really crazy about him."

"How long have you been working here?" Jerry asked.

"Oh, a while now. At least a year. You remember we came here together?"

"Yeah, I remember."

"Want me to give you a dance?" She was already on her feet.

Jerry showed her the fifty and said, "This is for you to dance, but only if you say your real name."

She smiled. "You know my real name."

Jerry tucked the bill deep into the front of her G-string, feeling the graze of stubble against the backs of his fingers. "Do it anyway," he said.

A slow song had just started, some pop-metal ballad. She leaned in close and whispered, "*Girlie.*"

It was what he had called her sometimes, as close as they had come to a pet name. Now, whispered in his ear, it electrified him. Her breath flowed down through his body and settled warm and low.

Annie slid the pedestal in front of him and mounted it. She pulled loose the bow on her teddy. She smiled at him and dropped the teddy onto his lap.

"I think about you sometimes," she said, working her hips

smoothly in a figure-eight that hinged around her navel. "I was sorry when you left."

Jerry couldn't think of anything to say, so he just glanced up at her face. He wondered if Betsy could learn that with her hips.

She danced for a while longer, then popped the clasp on her bra and slid it off. "You still going to meetings?" she asked.

"Yeah, sometimes," Jerry said. "How about you?"

"No. Not really. I drink sometimes now. Smoke a joint. But I've stayed away from the junk."

"That's good," said Jerry. "I have, too." She leaned in with her hands against the wall and hung her little pears in front of his face, twitching sideways to shake them. When she pushed away from the wall, she arched her back forward and let a nipple slowly brush his upper lip and the tip of his nose. The touch took on a charged aspect in the noisy club. She faced away from him and bent down. She looked at him over her shoulder and slapped her own behind, leaving red finger marks. She bent lower until her head touched her knees and her vulva was clearly outlined against the sheer, tiny G-string. Jerry's pager went off. He waited until the dance was over to check the number.

As Annie sat back down and fastened her bra a twinge crossed her face, something like shyness, as if her modesty was triggered more by dressing than undressing. Her eyelids fluttered. "I'd better get back to work. Let's stay in touch. When you come back in, ask for Nina." She stood up.

Jerry felt the warmth from her body on the seat next to him. "Thanks for the dance, Nina."

She kissed his cheek. She whispered, "I'm in the book under Lejeune," and stepped away. "Or just come back here," she said over her shoulder. "I'm here every weekend."

"Okay," Jerry said.

She sauntered away, swaying like a runway model, and leaned over into a group of suits across the room.

On his way to the payphone, Jerry decided to tell Betsy where he was. She would surely ask, and he was working on personal honesty.

"Are you coming over soon?" she asked.

"Probably not. I'm still with this guy."

"Where are you, a bar? I hear music."

"Yeah," he said, "we're at Sultan's, downtown."

"The strip bar?"

"Yeah, well, this is where he wants to be. He paid my cover. It's better than waiting in the car."

"I'll bet." She paused. "Are you looking at the women?"

"Well. There they are, right in front of me."

"Do you like looking at them?" Her voice took on a wheedling, falsely cheerful lilt that didn't hide her disapproval.

Jerry sighed. "Come on. What am I supposed to do, hate it? I'm not going to close my eyes while I'm in here. It's no big deal. Really."

"Okay, okay," she said. He knew she'd have more to say later. "Do you still want to come over?"

"Sure, when I get done. You want to leave the key under the mat for me?"

"Yeah, I'll do that. Wake me up and kiss me."

"I will."

"Be good."

"I will."

"You know that chick, huh?" Billy asked when Jerry got back to the table.

"Yeah, I used to hang out with her a while back. Before she worked here."

"We come here looking for my old girlfriend and end up finding yours. Ain't that a trip?" Billy smiled and shook his head drunkenly, a little sadly.

Most of the drunks Jerry dealt with in his job served only to reinforce his sobriety with their ugliness and helplessness, but something about Billy, beyond the biker clothes and long hair, re-minded Jerry of himself. Something in the way he drank: starting out festive, his good will contagious, then just putting one drink in front of the next. Jerry imagined joining Billy in drinking, and in-stead of the fear and disgust which that thought should have brought, he felt only hard-boiled nostalgia. For the first time in about half a year the slow, muscular body of his addiction began to stir in him—heat uncoiling in his chest. It was a shrewd cousin of panic. His eyes narrowed. He remembered his conversation with Betsy and became suddenly annoyed.

There was a lull in the music. Billy was finishing a drink. He had withdrawn steadily, brooding behind long-ashed cigarettes. He reached forward and stubbed one out in the ashtray. His head snapped up and he said abruptly, "We gotta go."

Jerry said, "Okay, whenever you say."

"I say now. We gotta get back to the rez." He looked as if he had been startled from a nightmare.

In the car on the way down Billy was restless, chain-smoking.

"It's probably nothing," Billy said, "but sometimes I get these feelings. Like something ain't right." He rested his elbow on the lip of the door and flicked his ash out an inch of open window. The sleeve-zipper of his motorcycle jacket clicked against the glass and smoke from his mouth rushed for the opening.

"Have these feelings been right in the past?" asked Jerry.

"They're always right. But it might not be anything serious."

"I hope not," Jerry said.

Billy fell silent. Jerry steered the car down the cold highway. He thought about home. Lately he had been sustaining himself through the long workdays, which began and ended in darkness, with thoughts of California. He had his trip figured out. He would see his sister and her family, showing up well-dressed and flush with cash, and with charm and gifts he would make up for his past de-linquencies. What friends he had left whose lives weren't too deep in the crapper would be impressed with the new Jerry, sober and sporting a beautiful intelligent girlfriend. Yes, it would be perfect if

Betsy went with him. People would be more likely to trust the transformation with her there as evidence.

When they turned into the dirt cul-de-sac where Billy lived, red and blue lights were playing brightly across the trees and snow from the driveway of a small house at the end. A cop car sat there. The flashing lights making no sound made Jerry feel deaf for a second.

"No, Jesus," said Billy. "Pull up there. Pull *up there!*"

Jerry pulled the cab up behind the cop car on the road and Billy jumped out. He ran across the trampled snow on the lawn, nearly falling at every step, his legs bowed out wide like a toddler's. He went in the front door of the tiny, box-like house. There was no one else outside. Jerry switched on the radio and America was singing, *"After three days . . . in the desert sun . . ."* He had missed the first two days.

Billy came running out of the house, ripped open the car door, and fell into the front seat. "The hospital in Shakopee!" he said.

Jerry turned the car around and headed back for the main road. "Is someone sick?"

"My grandmother. Jesus, get me there." Billy fumbled for a cigarette and lit it.

America was still singing. Jerry reached over and snapped the radio off.

At the Emergency entrance, Billy told him to wait and got out. Four people were smoking outside the entrance, and they greeted Billy and hugged him and spoke to him. Billy ran inside. One of the group, a woman of about forty-five with softly creased, beautiful features, walked over to the cab. Jerry rolled his window down.

"Are you waiting to get paid?" she asked.

"No, not really. He asked me to wait."

"Well, he's better off with us now. I can pay you whatever he owes and you can take off." She took a wallet from her coat pocket.

"I'd feel bad leaving. He told me to wait for him here. He's already given me plenty of money."

She sighed, "I'll go in and talk to him. I think he's going to want to stay." She walked inside. The doorway was empty now, the others finished with their smokes. Jerry waited. Billy and the woman appeared on the other side of the sliding glass door. She was speaking and he was shaking his head and backing away. The door slid open and Billy turned and walked outside. She followed him, screaming his name. As he came toward the cab, she grabbed the sleeve of his jacket and tried to pull him back. He bellowed like a small child and yanked his arm away. He climbed into the passenger seat.

The woman spoke through the window. "Billy. Think of what Grandma'd want. Don't leave her. Stay with us now."

Billy just shook his head, his eyes closed tightly.

She came to Jerry's window and he rolled it down again.

"Take care of him," she said. She had a bill folded in her hand and she pushed it at Jerry. "Don't leave him anywhere. Stay with him and get him home, please."

"Don't take that money," said Billy.

Jerry shook his head at the money and pushed her fist out the window, saying, "Don't worry. I'll get him home."

They went to an all-night diner. Billy told Jerry his grandmother had died in the ambulance.

"That old lady was the one who taught me everything. Her and my big sister. She taught me the old language, she told me stories of her childhood, and I was off looking at titties when she died. She was Grandma Burns. I should have been there."

Jerry didn't know what to say. He settled for, "There was nothing you could have done."

"She was always there for me," Billy said. "I could have been there for her."

The diner was a low brick building called Boogie's Kitchen. One wide, friendly waitress worked both the counter and the tables. Bars were still open, so the place wasn't crowded. They sat in a booth near a window and ordered breakfast. Jerry dug into his omelet hungrily, and Billy drank coffee and pushed his fried eggs around the plate, taking a few bites of the sausage links. He talked about his grandmother, his childhood. His mother had run off when he was an infant. His father had enlisted the help of his own mother to raise the two children. She had cared for them when their father was at work, and sometimes he was away for long periods of time on construction crews in far-off states. This had been before the casino. Billy's grandmother had forced them to learn some of their native language, practicing with them after school. "I always got into trouble, and she was the only one who never held it against me. When I came back from my time upstate she never said a word about it, never once."

As if on cue a squad car pulled into the diner's parking lot. Two cops got out and walked in the door. They were sitting down at the counter when one of them looked to the far end where Billy and Jerry sat. He approached their table.

"Oh, great," said Billy, not far enough under his breath for Jerry's comfort. "Fucking pigs."

The cop stopped in front of their booth. He had a thick blond mustache. "Hi, Billy," he said.

Billy looked up at him, then silently back down at his plate.

"I'm sorry about your grandmother. She was a real great lady."

Billy nodded his head and grunted.

"You're not driving, are you?"

Billy sighed angrily, his fork gripped tight and facing menacingly upward.

"No," said Jerry quickly. "I am. That's my cab out there."

The cop nodded. "Good." He paused a moment. That loaded cop pause. "Stay out of trouble tonight, okay Billy?"

Billy dipped his head lower and shoved his plate into the middle of the table. "Leave me alone," he muttered.

The cop laid a hand on Billy's shoulder before walking away.

Billy paid the check and told Jerry to take him to a bar in Shakopee, just up the road.

"I know it's not my place," said Jerry, "but don't you think it would be good to head home now?"

"I can call another cab if you want me to."

"No, that's all right. My girlfriend's asleep by now anyway."

"Good," said Billy. He peeled another hundred from his roll and gave it to Jerry. "Here," he said, "that other one's run out by now I guess."

McNeely's had its sign painted in Irish green, the interior small and dark and pub-like except for the bright booth in the back corner that sold pull-tab lottery tickets, and the Black Crowes blasting from the stereo. Billy took the only empty stool at the bar and Jerry stood next to him. The bartender knew Billy by name and served him his drink quickly.

"What'll you have?" the bartender asked Jerry.

"Just a coke."

"This is my buddy Jerry," Billy said to the bartender. "He's driving me home tonight."

"That's nice of you," said the bartender. He slid Jerry's coke across the bar. "On the house for designated drivers."

A fat, gray-bearded man built like a small bear swaggered over from a table near the back and slapped Billy on the shoulder. "Billy boy!"

"Don't touch me, Karl," Billy said, looking over his shoulder at the man. "I ain't in the mood to talk to you."

"What are you talking about?" the man asked.

"I just ain't in the mood to talk to somebody who fired me right now." Billy turned away from the man and put his elbows on the bar, spread apart as if expecting trouble.

"Fired you?" The man laughed. "Billy, that's ancient history. I thought we'd forgot about that."

"No, Karl. *You* forgot about that. I pretended to forget, and I ain't in the mood right now. So fuck off."

"Fuck *off?*" The man puffed out his powerful chest.

Jerry took a step between them. "Listen, his grandmother just died, okay? Maybe you could cut him a break." The man was half a foot shorter than Jerry, but solid. His was the kind of fat that hid strength.

"Grandma Burns? She died?" The man stepped back. "Jesus, Billy, come on. I'm sorry about that."

Billy finished his drink. "Fuck off, Karl," he said without looking back.

Karl stood steaming there for a moment, then turned and moved off shaking his head. "Fuck *you*."

Billy ordered another drink, but the bartender had seen the confrontation and cut him off. Billy pleaded with him, but the man stood his ground. Then Karl was back, suddenly there, with his hands on his hips, behind Billy.

"No, Billy," he said. "You don't get to talk to me that way. Your grandmother was a friend of mine, you know she was. You don't get to tell me to fuck off after I hired you when you didn't have no experience. And the only reason I kept you on for as long as I did was out of loyalty to your old man. Just because you got money comin' out your ass now don't give you the right to shit on me. You never did nothin' but cause your family trouble."

Billy spun on his stool, already swinging. His feet hit the floor and he lurched toward Karl, who stepped away from the punch and put his forearm in Billy's neck, slamming him to the floor. Karl hit Billy's face once, just a pop to stun him out of resistance. Jerry put his hand on Karl's shoulder to pull him off, and the big man whirled and stood quicker than Jerry would have thought possible and pinned Jerry against the bar, one hand on his throat, one cocked back in a fist.

"You want some too?" Karl rasped, his eyes wild with booze and adrenaline.

Jerry was ready to back down, but Karl's hand tightened on his throat, cutting off his air, and the older man's teeth were clenched and bared. Jerry had learned never to suppress an impulse in a fight, and he hit the side of Karl's left eye with an elbow-punch. Karl released Jerry's throat and shuffled two steps back like a man doing what he's told. His hand went to his eye, and Jerry put a boot in his balls. Karl knelt, croaking.

Billy was getting to his feet, and Jerry dragged him out the door, one arm around his waist.

In the cab on the way back to the reservation, Billy was quiet for a while, but as they pulled onto the road leading to the houses he let out a low groan, followed by a little yelp of pain, and banged his fist against the door.

"I got to get away from here," Billy said. "Tomorrow. I got to get down to Mankato. I got friends there. I'll give you three hundred bucks to take me there and another three hundred to pick me up when I come back. Unless you want to stay down there with me for a few days. My friends wouldn't mind. They party. They have a great time. They all ride."

"Sure, I could take you down there."

"We'll go in the morning. I can't stay here."

"I'll give you my pager number. You can beep me when you want to go."

"No. You come here at nine in the morning. I'll be ready to go." Billy pointed to a larger house across the street from his. "Drop me off there. That's my dad's house."

Jerry pulled into the driveway and shut off his lights. There were lights on in the house, giving it warmth among the other dark homes. He pulled a pen and a card from the visor over his head and wrote down his name and pager number. "Here," he said. "Call me if you want to change the plan."

"But you'll be here, right? Nine AM?"

"Yeah," said Jerry, "I'll be here."

"Thanks." Billy got out. Before shutting the door, he leaned back in, his feet shuffling to keep his balance. "I'll tell you something," he said. He wiped blood from his lip. "You don't ever want to see old Karl again."

"Okay."

Before he got off the reservation, Jerry stopped at a convenience store where they sold tax-free cigarettes. When he stepped out of the store, he slapped the pack against his palm and lit one. He let the cold air deep into himself along with the smoke. His cheeks started to ache. In front of him the car was idling. His nerves were still raw from the fight. It felt good, in a way that he had forgotten about, and he tilted his head back. The cold had expelled every trace of vapor from the atmosphere, and the sky was crazed with stars. He was a warm speck on the frozen prairie. It occurred to him that if he stayed there, he'd freeze solid very quickly. Maybe he had already begun to. He stood and smoked until he began to shiver.

Across the roof of the taxi, in the corner of the lot, he saw a pay phone set low with a long cord so it could be used from inside a car. He climbed in and pulled up to it. He finished his cigarette, put it out, then lowered his window, picked up the receiver and punched 411.

"Minneapolis," he said. "Yes. Lejeune. Anne Lejeune." He wrote the number down on a card with no name and tucked it into his wallet.

Betsy was asleep when Jerry got there. He undressed in the bathroom and slipped into the bedroom carrying his clothes. He stood quietly for a minute, his eyes adjusting to the darkness, until he could see her breathing form under the peach-colored duvet, which looked white in the moonlight from the window. Her cat was curled on the bed next to her, and he picked it up and dropped it on the floor. It stretched and jumped onto a chair in the corner and was sleeping again.

He stole into bed and lay facing the back of her neck. A few locks of hair streaked the smooth skin there, and the rest fell back in a tangle on the pillow. The top of her left ear caught the moon. He was swept up for a second, taken with her. He imagined growing old with her. He imagined being someone else. He stroked her neck, pressed his lips to her shoulder, and she took a deep breath. She moaned, turned over and mumbled, "Everything okay?"

"Yeah, baby."

Her eyes stayed closed, her breathing even.

"I love you, Jerry."

"Sleep now," he said.

The next morning Jerry got up at eight and dressed to go. He had vague memories of drug-filled dreams. Betsy woke up as he was

putting on his jeans. She yawned and stretched. One slender arm
reached back and straightened up over the headboard, ending in a
sleepy little fist. She was so beautiful, so out of place in his life.
Jerry turned away from her and sat on the edge of the bed to put
on his boots. She asked him where he was going.

"Work," he said.

"I thought you were going to take the day off with me."

"I was." He was having trouble getting the second boot pulled
on. "But this guy said he'd pay me six hundred dollars to take him
to Mankato and back. So I'm going to pick him up."

"The same guy from last night?"

"Yeah."

"I don't like him," she said.

"How can you not like him? You don't know him."

"He kept you away from me last night." She reached and hooked
her hand into the back of his jeans and yanked as if to hold him
back. "He took you to see naked ladies. And he's taking you away
from me again today. Come to think of it," she dragged herself over
and lay her cheek along his thigh, "I really hate this guy."

"Well, I guess I can understand that," said Jerry. Her cheek was
right where Annie's bare thigh had touched him. He slid a hand
behind him, unhooked her hand from his belt, and stood up.

"Don't go," she said.

"I can't turn down this kind of money right now," said Jerry. He
was suddenly angry at her. She let him finish dressing in silence.

When he had his jacket and wool hat on, he sat back down on
the bed and touched her shoulder. She turned onto her back and
sat up, holding the sheet over her chest. "Please." The look in her
eyes was one he'd never seen before. She was testing him.

"Okay, listen," he said. "This guy's been through a lot. I promised
I'd pick him up. I'll just drive down there and tell him I can't do
it. Okay?"

"It's all right. You need the money. Go ahead."

"I'm not going. I want to be with you."

"I don't want to hold you back. Don't worry about it."

"Jesus Christ. Come on." He stood up and stepped to the bedroom door, his anger turning over on itself. "I'll be back in an hour or two."

Betsy sighed and nodded, looking at him. Her arms were crossed, and the crooked smile crept across her face. She dropped the sheet to her thighs. "I'll be here."

Insulating cloud cover had moved in, and the morning was less cold than the previous night, the temperature now just above zero. He didn't let the car warm up, and when he eased off down the street the engine sounded raspy as it struggled to circulate the congealed oil. He stopped for gas at a station by the highway entrance. A tanker truck was backed up to the pumps, and the driver waved him off. He pulled up by the door and went in. The counterman was old and shiny-faced, and his black hair looked dyed above his gray eyebrows.

"How long till I can get gas?" Jerry asked.

"Oh, a few minutes yet," the man rubbed one drooping cheek with his fingers thoughtfully, calculating. "Six or seven, maybe."

Jerry bought a pint of steering fluid and listened to the car's running engine suck it up as he poured it in. He pulled out and drove around the block taking the turns tightly, testing the steering. Wind whistled in the imperfect seal of his door. When he came around, the tanker was pulling out.

He had forgotten his gloves at Betsy's, and the pump wouldn't hold itself open, so he alternated hands. It was a big gas tank, and by the time he finished, both hands were completely numb. He went inside and paid for the gas, along with a Styrofoam cup of coffee.

Back in the car, he flipped open the tab on the lid of the coffee and took a sip; warmth spread through his chest. He lit a cigarette. The first drag sent a wave of comfort through his system and he took another quickly to boost it. It felt as only the first cigarette of the day can. He sat for a moment with his two substances. He thought of what the first hit of junk used to feel like when he was strung out, especially when he had thought to save himself a bump for the morning. The best first cigarette was only a feeble imitation of that.

The highway on the way south was not crowded on a Saturday morning, and the farther he got from the city the more empty it became. He began to feel his hands again as the car warmed up inside. He didn't turn on the radio, drinking in instead the hum of the snow tires on dry pavement and the deep growl of the V-8. The light from the overcast sky was diffuse, graying everything like an invisible mist. Suburbs slid past, strip malls, flat, frozen fields. If he stayed on it, this road would take him all the way to Mexico. He wondered how he would make his lease payment to the cab company on Monday, if he was in Mankato with Billy. The taxi rode up onto the bridge, and he tried to feel the exact moment when the gentle arch reached its peak, but then he was beyond it; as he came down the other side, the river passed under him, white and serpentine and hard, and, somewhere below feet of ice, moving.

MAKE A WISH
by
ELIZABETH TIPPENS

YOU ARE HERE.

Or so it says on the Level 2 directory.

I wear bright red lipstick and no other makeup until another sales associate, a girl named Bailey, tells me that my eyes, and not my lips, are the feature I should accentuate. Bailey is not the kind of girl I would have been friends with in high school. She uses expressions like "Sweetie" and "P.S." But here, now, on Level 2, things are not high school. Things are different.

"Sweetie, I could tell you stories," Bailey says. And then she does.

Bailey is a one-girl FBI who has accumulated massive amounts of personal information about the employees of Level 2, like which employees shoplift, who's gay (male and female), who's a slut (male and female), who's a parking lot whore, who just looks like one but is really a nice person, who binges and purges, who's listening to Prozac, who isn't but should be, who's about to get fired, promoted, demoted, engaged, dumped, cheated on, stabbed in the back, used for sex, or taken away from all this by a very rich customer, which has happened, according to Bailey. And abortions. Bailey can tell who is even a little bit pregnant, and then two days later, who is not anymore.

"P.S., try dark black eyeliner and just a little bit of clear lip gloss," she tells me.

I do. I try this.

When mornings are slow Bailey tells me all about her sex life with her boyfriend, Duff. Now I know so much about what Bailey likes Duff to do to her, and what Duff likes to do to Bailey, that I feel as though I have had sex with both of them. Duff has a motorcycle.

Bailey and I arrange the accessories rack, straightening out a tangled mess of ugly belts and cheap scarves. She gives me advice, like when a guy is hazardous to your health, watch, and the little hairs on your arms will stand up straight.

Bailey has a chubby little stomach, but because she wears a navel ring and cropped-off sweaters, it took me forever to make this simple observation. That's something I've noticed, here on Level 2. If a girl markets herself as cute, if by wearing a navel ring, for instance, she telegraphs her own belief in the attractiveness of her stomach, there will be a lag time until reality hits the eye of the beholder. If it ever does.

The store manager, a short, wired woman named Robin, has no marketing strategy for herself. What she does have is actually a lack of personal style. Her outfits are anti-personal, like somebody's boxy, generic uniform, passed along apathetically from one employee to the next. Robin is a corporate misfit who believes in misguided sales techniques she invents herself, like, "Disco sells clothes." Does this mean that disco makes customers more inclined to buy, or that with disco hammering at our brains, we are more inclined to sell? The answer, like everything else lately, lies in the realm of Divine Mystery.

I heard somebody say, Burn baby burn, Disco inferno, Burn baby burn. It plays over and over. "An endless loop of disco madness," Bailey calls it.

Robin puts Bailey and me up front to sell coats.

Who could have guessed that I would actually excel at something like this? My ability to sell coats has come crashing out of nowhere, meteor-like, and has nothing to do with any previously known talent of mine, or with my actual personality, which is what you would call introverted. It all happens in a kind of trance. While this new, outgoing coat-selling girl works the floor, I seem to disappear altogether.

Later, when my impressively high sales are tallied, I have no clear memory of what I could have said that was so persuasive and convincing. It's a blur. With disco.

My mother and I just bought the exact same ones! One night, right before I am about to fall asleep, I remember saying this. Apparently I will say anything at all to sell a coat. I appear to be a genius at the mother/daughter double sale.

I sell a lot of coats.

The president of the company sends me a congratulatory letter, which leaves me, and even Bailey, nearly speechless in its pathetic sincerity.

"P.S., you can't even make fun of something this banal," says Bailey.

I win a prize.

For lunch I insist on eating the exact same thing every day: a very large, very sweet wedge of cheese Danish, and an extra tall cup of coffee with extra cream and sugar. I get my Danish and coffee in the Food Court at a small store called Alpenhaus.

Just to get their German-Swiss-Austrian-whatever theme across to the one last mall customer who might have missed it, Alpenhaus has hired a dwarf to parade back and forth outside its entrance wearing an Alpenhaus sandwich board, lederhosen, and a little green Alpine hiking hat. With a feather. And I have to pass by this reeking medieval indignity in order to get my Danish and coffee. But this is how badly I want my Danish and coffee. It is my one and only pleasure of the day, and while I actually do care that it is sickening and unhealthy and causes an intense sugar/caffeine rush/ crash, and that I have to witness human debasement in order to get it, I feel physically incapable of ordering anything else.

Once I have made it past the dwarf, a relief you can't believe, I get to see the boy behind the counter. I find his hostility refreshing after a morning of being NICE to the general public. I find it bubbly, like Sprite. His ears, his eyebrows, and his nose are all pierced. He will be the one to inflict the pain here, NOT YOU. I call him the boy who hates everything. He is a little younger than me, and very tall, with big feet and hands, like a puppy. He acts bored and tired, and he speaks softly, forcing the customers to crane their necks to hear what he is saying. But the boy who hates everything likes me. It's the kind of acknowledgement you shouldn't feel honored by, but you do anyway. We have a mental crush on each other, which you can actually feel the purity of. Each day we have a brief yet satisfying conversation.

"Will you be dining *in* today?" he says.

Together we eye the dining conditions. One sticky plastic table and two metal folding chairs.

"I believe I'll be dining *out* today," I answer.

This portion of my daily routine is what you would call a highlight.

The mall is a space station. No day. No night. A synthetic habitat of regulated, piped-in weather. I eat on a white bench by a fake pond with a fountain that drips down onto copper lily pads. If someone sits down beside me on the bench while I am eating my cheese Danish and drinking my coffee, my lunch is ruined.

I listen to the persistent sound of water hitting copper as it echoes everywhere. It is an open, hollow sound. Children come by with their mothers to throw coins into the fountain.

Make a wish.

After lunch I usually go by Pop Cowboy to visit my boots. My boots are beautifully constructed from dark, red leather, and not something I would actually be able to afford, not with my pathetic paycheck. But the boots and I have a relationship anyway. They sing to me from their little perch behind the glass window, ditties about the open trail, which are not their real personality, but pseudo cowboy junk they have picked up at the pseudo cowboy store, and sung with a scary, forced enthusiasm, alarming if you're not expecting it. Like pick-up lines. Like, Hey, Good Lookin'. The boots can be obnoxious, but they are so pretty, you can overlook it most days. They are always Happy Trails.

For one strange, exhilarating moment not one customer is in the store.

"Oh, Miss. Miss sales*gal*, can you help me?" Bailey screams, pulling up her tartan skirt, and twirling around in a circle. She's got on men's underwear, the white Jockey kind with the blue line around the waistband.

"Wa-hooooo," she shouts, "excuse me while I kiss the sky."

I love her for this.

Later, when the gate is pulled down and Robin is vacuuming in her tight black skirt and stocking feet, and Bailey is hand-steaming wrinkled skirts with her Walkman on, and I can't remember what I said that made all those women buy all those coats, I become extremely tired, shy again, more or less who I consider myself to actually be, wordlessly folding sweaters into perfect squares and stacking them into neat, fluffy piles. It is somehow satisfying to look at a neat stack of things, any things, that are all the exact same color. I linger over this tiny study in order and perfection.

Then I go home.

"Mind if I sit down?" he says.

My lunch, and therefore my entire day, are in danger of being ruined by a man in a big, white cowboy hat. That is, if I'm seeing things right. I mean, I know I am, but you have to question a hat like that. You just have to.

"It's a free whatever," I say.

"A free country?"

"That too."

I've seen this guy around the mall, strolling the lower levels in his unsullied cowboy boots, lurking noticeably, in that big hat, in the background of things. His mustache is thick and bushy, but carefully combed, well-manicured, like a lawn. He wears clean jeans and a good leather belt, its big silver buckle coiled into the shape of a sleeping snake.

"I'm trying to guess which store you work at," he says. "I keep seeing you on this bench."

Someone from another level drops a penny into the fake pond.

"I bet you work at Paraphernalia," he says, "Or The Sox Box."

"Wrong," I say.

"Then I bet you work at Talbots. No," he says, "Laura Ashley. You're the Laura Ashley type. The classic type. The good-bone-structure type."

"Wrong," I say.

"You tell me then, Beautiful Girl."

"If you must know, I work at Steinway," I say. "I play the pianos so the customers can hear how the instruments sound. It's not really that fun, but I'm working my way through college on a music scholarship, and they really pay a lot."

"Really?" he says.

"Uh huh."

"How come I don't believe you?"

"I don't know," I say, shrugging.

"I bet you really work at one of those little shitholes for minimum wage and no benefits," he says.

"I guess you're a real cowboy then," I say.

"Darlin', there are no more real cowboys," he says, "only outlaws in cowboy hats."

"Is that what you are?"

"What's your name?" he asks me.

Once, Bailey wore a nametag that said, PURPLE HAZE. Jimi Hendrix is her hero, the guitar god for *all time*. Five days went by before Robin noticed the nametag and delivered a hyperactive lecture on acting more professional. Before that though, the two of us were giddy, almost free.

"Bailey," I tell him.

"What's your real name?"

"Why can't Bailey be my real name?" I say.

"Because it's not the truth," he says. "Why can't I be Willie Nelson?"

"You're not?" I say.

I look, but I can't see his eyes behind the dark gray lenses of his glasses, the aviator kind.

I am surprised by how much time goes by while my car spins around and around on the frozen road. I've hit an ice patch on the exit ramp, coming off of the highway.

In the movies, action of this kind takes place so quickly, but here, in real life, there appears to be plenty of time to think about things, like, Can this really be happening? Am I really here? I have enough time to become totally aware of the darkness of the highway, the absence of other vehicles, of drivers, of people, of anything but frozen road, my car, and me. Driver's ed, taken in summer school, comes back to me. There is that kind of time. Time to recall a whole summer with friends two years ago, and driving around on the black-top, bashing into bright orange cones and laughing like maniacs. Take your foot off the brake, I think. Isn't that what you're supposed to do on ice? And finally the spinning stops, and I begin a strange, silent drift, sliding off of the road and onto the ramp's shoulder, where I sit completely unharmed, and singing to myself the same song I was singing before the wheels of my mother's old VW Rabbit hit the ice and began to spin.

"Carrie," they shriek.

I try to get away from them by hiding behind one of the round coatracks. I keep circling, around and around, but the little stalkers circle too.

"Carrie?" They are still shrieking.

"Carrie, it's us," one of them says. They have me sandwiched in between them, trapped, like bologna.

I find I can't remember their names. For some reason I think that they must all be named the same thing. Either they are all named Ashley or Amber, or Ashley-Amber with a hyphen.

"From last year. From Senior Choir." Then all together, "From *high school*," they say, laughing.

"We heard about your mother," says Ashley-Amber, her mood suddenly solemn.

"Heard what?" I say.

"Well, that she died."

"You heard that?"

"Well, yeah," one of them says softly.

"She didn't die at all," I say. "She almost died. She was sick. She had cancer. But she recovered with a combination of macrobiotic food and chemotherapy. She had a radical mastectomy, but she's doing really great. She's getting total reconstructive surgery, but in the meantime, she and I went shopping for all these new bathing suits and bras with falsies in the front. Then we bought a bunch of matching stuff, like coats. Now she and my dad are on vacation, like a second honeymoon in the Caribbean."

"Which island?" asks one of the girls.

"Ashley," another says, hitting her.

"St. Barth's," I say.

"Well, that's so great then," one of them says gently.

They like the word "great." I remember that, how much they liked the word "great."

"God, I'm like, so glad," says another. "That's so *great*."

"So, where are you going to college?" It's the same one who asked which island.

"My parents wanted me to go away, but I decided to stay home and help them out."

They just stare at me.

"What does that mean?" one of them asks. Bailey has me wearing a nametag that says, FOXY LADY, which Robin is too freaked out with her incoming shipment of hideous sweaters to have noticed yet.

"It's like a joke," I say. "Jimi Hendrix." They all stare at the joke.

"Who's Jimi Hendrix?" they ask.

"A famous architect," I say. "He built this mall."

"Great."

"I've got to go," I say, "I've got to go unlock a dressing room." I back away from them, calling out how great they all look. How totally great. And wasn't it great to run into each other? Everything is so unbelievably great.

I unlock the dressing room door and stand in there with my forehead resting against the cold, smooth mirror. My legs go, and I let myself slide against the carpeted wall to the floor. Robin is out there, pounding on the door. "Are you in there? What is going on in there?" I am definitely wearing too much eye makeup. Black mascara and black eyeliner hollow out my eyes and make my skin look pale. I can no longer seem to tell what looks good. As opposed to what looks bad.

I need a marketing strategy.

P.S., my skin is breaking out.

I close my eyes and listen to the sound of drizzling water as it echoes inside the mall. It's like water inside a cave. When I open my eyes he will be there.

"Wake up," he says. He's there. *He's there.*

"Do I look like I'm asleep?" I say.

"Yeah, you do," he says. "Sleeping Beauty takes a nap." He sits down on the bench beside me.

"Do you know that it ruins my day completely if someone sits down on this bench while I'm eating my lunch?"

"You call that shit lunch?"

I notice how pointy his snakeskin boots are. He is short, and those little stacked heels give him a slight boost in height, not that cowboy boots on short guys ever really fool anyone. I notice things I didn't notice before, things you can't notice when you are bombarded with the big picture. Or the big hat. Now I notice details like the small size of his hands, and the rings. He's got on silver rings. One ring is a cat's face with tiny rubies for eyes.

"If I didn't work here," I tell him, "I'm pretty sure I wouldn't be hanging around on this bench criticizing what the salespeople eat."

"I'm rich," he tells me.

"So," I say.

"So, rich is nothing to sneeze at."

"Do I look like I'm going to sneeze?"

"You could sneeze," he says. "That's a good name for you, Sneezy."

"That's amazing," I say, "because Sneezy really is my name. See, it says so, right here on my nametag." Actually, my nametag is missing again. I keep losing them. Today my nametag says LASHONDA BROWN, the name of an employee who was fired for having sex in the bathroom at the Food Court.

"It may say Sneezy, or it may say Sleeping Beauty," he says.

"Can't you read?" I say.

"No ma'am," he answers. "I can't read or write, but I can pay someone to do it for me. Muhammad Ali said that," he tells me.

"I think Muhammad Ali had dyslexia," I say.

"There's something real special about you," he says.

"I bet you say that to all the girls," I say, taking another large sip of coffee.

"I don't need to say it to all the girls," he says. "I'm saying it to you because I can see you're different."

I am sure this guy is known among the salesgals of this world as one gigantic joke, something to laugh and laugh about later with Bailey.

"Can I give you a ride home after work?" he asks.

"Of course," I say. "I'll meet you in the parking lot at nine."

"I'm serious," he says.

"I'm not," I say.

"Why not?"

"First of all, I have my own car," I say. "And besides, my mother says never to take a ride with a stranger."

"Do you always do what Mama says?"

I take the last sips from the bottom of my cup, which is basically crystals of coffee-soaked sugar. In high school I used to drink carrot juice.

"What if you got to know me?" he says.

"You say there are no more real cowboys, right?" I say.

"That's right, darlin'," he says.

"So, if there are no more real cowboys, then soon there will be no more pseudo cowboys, right? I mean, who are all the pseudo cowboys going to imitate?"

"Darlin', I'm afraid we're on the very verge of extinction," he says, holding up his hand and pointing it at me like a gun. He smiles a little, like a smirk. "Pow," he says. "You better get it while you can."

I visit my boots. They are mute today. Worn out, and not in the mood for little songs.

The store is just about to open and Robin decides to give a panicked motivational speech that she calls "Selling to the Upscale Customer."

"No woman is ever just looking," she tells us, "she's looking to buy. Now, let's have the best sales week ever."

She raises a lame little power fist. She looks especially anemic today.

Within an hour, Bailey and I are buttoning up blouses and picking up sweaters that the upscale customer has strewn all over the dressing room floors.

"Could this be more like vomit?" she says, holding up a white silk sweater, which has been smeared around the collar with punch-pink lipstick.

"Gross," I say, as though that would even begin to express it.

Here he comes, big, fake cowboy, into the store, looking not at all red in the face to be touching girls, things, running his fingers up and down the arms of a silk sweater. Bailey throws a gum wrapper at my head. She cannot believe what she is seeing. Bailey cannot believe her good luck, because she is always waiting for exactly this kind of walking spectacle.

He's wearing a black Harley-Davidson T-shirt, which fits tight across his small, muscular chest and arms. His jeans are black and tight and he rolls when he walks, from his heel, through to the pointy toe of his cowboy boots.

Bailey's way of snickering is to way over-smile at things. She laughs behind a huge, fake grin, which makes her peace-sign earring shake. She marches right up to him, and smiling hugely, asks if she can help him find something nice for his wife or his girlfriend today. Then she starts asking rude questions about the authenticity of the hat, and he lets her try it on, and she shouts "Ya-hoo," and any other cowboy thing she can think of. He has his own way of snickering, which is to barely smile at all.

Bailey checks herself out in the mirror.

"I'm starting to like this. It's fresh," she says.

"Hey, cowgirl," he says.

Bailey is playing with him, but he is playing with her, too, and it surprises me that she thinks she's the only one having fun.

He circles around the store a few more times, rolling on his boots, taking his time on his way out. He is like a time bomb in here, something waiting to go shooting off. Robin is watching him now, glaring from behind the cash register.

"I knew I'd find you," he whispers. His breath hits my ear and a flash of heat shoots down my neck and into my spine, where it sits in the small of my back, like a guy's hand while you're dancing.

Bailey comes bouncing over, full of a good time, "What did he say?" she asks.

"I don't know," I say. "He's crazy."

"He likes you," Bailey says, poking me in the arm. "He was staring at you the whole time."

"He likes *you*," I say.

"Secret boyfriend, secret boyfriend," she says, clapping her hands and jumping.

"That's right," I say, relieved to see him go, "he's my secret boyfriend."

"He's a drug dealer," Bailey says, leaning her body out into the mall to see where he's gone. "The sluts at the Food Court buy coke off him. And that's not all they do."

Robin is marching across the floor, coming right for us.

"He's got a good bod," Bailey says. "He wouldn't be so bad without all the cowboy paraphernalia." She leans out even farther. "Come back, secret boyfriend," she calls, "come back."

Robin grabs Bailey's arm, and physically pulls her back into the store.

"I was *leaning* out," complains Bailey. "My feet were still inside the store. Carrie can testify on my behalf. My feet were in. My feet were in."

What passes for fun, here on Level 2, is now over, and Bailey and I return to the task of picking up the clothes other women have decided it was okay to throw on the floor. I zip up pants and hang them back on hangers while I think about the boys I slept with in high school. There was one boy who said I love you, but then I found out he loved everyone. Boys, some of them with beautiful long hair in ponytails, and soccer team legs—boys, but not one man. I have never kissed anyone with small creases around his eyes and actual pick-up lines and in his head Willie Nelson singing the soundtrack to the movie of his life. I've never kissed anyone with such a fully realized mustache. I look down and see the faint imprint of his boot in the carpeted floor. I put my foot inside the impression. His boots were my boots, my red boots from Pop Cowboy, the ones that sang to me, and made me delirious with "consumer lust." Bailey's term, but I've already made it my own.

Bailey gets a personal call and comes back out onto the floor with black mascara tears running down her bright pink face. I watch while Robin, in defense mode, crosses her arms over her chest. I listen while Bailey pleads with her for the rest of the day off.

"I just can't let you go," Robin says.

"Jesus Christ," says Bailey, sobbing.

"I really wish I could," says Robin, "but the store. I have no one covering the back of the store."

"My boyfriend crashes his bike into a fucking telephone pole and all you care about is the back of the store."

"The back of the store is my job," says Robin, who is sobbing now too.

"You think I'm going to stand around in the back of the store while Duff lies there in a coma?"

"I'm sorry about your boyfriend, but I just can't let you out, not this afternoon."

"Fuck you," Bailey screams. "You people are heartless, fucking pigs."

Bailey storms into the back to get her stuff out of her locker. On her way out of the store she stops by the coats to give me a big hug in her little rabbit fur jacket, so soft, so helplessly soft.

"Duff will be all right," I say. I never know what to tell people, except to repeat all the things people said to me.

"Oh, sweetie," Bailey says, clinging to me. Her tears are all over me. Her tears are all over my face.

Later, I watch a girl about my age shoplift a thin pink belt, which is missing its plastic antitheft device. I lean against the coat rack, watching, while she rolls it neatly around her hand and stashes it away inside her backpack.

Saturdays are the busiest days of the week. Sales associates are required to arrive two hours prior to opening in order to attend various seminars with titles like "Sweater Folding," "Accessorizing," and "Staying Psyched." Without Bailey to stand behind Robin and make faces, the seminars are in danger of being taken even the tiniest bit seriously. My eyes are already burning from the dry air and fluorescent lighting, and the fact that it is way too early in the morning.

"Purple is to be referred to as 'Eggplant,' " Robin says. She is twitchy in her scuffed high heels, which you can tell were cheap to start with, shifting her weight nervously from one leg to another. "There is no *purple* in this store," she says. "Got it?"

"Is this 'Sweater Folding,' or 'Staying Psyched'?" asks a girl named Breck. She is new and takes notes.

Robin looks as tired as the rest of us, fueled by nothing more substantial than coffee and sugar, burning out before our eyes.

"Pantyhose. Pantyhose," she repeats, unaware that she is caught up in the middle of an incoherent rant about a pair of pantyhose so dirty they will stand up by themselves.

Near tears, Robin says, "Some people don't even have three minutes to wash out a pair of pantyhose."

I whisper to Breck, "See, it's good to have role models."

Outside it has begun to snow. I know this only because thick hair goes bushy, thin hair goes flat, and everybody complains that they have the wrong kind of hair. *How about a new coat? How about a new coat on sale? Burn baby burn.*

Now it is just me up front, selling coats to snowed-on women. Cheap, trendy coats that are not well made, that are not anything substantial, not anything that is going to last or hold up. Coats that will lose buttons and stays and little tacked-on velvet bows. Coats that will unravel. In my mind I can see them all unravel.

Last night, on my way upstairs to my bedroom, I passed by my mother's old room. My father doesn't sleep in there anymore. He sleeps downstairs on the couch with all of the lights on. When I looked in, I noticed that white powder from a blue box of hers had spilled all over the bureau and mingled with the dust. I wonder if my father opened the blue box, trying to recall the way she smelled when she was still here, and when she still used those things. From the doorway I could see the glass bottles of perfume. They sat untouched. Other things she threw away in a fit of disgust at things of beauty, at life, at the world, but these she left to turn old and dark from time and heat and too much light.

Robin is clapping her hands in front of my face. "Wake up," she says.

People keep telling me this.

"It's the busiest day of the week and you're standing around here daydreaming," she says.

I'm looking at Robin, thinking, She has got to stop using brown mascara, because it smudges, and then all it does is make her face look dirty.

"I put you up front to sell coats," she snaps. "Now if you don't want to stand in the back, you better WAKE UP."

"Robin, you need a day off," I tell her.

"I need some salespeople," she says, snapping her fingers at me. "Now, let's wake up and smell some coats."

"You mean, sell some coats," I say, correcting her.

"Listen," she tells me, "Your sales have gone way downhill lately. You better get it together, girl."

"I don't think you want that coat," I tell a woman whose huge hat hair is wild with static electricity. "It is a total waste of money," I tell her. "The style is over. It will look like a joke next fall."

The woman looks angry, as though she is being tricked.

"Can't you see it's not well made?" I say. "Can't you see that?"

"Is there a coat in this store you could recommend?" she asks, gesturing sarcastically.

I shake my head no.

"I appreciate your honesty," the woman says, "but I still want the coat. *I* like it."

"Take it then," I snap. "Who's stopping you?"

"What?" she says.

"Panty-Ho," I call her. I have just made this up, and start laughing.

"You're being abusive," she says. "Where is the manager? I want the manager."

"Still want the coat?" I ask.

"I like it," she says, clutching it to her chest. I watch her scurry across the sales floor to the register.

Burn baby burn. Maybe disco does sell clothes.

No cheese Danish today. I can no longer face the dwarf, the sight of him standing there in the sandwich board. I don't feel like a witness anymore. I feel like, just seeing him, I am part of the crime. And the boy who hates everything, his wrists with their jagged purple scars, zigzags and small dots that look unreal, drawn-on in Magic Marker. I no longer want to look or know or care or imagine. I don't want to have little conversations anymore.

I fall in with a group of mall walkers, old people dressed like fuzzy babies in pastel pink and blue. People brush up against me with their big bags. Purchases. The boy who hates everything passes me, loping along, and we nod, one mall employee to another. His T-shirt says GRAVITY SUCKS. I turn and watch him walk through the mall, until it's just the top of his half-shaved head, disappearing down the escalator.

My mother floats up the escalator, at her worst, with no vanity left in her, tubes in her nose and her arms, colorless tufts of hair on her head, big, vacant eyes staring out at a spot on the wall, where she seems to be watching something that no one else can see. My father is sitting on the end of my bed. The phone rang at an odd hour and I knew to try and stay asleep as long as I possibly could. Later, my father came into my room, which he never did, because it was a girl's room and embarrassed him. He sat on the end of my bed. I knew he was sitting there, and he knew I was only pretending now to be asleep, postponing hearing it for as long as I could. We froze like this for hours, I think.

I walk through the big department store, hoping to hear her voice there. *Ladybugs bring you luck,* she might say in her low, breathless voice, rough and soft, like tiny grains of sand pouring through your open fingers. I wonder where the sound of her voice might be, because for a while, it lingered here and there. For a while you could catch a trace of it, a faint half-whisper at the cosmetics counter, near the perfume. You could catch a trace of it. It lingered. I swear.

I let the women run their smooth, cool fingers over my eyelids, contouring my eyes, they tell me, with three different shades of beige. I inhale the smell of expensive perfumes. Flowery, lemony, cinnamon smells. I wait in the makeover chair for what could be hours. I wait until the white-coated women look annoyed, then concerned. I wait until a plainclothes security guard (good suit/bad shoes) approaches me, asking if everything is all right.

"Just waiting for someone," I tell him.

"Looks like that person is a no-show," he says.

But for a while it lingered right here.

"Guess so," I say.

On my way out to my car I see the dwarf and the boy who hates everything getting high behind a giant orange dumpster.

In the underground parking lot I hear his voice. It echoes, ricocheting off of parked cars.

"Hey, girl, can I give you a ride home?" Bing, bing, bing, and bing, and it's everywhere.

"No," I say, looking around, wondering how long I have been sitting in my car, running my hairbrush through my hair.

He is in the shadows, behind a concrete pole that says LEVEL 2 in huge blue letters.

I lock my doors.

I sit with the key in the ignition, wishing I could remember certain things that I have forgotten, but I can't even seem to remember what to remember. I rest my forehead on the steering wheel and accidentally blow my car horn.

He appears at the window in his absurd white hat, and I realize that a joke doesn't have to be funny to still be a joke.

"Unlock the door," he says through the window.

"Go away," I say.

"Go ahead, unlock the damn door."

I do. I do this.

He opens the car door, pulling it hard because it sticks badly. He tosses a bunch of empty Diet Coke cans into the back seat, and slides in beside me. He is wearing the warmest looking coat I have ever seen, a thick, shearling-lined jacket made of soft tan leather, a coat too good to ever unravel.

He stretches out in the seat beside me, and blows on his hands for warmth. "Sometimes life gives you shit," he says.

"What are you talking about?" I say.

"You know what I'm talking about, since you drive this shitty car."

"Does it make you feel superior to criticize everything?"

"I want to show you something," he says.

"Like what?" I answer.

"Like my fish," he says. "Each one of my fish is named for a character on *All My Children.*"

"You're a drug dealer," I say.

"You're a little liar," he says.

"I really did work at the piano store," I say, "but I changed jobs because they wouldn't let me off work when my boyfriend crashed his motorcycle. I lost it, and started screaming at the manager what a heartless pig he was, and then I stormed out of the store and never went back."

"What happened to your boyfriend?" he asks.

"He died," I say, feeling unexpectedly satisfied by the sound of it.

"Really?" he asks.

"Yes, really," I say. "He was this incredibly gifted person whose life was completely wasted."

"I want to know your real name," he says.

"Aren't you missing *All My Children?*" I ask.

"It's Saturday," he says.

"What about weekdays?"

"I tape," he says. "Where's your coat at?"

"I lost it," I say. I can see my breath, and I realize how cold I am, and that I will never see my coat again, because my coat is hanging in the locker room in the back of the store, and I have just decided that I am never going back. "I won my coat in a contest," I say, "a coat-selling contest."

He takes his coat off and wraps it around my shoulders. It is heavy and smells of sheared wool and expensive leather.

"I don't do drugs," I say.

"Tell me your name."

"Drugs bore me. Cocaine is passé. You should sell heroin."

"If I knew your name, I could name a fish in your honor."

"Won't I have to join the cast of *All My Children*?"

I want to settle into the coat, pull it tightly around me, give into to its soft, thick lining, but I let it sit, resting stiffly on my back.

"You're pretty enough to," he says.

"Right," I say.

"You shouldn't be running yourself down," he says. "I don't like to hear you running yourself down."

"It's so none of your business what I do."

"I want to touch your hair," he says. "Right now, in my mind, I'm touching your hair."

"Get out of my car," I say.

"Do you want to see my fish?"

"Are you high, or just insane?"

"None of the above," he says, reaching toward me. "Now, go ahead and take my hand." A flash of silver rings, of cat's-eyes and rubies. "Go ahead, take it."

I reach to turn the key in the ignition, but he grabs my wrist and pulls me toward him.

"Get out of my car," I say.

"Your teeth are chattering," he says. "You're shaking all over."

He gathers the coat by its lapels and pulls me, wrapped up in it, toward him.

Even so, there is still time to put a stop to stupid compliments, and all of the rest of it, none of which makes any sense in the world. I know I could still get out of the car. I could turn, I could walk, I could run, before his mouth becomes the only warmth in the world.

y's STORY
by
SYLVIA FOLEY

THE LETTER j WAS MY UNDOING: HER LIQUID STROKE, THE ORIGAMI beauty of the fold at her throat, the way her eye-dot bobbed along above her, never falling, never failing her. It was a part of her and yet apart from her. She carried it everywhere. It was her buoy and her mantra; it gave her courage, and kept her afloat in the White Sea.

I was living inside an abandoned zero in the dump just outside Ysto, a town on the northern seacoast. I made my nest out of tangled fishing line and steel wool and cast-off punctuation. Of the last, I preferred the commas for the way they curved softly against me, took my form for their own. The semicolons stung my foot and mocked me. "We are not alike," I told them. "Ah, but we are just like you," they said. "You've curled your tail, is all." I fumed and sputtered, but could think of no adequate response. I did not want them to know the true depth of my feeling for her.

Others lived in the dump as well: solitary, silent *e*'s struck from the likes of *judgment* and *story;* stealthy *gh* pairs, hounded from *thruway* and *nite;* and my cousins, those beggar *y*'s, neither entirely vowel nor consonant, caught riding the backs of *voyeur* and *coyote.* They were outcasts, as I was. Driven off for homonymic thefts of trust, for acts of trespass or infidelity, in the eyes of the world they were guilty of moral weakness. I tried not to judge them. They were what they were, what they had been made for. Their only crime was loneliness. Underneath my elastic skin, the placid exterior I presented, I too mourned for lost freedom. Yet because of who I was, a capital's bastard, even they did not entirely accept me.

My father was a rarity, a lowercase who had risen above his type. His transformation was complete long before I was born. There were stories about how he'd blunted his serifs driving himself against the etched blue sky until it cracked open; and he'd never looked back, though he never forgot where he came from. He headed up Ysto until old age weakened his proud posture. There were signs presaging his decline. He began to fancy himself the stalked prey of b's and d's, those letters of the ascendancy that live entirely above the line. My father thought highly of them, all born descenders did, we couldn't help it; and so he thought less of himself. Most descenders are known for their stalwart yet easily subjugated nature. In my youth I was defiant. This worried my father greatly. Watch the p's, he'd tell me; study their willingness to work in yoked teams for the sake of *appurtenances, appendices,* and *appliances,* laboring in foreign lands like *Appalachia* and *Parsippany.* He lectured me and uttered pronouncements: "Be like them!" As his health failed, he developed a stutter that made us weep. We fed him motor oil, 10W-40, the highest viscosity, which gave him some relief. I wanted more out of life than this. I left his house the day he died.

Every Ystorian learns to sing the erot by heart. We learn it as we study our forms, print and cursive. Our hearts beat hard, our limbs wobble as we learn to stand alone and then to swim together in the Great White, scrolling and looping and dotting and crossing until we shake with exhaustion. Learning one's print form develops individual character and stamina; hissing or huffing, teeth bared or nearly swallowing our tongues in fear, we practice balancing on the blue tightropes, whispering our names to ourselves: aaaaaaaa / bbbbbbbb / cccccccc. By assigned place, I was too far away from j to know her then; I was y, and barely knew that much. I was still learning what it meant to have a body: its awful and glorious cleft mouth, which gives me a lusty appetite but leaves me constantly hungry; its serif-eyes, which grant wide lateral but poor binocular vision; the long leg my kind value for the speed it affords us on the shoals. Running was my planned salvation. And when I raced, I won, coming in last time and again, as *y*'s have for generations.

But it's when we learn cursive that we first become more than ourselves. In cursive we embrace all the sensual miscellany of language: the proximal kiss, which links us and gives us temporary, incarnate lives in words; same-letter coupling, so homoerotic; the orgasmic vocalizing of the long vowels; even the selfish lovemaking of punctuation, whose vows of same-mark celibacy resign them to fucking us. (I was taught to respect punctuation, owing to our frequent adjacency; perhaps this was for my own sake as well as my father's.)

And here is the riddle: Are we many or one? I cannot answer for all; but some letters, in the manner of fungi and suns, can send forth their minions without diminishing: such a one was j. A trillion times her twins appeared and disappeared in daily usage, paling slightly as they surfaced, their eye-dots drying out in the air of countless overheated jury rooms, their tails switching in the mouths of jockeys. Yet no matter how many of her existed at any given moment, she was never any less than herself, solely and rapturously herself, as she plied the sea. And I? I am easily confounded by doubt: *And sometimes y*, the references say.

I was soon proficient in both print and cursive, and for a time indulged in much heady converting from one to the other and back again, as the young will. And the longer I practiced, the slower I became. Language requires languidity; we believe it is a kind of time. I was a runner and loved its flow. I liked to run laps early mornings around the dump, when no one would be watching, as I was still rather awkward and easily shamed. But because I was known for my insatiable hunger, the others were wary, and soon left me alone. Then one day, looking up from my makeshift starter's blocks, I saw her.

Desire cast its rough blur around me like a net. My ears went numb; I could not feel my foot in the sand. I wanted her: That was all I knew. I had no language for love then. She was gliding by on a crest of blue, her eye-dot bobbing in the moonlight, and as she passed I caught a glimpse of the waxy white sea below her. Then, for no reason I could discern, she slowed, treading, and turned to look at me, waiting for words to come.

Even at our closest, in *joy,* we were never together. A conundrum stood between us: o, who holds the universe and all its emptiness within him, who despises intimacy, even in his cursive form, he hangs and pulls on his joining rope. But from across the divide of his vast, vacant soul I could at least see her, could hear the faint lashings of her tail as she looped into cursive, could smell her longing. She kept her back turned to me, no matter the hour, protecting the soft lead of her belly. The word rose at its fixed time and was spoken, or thought, and when it fell back into the sea, I lost her in the pounding surf.

Yet as her eye swivels its 360 degrees, I know she sees me. It proceeds majestically above her, never falling, never failing her. When we float above the white shoals, I can hear the taunting whispers of the others: *jealousy jittery japery jokey jury,* they say. She only stretches her throat-fold. As for the rest of us, on black nights in the Ysto dump we seethe, we seek, we long, we touch, we nose one another's genitals like dogs, and come alone, rarely in ecstasy and always in silence. I swear my love for her. I feel the erot's thrill and flush come over me whenever she's near. It is not enough. But I am used to hunger.

PLANE CRASH THEORY
by
DANI SHAPIRO

THESE ARE THE FIRST WORDS I'VE WRITTEN SINCE J. FELL DOWN THE stairs, unless you count lists. I have lists in my pockets, lists tacked to the bulletin board above my desk. Small lists on Post-its ruffle like feathers against walls and bureaus. Chunky baby food, milk, Cheerios, Diaper Genie refills. Huggies overnight diapers. This is what I do now. I cross things off lists. The more items I cross off, the better I can breathe.

J. was just seven weeks old when we moved from Manhattan across the river to Brooklyn. We bought an old, four-story brick townhouse with a dogwood out front. A green-painted front door with glass panels led into a foyer with a pale pink chandelier dangling overhead. An antique cherry banister curved in one fluid line up two steep flights of stairs. The staircase itself was polished, with creaky, uneven steps.

My husband and I looked at a lot of places before we decided to live in Brooklyn. Manhattan was out of the question—we needed four bedrooms—so we explored Montclair, South Orange, Hastings-on-Hudson. We considered the country. Litchfield, Sag Harbor. During a trip to Seattle, on a sunny day when we could see the mountains, we thought about moving out West. We kept reminding ourselves that we're writers, and writers can work from anywhere. But Brooklyn won us over—so close to our friends, to everything we knew. And then, after a parade of realtors showed us dozens of narrow dark Victorians, we fell in love with the brick house. The night after I first walked through the house, it filled my dreams. I was in my eighth month of pregnancy, and my dreams had become colorful, baroque. I floated through each room, focusing on the wide-planked orange pine floors, the intricate, crumbling moldings.

We ran out of money shortly after J. was born. It was my fault. I was giddy, on a postnatal, hormonal high. I was a mother! I wanted everything to be just right for my little family. The parlor needed an armoire for Michael's record collection. The baby's nursery had navy blue curtains hanging to the floor and a hand-loomed rag rug. We had thousands of books, so we found a carpenter to build in shelves. And as long as he was already there, we had him install library lights, extra electrical outlets. You never know when you'll need them. I pored over "shelter magazines": *House & Garden, Metropolitan Home.* I looked at photographs of other people's shelters. A shelter with a small Mondrian above the mantel. A shelter with an eighteenth-century writing desk in a child's room. We relined the fireplaces, built closets, installed an alarm system, and before I knew it, we were broke.

Eighteen steps lead from our front hall to the second floor, to J.'s nursery and our bedroom. They are steep and creaky. Along the curve of the wall, near the top of the staircase, there is an indentation in the wall shaped like a tablet, like half of the Ten Commandments. I am told it's called a coffin.

Things don't go wrong all at once. There are small things—invisible things—that constantly go wrong. Wires fray inside a wall. A van speeds through a yellow light. Someone leaves a Q-tip in the baby's crib. These small things almost always just scatter and disappear. Big wind comes along and—poof!—they're gone. But once in a while, they start sticking to each other. If this happens, you find yourself with a big thing on your hands.

Whenever we're on an airplane taxiing down the runway, I ask Michael to explain this to me. He calls it Plane Crash Theory. I know he wonders why I need to hear it again and again. But I do. His theory is simple, scientific: in order for a commercial airliner to crash, many things have to go wrong in sequence. Many unlikely things. No single event causes an accident. It is the sheer coincidental accrual and velocity of these failures that sends two hundred people plummeting into the ocean. This makes Michael feel better. He finds comfort in these odds as he settles into his seat and cracks open a newspaper as the jet takes off. Me, I think it's as likely as not that I'll be on that particular plane.

Michael and I have always lived hand to mouth, though from the outside it doesn't look that way. We occasionally get a big check, then go months—sometimes years—without any money to speak of coming in. We bought the house with the expectation that a big check was on its way from Hollywood. It was a done deal. What we didn't realize was that done deal, in the language of Hollywood, does not, in fact, signify a deal that is done. The producers are on vacation in Hawaii. Larry (who's Larry?) is on the golf course and can't be reached.

Here are the things we didn't do when we moved to Brooklyn, because the check didn't come. I still have the list tacked to the refrigerator: fireplace screens, seed garden, repair roof hatch, basement beam. Last on the list was runner for staircase.

J! He was perfect, with a burly little body. Late at night, while Brooklyn slept, he burrowed into my soft belly as he nursed, and I watched him with bewilderment and joy. Where had he come from? He seemed to have inherited a temperament that didn't exist in either my husband's family or my own. From a grumpy, depressed bunch of people comes this smiling boy. In the darkness of his nursery, I stared out the window at the glowing red face of a clocktower in the distance, and thought obsessive thoughts of all the things I had read about in the baby books. He could choke on a button, or the eye of a stuffed animal. He could suffocate in his own crib sheet. He could strangle himself with the cord of his purple elephant pull toy.

This is what I do with happiness. *Kayn aynhoreh,* my grandmother used to say, repeating this magical Yiddish phrase to ward off evil. *Kayn aynhoreh.* I need to think of the worst case scenario. If I think about it hard enough, it won't happen.

There is a cage in our basement. I've never gone down there. The stairs are dark and rickety; the third step from the top is loose. The cage is made of rotting wood poles and chicken wire. It was built earlier in the house's history, a less affluent time. Maybe it was once a rooming house. When we moved in, Michael found an axe propped in a corner of the basement. He's not in the least spooked by it. This is one of the reasons I married him. He's been using the axe to tear the cage down. Sometimes, I hear the crash of metal and he emerges, covered with dust.

We come from money, my husband and I. Not huge family fortunes, but from first- and second-generation Jewish parents who made good, who have more than one house and drive the cars they swore they would never drive (those Nazi-mobiles) and take first-class round-the-world trips. Parents who wish we had become doctors or lawyers instead of writers. I'm saying this because we could have put our pride aside and asked. We could have said Mom, Dad, we're low on cash. We need a couple of thousand. The staircase is slippery. We should do something about it. Put up a runner.

We settled into the new house over the long, hot summer. I rarely left. I was captivated by J. and spent hours doing nothing but singing the Winnie-the-Pooh song to him. Saturdays, we had a routine: We walked with J. in his stroller to a farmer's market at Grand Army Plaza; I circled the market buying goat cheese, banana muffins, grape juice while Michael and J. played in the shade. It was the first time in my adult life I had a full refrigerator. I kept the grapes in a Provençal bowl we had brought back from our honeymoon.

One day during that summer, Michael and I were driving through the city, heading home after visiting friends who had just given birth to a premature baby. Michael turned right from Thirty-fourth onto Broadway, and drove straight into a swarm of police officers. They had set up a trap and were pulling cars over for making an apparently illegal turn. Michael, usually a calm guy, lost his temper. He screeched to the curb, and got out of the car. Maybe it was sleep deprivation, or the heat, or visiting a three-and-a-half-pound in the neonatal intensive care unit. I saw him waving his hands at the traffic cop, who didn't meet his eye, shrugged, and began to write a ticket. Michael opened the car door, grabbed a camera we happened to have handy, and began snapping photos. The corner of Thirty-fourth with no sign. The traffic cop himself. He got back in the car. "I'm going to fight this," he said. I wondered if he'd bother, or just forget about it.

That coffin, that empty space, bothered me. Broke as we were, I decided that something belonged there. But what? Fresh flowers? An empty vase? I gave it a lot of thought. Then, I bought an arrangement of dried sprigs of herbs, baby roses, big bulbous things that I didn't know the name of that dropped from the edges of a cracked white urn. I placed it in the coffin and it filled the space nicely, with some of the dried arrangement pushing out into the stairwell in a burst of color. A bit precarious, perhaps, but hell, it looked so good that way. I could picture it in one of those shelter magazines.

September. Back-to-school time for me. Leaving for my teaching job in the city was impossible. I would walk down the front steps of the house while Michael and J. waved bye-bye from the door. I could barely breathe, but I didn't say anything. Just waved at them, blew kisses at J., and wondered if I would ever see them again.

On the subway, I would hang on to the pole and stare out the smudged window at the graffiti on the tunnel walls. I thought of J., of Michael, of anything safe and good, anything to pull me back, but thinking of them only made it worse. I was underground, with no way out. Moving farther away from them by the minute. Was this what having a family meant?

Of course, J. needed a babysitter. We interviewed fourteen women for the job. Who do you trust? We talked to cousins, sisters, best friends of babysitters of friends, and friends of friends. Finally we chose Marsha. She was young and pretty, with a Louise Brooks bob and big brown eyes. She was so gentle, so sweet that her eyes seemed to be constantly brimming with tears. She had a little girl of her own. She pulled a photo from her wallet; I liked how proud she was of her child. Marsha would never be one of those babysitters I saw in the park, talking to her friends with her back turned to my baby.

One morning, when the train pulled into the station, I stood on the platform, paralyzed, watching as the doors opened, the rush hour crowd pushed its way in, and the doors slid shut again. This had never happened to me before. I climbed back upstairs and stood on the street. I wondered if I should just walk the two blocks home. Call in sick. Give up for the rest of the semester. It was too hard. I didn't know what was wrong with me. An off-duty cab was approaching and, impulsively, I flagged it. The driver stopped for me. As we rolled down Flatbush, we got to talking. He said his name was Tony. He came from Nigeria. He lived nearby, and was on his way into the city to begin his shift. By the time he dropped me off at school he had given me his number. I told him I'd call him the following week to pick me up on his way in. Maybe that would make it easier.

On her first morning working for us, Marsha put too much detergent in the wash while she was doing the baby's laundry. The water flooded my office and dripped through the old floorboards to my bedroom closet below. As we frantically mopped up the mess, I tried to comfort her. I told her it was just an accident. Nothing was ruined. It could have happened to anybody.

That afternoon, Marsha and I pushed J. in his stroller to the park. I wanted to give her my guided tour of the neighborhood. The health food store, the pizza place, the Key Food. It was a warm day, just past Halloween, and the playground was full of moms and kids and babysitters. I lowered J. into the baby swing, and he laughed and laughed as I pushed him. He has the most unusual laugh I've ever heard in a baby. It's like, he cracks himself up. Everything was funny that day: The leaves falling off the trees were funny. The little girl with her orange plastic pumpkin was funny. Mommy making her silly faces was very, very funny. He was wearing a Red Sox baseball cap and a blue denim jacket. Already, at six months old, he wanted to go higher and higher.

On the morning of Marsha's second day, we take a family nap together before she arrives. J. falls asleep between us, his little mouth open, his eyelashes blond and long. We hold hands across his sleeping body.

It is a teaching day. I dress in black cargo pants, a black turtleneck sweater, black boots. Tony will pick me up at nine o'clock. I feel pretty pleased with myself at this arrangement. Marsha arrives a few minutes late. Michael is going to catch a ride into the city with me; today is his court date to fight that traffic ticket, and he seems strangely energized by it. J. is in his high chair, being fed strained plums. I take the dog out for a quick walk, rounding the corner by the bodega. A truck honks. You look beautiful! the driver yells. I'm in such a good mood— I've figured out my life!—that I yell back Thanks!

We cross the Brooklyn Bridge, and for once I feel at peace on my way to school. Michael is in the back of the taxi next to me. Tony is an excellent driver. And Marsha is at home with J., feeding him strained plums in his safe, ergonomically designed high chair. It's a perfect day. The city is a jagged, sparkling cliff along the East River and I notice things I don't notice on the D train when it crosses the bridge. The small boats, the abandoned Brooklyn Navy Yard, the faint outline of the Statue of Liberty off to the left in the distance. I feel, for a moment, lucky.

We drop Michael off somewhere near the courthouse. He gets out of the taxi, a manila envelope containing proof of his innocence—photos of the corner of Thirty-fourth and Broadway—in his hand. He has graying hair and a mostly-gray goatee and he's put on some weight since the baby was born. He's wearing his usual blue jeans, black T-shirt, green army jacket. We pull away from the corner and, as I always do, I turn and watch as he walks away. In our marriage, I am the one who turns around and watches. He is the one who walks deliberately, in the direction of wherever it is he's going.

This is the first morning since J. was born that we have both been out of the house at the same time.

As I speed farther and farther away from my neat and well-appointed house (the bookshelves, the sheer white bathroom curtains, the ficus thriving in the South-facing window, the dried flowers bursting forth from the coffin in the stairwell) up the West Side Highway past terrain more familiar to me than my Brooklyn neighborhood where even the silence and the birds chirping and the car alarms in the middle of the night still feel strange and new—I close my eyes.

When my cell phone rings, it surprises me. It rings from deep inside my briefcase, which is a bag I use only once a week, when I teach. I unsnap the briefcase and pull the phone out from its own special little pocket inside. I'm thinking, it's Michael. He's forgotten something. We are speeding toward the Seventy-ninth Street boat basin. The traffic is light. I flip the phone open.

Even when I hear the screams on the other end of the phone, I don't get it. Marsha is screaming, J. is screaming. There's static on the line. I can barely hear anything but the screaming, and I'm thinking, we just left twenty minutes ago. Nothing terrible could happen in twenty minutes. Her voice is shaking so hard all I can hear is, I fell, and stairs, and he hit his head, and I'm sorry, I'm sorry, I'm sorry.

I notice that Tony has wordlessly turned off the West Side Highway and is heading downtown, back toward Brooklyn, pedal to the floor. I tell Marsha to call 911. She's crying so hard, hyperventilating, that I have to keep my voice gentle, ask Can you do that? Can you do that for me? I tell her I will call her back in three minutes.

I try to think. The world shrinks around me. I call J.'s pediatrician. I can practically see her office from where I am right now, in the back of Tony's car. We haven't switched to a local pediatrician, believing irrationally in Manhattan doctors over Brooklyn doctors. While I'm on hold, I try to catch my breath, because I can't think clearly, and my heart is going to explode. I'm going to have a heart attack right here in the back of a taxi and that won't do anybody any good, will it?

Kids hit their heads all the time, J.'s doctor tells me in a professional, soothing tone, like she's talking someone off a ledge. Tell the babysitter to put some ice on it. Is he crying? Well, that's a good thing. It's when they're not crying that you worry.

I call Michael's cell phone. He's at a diner, just about to go into the courthouse. And I say there's been an accident, that it's going to be okay, but that it appears that Marsha has slipped and fallen down the stairs while holding J. and EMS is coming, and I'm on my way home. Michael is halfway out the diner door before I've finished the first sentence, and is springing in his green army jacket to the subway. And I am somewhere on lower Broadway. Tony is weaving in and out of traffic.

The stairs. There are eighteen. Have I mentioned eighteen? Maybe she fell near the bottom. If she fell near the bottom, on the last few steps and landed on the small rug in the foyer, that wouldn't be so bad. What part of his head? Babies have soft spots. All I can think about as we pass the Tower Records building and make a few quick turns and speed down the Bowery is, please, not the curve at the top of the stairs, the place where it would be most likely to fall, the place where the steps are narrow and the dried flowers make the passage even narrower, and it's a long, long way down. Please, not that.

He was screaming. Screaming is good. Screaming is the best thing. That's what you want to hear. Big, loud, shrieking sounds.

I call my home and a stranger answers the phone. A strange man. A strange police sergeant man. He asks me who I am. I say I am the mother. How's my baby? He says, Ma'am, your baby has quite a bump on his head. I melt for this man, I want to collapse into his big, blue chest. His voice is not shaking, he is calm, he is imparting information to me, information I need. Quite a bump. We can deal with quite a bump.

I call the school. I won't be able to teach my class. Baby fell down stairs. Baby fell down stairs trumps all. Trumps viruses and flus and the dog ate my students' homework. I call back the doctor. They're taking him to the hospital, I tell her. She seems annoyed. After all, she's certain that I'm a hysterical mother, that this is only a minor bump. And it occurs to me, not for the first time, that this doctor is younger than I am. When I was in second grade, she was in kindergarten. What is she doing, taking care of my son?

I grew up in a home where prayer was where you turned in moments like these. But I have never been in a moment like this, and I do not know how to pray.

I catch Tony's eyes in the rearview mirror, and then notice for the first time a yellow plastic taxi, dangling there. It looks like it's flying, floating against the pale blue sky. I keep staring at the cheerful taxi, imbuing it with supernatural powers. Nothing bad will happen if I just don't take my eyes off the taxi and keep repeating Please God over and over again.

We pull up to the emergency room of a hospital somewhere in downtown Brooklyn. All I have in my wallet is a twenty, and the meter is much more than that, but I hand Tony the twenty with an apology and he turns around and looks at me like the father of four children that he is. He says, I'm not leaving until you come out and tell me about the baby.

There were eight of us, friends and acquaintances, who were pregnant at the same time with our first babies. Something about the age thirty-six. Thirty-six means, get serious. Thirty-six, at least in New York City, means that you're still young enough to do it, with any luck, without fertility doctors and injections and in vitro and all that stuff of middle-aged motherhood. Thirty-six is still normal. And so I would think, sometimes, about my pregnant friends, and then I would think about statistics. Most of us would be fine: a little morning sickness, indigestion, varicose veins. Half of us would end up with C-sections. One or two would have some serious complications during pregnancy: gestational diabetes, preeclampsia. The sort of thing our mothers didn't even know about but that we, with our shelves of pregnancy books, our middle of the night online surfing, know only too well. I would think about the odds. Then, the woman whose due date was just before mine developed severely high blood pressure during her birth and she very nearly died. I felt, in a completely unscientific way, that she had taken the fall for all of us.

J. is on a tiny bed in a tiny curtained-off area in a tiny E.R., and he is not crying. He is not shrieking. His eyes are closed, and he is just lying there. Why isn't anybody doing anything? Marsha is sitting on a plastic chair by the window, a tissue pressed to her nose. Her eyes are red, and she looks like her life is over. Two police officers are standing near the door. Sit down, Mommy, one of the nurses tells me.

I pick up my baby. He is unconscious. But he was screaming just a little while ago! Screaming is good. What happened? I don't want to shake him. Shaking is bad, I know. I clutch him to my chest, feel his breath, whisper in his ear, "Mommy's here. It's going to be all right. Mommy's here." His eyes flutter open slightly, and he lets out a pathetic little whimper. "Look at me," I command him, my six-month-old whose entire vocabulary consists of "Ga."

Michael rushes in. His face is white, his eyes are huge. He hugs me and J. together, he turns to the doctor, a Pakistani named Noah, and asks what's going on. "We've ordered a CT scan," says the doctor. "Does your baby have any allergies?"

While J. is sedated and taken in for his CT scan, two men in suits approach me. They introduce themselves as police detectives. They are lumbering, uncomfortable. Ma'am? Can we just ask you a few questions? Your babysitter. How long has she worked for you? Two days, I say. They exchange a glance. Ma'am? You don't think . . . well, you don't think she did anything.

Our pediatrician calls the Brooklyn Hospital. She wants J. transferred to the Upper East Side Hospital where she works, the hospital with the best neonatal intensive care unit in the city. Suddenly, she is no longer calling this a minor bump. She is no longer sounding annoyed. She says she's sending an ambulance, a team.

I don't want to hurt Dr. Noah's feelings. I don't want him to think that we believe his hospital to be inferior to the Manhattan hospital where we are about to transfer our baby. Our pediatrician wants to see him, I shrug apologetically, marveling at my own ability, even in a moment like this, to be polite at all costs. It's my nature. I have a nice surface. Dinner party, emergency room, it really makes no difference. Can I get you something to drink? You look tired. Here, put your feet up.

Marsha gets up from her plastic chair by the window where she has been interrogated by two detectives from the 77th Precinct and walks toward me. Her whole face has crumbled, and she looks like a completely different woman. Not young. Not pretty. Her arms are outstretched, and I realize that she wants me to hug her. And so I do. I wrap my arms around this trembling woman who fell down the stairs, who doesn't know how it happened, who was wearing socks on the slippery, slippery wood. Who let go of my baby so that he tumbled by himself from the sixteenth or seventeenth step down who knows how many steps before she grabbed onto his arm and caught him. Are you okay? I ask her.

Tony waits outside. At least an hour has gone by, and he's sitting there in his taxi, meter turned off.

This is how they transport a baby in the back of an ambulance: I lie on a stretcher, and they tie me down. Then they hand me J., bundled up in the pajamas he was wearing this morning. Blue pajamas the color of the sky, printed with clouds shaped like white sheep. I cradle him in my arms, his head resting against my breast. His hair is tangled, his upper lip is rubbed raw from crying. The bump is getting bigger. The team—a driver, a paramedic, a nurse, and a doctor—lifts us into the back of the ambulance. I watch through the window as we are driven away from the Brooklyn hospital, siren going, through the congested streets of downtown Brooklyn, over the bridge once more, and up the East River Drive. The doctor, a lanky, dark-haired woman with a big diamond on her finger, keeps checking J.'s vitals, while I keep myself sane by asking her where she went to medical school, how long she's been out, what she wants to specialize in.

I don't want to be a writer anymore. I want to be her.

Hellooooo! coos the pediatrician as she parts the curtain in the I.C.U. Her face is scrunched into her practiced, good-with-babies grin. Let's see that bump. Oooh, that's a nasty bump. J. is in a hospital crib, and I have lowered the rail and crawled in there with him. If I tuck myself into the fetal position, it's not such a bad fit. The pediatrician opens her wallet and passes around a photo of her own six-month-old daughter. The nurses coo, then hand me the photo. She's not a cute baby, not cute at all, and she's sitting up against one of those department store backdrops of lollipops and balloons. I keep looking at the doctor, J.'s doctor, wishing I were the kind of person who would say excuse me, but what the fuck are you thinking?

At night, friends bring bagels and lox. Chocolate bread. Cheeses. A cheese board, a knife. We have a party in J.'s room. He's coming to, coming out of that gray place where he went to. He gives everybody a weak little smile.

The phone rings. It's Tony, checking on the baby.

The pediatric step-down I.C.U. is festooned with photos of its long-term patients. Birthday parties, staged plays, tired-looking nurses wearing clown hats. In some of the rooms there are special video monitors, so that parents and children can hook up to say good night. I sleep curled up with J., waking every hour as a nurse comes in to lift his lids, check his pupils, take his blood pressure and pulse. Michael wanders the corridors, talking to the children. An eleven-year-old who has lived in the hospital for nearly the past year, waiting for a heart and a liver, tells him about her seven-year-old friend down the hall, who she feels sorry for, because she's only seven, and she hasn't had a chance to live yet.

J. has had a normal CT scan, but they decide to do an MRI as well. That's why we're here, with the big guns, isn't it? My husband goes in with J., into the noisy, noisy room where we get three-dimensional color pictures of his brain. My husband is instructed to remove all metal from his body: watch, coins, belt buckle, wedding band. I put his ring on my thumb, twirling it around and around as I wait.

The MRI shows a contusion on J.'s brain, just below the nasty, nasty bump. Wait a minute. Contusion is a fancy word for bruise, right? And bruises bleed. Bruise on his brain?

We're talking fractions, here. I was never good at math. We're talking an infinitesimal distance between healthy baby and dead baby. That's what we're talking.

Kayn aynhoreh.

In the morning, we check out of the hospital. We are wheeled, J. and I, down the long white corridor. I've pulled a striped knit cap over his misshapen head, and he's grinning, flirting with the nurses who wave and call out There he goes! There goes our boy! like he's on a float and this is a parade. The two transplant girls wave good-bye too, in their robes and slippers. The head nurse gives him a kiss. They are all so happy, so happy to see him go.

When we pull up to our house and bring the baby inside, I feel as though I'm walking into a crime scene. The police officer left his card on the kitchen table, under that jar of strained plums with a plastic spoon still stuck inside. The kitchen tap is dripping. Yesterday's newspaper is open to the metro news. I carry J. upstairs. The steps are so old, so creaky and uneven. And the dried flowers look like tumors, like malignant growths on an X ray, egg-shaped and prickly. I watch J.'s eyes for any flicker of fear but he's focused on the ceiling.

Marsha called that night to ask how J. was doing. Michael said he was fine. He didn't want her to worry. Then he fired her. It wasn't easy. We felt bad about it. When she asked why, her voice gentle and resigned, the only answer—you almost killed our baby— seemed like more than could be said.

The socks, the stairs, the dried flowers, Michael's traffic ticket, our empty bank account, the strained plums, my subway panic. It all adds up to something. Doesn't it? It adds up to almost died.

Kayn aynhoreh.

The Hollywood check finally arrived. The first thing we did was buy a very nice runner for the staircase. It's a pale brown the shelter magazines might call "sand" or "birch" and there are pastel stripes running up the sides. I yanked out the brown, bulbous things that hung over the edge of the cracked white urn, and pulled out some of the roses until there was nothing pushing its way out of the coffin.

I stay pretty close to home these days. Downstairs, J. is laughing. Have I mentioned that he has the most unusual laugh? The sun is streaming through the tall parlor windows. It's early afternoon, almost time for his nap. I can picture his sleepy eyes, the way he bangs on his plastic butterfly when he gets tired. I can't write anyway, so I go downstairs to see him.

I rock my baby while he sucks down his bottle. The bump is gone. Sometimes, I think I can still see a bluish stain on his forehead. This is what I do, every single time I put him to sleep: I sing him three rounds of "Hush Little Baby," four rounds of "Twinkle, Twinkle, Little Star." Then I count backwards from fifty. When I get to one, I finish by saying Thank you God. Please keep this baby safe. Please watch over him and keep him safe. I repeat it over and over again while I rock. I can't alter the routine, and if it's interrupted, I have to start all over again. I imagine an invisible hand cupping my baby's head, softening the blow by a fraction as he smashed into the corner of a stair. Whose hand? What grace?

The house is quiet. Outside, birds are chirping, pecking at the grass seeds we've scattered in the backyard. I'm not sure where Michael is. He's around here somewhere. He's always doing something practical around the house. Maybe he's in the basement, taking down the last of the cage I have never seen.

DEARTH
by
AIMEE BENDER

THE NEXT THING IN THE MORNING WAS THE CAST IRON POT FULL OF potatoes. She had not ordered them and did not remember buying potatoes at the grocery store. She was not one to bake a potato. Someone must have come in and delivered them by accident. Once, she'd woken to meadowsful of sunflower bouquets all over her house in glass vases and they turned out to be for the woman next door. Perhaps the woman next door had a new suitor now, one who found something romantic in root vegetables.

Our woman checked through her small house but it was empty as ever. She asked her neighbor, the one whose windows were still buttery with petals, but the neighbor wiped her hands on a red-checkered cloth and said no, they were not for her, and she had not ordered any potatoes from the store either, as she grew her own.

Back at the house, the potatoes smelled normal and looked normal but our woman did not particularly like potatoes and did not want them around so she threw them in the trash and went about the rest of her day. She swept and squared and pulled weeds from her garden. She walked to the grocery store and bought milk. She was a quiet person, and spoke very few (five) words throughout the afternoon: Thank You, Good-bye, Excuse Me.

The next morning, when she woke up, the potatoes were back. Nestled, a pile of seven, in the cast iron pot on the stove. She checked her trash and it looked just as it had before, with a folded milk carton and some envelopes. Just no potatoes. She picked up all seven potatoes again, and took them across the road and pushed them one at a time into the trash dumpster, listening as they thumped to the bottom of the bin.

That afternoon she walked past rows of abandoned cabins to her lover's house. He was in his bedroom, asleep. She crawled into the bed with him and pushed her body against his until he woke up, groggy, and made love to her. She stared at the wall as the desire built bricks inside her stomach, and then burst onto him like a brief rain in drought season. Afterward, she walked home, and he got ready for his night job of loading supplies into trucks and out of trucks. She stopped by the cemetery on the way home to visit her mother, her father, her sister, her brother. Hello mother, hello father, hello sister, hello brother. Good-bye now.

The next morning, the potatoes had returned. This time she recognized them by the placement of knots and eyes, and she could see they were not seven new potatoes, but the same seven she had, just the day before, thumped into the Dumpster. The same seven she had, just the day before that, thrown into the small garbage of her home. They looked a little smug. She tied them tight in a plastic bag with a knot, and dropped them next door on the sunflower woman's front stoop. Then she repotted her fern. For the rest of the day, she forgot all about them, but the next morning, the first thing she checked was that cast iron pot. And what do you know. And on this day they seemed to be growing slightly, curving inward like big gray beans.

They were bothering her now. Even though she was minutely pleased that they had picked her over the sunflower neighbor. Still, this reoccurring potato visit was a hindrance in the rhythm of her day.

"All right," she spoke into the pot. "Fine."

Oven. On.

Since she did not enjoy the taste of baked potatoes, when they were done she took them into the road and placed all seven crispy purses in a line down the middle. The summer sun was white and hot. At around three, when the few cars and trucks and bicycles came rolling through town, she swayed and hummed at the soft sound of impact, and that night, she slept so hard she lost her own balance and didn't wake up at sunrise like usual but several hours into the morning. There was a note slipped under the door from her lover who had come to visit after work. He forgot to write love before his name. He had written sincerely instead.

Settling down to a breakfast of milk and bread, the woman looked into the pot almost as an afterthought. Surely, they would not survive the oven *and* the tires *and* the road. But. All seven—raw, gray, growing. Her mouth went dry, and she ignored them furiously for the rest of the day, jabbing the dirt with a spade as she bordered the house with nasturtium seeds.

Later that day, she stapled them in a box and lugged them to the post office and mailed them to Ireland, where potatoes belonged. She left no return address. When they were back in the pot the next morning, she soaked them in kerosene, lit them on fire, and kicked them into the hills. When they were back again the next morning, she walked ten miles with them in her knapsack and threw them in a pond at the county line, into the next county. But they were back again by morning, and again, and again and again, and by the twentieth day, they curved inwards even more and had grown tiny sketches of hands and feet. Unfurling. Her heart pulled its curtain as she held each potato up to the bare hanging lightbulb and looked at its hint of neck, its almost torso, its small backside. Each of the seven had ten very tiny indented toes and ten whispers of fingertips.

Trembling, she left the potatoes in the pot and fled her house as fast as she could. She found no comfort in the idea of seeing her sincere lover so she went to the town tavern and had a glass of beer. The bartender told her a long story about how his late wife had refused to say the word love in the house for fear she only had a certain amount of times in a life to say the word love and she did not want to ever use them up. "She instead said she liked me, every day, over and over." He polished a wine glass with a dirty cloth. "I like you is not the same," he said. "It is not. On her deathbed even, she said, 'Darling, I like you.'" He spit in the cloth and swept it around the stem. "You'd think," he said, "that even if her cockamamie idea were true, even if there were only a certain amount of loves allotted per person, you think she could've spent one of them then."

The woman sipped her beer as if it were tea.

"You say nothing," he said.

On the buzzy woozy walk home, she stopped by the cemetery to pat headstones and on her way to see her family she passed the bartender's wife's grave which stated, simply, She Was Greatly Loved.

Back at her house, holding her breath, she sliced all seven potatoes up with a knife as fast as she could. The blade nearly snapped. She could hardly look at the chubby suggestions of arms and legs as she chopped, and cut her own finger by accident. Drunk and bleeding, she took the assortment of tuber pieces and threw them out the window. She only let out her breath when she was safely back inside.

Gasping, gasping.

Only one little piece of potato was left on the cutting board, and she ate it. Apple-like, spiteful. The rest of the evening she swept the stone floor of her house, pushing every speck of dirt out the door.

She woke at the first light of day and ran into the kitchen and her heart clanged with utter despair and bizarre joy when she saw those seven wormy little bodies, whole, pressed pale gray against the black of the cast iron. Their tiny toes one second larger. She brushed away the tears sliding down her nose and put a hand inside the pot, stroking their backsides.

In the distance, the sunflowers on the hill waved at her in fields of yellow fingers.

August came and went. The potatoes stayed. She could not stand to bother them anymore. By the fourth month, they were significantly larger and each had a squareish box of a head with the faintest pale shutter of an eyelid.

Trucks, big and small, rattled through the town but they did not stop to either unload or load up. She hadn't seen her lover in a month. She hadn't been to the cemetery in over a month either, and the weeds on her family were probably ten feet high by now, a clear sign to the heavens of who wasn't doing her job.

With summer fading from her kitchen window, the woman saw her neighbor meet up with the latest suitor, yellow petals peeking out from her wrists and collar, collecting in clusters at the nape of her neck. He himself was hidden by armfuls of red roses. They kissed in the middle of the dirt road, a ruby-and-gold brooch of arms and lips.

Inside her house, the woman shivered. She did not like to look at so many flowers and the sky was overcast. Pluck, pluck, pluck, she thought. Her entire floor was so clean you could not feel a single grain when you walked across it with bare feet. She had mailed her electricity bill and bought enough butter and milk to last a week. The nasturtiums were watered.

The smacking sound kept going on by the window. Wet.

It was lunchtime by now, and she was hungry. And you can't just eat butter by itself.

She put the potatoes in the oven again. With their bellies and toes. With their large heads and slim shoulders. She let them bake for an hour and a half, until their skin was crisp and bright brown. Her stomach was churning and rose petals blew along the street as she sat herself down at her kitchen table. Noon. She used salt and pepper and butter, and a fork and a knife, but they were so much larger now than your average potato, and they were no longer an abstract shape, and she hated potatoes, and the taste in her mouth felt like the kind of stale dirt that has lost its ability to grow anything. She shoved bite after bite into her teeth, to the sound in her kitchen of the neighbor laughing, through such dizziness she could hardly direct the fork into her mouth correctly. She chewed until the food gathered in the spittle at the corners of her lips, until she had finished one entire enormous potato. The other six crackled off the table and spilled onto the floor.

That night, she had a horrible stomachache, and she barely slept. She dreamed of a field of sunflowers and in each pollened center was the face of someone she had once loved. Their eyes were closed.

At dawn, when she walked over to the stove, as she did every morning now, pulling her bathrobe tighter around her aching stomach, there were only six potatoes in the pot. Her body jerked in horror. She must have miscounted. She counted them over. Six. She counted again. Six. Again. Six. Six. Again. Six. Her throat closed up as she checked under the stove and behind the refrigerator and around the whole kitchen. Six. Not one more; not one less. She checked all their markings until it was clear which one was missing. The one with the bumpiest head, with the potato eye right on its shoulder blade. She could feel it take shape again inside her mouth. A wave of nausea swept over her throat, and she spent the rest of the day in the corner of the old red couch, choking for breath. She ended up throwing up by evening from so much crying, but the seventh potato never came back.

The sunflower fields browned with autumn, and within a month, two other potatoes were expelled from the pot. These were the two smaller ones, and they lolled on the stove top, and stopped growing. There was simply not enough room for all six in the pot anymore. She had done nothing this time. She didn't want to put them outside, bare, in the cold, so when they were soft enough, she buried them deep beneath the hibernating nasturtium seeds. They never came back either. The four remaining in the pot seemed to be growing fine but it was unsettling to look in and see only four now; she had grown so used to seven.

By the eighth month it was raining outside and she was having stomach cramps and the potatoes were fully formed, with nails and feet, with eyelids and ears, and potato knots all over their bodies. They rotated their position so that their heads faced the mouth of the pot. On the ninth month, they tumbled out of the pot on the date of their exact birthday, and began moving slowly across the floor. They were silent. They did not cry like regular babies and they smelled faintly of hash browns. She picked them up occasionally, when they stopped on the floor, legs and arms waving, but mostly she kept her distance. They tended to stick together, moving in a clump, opening their potato eyes to potato pupils that were the same color as the rest of them.

The four were mostly similar, but you could distinguish them by the distribution of potato marks on their bodies, and so she named them One, Two, Three, and Four. Two also had a tiny wedge missing from its kneecap, in the shape of a cut square.

When she left to go mail a letter or pick up some groceries, the potato visitors went to the windows like dogs do, and watched her walk off. When she returned, they were back at the window, or still at the window, waiting. Their big potato heads turning as she walked up and opened the door. Potato eyes blinking fast to welcome her home. She went through her mail and fell into a corner of the rotting old red sofa and they walked over and put rough hands on her shoulders, her knees, her hair.

The five of them spent the winter like that, together in the small house, watching the snow fall. She tried to send them outside, to find their fortune, but they always turned right around and came back. They only slept when she slept, making burbling noises like the sound of water warming up. They were dreamless, and woke once she awoke.

On the first day of spring, the bountiful neighbor came over with lilies woven into her hair, asking to borrow some matches. The woman had the four hide in the bathroom. She tried to talk to the neighbor but had very little to say and instead the neighbor filled the small house with chatter. The neighbor was in love! The neighbor liked the weather! The neighbor asked to use the bathroom and the woman said sorry, her bathroom was broken. The neighbor talked at length about broken bathrooms, and how difficult, and if she, the woman, ever needed to use her bathroom, she was welcome anytime. Thank you. You're welcome! When the neighbor left, the woman's ears were ringing. She went into the bathroom to pee and was somehow startled to see the four in there, blinking beneath the silver towel rack.

"Get," she said, brushing them away. "Get away from me. Go!"

They bumped out the door and waited in the living room. She

put them in the closet and went about her day, and there they stayed, waiting. The following morning, after a sleepless night when they gazed at her with white pupils, she pushed them out the front door to the side of the house where there was a strip of dirt that the neighbor could not see. The woman picked up her gardening shovel and dug a hole in the earth, as deep as her knee. She looked at One.

"Get in," she said.

He stepped into the hole.

"Lie down," she said. He looked up at her with wondering eyes and she filled the hole with dirt over him.

"Go back to where you came from," she said, as she shoved more dirt over his grayish body. She looked at Two. Dug another hole. "Go," she said, "and don't you come out," and her voice shook as she said it. Two hopped in without pause. As did Three and then Four. She filled the holes up fast and then strode into her house and locked the door. Fine, she said to herself. Fine, Fine. FINE. She ate dinner alone and slept alone and woke alone, and the cast iron pot was empty when she checked. They wouldn't fit in it any-more anyway. She couldn't even eat them now; they would just walk right out of the oven, right out of her mouth. Go back to where you came from, she told herself. Thank you, Good-bye, Excuse me. She swept endlessly, and trucks rolled past her window.

In the morning, with spring rolling off the hillsides in bright puffs, she went outside to the strip of dirt. No movement at all. She set a rock at each site, one rock for One, two for Two, etc. She sat for long spells, over the course of the next week, and watched the sky drift overhead. It all felt very familiar, and she recognized the shape and texture of her life before, but it was as if someone had put her old life in the laundry and washed it wrong. The color was slightly off. The fit was off. The sleeves were now too short.

At the end of the week, she kicked off the stones and got out her big shovel. Her neighbor was hanging up clothing on her laundry line, green dresses and blue scarves. The wind whisked her hair around.

"How's that broken bathroom?" she yelled.

"Oh," said the woman. "Well. There was never any broken bathroom."

The neighbor raised her eyebrows.

"I was hiding my children from you," said our woman.

"Children? What children?" said the neighbor, wrapping her neck in a rose-colored scarf. "How sweet! How many? Where are they?"

"I buried them," said the woman, waving her shovel.

"You what?"

"I buried them," said the woman. "And now I am going to dig them back up."

She went to the side of the house, and dug up One first. He sat right up when the shovel touched his arm and dirt fell from his face and legs. He blinked at her, as if no time had passed at all, and she held out her hand and pulled him up. She dug up Three, and Four. She thought briefly of leaving Two there forever, letting weeds grow all over him, but the other three were looking at his spot expectantly, so she dug up Two, too.

The woman looked at each in turn as the wind blew against the tree branches. The layers of dirt became them.

"Okay," she said.

They stepped into her open arms, solemn as monks. She let them nestle and burrow into her neck, where they smelled of clay and old sun. The neighbor poked her head around the corner of the house, draped in a clean sheet.

"Oh!" she said. "Look at this! I didn't think you could be serious."

The woman glanced up with Three on her back and Four clinging to her shoe. One ran his hand down her hair, and Two curled into her lap.

"I am always serious," she said, and adorned in pale berries of potato babies, she returned to her house, leaving the neighbor on the front stoop, fluttering.

Inside, the woman dressed the four in clothing even though they had no hair or blood and would never look normal, dressed or un-dressed. Still she put them in pants and shirts she had sewn herself, in hats and shoes and belts.

She took their slow-moving hands and walked out the door again. They blinked and ducked under the lemony March sun. Already, like clockwork, the very first buds of green were pushing up from the soil, a ring of nasturtiums and dead potato babies to border her house. She'd never told the others about the two they had expelled in the seventh month, the two that were softening right there at their feet. She never told even herself about the one she had chewed in her mouth until it became a part of her own skin and bones. Only the wedge missing from Two served as a constant reminder of some-thing important to forget.

Halfway down the block she turned and glanced at the neighbor, who was wearing a straw hat, planting tomatoes. The four glanced with her. The neighbor's clothesline, ballooning in the wind, was a ballroom of colorful ghosts. The woman waved to the top of the hat, and pulled on her group to keep walking.

The rest of the town was quiet and drowsy on the walk over, and the five entered the park of colorless ghosts all in a line. Holding hands. They passed She Was Greatly Loved, and steered right over to the tallest rows of weeds.

The woman cleared her throat.

"Mother," she said. "Father. Brother. Sister. I'd like you to meet my children."

The weeds swayed to and fro. A green amassment of hair. The potato children stood by the headstones and lay their hands on the dirt. They seemed interested, even pleased, by the new setting. They had no traumatic recollections of their past week buried alive. In-stead, they brought fingers dusted with soil to their noses and smelled appreciatively. The air was ripe with spring. The woman told her parents and siblings she had given birth to four babies, four grandchildren, four nieces or nephews, four like no one had ever seen before. "They seem to stay," she said. She held onto the hands of two, who clasped and reclasped her fingers, while the others felt the soft prickle on the inside fold of a blade of grass.

After a while, it began to rain. There were no trees close by, so the woman sat herself down. She tried to shelter her brood, but they formed a circle around her instead. They did not seem to mind getting wet, and tilted their faces to the sky. Water rolling down off dirty potato skin smelled just like mother at the sink, in the early hours of morning, before breakfast. Getting up and lighting the new fire. The sound of her humming. Peeling. Scrubbing. When the world was full of people, always, and the word love could never run out.

PLANET BIG ZERO
by
JONATHAN LETHEM

MY HOUSE IS PROTECTED FROM THE STREET BY A WOODEN FENCE SIX feet high, so solidly built that it's practically a wall. You can't look through it. The fence gate swings open smoothly, an inch from the paved walkway, without sticking or wobbling. Returning home a few days ago, I stepped up and pushed the gate open, as I always do, without breaking my stride. This day the gate bumped hard against something on the other side.

Annoyed, I pushed harder, and stepped through the space I'd wedged open. Lying on the walkway, rubbing his head, was a bum. I'd whacked him on the top of his skull with the gate. After a confused moment I grasped the situation: he'd ducked in from the street, then stretched out to warm in the sun in the first place he found. I live next door to a supermarket. He was probably napping after a meal of salvage from the Dumpster in the alley. I knew that bums sometimes slept the night in the alley, though they always kept out of sight.

He wasn't knocked out. He made a sort of rasping, moaning sound and rolled onto his side.

Then we had the strangest conversation.

"You okay?" I said, defensively gruff.

"Yeah," he said. He was bald on top, so I could see that there wasn't a gash.

"That's a hell of a place to be," I said, justifying myself.

He said something I couldn't quite make out. It sounded like, "Every place has its price."

"What?"

"That's the price of this place." Or something. I was already walking away, toward my door. I'd seen that he was both unharmed and harmless.

"Well, take care of yourself," I said.

"Don't worry about me," he said.

Then I went inside, and for the briefest moment tried to think about what had happened. *I just hit a man in the head with a big piece of wood,* I told myself. A part of me insisted that it was a notable event, something disturbing, something extreme. I'd certainly never done anything like it before.

But that part of me lost out. My attention just slid away. I literally *couldn't* keep my mind on it.

I mention this because of the light it sheds on what happened with Matthew.

When Matthew and I were in high school we had a running joke that I think epitomized our sense of humor. Our school featured special programs for musically talented students. For that reason, or for no reason at all, there was a bust of Toscanini in the middle of the main hall of the building. It was a dingy bronze, slightly larger than life-size. Toscanini gazed out with a stolid, heroic air, his thick oxidized hair flowing back in the sculptor's imaginary breeze. He could have been a general, or a football coach, but a plaque on the pillar informed us that it was in fact Toscanini. It was typical of Matthew and me that we even *noticed* the sculpture. I doubt if any of the other students could have confirmed its existence if we'd mentioned it to them. We never did.

The joke was exclusively between us and some unseen janitor or security guard. Every week or so for a whole term, on our way out of the building after our last class, Matthew and I would hurriedly tape a pair of eyeglass frames, crudely fashioned from torn notebook paper and scotch tape, across Toscanini's glaring eyes. The glasses were never there when we returned in the morning. They were probably torn away within minutes, but that didn't matter to us. The sight

of the paper glasses on the bronze was funny, but only initially was
it the point of the joke.

The real point was saying it, again and again. "Toscanini's glasses." As though those glasses were a landmark, the one certainty in an uncertain universe. Whatever subject was at hand, the glasses were the comparison we'd reach for first. "What didn't you understand? It was as clear as Toscanini's glasses." Or, "Cool, man, like Toscanini's glasses." Or, "No more urgent than, say, Toscanini's glasses." If one of us forgot what he was going to say, the other would gently suggest, "Something about Toscanini's glasses?"

It was a joke about futility, and at the same time a joke about will, and subjectivity. If we filibustered the glasses into existence between us did it matter that the paper-and-tape glasses didn't persist? Worlds seemed to hang in the balance of that unspoken question, and in a way they did. Our worlds. The glasses stood for our own paper-thin new sensibilities, thrust against the bronze of the adult world. Were we viable? Did we have to convince others, or was it enough just to convince ourselves?

The question was made immediate by our careers as students. Did it matter that you were smarter than your English teacher if she could fail you for cutting class to smoke pot in the park? Matthew and I gave her that chance, and she took it. When college application time rolled around, the costs were suddenly apparent. You couldn't get into an Ivy League school on the strength of private jokes.

Actually, I did. For the essay section of my Yale application I drew a ten-page comic, of the soul-searching, R. Crumb variety. It took me three weeks, and it was by far the most sustained effort I'd made in the four years of high school, or in my life to that point. I remember Matthew calling me at home during those weeks, wanting to know what was wrong. I couldn't explain.

The comic led to an unusual interview with a Yale scout. The first question he asked was what my favorite single book was. I said *Travels in Arabia Deserta*, which I'd never read. He looked taken aback. "That's *my* favorite book," he said. "I didn't realize anyone your age was reading it."

"Yeah, well," I said. "I'm an autodidact." I hoped that would account for my grades. I don't know if it did, but I had the scout eating out of my hand after the lucky coincidence. Fortunately he didn't ask me what I liked about *Arabia Deserta*.

Matthew got into Reed. I helped him get the application out, in one desperate night before the deadline. Reed is one of those colleges where they don't give grades, where you can major in things like harmonica or earth sculpture. It's in the Pacific Northwest, far from New York, which probably would have been good for him. But he didn't go. He convinced his parents that he needed a year abroad before he could decide what to do. Sending him to college would have cost about the same, so they went for it. He and his marijuana fumes were out of the house either way.

Matthew was talking about becoming a Zen monk a lot at that time, and he even carried around an Alan Watts book called *The Wisdom of Insecurity* for a while. I'm sure he thought our pranks were a form of native Zen. An example: we took an 8 by 11 sheet of clear mylar to the Xerox shop and asked for a copy. The clerk indulged us. The result was a photograph of the inside of the machine, of course, but Matthew insisted on calling it "a copy of nothing." Just like one hand clapping, see? He cared nothing about Buddhism, needless to say. If there had been such a thing as a Dada monk he would have wanted to become that. But Zen it was, so he went to Asia.

Matthew visited me once at Yale, junior year. I lived in a suite with a roommate, and I was embarrassed to have Matthew stay there. He and I were beginning to look different. He was sunburnt and wiry and seemed quite a bit older. He was still dressed like a boy but he looked like a man. At Yale we all dressed like men but looked like boys, except for a few who were working on beer stomachs.

Matthew was back temporarily from Thailand, where, he explained excitedly, he'd gotten involved with a charismatic drug lord named Khan Shah. Khan Shah was more powerful than the government, Matthew said, and was trying to legitimize his rule by making poppy cultivation legal. He was a man of the people. Matthew was learning to speak Thai so he could translate Khan Shah's manifestos.

This didn't sound like Zen to me, and I told Matthew so. He laughed.

"Are you doing what you want to do?" he asked me suddenly.

That question didn't compute for me at the time. Matthew was making me very, very nervous. I could still admire him, but I didn't want him in my life.

Cracking old jokes for cover, I hustled him back down to New York with excuses about a girlfriend's demands and a paper I had to write. He spent just one night.

That was the last I saw of him for eight years. Except for postcards. Here's one from a few years back. The front shows Elton John, in spangled glasses. In Matthew's hand on the back it says "Vacant Lot/Living Chemist." No return address. The postmark is Santa Fe, New Mexico.

I had only an hour's warning. He got my number from information, he explained on the phone. I gave him the address. An hour later he knocked on my door.

He wobbled slightly. "I parked in the green zone," he said.

"That's fine, it's two hours." I stared. He was still tall and bony, but his face was fleshy and red. I immediately wondered if I looked as bad, if I'd lost as much.

"Here," he said. "I brought you this."

It was a rock, fist-sized, gray with veins of white. I took it.

"Thanks," I said, checking the irony in my voice. I didn't know whether I was supposed to think it was mainly funny or mainly profound that he'd brought me a rock.

If it was high school there would have been a punchline. He would have led me out to the curb to see the trunkload of identical rocks in his car.

Ten years later, that kind of follow-through was gone. Matthew's gestures were shrouded and gnomic. Trees falling in forests.

"Come in," I said.

"I saw the Piggly Wiggly when I parked," he said. "I thought I'd get some beer."

It was two in the afternoon. "Okay," I said.

A few minutes later he was back in the doorway with a rustling paper bag. He unloaded a six-pack of Sierra Nevada into my fridge and opened a tall aluminum canister of Japanese beer to drink right away. We poured it into two glasses. I wrote off getting anything accomplished that afternoon.

He leaned back and smiled at me, but his eyes were nervous. "Nice place," he said.

"It's a place where I can get work done," I said, feeling weirdly defensive.

"I see your stuff whenever I can," he said earnestly. "My parents clip them for me."

I draw a one-page comic called *Planet Big Zero*, for a free music magazine produced by a record store chain. Once a month my characters, Dr. Fahrenheit and Sniveling Toon (and their little dog, Louie Louie), have a stupid adventure and review a new CD by a major rock act.

Somewhere in there you might detect the dying heartbeat of Toscanini's glasses. It's a living, anyway. Better than a living recently, since a cable video channel bought rights to develop *Planet* into a weekly animated feature, and hired me to do scripts and storyboards.

"I didn't realize your folks were into rock journalism," I said.

"My parents are really proud of you," Matthew said, working diligently on his beer. He wasn't being sarcastic. There was nothing challenging left in his persona, except what I projected.

He told me his story. Since Santa Fe he'd been in Peru, taking pictures of plinths and other ancient structures. He talked a lot about "sites." The term covered a sculpture in Texas made of upended Cadillacs half-buried in the desert, stone rings in Tibet, a circular graveyard in Paris, and Wall Street skyscrapers. He'd shot hundreds of rolls of film. None of it was developed. He was trying to get funding to create a CD-ROM. In the tales he told there were ghosts, mostly women, scurrying out of the frame. An expatriate

English woman he'd lived with in Mexico City who'd thrown him out. A female journalist who'd been his collaborator, then disappeared with his only photos of an Inca burial site that had since been destroyed. And the bitch in the Florida Keys just now who'd stolen his camera after a shared three-day drunk.

I live in Connecticut, an hour out of the city if there's no traffic. Matthew had driven up to see me in his parents' car. He was in New York trying to convince his parents to cash out ten thousand dollars in zero-coupon bonds they were holding in his name, presumably for when he married and bought a house. He was willing to take a hit on early-withdrawal penalties, so that he could use what remained to fund his return to Peru.

He'd become some combination of an artist with the temperament, but no art, and Thor Heyerdahl without a raft.

The Japanese canister was empty. Matthew went into the kitchen for the first of the Sierras, unapologetically. He wasn't drinking like he was on a tear, or wanted to be. It was as though the beer was a practical necessity, like he needed it for ballast.

"If you don't want to drive back down tonight you can stay in the garage," I told him. "It's set up as a guest room. You can pee in the sink in there. I'll give you a key to the house so you can shower or whatever."

"That's great," he said. His look was humble and piercing, both. "You know, it's really amazing to see you again."

I sort of flinched. "The same," I said.

"It's amazing how little has changed after all this time."

I wasn't aware of that being the case, in any sense at all. But I nodded.

That night we got on a roll in safe territory, talking about high school. The Water Fountain Trick. The Literary Excuse Me. Mother Communication Hates You. Falling Down Jesus Park. Toscanini's Glasses. Then, fueled by beer, I told him a bit about my life, my short marriage, the novel I couldn't sell, the years of legal proofreading. Matthew drank and listened. He listened well.

Then he started telling me about his idea for a screenplay we were going to write together. "Has there ever been a thriller set in Antarctica?" he asked, eyes burning.

"*Ice Station Zebra,*" I said. "Rock Hudson's in it. It's really bad. Listen, I'm bushed."

He slept in. I was working at my desk for hours before I heard him go in through the kitchen, up to the bathroom for a shower. The water ran for almost twenty minutes. I'm not sure, but I think he must have come out while I was on the phone with my Hollywood agent.

As I get older I find that the friendships that are the most certain, ultimately, are the ones where you and the other person have made substantial amounts of money for one another. Those histories have a breadth, an unspoken ease that others, even siblings or ex-wives, just can't match. My Hollywood agent is about my age, and when I talk to him I feel he knows who I am, because he helped make me who I am. We're a conspiracy, and a much more reliable one than most.

Some time after I'd hung up the phone, I became aware of Matthew standing in the doorway of my office. "Did you hear me talking to you?" he said.

"Uh, no."

His eyes were ringed and dark. He didn't speak.

"There's coffee in the kitchen," I said. "It's still hot."

When he returned with the coffee he came all the way into the room and stood in front of me. He seemed disconcerted.

"I think I'll go check out that old foundry today," he said. "There's some wrecked equipment I always wanted to take pictures of."

"No camera," I reminded him.

"Well, I guess I'll just go look at it."

Ruins, I thought. Wrecks, shambles, margins. Zen junk.

"That's fine, I'll be here," I said. "I have some stuff to do. We can go out for dinner tonight."

"We could cook something," he began. I could see him grasping, trying to frame some larger question.

"I'd like to take you out," I said—magnanimity being one of the most effective ways of ending conversations. I was thinking of my work. I had to get back to harnessing our high school sensibility to the task of selling compact disks.

He was back at five, with another bag from the Safeway. Inside was a full six-pack, and another one full of empties. He'd been out all day looking at sites and drinking beer from a paper bag. He put the empties on the porch and the six in the fridge, like an obedient dog moving slippers to the bedroom.

I'd arranged for us to meet a couple of friends for dinner. A science fiction writer who does scenarios for interactive video games, and a screenwriter. We all have the same Hollywood agent, which is how we met. I figured the screenwriter could sober Matthew up about his script ideas. I didn't want to eat dinner with Matthew alone anyway.

We met for drinks first. By the time we got to the restaurant Matthew was lagging behind, already so invisible that the maître d' said, "Table for three?"

He barely spoke during dinner. At the end of the night we parted at my driveway, me to my front door, Matthew to the garage.

"Well, good night," I said.

He stopped. "You know, I realize I don't have everything quite together," he said.

"You've got a lot of interesting projects going," I said.

"I'm not asking you for anything." He glared, just briefly.

"Of course not."

"I feel strange around you," he said. "I can't explain." He looked at his hands, held them up against the light of the moon.

"You're just getting used to the way I am now," I said. "I've changed."

"No, it's me," he said.

"Get some sleep," I said.

I didn't see him in the morning, just heard the shower running, and the door to the refrigerator opening and closing.

About a week later, I hit on the idea of putting Matthew into *Planet Big Zero* as a character. It was a way of assuaging my own guilt, and of compartmentalizing the experience of seeing him again. I guess I also wanted to establish the connection between our old wide-open, searching form of humor and my current smug, essentially closed form.

As I drew Matthew into the panels it occurred to me that I was casting him into a prison by publishing him in the cartoon. Then I realized how silly that was. If he was in a prison he was there already, and the cartoon had nothing to do with it. He'd be delighted to see himself. I imagined showing it to him. Then I realized I wouldn't. Anyway, I finished the cartoon, and Fed-Ex'd it in to my editor.

Who hated it. "What's that guy doing there?" he said on the phone.

"He's a new character," I said.

"He's not funny," said the editor. "Can you take him out?"

"You want me to take him out?"

"He's not intrinsic to any of the scenes," said my editor. "He's just standing around."

That was two months ago. The point is, it wasn't until just the other day, when I hit the sleeping bum on the head with the gate, that I really gave thought to the way things turned out. So much of what we do is automatic, so much of life becomes invisible. For instance, I've been buying six-packs and putting them in the fridge, but it isn't me drinking them. The empties pile up on the porch. I always forget to bring them out to the curb on recycling day. Sometimes the bums prowl around for bottles and do my work for me. I think somebody somewhere gives them a nickel apiece for them—another invisible operation, among so many.

Matthew's parents' car got towed after two weeks. It must have had ten or fifteen tickets pinned under the wiper. The authorities are pretty vigilant about that around here. As for Matthew, he's still in the garage. But he's been rendered completely transparent, unless, I suppose, you happen to be wearing Toscanini's glasses.

DREAM OF MEN
by
MARY GAITSKILL

———————

LAURA WAS WALKING AROUND HER APARTMENT IN A COTTON NIGHT-gown with green and yellow flowers on it muttering "ugly cunt, ugly cunt." It was a bad habit that had gotten worse in recent months. She caught herself muttering while she was preparing her morning coffee and made herself stop. But it's true, she thought to herself. Women are ugly. She immediately thought of her sister, Anna Lee, making herself a chicken salad sandwich to have with a glass of milk. Anna Lee was not beautiful, but she wasn't ugly either. She thought of her mother, frowning slightly as she sat at her kitchen table, drawing a picture of fruit in a dish. Her mother had a small, dear bald spot on the top of her head. If anyone had said "ugly cunt" to her sister or her mother, Laura would have hit him. She would hit anyone who said it to her friend Danielle. Well, she didn't really mean it when she said it. At least not in the normal way.

She put her foot up on the table and drank her coffee out of a striped mug the size of a little bowl. She had to be at her job at the medical clinic in half an hour; she wasn't late, but still, her body was racing inside. Even though she'd been at the clinic for five years, every morning her body acted as if getting out the door and into the world was an emergency. This was even more true since her father had died. The death had turned her inside herself. Even when she was in public, talking to people, or driving through traffic, or carrying forms and charts and samples in the halls of the clinic, she dimly sensed the greater part of herself turned inside, like a bug tunneling in the earth with its tiny sensate legs. All through the earth was the dull roar of unknown life forms. She could not see it or hear it as she might see and hear with her human eyes and ears, but she could feel it with her fragile insect legs.

She finished her coffee and got out the door. Houston in the summer was terribly hot and humid. The heat made her feel grossly physical and ugly. She gave a tiny grunt to express the feeling; it was the kind of grunt her cat made when she lay down and settled in deep. She opened her car; there were cassettes and mixed trash on the floor and the passenger seat, and she thought there was a sour smell coming from somewhere. She let the air conditioner run with the door open, sitting straight up in the seat with her legs parted wide under the tented skirt of her uniform. Across the street, there was a 24-hour flower market in an open shack; dimly, she could see the proprietor inside, wiping his brow with a rag. He looked like he was settled deep into something, too.

Last night she had dreamed of two men in a vicious fight. At first they had been playing basketball. One of them seemed the apparent winner; he was tall, handsome and well-developed, while his opponent was short and flabby. Watching the game, Laura felt sorry for the little one. Then the game became a fight. The men rolled on the ground, beating each other. The little flabby one proved unexpectedly powerful, and soon he had the tall handsome man pinned on the ground. As Laura watched, he pulled out a serrated knife and began to cut the top of the handsome man's skull off. The handsome man screamed and struggled. Laura ran to them and took the knife away from the small man. He pulled out another knife and tried to stab her. She cut him open from his neck to his crotch. He remained standing; blobs of brown offal fell out of his opened body.

She lit a cigarette and closed the car door. Her father had been a small man. When he was younger, he would strike boxing poses in front of the mirror, jabbing at his reflection. "I could've been a Bantam weight," he'd said. "I still have the speed."

Laura lived in a run-down neighborhood that was usually slow, but today there was heavy traffic. She talked to herself as she negotiated the lanes, speeding and slowing in a lulling rhythm. When she talked to herself, she often argued with an imaginary person. This time, she argued about the news story concerning the President's lewd affair with a twenty-two-year-old intern. "Personally, I don't care," she said, "it shouldn't really matter what they're like as people. Besides, they all do it." Stopped at the red light, she glanced at the people waiting for a bus. They looked tenacious and stoic as a band of ragged cats, staring alertly down the street or pulled tidily into themselves, cross-legged and holding their handbags. "When things are private like that, it's hard to tell what really went on between the two people anyway," she continued. "Sometimes things that look really ugly on the outside look different when you get up close."

Her father had started dying in a hospital in Tucson. By the time Laura had gotten there, her sister was fighting with the doctors about his treatment. He was too weak to eat so they'd stuffed tubes down his nose to feed him something called Vita Plus. "His body doesn't want it." Anna Lee was talking to the nurse. "It's making him sicker." It was true. As soon as Laura looked at her father she knew he was going to die. His body was shrunken and dried, already half-abandoned, his spirit stared from his eyes as if stunned. "I know," said the nurse. "I agree with you. But we have to give it to him. It's policy."

"Hi Daddy," said Laura.

When he answered her, his voice was like an old broken sack holding something live. He was about to lose the live thing, but right now he held it, amazed by it, as if he had never known it before. He said "Good to see you. Didn't know if you'd come."

She stopped at a crosswalk; there was a squirrel crossing the street in short, halting runs. She stopped traffic for a minute, waiting for it. A woman sitting on a public bench smiled at her. The woman sat with her knees tensely open and her feet poised on their balls. In her pointy shoes her feet were like little hooves. It made sense she was on the squirrel's side.

They brought their father home to be cared for by hospice workers. By that time, he was emaciated and filled with mucus that he could not discharge through his throat or nose. It ran out of his nostrils sometimes, but mostly they heard it, rattling in his lungs. He couldn't eat anything and he didn't talk much. They put him in the guest bedroom, in a big soft bed with a dust ruffle. The sun shining in the window made his skin so transparent that the veins and spots on his face became more present than the skin. He blinked at the sun like a turtle. They took turns sitting with him. Laura stroked his arm with her fingertips, barely grazing his fragile skin. When she did that, he said "Thank you, Laura honey." He had never called her honey before.

He was so weak he couldn't turn himself, so two hospice workers had to turn him. When they did, he got angry; his skin had gone so thin that his bones felt sharp, and it hurt him to be moved. "No, leave me alone," he'd say. "I don't care, I don't care." He would frown and even slap at the workers, and, in the fierce knit of his brow and his blank, furious eye, Laura remembered him as he had been 25 years ago. He had been standing in the dining room and she had walked by him wearing flowered pants that were tight in the seat and crotch. He said "What're you doing walking around with your pudenda hanging out like that? Nobody wants to see that."

She arrived at the clinic early and got a good place in the parking garage. On the way up to the 17th floor she shared the elevator with Dr. Edwina Ramirez, whom she liked. They had once had a conversation in the break lounge, during which they both revealed that they didn't want to have children; Dr. Ramirez had looked at Laura suddenly, a deep, bright spot inside her eye. "People act like there's something wrong with you," she said. "Don't they know about over-population? I mean, yeah, there's biology and shit. But there's other ways to be a loving person." She had quickly bent to take her candy bar out of the machine. "You know what I mean?"

Ever since then, Laura had felt good around Dr. Ramirez. Every time she saw her, she thought "ways to be a loving person." She thought it as they rode up in the elevator together, even though the

doctor stood silently frowning and smoothing her skirt. When they
got to the floor Dr. Ramirez said "See you" and gave Laura a half
smile as they strode in opposite directions.

Laura went to the lounge to get a coffee. Some other technicians
and a few nurses were sitting at the table eating donuts from a box.
Newspapers with broad, grainy pictures of the White House intern
lay spread out on the table. In one of the pictures, the girl posed
with members of her high school class at the prom. She stood very
erect in a low-cut dress, staring with focused dreaminess at a spot
just past the camera.

"She's a porker," said a tech support. "Just look at her."

"Beautiful hair though," said a phlebotomist

Laura lingered at the little refrigerator, trying to find the carton
of whole milk. Everybody else used 2%.

"It makes me sympathize with him," said a nurse. "He could
have anybody he wanted, and he picks these kinds of girls. Like,
they're not models, they're not stars."

"That makes you sympathize? I think that's what's gross about
it."

"But it might not be. It might be because he wants somebody to
be normal with. Like somebody who's totally on his side who he
can, like, talk about baseball with. Somebody who's pretty in a normal way"

"What? Are you nuts? She was a fat girl sucking his dick!"

Laura settled for edible oil creamers. She took a handful, along
with a pocketful of sugars and a striped stir-stick. She walked down
the empty hall whispering "Ugly cunt, ugly cunt."

The day they brought their father home, the plumbing in the bathroom backed up. Sewage came out of the bathtub drain, water
seeped into the chenille tapestry their mother had put up around
the window. The sight of it made Laura's heart pound.

During the eight days that Laura stayed there, she slept in the bedroom of her girlhood, sharing the bed with Anna Lee. She and Anna Lee had slept close together in the same bed until Laura was fifteen and Anna thirteen. Even when they got separate beds, they sometimes crept in together and cuddled. Now they lay separate even in grief.

They talked though. The night before their father died, they talked until four in the morning. Anna Lee talked about her six-year-old, Peter, an anxious, overweight child with a genius IQ. The kid couldn't make friends; he fought all the time and was often beaten. He'd set his room on fire twice. She was talking about a psychiatrist she had taken him to see. In the light from the window, Laura could see her sister's eyelashes raising and lowering with each hard, dry blink. She could smell the lotion Anna Lee used on her face and neck. The psychiatrist had put Peter on a waiting list to go to a special school in Montana, a farm school with llamas the children could care for and ride on.

After Anna Lee stopped talking there was a long silence. Laura could feel her sister's body become fractionally softer and more open, relaxing and concentrating at the same time. Maybe she was thinking of Peter, how he might get better, how he might grow happy and strong. Laura had met the child once. He'd frowned at her and looked down at the broken toy in his hand, but there was curiosity in his mien, and he was quick to look up again. He was already fat and already bright; he seemed too sad and too angry for such a young child.

"I had a strange thought about Daddy," she said.

Anna Lee didn't answer, but Laura could feel her become alert. In the scant window light, Laura could see that the muscles around her eyes were alert. Laura knew she should stop, but she didn't. "It was more a picture in my head," she continued. "It was a picture of a vagina that somebody was slashing with a knife. Daddy wasn't in the picture but—"

"Oh Christ, Laura." Anna Lee put her hands over her face and turned away. "Just stop. Why don't you just stop."

"But I didn't mean it to be—"

Her voice was raw and hard; she thrust it at Laura like a stick. Laura pictured her sister at twelve, yelling at some mean boys who'd cornered a cat. She felt loyalty and love. "I'm sorry," she said. Her mouth frowned, a weak, spasmodic grimace in the dark. "I'm sorry."

Anna Lee reached back and patted Laura's stomach with her fingers and half her palm. Then she withdrew into her private curl.

Laura lay awake through the night. Anna Lee moved and scratched herself and spoke in urgent, slurred monosyllables. Laura thought of their mother, alone upstairs in the heavy sleep brought on by barbiturates. Tomorrow she would be at the stove, boiling Jell-O in case her husband would eat it. She didn't really believe he was dying. She knew it, but she didn't believe it anyway.

Carefully, Laura got out of bed. She walked through the dark house until she came to her father's room. She heard him breathing before her eyes adjusted to the light. His breath was like a worn moth feebly beating against a surface. She sat in the armchair beside his bed. The electric clock said it was five-thirty. A passing car on the street filled the room with a yawning sweep of light. The wallpaper was yellow flowers. Great Aunt's old dead clock sat on the dresser. Great Aunt was her father's aunt who with her sister Dorcas had raised him. Two widowed aunts and a little boy with no father. Laura could see the boy standing in the parlor, all his new life coursing through his small, stout legs and trunk. The dutiful aunts, busy with housekeeping and food, didn't notice it. In his head was a new solar system, crackling with light as he created the planets, the novas, the sun and the moon and the stars. "Look!" he cried, "look!" The aunts didn't see. The more he tried to show, the more they wouldn't see. The boy hesitated, unsure of his new system, and with his uncertainty, it began to break. Thrown off its trajectory, the sun became erratic and the planets went cold. The stars burned fiercely in the cold dark, but the aunts didn't notice that either.

Another car went by. Her father muttered and made wet noises with his mouth. She imagined him saying "When I was broken, then they loved me."

"No wonder you hated them," said Laura softly. "No wonder."
Except he hadn't hated them at all.

Behind the reception desk, there were two radios playing different
stations for each secretary. One played frenetic electronic songs, the
other formula love songs, and both ran together in a gross hash of
sorrow and desire. This happened every afternoon by around one.
Faith, who worked behind the desk, said it was easy to separate
them, to just concentrate on the one you wanted. But Laura always
heard both of them jabbering every time she walked by the desk.

"Martha Dillon?" She spoke the words to the waiting room. A
shabby middle-aged man eyed her querulously. A red-haired middle-
aged woman put down her magazine and approached Laura with a
mild, obedient air. Martha was in for a physical, so Laura had to
give her a preliminary before the doctor examined her. First, they
stopped at the scale outside the office door; Martha took off her
loafers, her socks, and her sweater, to shave off some extra ounces.
A lot of women did that, and it always seemed stupid to Laura.
"Five four, one hundred and twenty-six pounds," she said loudly.

"Shit," muttered Martha.

"Look at the bright side," said Laura. "You didn't gain since last
time."

Martha didn't reply, but Laura sensed an annoyed little buzz from
her. She was still buzzing slightly as she sat in the office; even
though she was small and placid, it struck Laura that she gave off
a little buzz all the time. She was forty-three years old, but her face
was unlined and her eyes were wide and receptive, like a much
younger person's. Her hair was obviously dyed, like a teenager
would do it. You could still tell she was middle-aged though.

She didn't smoke, she exercised three times a week, she drank
twice, wine with dinner. She was single. Her aunt had diabetes and
her mother had ovarian cancer. She had never had an operation, or
been hospitalized. Her periods were regular. She had never had any
sexual partners. Laura blinked.

"Never?"

"No," said Martha. "Never." She looked at Laura as if she were watching for a reaction, and maybe holding back a smile.

Her blood pressure was excellent. Her pulse rate was average. Laura handled her wrist and arm with unusual care. A forty-three-year-old virgin. It was like looking at an ancient, sacred artifact, a primitive icon with its face rubbed off. It had no function or beauty, but it still felt powerful when you touched it. Laura pictured Martha walking around with a tiny red flame in the pit of her body, protecting it with her fat and muscle, carefully dying her hair, exercising three times a week and not smoking.

When the doctor examined Martha, Laura felt tense as she watched, especially when he did the gynecological exam. She noticed that Martha gripped her paper gown in the fingers of one hand when the doctor sat between her legs. He had to tell her to open her legs wider three times. She lay with her head sharply turned so that she stared at a corner of the ceiling. There was a light sweat on her forehead.

When she changed back into her clothes though, she moved like she was in a women's locker room. She got up from the table and took off the paper gown before the doctor was even out of the room. Laura stared at her. Martha suddenly looked right at her and smiled as if she'd won something.

"She's probably really religious or maybe she's crazy." That's what Beatrice, the secretary thought. "At this day and age? She was probably molested when she was little."

"I don't know," said Laura. "I respected it."

Beatrice shrugged. "Well, you know, everybody has the right." She lowered her dark, heavy lashes and continued her graceful movements at her desk.

She imagined her father looking at the middle-aged virgin and then looking away with an embarrassed smile on his face. He might think about protecting her, about waving at her from across the street, saying "Hi, how are you?" sending protection with his words. He could protect her and still keep walking, smiling to himself with embarrassed tenderness. He would have a feeling of honor and frailty but there would be something repulsive in it too because she wasn't a pretty young girl. Laura remembered a minor incident in a novel she had read by a French writer, in which a teenage boy knocked an old nun off a bridge. Her habit was heavy and so she drowned, and the writer wondered, with a stupid sort of meanness, Laura thought, if the nun had felt shocked to have her vagina touched by the cold water. She remembered a recent news story about a man who had kidnapped a little girl so that he could tie her to a tree and set a fire at the foot of the tree. Then he went to his house to watch her burn through binoculars until the police came.

Instead of going back to the waiting room, she went to the public bathroom and leaned against the small windowsill with her head in her hands. She was forty; she tried to imagine what it would be like to be a virgin. She imagined walking through the supermarket, encased in an invisible membrane that was fluid but also impenetrable, her eyes wide and staring like a doll's. Then she imagined her virginity like a strong muscle between her legs, making all her other muscles strong, making everything in her extra alive, all the way up through her brains and into her bones.

She lifted her head and looked out the small window. She saw green grass and the tops of trees, cylindrical apartment buildings and traffic. She had not wanted her virginity. She'd had to lose it with three separate people; it had been stubborn and hard to break.

She brushed the dust and particles from the windowsill off her elbows. "I was a rebellious girl," she said, "and I went in a stupid direction."

She thought of the Narcotics Anonymous meetings she had attended some years ago. People talked about the things that had happened to them, the things they had done on drugs. Nothing was too degrading or too pathetic or too dull. Laura had talked about trying to lose her virginity. Her friend Danielle had told a story about how she'd let a disgusting fat guy whom she hated try to shove a can of root beer up her vagina because, he'd suggested, they might be able to fill cans with heroin and smuggle them.

Laura smiled a little. After the meeting, she'd asked Danielle, "Who tried to stick it in, you or him?"

"Oh," said Danielle, "we both tried." They laughed.

Such grotesque humility, she thought. Such strange comfort. She remembered the paper plates of cookies, the pot of coffee at the low table in the back of the room at N.A. She loved standing back there with Danielle, eating windmill cookies and smoking. Laura looked at herself in the bathroom mirror. "A stupid girl," she said to her reflection. Well, she thought, but who could blame her?

She thought of a teenage girl at the intergroup shelter where she volunteered as a receptionist. She didn't remember the girl's name, but she remembered her thick brown hair knotted with beads, bubble-gum trinkets and a small, rusty key. She drank a Styrofoam cup of cocoa as she answered Laura's intake questions. She said she'd brought her kitten with her when she ran away from home, but that she'd given it away to somebody on the street.

"Why'd you do that?" asked Laura.

The girl shrugged. "You know, be friendly."

Laura had wanted to touch the girl's face. She looked down as she drank, a heavy piece of hair fallen forward.

When Laura was still a teenager, her mother had asked her what it had been like for Laura to lose her virginity. She wanted to know if the experience had been "special." It was late and the living room was dark. They had been watching TV together. Laura was startled by the question. Her mother had looked straight ahead while she asked it, but Laura could see her expression was unhappy. "Was it someone you loved?" she asked.

"Yes," said Laura. "Yes, it was."

"I'm glad," said her mother. She still looked straight ahead. "I wanted you to have that." It seemed like she knew Laura was lying, and that the lie was okay with her.

She went back to the waiting room and got the grouchy middle-aged man. He didn't bother to take off his shoes when he weighed himself. He was there, he said, only because his wife had made him come. He had taken off from work and shot the whole day. "My wife loves going to the doctor," he said. "She had all those mammograms and she lost her breast anyway. Most of it."

"Well, but it's good to come in," said Laura. "Even if it doesn't always work. You know that. Your wife's just caring about you."

He gave a conciliatory little snort. With his shirt off, he was big and flabby but he carried it as if he liked it. His blood pressure was much too high. As she worked, Laura let her touch linger on him longer than was necessary because she wanted to soothe him. She felt him respond to her touch; the response was like an animal turning its head to look at her, then looking away again. She thought he liked it though.

When the man was gone, she asked Dr. Phillips if she could go outside on her break. He usually didn't like her to do that because she was always a little late getting back when she went out, but he was trying to be extra nice since her father died. "Okay," he said, "but watch the time." He turned and strode down the hall, habitually bristling like a small dog with a dominant nature.

Outside the heat was horrible. She started sweating right away, probably ruining her uniform for the next day. Still, she was glad to be out of the building. The clinic was located between a busy main street and a run-down slow street occupied by an old wig shop, a children's karate gym and a large ill-kept park where aging homeless men sat around. She decided to walk a few blocks down the park street. She liked the trees and she was friendly with a few of the men, who sometimes wished her good afternoon.

She walked and an old song played in her head. It was the kind of old song that sounded innocent and dirty at the same time. The music was simple and shallow except for one deep spot where it was like somebody's pants were being pulled down to show their ass. "You got nothing to hide and everybody knows it's true. Too bad little girl, it's all over for you." The singer laughed and the music laughed too, laughter spangled with pleasure and contempt.

Laura had loved the song, she had loved the thought of it being all over and everybody knowing. A lot of other people must've loved it too; it had been a very popular song. She remembered walking down the hall in high school wearing tight clothes; boys laughed and grabbed their crotches. They all said she'd sucked their dicks, but really she'd only screwed one of them. It didn't matter. When her father found out, he'd yelled and hit her.

"Was it someone special?" asked her mother. "Was it someone you loved?"

She stopped at a curb for traffic. Her body was alive with feelings that were strong but that seemed broken or incomplete, and she felt too weak too hold them. "You can leave little girl, I don't want you around no more."

A car pulled up beside her, throwing off motor heat. The car was full of loud teenage boys. The driver, an Hispanic boy of about eighteen wanted to make a right turn but he was blocked by a stalled car in front of him and cars on his side. He was banging his horn and yelling out the window; his anger was hot and all over the place. Laura stared at him. His delicate beauty was almost too bright, lit by his intense youth and maleness. He had so much light that it burned him up inside and made him dark. He yelled and pounded the horn trying to spew it out, but still it surged through him. It was like he was in war, like he could kill in great bursts, without any understanding in his mind or heart. In a real war, thought Laura, he would rush into danger before the other men and be called a hero. Her thought folded over unexpectedly, and she pictured him as a baby with his small mouth on his mother's breast. She pictured his fierce nature deep inside him, like dark, beautiful seeds feeding off his mother's milk, off the feel of her hand on his skull. She thought of him as a teenager with a girl; he would kiss her too hard and be rough, wanting her to feel what he had inside him, wanting to show it to her.

He turned in his seat to shout something to the other boys in the car, then turned forward again to put his head out the window to curse the other cars. He turned again and saw Laura staring at him. Their eyes met. She thought of her father showing his aunts the stars and all the planets. "You are good," she thought. "What you have is good." The boy dropped his eyes in confusion. There was a yell from the backseat. The stalled car leapt forward. The boy snapped around, hit the gas and was off.

Laura crossed the street. She thought: I told him he was good. I told him with my eyes and he heard me. She flinched under a second of embarrassment; to think that she could give that guy anything he might want! But then she thought of the middle-aged virgin jumping off the examining table and smiling like she'd won something, and she felt okay again.

She walked up the block sweating and grateful without knowing why. Again, she pictured the middle-aged virgin, this time at home at night, doing her meticulous toilet, rubbing her feet with softening cream. She pictured herself at home, curled on the couch, watching TV and eating ice cream out of the carton. She pictured the men in her dream, fighting. She pictured herself kneeling to hold the handsome man's cut-open head. She would pass her hand over his broken skull and make an impenetrable membrane grow over his exposed brain. The membrane would be transparent, and you would be able to see his brain glowing inside it like magic stones. But you could never cut it or harm it. She pictured her father, young and strong, smiling at her, the planets all around him.

Deep in the park she saw the homeless men moving about, their figures nearly obscured by overgrown grasses and trees. For a moment she strained to see them more clearly, then gave up. It was time to go back; she was late.

THE WITCH
by
FRANCINE PROSE

———————

IT'S GOT TO BE A BAD SIGN WHEN YOUR WIPER BLADES START TALK-
ing. Getting killed would be a worse sign, a billboard lit up by that
final flash, giant letters spelling it out: Zip's pushed his luck too far.
He should have taken early retirement, he's been eligible since July,
but he refused—a huge mistake about to be corrected when his
patrol car wraps itself around the nearest tree. Right now, he could
be home in bed watching TV with Irene, or playing computer games
with Charlie, if the kid's still awake, instead of driving through a
storm just because Jerry Greco's wife, Marianne, called in crying
that Jerry was trying to kill her again.

Wind crashes into the car door, snow weighs down the wipers
now barely clearing one frosted saucer of glass. The road is slick as
a tablecloth, and naturally Zip has to wonder what's to keep God
from yanking it just to see everything slide.

Lately, Zip's been getting superstitious. It's genetics kicking in,
like one of those time-bomb chromosomes you pray your kid won't
inherit. Zip's grandmother couldn't leave the house without first
touching every icon, every raccoon-eyed Virgin, every bearded saint
famous for slaying a dragon or bringing the Cyrillic alphabet to the
Slavic people. These days Baba would have a diagnosis: obsessive-
compulsive disorder. The family's diagnosis came closer: a lunatic
and a witch. Zip's mom believed Baba could *do* things; once, when
Zip's mom was driving her to a doctor's appointment, Baba started
mumbling gibberish and Zip's mom drove off the road. Obviously,
Zip comes from generations of thinking that magic spells count for

more than, say, driving experience or skill. Twenty years as a state trooper, eighteen of marriage, a kid who's almost fourteen, a lifetime as a normal guy, and Zip's turning into Baba.

Zip sucks on his doughnut-shop coffee. The caffeine doesn't help.

Who says snowstorms are quiet? This one's making a racket, the plop of sodden flakes, the shrieking wind competing with the groans from the trees. As a kid, Zip was scared of driving in weather like this. Then for years he got used to it, and now he's scared again. Some chemical change has turned him into one of those paranoids who think Fate's got nothing better to do than smack you around for staying too long at the party. Is it Fate? Or statistics? You always hear about cops getting killed with two weeks until retirement.

More like water than solid ground, the blacktop slips beneath him. It would help if Zip knew the road, but though he's lived in the county all his life, he hardly ever gets out here. Certainly, he's never been to Jerry and Marianne's. He sees Jerry at the barracks and at meetings. Maybe once a year, at Christmas parties and such, he talks to Marianne—boozy, sociable conversations that, strangely, he finds himself thinking about later. But they're not the type who give the jolly hot-dog-and-beer summer cookouts. The far edge of the county is the perfect place for the Grecos. They could kill each other every night, and no one but their kids would hear them.

The last time he drove this road, it was a gorgeous spring morning. A little girl had come into school claiming she'd seen a human head in a plastic bag in the woods by her bus stop. A pathological liar. But you have to check this stuff out. The grade-school principal, Sally Mayhew, rode beside him in front, and they both half pretended Sally wasn't gay, unseriously flirting, while the kid in the back babbled on about her mom's movie star friends, all her dad's new cars, the lady's head with blond pigtails—the little girl had blond pigtails—in the pumpkin leaf bag.

She'd led them to a spot by the side of the road. "Oops," the kid said. "She's not here anymore."

Zip is just as certain that there won't be a corpse when, and if, he gets to Jerry Greco's house. Every couple of months, for years, somebody's had to go out there. It's always a little . . . delicate, since Jerry's on the force. Headquarters tries to send Lois Ryan, when she's on duty, because this isn't your high-risk domestic violence, the crackpot waving the broken bottle, it's some chick thing, Marianne Greco loaded on vodka and pills, crying that her life is shit, while Jerry, also hammered, paces around the edges, yelling that Marianne needs to check herself into a dry-out clinic. The whole force knows about it, and they all pretend they don't. It's a small division. They've got to work together.

How can people live like that? Zip can't understand it. When he and Irene have an argument—for example, the one that grew out of her asking why Zip all of a sudden wanted to lose so much weight, the fight that escalated into Zip saying Irene knew goddamn well *she* didn't want him taking early retirement, and Irene saying well, actually, what did Zip plan to *do* with his time?—Zip feels gloomy and tired for days. Some people must like drama. The fighting. The making up.

Marianne and Jerry probably have every reason to want to kill each other. Jerry's got girlfriends all over the county, amazingly, since Marianne's got him on such a short leash that when Jerry's an hour late for dinner she calls in to the station and asks if there's been an accident on the road. Zip's pretty sure that Jerry is harmless. But there's always that guy everyone swears wouldn't hurt a fly until the night he chops up his wife into little tiny pieces. Plus Jerry's a fellow trooper, and if something did happen and Zip got there, let's say, twenty minutes late, the story would be all over the state, he might as *well* retire.

And finally, there's this: Marianne called in, as she always does, and then Jerry called in, as he always does, and said to ignore Marianne, as he always does, and then he called back a few minutes later and said maybe they should send someone out. Which he never does. *Ever.*

Zip turns right, the wheels go left. Zip thinks, I'm dead, until adrenaline jump-starts his instinct and he lets the car do what it wants. The wheel spinning in his hands makes him feel like a circus bear driving one of those tiny cars. But he's not a bear anymore, he's dropped twenty pounds in six months on the "Zip" Ziprilic diet: all the coffee he can drink. His doctor's thrilled, his cholesterol's dropped, Zip likes the way he looks. For the first time in his life, his nickname doesn't seem like a joke. Only Zip's heart doesn't like it. It's been doing this trippy salsa beat, down low, so maybe it's only his stomach. Irene thinks the weight loss means he's having an affair, which he isn't. Though lately he's had the feeling that there *is* less . . . interference between him and other people, especially women, which is why he could flirt like that with Sally Mayhew as he drove around thinking that he was a lucky guy, a grown man getting paid to cruise a lovely country road with a nice-looking friendly lesbian grade-school principal on a beautiful spring morning.

Tonight Zip feels less lucky as he tries to convince himself that the storm is letting up and that by some miracle he'll find the house. The mailboxes are miles apart and already buried in snow. He'll drive around forever and then get stuck at the bottom of a hill, radio in, freeze his ass off in the car all night until the roads are plowed and somebody comes to get him.

The house should be somewhere around here. He slows down, but not enough to lose the power he needs to get up the inclines.

Suddenly, just as Zip is driving by, a gust of wind lifts the snow off the top of a mailbox, and he sees the name: GRECO. Come on, how freaky is that? Maybe it's God trying to help him save Marianne Greco's life, or Fate sadistically ushering him from one death trap into another.

Through the veiled windshield, clumped with white, Zip makes out your basic prefab split-level—a cheaper and less cared-for version of his own. The Grecos' downstairs lights are blazing, the upstairs windows are dark.

Zip parks at the bottom of the driveway. Later, Jerry can help dig him out. He honks the horn—a big friendly shave-and-a-haircut how-are-ya—just as he was taught during that wasted weekend of Domestic Violence Training. Don't surprise somebody high on all the ordinary substances plus the domestic-violence chemicals. Zip can't imagine hitting Irene, their fights don't go like that, either she sulks for three days or becomes so logical that, all right, he's had fantasies of wringing her neck, just to make her shut up. The fantasy passes in a heartbeat—as it does for Jerry, Zip hopes. Zip couldn't imagine hurting Irene. Lately she's seemed so fragile, first the lactose intolerance, then the wheat allergy. That's why she doesn't want Zip around the house, it must take her all day to figure out what she can and can't eat. That's not fair. Zip loves Irene. He wishes he were with her and Charlie right now. Maybe that's why he kept working—so he could feel this desperate, lonely longing to be home.

He puts on his jacket, pulls up the hood, and heads up the drive. The snow is halfway up his calves and keeps melting into his boots. Thank God he lost the extra weight, it's tough enough trudging through the drifts, and it's so humiliating to show up huffing and puffing. There's a place by the front steps from which Zip can see into the living room window, and that's where he pauses to catch his breath. His heart is jumping again.

Didn't they hear his car horn? Why aren't they looking out? Jerry's on the sofa, Marianne on the love seat, both just sitting there. Stunned. Not talking. Nothing looks torn apart, Marianne's face is okay, everything fine and dandy.

Except for the two handguns, one on the end table beside Marianne, the other on the couch next to Jerry. Two guns. Enough bullets for everyone and the kids, as well. If Zip had any brains, he'd turn around and get back in the car and take early retirement tonight.

Zip knocks, gently but firmly. Jerry lets him in. How warm and bright the house is! Shelter from the storm! Jerry flashes Zip a big goofy smile that might be more welcoming if not for Jerry's pointy little cat teeth, which go right along with his caged-bobcat nervous energy, the scary ratio of tension and instinct to brains that has always put Jerry Greco near the bottom of the list of guys Zip would want to work with.

Jerry's T-shirt and jeans look slept in, or grabbed off the bedroom floor. He squeezes Zip's shoulder and says, "Man, am I glad to see *you.* What a night, huh? They're predicting a foot and a half, but what the hell do *they* know?"

Zip follows Jerry into the living room and gets as far as the doorway. That's when he sees the icons jammed into every corner, all the old familiar faces, Our Blessed Virgin of Whatnot, St. Michael and St. George, the two tall guys with the long white beards. What are *they* doing here? He hasn't seen them since Baba died. Obviously, a coincidence. Zip feels oddly dingy. Too much caffeine, for a change. He doesn't want his hands shaking, especially if he has to separate the Grecos from their guns.

Fortunately Marianne and Jerry are too out of it to notice where Zip's looking. So there's no need for a little group excursion down memory lane, back to somebody's Orthodox childhood, that sinkhole of superstition that Zip's been running from ever since. Whereas someone in *this* house—it's got to be Marianne—has never left that place where you tear out big fistfuls of hair, crying to a Madonna who, any moron could tell, has more problems than you do.

Jerry's sunk back into his couch. The spazzy way he keeps reaching out and touching his gun is exactly how Zip's grandmother used to poke you at inappropriate random moments. Might as well add Tourette's syndrome to Baba's diagnosis. His grandmother's got his attention now, from beyond the grave, and while he's spaced out and distracted by this voodoo paranoia, Jerry Greco will pick up his gun and blow them all away. Baba's last little joke.

Baba was a witch, which is, come to think of it, what Marianne Greco looks like with her long, crazy black hair, her dark eyes ringed with smudged makeup.

Marianne says, "Hey, Zip, good to see you. Would you mind taking off your boots?"

Would Marianne mind go fucking herself? He's not dropping by for a beer! Then he looks down and, sure enough, his boots are seeping grainy black puddles into the grayish wall-to-wall. Zip crouches and unlaces his boots, clumsily shakes them off. He feels like Jack in "Jack in the Beanstalk." He'll never leave here alive. He looks around at this giant's lair—functional, modern, somehow institutional despite the children's sneakers and toys piled up in the corners.

"Jesus, Zip," Marianne says. "You lost a ton of weight."

"No cake," says Jerry. "That's all it took. Am I right?"

"That's all it took," says Zip.

"Please," says Marianne. "Sit down. You want something? Coffee? A beer?"

Zip would love some coffee. "No thanks. You guys called in?"

"Sit." Jerry gestures at a recliner placed conveniently between Marianne's love seat and Jerry's couch. Not so conveniently, as it turns out, because when Zip sits and the couple begins to talk, Zip has to swivel between them while still trying to keep one eye on the guns.

"Well," says Jerry, "we were sleeping."

"*You* were sleeping," says Marianne. "You know I haven't slept in, like, six months."

"You were snoring," says Jerry.

"Fuck you," says Marianne.

"Marianne," says Jerry. "Give Zip a fucking break."

"All right," says Zip. "You guys called into the station. That's what this is about."

"Okay," says Jerry. "I was sleeping. I heard noises downstairs. Someone walking around. Maybe I was still dreaming, but I was sure I could hear the fucker moving from room to room. I asked myself a million times, was I awake, and then I got my gun out of the nightstand, got dressed, and went downstairs to look around."

"Did Jerry say anything to you?" Zip asks Marianne.

Marianne props her elbows on her knees and leans forward. The cuff of her pink terry bathrobe falls back, revealing her thin forearm, on which she's wearing a thin gold bracelet.

"Marianne," says Jerry, "you're falling out of your clothes." Zip looks up just in time to see the tops of Marianne's breasts before Marianne makes a face at Jerry and tightens the sash on her robe. She doesn't look like a pill freak. She and Jerry seem all too sober.

"I don't know," she says. "Maybe I dozed off. Anyway, I finally heard it, too. Footsteps downstairs. And Jerry wasn't in bed. I figured it was Jerry going to get a snack, but I don't know, something felt weird, something *told* me to check for Jerry's gun. It wasn't in his nightstand. So right away I got nervous. What if something happened to Jerry, and it wasn't him down there, but some other guy, some stranger—"

"Wishful thinking, ha ha," says Jerry.

Marianne rolls her eyes. "So I'm not, like, about to yell, *Oh Jerry, dear. Is that you?* Let the guy know where I am. So I get *my* gun from *my* night table."

Marianne's looking hard at Zip, but strangely, he doesn't notice until she cuts her eyes to the gun and he realizes that he and Marianne are in intense visual communication. He sees Jerry noticing, too. How ironic if Zip, who never cheated on Irene, got blown away on duty by a jealous hothead like Jerry Greco.

Jerry says, "I got her the gun after Lorraine Prentiss got held up down in Reedsville—"

"It wasn't then," says Marianne. "It was when that kid down the road was doing all that half-assed breaking and entering—"

"Craig DeBellis," says Jerry.

"You know something strange?" says Zip. "Last spring, I got this call, this kid from the grade school said she'd seen a human head at her bus stop. Heather DeBellis. Isn't it weird I'd remember the kid's name?"

"Everyone on this road is named DeBellis," says Marianne. "Except us. Gross. Was there a head?"

"No," says Zip. "People imagine things all the time."

"Tell me about it," says Marianne. "Anyhow, I got my gun and kind of snuck downstairs, and I hear this noise and turn toward it, and so help me Jesus Christ I'm just about to aim and shoot when the sensor light, you know, the security light, goes on outside. A deer must have passed or something. And I see it's Jerry, backlit, pointing his gun at *me*."

"We could have killed each other," says Jerry. "We could have

fucking killed each other. Man, we came as close as *that* . . ." He
pinches the air with his thumb and forefinger.

Something is wrong with this story. Zip's got it. A deer in a snowstorm.

"But you didn't," Zip says. "Kill each other. And the intruder?"

"Must have been the wind," says Jerry. "Listen to it out there."

Zip says, "So Marianne calls in because . . . ?"

"Flipped out. Hormones. As usual. She's like one of those sports
cars goes from zero to seventy in six seconds. Totally bananas, crying, blubbering, saying I'm trying to kill her. I don't love her. I hate
her. The usual shit. Women. Shit."

Zip can't look at Marianne. "But you weren't trying to kill her,
Jerry. And then you called in."

"Okay," says Jerry. "This is the hard part. But you're right, I
called in, so fuck it, I might as well deal with it. Right? I was scared.
I mean it. I thought: You know, if Marianne and I *did* kill each other,
there wouldn't be a single person in the whole world, probably not
even our own kids, who wouldn't think we'd done it on purpose.
Everyone would say: All right. They finally did it. What the hell
took them so long? And I'll be honest. That scared the shit out of
me. It fucking terrified me, man."

"Terrified," says Marianne. "*Now* he gets fucking terrified."

Zip's a little nervous himself, because *he'd* also been thinking
that Jerry and Marianne probably had a million reasons to murder
each other, and if they'd wound up dead, accidentally or not, everyone would have assumed that they'd done it on purpose. . . .

"Are you okay?" Marianne asks. "Oh, God, are we freaking *you*
out?"

"Yes," Zip says. "I mean no. I'm fine."

"Christ, Marianne," Jerry says. "Zip's a cop. Not a fucking marriage counselor."

As if on cue, a series of shrieks float downstairs. "Daddy! Daddy!
Daddy!"

"It's Chris," says Marianne. "For you."

"Duh. I know it's Chris," says Jerry. "Can't *you* go? See what he wants. I'll owe you one."

"One," says Marianne. "You'll owe me *one*. I can tell you what he wants. He wants you."

"Who would *you* want?" she asks Zip. "The dishrag mom who washes your socks and wipes your ass and gets dinner on the table? Or the dad who comes home in a uniform with the snappy hat and gun and handcuffs and shiny badges? What would a seven-year-old boy want? Who would *anyone* want?"

"Okay, buddy," Jerry yells upstairs. "Dad's coming. I'm on my way." He shrugs at Zip, then takes off, leaving his gun on the table. If these were strangers, Zip would pocket the gun, telling the wife he was just holding it for safekeeping. But with Jerry and Marianne, that would be . . . socially awkward.

Marianne listens with the back of her head till the noise upstairs dies down. She rakes her hand through her hair, then jackknifes forward and wraps her robe tighter. Okay, there's that witch thing, but there's something else, too, some restless dissatisfied energy animating her long skinny body that—if this were any other situation and anyone but Marianne Greco—Zip thinks he might find sexy. Interesting, at least.

Silence. Silence. More silence. Marianne looks at her gun.

Zip says, "How old are the kids now?"

"Besides Chris?" says Marianne. "Zack's fifteen. Patty's eleven. What's Charlie now?"

"Twelve?" says Zip, then thinks: Thirteen.

After another silence, Marianne says, "Seen Lois lately?" But she's not really asking. It's shorthand to find out if Zip knows how often Lois Ryan has driven out here in the line of duty.

"Lois is fine. Off tonight, I guess."

"Lucky her," says Marianne. "You know the real reason he got me that gun? Because he's never home."

Is Zip supposed to admit he knows? "Marianne . . . ," he says.

"Let me talk," she says. "I assume you figured out that Jerry's not being on his side of the bed was not exactly a once-in-a-lifetime event."

"I got that much," Zip says.

Marianne shivers, grabbing her arms, though the house is over-heated—as Zip notices only now. It must cost them a fortune to keep the place like this, with the wind raging outside, flinging snow against the windows. Zip wriggles out of his jacket, trying not to interrupt the conversation. Marianne's shoulders ripple, reflexively mirroring his, and her bathrobe gaps again to reveal a curve of breast arcing under her nightgown.

"Mostly it's fine with me," she says. "I'd rather be alone. You know . . ." Her pause is a warning. Zip doesn't want to hear what's coming. "I'll bet you think Jerry's a normal guy, a sane, normal guy. That's what everybody thinks, especially his girlfriends. Even the guy's own kids don't know how nuts he is. But trust me. The guy's insane."

"Marianne . . ." Zip tries again.

"Please, Zip. Don't Marianne me. You wouldn't believe the crazy shit he says. All this stuff"—she waves at the icons—"they're his. Jerry's a believer. I feel like I married my grandmother. And that's the *sensible* part of him. He's way more fucked up than that. He goes into these jealous rages, saying I'm some kind of witch, that I'm making guys think about me, look at me, which wouldn't even make sense even *if* we ever went anywhere where guys *could* look at me. At some point tonight, probably the minute you leave, he's going to come out with some paranoid bullshit about how I brought you here with my magic powers."

Zip misses the next few sentences. Once more he's distracted by Marianne's saying that Jerry thinks she's a witch when he, Zip, has been thinking that's what she looks like. Well, Marianne looks like a witch. Anyone would think it.

". . . and it's not exactly like I need a black cat to go out and spy around. My girlfriend calls one day, and it takes me half an hour to figure out she's trying to tell me that Jerry's fucking that teenage nympho slut from the beauty parlor in Loudonberg."

Even Zip knew about that one. Word got around the force that Jerry was giving this big-haired high school jailbait free rides in his patrol car.

"You knew, right?" says Marianne.

"You mean Amy Fisher?" Zip likes making Marianne smile.

"So it wasn't exactly top secret. But this time I couldn't stand it. So one day I drive into Loudonberg and walk right into Quickie Cuts, No Appointment Necessary, and tell her I want my hair cut. Of course she knows who I am, I know who she is. It's one of those moments, everybody knows everything, no one says a word. You tell me how ballsy that is, letting some slut your husband's fucking get her hands on your hair."

Zip looks at Marianne's tangled hair. No one's had their hands on it in a while.

"This was last year," says Marianne. "I ask for a trim. We go through the whole charade, she washes my hair, takes off a quarter inch, exactly like I tell her. Finally I check the mirror and say, Perfect, great, could I borrow the scissors? There's this one teensy stray hair I need to get . . . I liked how she got nervous, but only for a second, because we were both so good at pretending that I just happened to be some woman who wanted a haircut, and she just happened to be some little whore who cut hair.

"I took the scissors and threw them across the room. They landed right between the eyes of this blond model in a poster for some bullshit pixie haircut. And they stuck there, the scissors stuck there, kind of . . . twanging in the wall."

Would scissors do that? Zip wonders. You'd have to throw them hard.

Marianne says, "I can't throw. I can hardly play catch with the kids. So maybe Jerry's right, maybe I am a witch. Everyone thinks I am, so I might as well be. But listen, let me ask you: If I *was* a witch, if I had magic powers, why would I let my marriage get to the point where I was flinging scissors around some low-rent beauty parlor in Loudonville? The point where I believe that the fucker is trying to kill me. Listen, when I call into the station, I *mean* it, and then a couple days pass, and I forget until it happens again. You think a witch would live like that? An abused wife lives like that."

Zip can't help it. "Marianne, has Jerry ever . . . ?"

"Jesus. Please," says Marianne. "That's not what I'm saying at all. If I was using my powers to get you out here, wouldn't I have fixed myself up first? You think I'd look like *this?*"

"You look fine," says Zip. "Anyhow, you and Jerry *called.*"

"I rest my case," says Marianne. "But okay. As I was saying. It was like something guided my hand and *put* those scissors between the model's eyes on that poster. And it was pretty soon afterwards that bitch dumped Jerry. For which, needless to say, he blamed me."

Marianne leans forward, and now Zip does, too. She says, "I'll be honest. There's been a million times I wanted to shoot him. But it just so happens that tonight wasn't one of them. But I thought the same thing he did. That if he and I killed each other everybody would think we meant it. I figured *that* out before he did. And Jerry's right. It was scary."

Zip feels something like . . . jealousy. But what could he possibly envy?

"And that's when I thought: he's killing me, and I called in, and Jerry called. And then he called back. How many times has *he* called in when we were having trouble?"

Zip shrugs. What's he supposed to say?

"Never," says Marianne.

There's something Zip's not getting, the step that leads from their not killing each other to Marianne thinking Jerry is—thinking it seriously enough to call in to the station. But that's how they play it out here. Some people count to ten when they're mad. Others throw dishes. Some pick up the phone and call the troopers their husbands work with.

Marianne makes a cup with her hand and presses it over her eyes. "Jesus Christ," she says. "Do you know how embarrassing this is?"

"Don't be embarrassed," Zip says. "Marriage isn't easy." What the hell is Zip talking about? And what's made Marianne take her hands from her face and stare at him across the room? What is she seeing in his face? Zip doesn't have a clue. Still, there's something exciting about a woman looking that long until Marianne ends their little moment by bursting into tears.

"What am I supposed to do now?" she says, between gulping sobs. "I'm forty-one. I've got three kids. Am I supposed to start over? Look for anther guy? Go back to shaving my legs?"

Zip sneaks a look at the fine dark hair climbing up Marianne's calves. Ordinarily, he doesn't like hairy legs. Irene gets hers waxed at the mall, he thinks guiltily—guilty because an unprofessional, inappropriate, tiny . . . hiccup of lust is making him want to push up Marianne's robe and see. Ordinarily, for that matter, he doesn't like women crying. Irene did lots of crying before her crackpot nutritionist figured out about the wheat allergy. Suddenly, it occurs to Zip: Irene has a crush on that nut.

Zip has heard guys say that when their wives or kids cry, it makes you want to give them something to cry about. Whereas Zip just wants to be somewhere, with anyone else but Irene. That's what women's tears do to him. Yet right now, for some reason, he thinks it would be criminal, pitiless—inhuman—not to get up and cross the room and sit down next to Marianne and put his arm around her.

Under Zip's hand, Marianne's thin shoulder trembles like a hamster, trapped in fuzzy chenille. Marianne leans against him, at which point Zip's soul vacates his body and watches it hugging his co-worker's wife. The only way he can come down is to convince himself he's just seeing a trooper comforting a domestic 911.

"Feel this." Marianne takes his other hand and puts it inside her robe. Zip's hand is twice the size of hers, but it lets itself be led, burrowing into the warm dark place between soft robe and softer skin.

"Feel my heart," says Marianne.

Zip can't feel a thing. And then he thinks he can: a bubble swelling and popping lightly against her rib cage. Or maybe it's his own heart, doing that dance the coffee's taught it.

It started before the coffee. That's why Zip lost the weight.

"Feel how unevenly it's beating," says Marianne. "That's what I mean: he's killing me. I'm not saying that just to *say* it! What else can I do but call in?"

Of course, it's then that Jerry appears, bouncing down the stairs.

"Great," says Jerry, meaning *them,* meaning Zip's arms flying from around Jerry's wife's shoulders and out from under her robe. "Would you look at this? Is this beautiful, or what?"

"Marianne was upset," Zip says, jumping up and springing back to his chair, trying at the same time to keep semi-focused on Jerry's gun.

But it's one of those times that Marianne was just describing. Everyone knows everything, and no one says a word. It's clear that Jerry doesn't want to kill Zip. He doesn't want to kill Marianne. If he did, this would be the moment. No one's getting killed, except maybe Zip, who could still get creamed driving home in the storm. Neither of those guns will be fired tonight. Zip can cash it in, and take off.

"I'm really sorry, man," Jerry says. "Dragging you out in weather like this. Shit, I don't know what got into me. Into Marianne. You don't need to drive home in this. Want to spend the night?"

Looking over at Marianne isn't anything Zip can control. And Marianne's staring right back at him. So it's not all in his mind. Something's going on here. No one says it has to make sense. He would give anything to know what Marianne's expression means. But what *doesn't* he know, exactly? It means she wants him to stay. Really, it would be smarter to stay. He could call Irene. Irene would rather he stay over than try to get back in this blizzard.

"That's okay," says Zip. "I'll make it. Don't worry about it."

All this time, he's looking at Marianne, whose disappointment is so visible, it's as if they've had a long affair and he's just told her he's leaving. What's worse is, Zip is horribly sure that the same look is on his face.

"Are you positive?" says Marianne. "You could stay on the couch. Or Chris could sleep with us, he'd love it, and you could have his room."

"Positive," says Zip. "I've got to get back."

"Fine, then," says Marianne.

"I'll walk you to the car," Jerry says. "I'll bring a shovel, just in case."

Doesn't Jerry see what's going on? So what if he does? Zip's leaving. Jerry goes to get his coat. Zip follows him into the hall. Marianne rises, then stops in the living room doorway, the gold icons winking behind her.

"Well . . . thanks . . ." Marianne's voice trails off.

"Don't mention it." Zip's manly response is undermined by the awkwardness of putting on his boots.

"Ready?" says Jerry.

"Drive carefully," says Marianne.

"See you," Zip says, without turning.

But when at last they get outside, and the wet snow whips their faces, it takes all of Zip's self-control not to turn and look back to see if Marianne's watching. The warmth they've brought with them from inside lasts about a second before the cold sneaks under their jackets and their teeth start chattering lightly, a reflex that neither Zip nor Jerry wants the other to see. They take the first few steps boldly, stomping in and out of the drifts, but soon slow up and stagger down the drive, bending almost double against the stinging wind.

"Motherfucker!" Jerry shouts at the wind.

Zip doesn't have to answer. His only job is to get to the car. Finally he succeeds. He brushes the snow from the windshield and climbs inside.

"Get in," he tells Jerry. "At least while I try to start this."

Jerry props the shovel against the car and slides into the passenger seat. Miraculously, the car starts up and eases forward out of its space.

"Okay, then," says Zip. "Take it easy, man." But Jerry isn't moving.

"I need to tell you something," he says. "About what happened tonight. This is going to sound crazy. But trust me on this. Marianne's a witch. I *told* you, I know it sounds crazy, but I've seen her do shit you wouldn't believe. . . . Listen, the first time I met her mother, this was back in Brooklyn, her mother tells me that when

Marianne was a kid, they'd go to church on Sunday, this is in the Orthodox church, where everybody stands up—"

"I know about it," says Zip.

"Her mother tells me that every Sunday, in the summer, a bunch of people would faint, and it was always the people standing directly around Marianne. And she always thought it *was* Marianne. Clearing herself some room. Her own *mom* tells me this, and I don't listen!"

Mother of God, it's Zip's dead grandmother speaking to him in the voice of a not-very-smart and probably crazy cop! Baba always talked like that, blamed the neighbors for souring the milk by looking at her funny. And there was always that same wild look, that same wacky glint in her eyes. Isn't that what Marianne said? *It's like living with my grandmother.* Zip remembers his mother—dead for how long now? Could it really be five years?—telling him how Baba's mumbling made her drive off the road.

Zip's attention drifts briefly, but snaps right back when Jerry says, "How do you think *you* got here tonight? Man, you cannot *believe* how many guys get lost around here, the FedEx man, the UPS man, the electric-meter reader, they're always knocking on the door, Marianne's *bringing* them up here, and I know it's just a matter of time before one of them decides to stay. Or comes back. Or calls her. And if she leaves me, it'll kill me. I swear. Look, I know what you're thinking. I'm not exactly a saint. But let me tell you: there's a difference between nookie and a woman who can make weird shit happen. The mother of your children."

It's not that Jerry could say this stuff, but that Jerry *believes* it, and the naked longing that creeps into his voice when he talks about Marianne, the love and terror, respect and desire, all knotted and gnarled up together. Jerry doesn't care if Zip hears. He doesn't care who's watching. How slow Zip's been to understand: Jerry loves his wife. He's terrified of losing her, and who's to say he isn't right? Jesus, what went *on* at that house? What happened between Zip and Marianne? Zip feels a bolt of sheer longing sizzling through his chest. Was Marianne at the Christmas party this year? Why didn't he pay attention? It's another year—eleven months—till Christmas comes again.

Maybe Jerry's right about her. Some people have strange powers.

Zip says, "I don't know, Jerry. I don't think Marianne's planning to leave you. Like we were saying, people imagine things. And Jerry . . . there aren't witches, really. No one believes that shit. Your grandmother believed it. Think about it, Jerry—"

"Oh, really?" says Jerry. "*Really?* How *did* you get here tonight?"

"You and Marianne called, remember? Picked up the phone and called. That's a little different from her dragging me out here by magic."

"I mean, how did you find the house, wise guy? This weather sucks. You can't see two feet. The mailbox is covered with snow." Zip sees an image, clear as film. Snow gusting off the mailbox just as he drives by. He shakes his head to get rid of it.

"Homing instinct," he says. "Speaking of which . . ."

"All right," says Jerry. "I'll let you go. Hey, man, listen. This is, like, our little secret, right?"

"Sure," says Zip. "No problem. Who am I going to tell?"

"Okay, then. Drive safely, man. Thanks again. See you at work." Jerry gets out of the car.

"Take it easy," says Zip.

Zip waits with the engine running until he's sure that Jerry's back home. A shiver crawls down his spine. Is it cold—or fear? What if Jerry kills Marianne—and Zip never sees her again? Then he gets out and takes a piss, looking up at the house.

If Marianne Greco were a witch, why would she live in that dump? It's not the gingerbread cottage, not the hut on chicken legs. Because she isn't one, Zip thinks. There are no bolts of magic sparking around that split-level. There was no head in the trash bag. Just people making up stories and telling them until they believe them. No evil vibrations crackling, except between the Grecos, no deer in the security light, no intruder downstairs, no scissors twanging between the eyes of a model in a poster, no grandmother playing with Zip's head from beyond the grave.

How he wishes there *were* all those things. But he knows there aren't. There is only a plain, thrown-together house, not so different from his own, disappearing, inch by inch, under the deepening snow.

THE LEAST YOU NEED TO KNOW ABOUT RADIO
by
BEN MARCUS

BY TUNING A RADIO, YOU CONTROL THE AMOUNT OF WIND IN YOUR house, and, to a lesser degree, the language spoken there. You dial in the wind and regulate which rooms it will enter, how hard it will blow, and the form it will take: shouting, singing, silence, breath, whispering, aroma. The antenna on radios is long, thin, and retractable because it measures the level and style of breathing people do near the radio. When too many people gather near a radio, one of them will feel short of breath, clutch her throat, wobble, swoon to the floor. She is referred to as Julie. Often she carries her own antenna, which looks like a key and opens the front door of her house. If a family collectively holds its breath, known as "getting ready for bed," no sound will be possible in their house. A father loses his temper if his family does not breathe fast enough, if they are dull and seem exhausted, when their breathing is shallow. He fears his house will collapse, so he frightens his children, to quicken their breathing, by striking the furniture with a long, flat stick. His anger operates as a bellows inside his children's chests and is referred to as a "radio-driven mood." This is why he claws and growls outside their doors in the morning. This is why they hear noises in their sleep and wake up feeling uneasy.

Children are resistant to the strangled sounds of radio, because they have not yet shed their windproof layer, referred to in Indiana as baby fat. When adults practice their knife work at waist-high countertops, chopping, slicing, and shredding objects they will later warm in clear fat and present to the regard of their families, children hiss at each other in radio static, their mouths gaping. Children's teeth are small because the flow of radio static chisels them down and keeps them from growing into hard, square bones. This is why they cannot dismantle entire animals with their mouths. After repose, when adults maneuver from their beds to an upright position and align their heads next to radios tuned to static, they are able to remember the first wind of their childhoods: its height and color and sound, what part of their bodies it targeted, and how weak it made them feel. If you held a microphone to your father's neck, you would hear a muted, crackling static: the sound of a lifetime of wind that has flowed over his body. Wrapping his neck in a scarf will briefly mute the sound, allowing for short conversations to occur.

Most speech that occurs in the home can be attributed to one or another call sign on a radio. The numbers are old American words used to procure food, express alarm, and soothe frightened animals. A store-bought radio with a digital tuner can dial in many of the conversations of today's American homes. If Mother controls the radio, she determines what will be discussed in the kitchen, the living room, and the den. Of special note is her remote control: a long, slender fin with hinged digits called a "hand." On holidays she colors the nails on her hand, dips it in ointment, wraps it in gauze, then pounds it against the table to neutralize it. It expresses a milky color and blends in with the rest of her body, appearing to extend from her arm. She waves her hand, buries it in her pocket, collides it against the faces of her children, and the speech in the room comes quietly under her command. When Mother is alone at her window, she can be overheard muttering numbers, which is her way of planning the moods her family will have throughout the day and week. She confines herself to the lower, monosyllabic numbers, to prevent the occurrence of actual fires in her home, a physical reaction at the far end of the mood scale.

Different radio stations collect different kinds of wind, then break it up and slow it down until it sounds like a song or a man talking. This kind of wind does not blow under its own power; instead, it must be broadcast weekly in the evenings when houses have surrendered their father-free shields, when their listening block is lifted. The term "broadcast" was first used to describe a special muscle in the face that gave propulsion to sound generated in the mouth; mostly words, but also yelling and singing. Men and women inspect their broadcast muscles by pushing a fist into each other's mouths and opening up their hands once inside. With their free hand, they grasp the back of their partner's head and impale their hands farther into their faces so that the head is worn in the manner of a glove. A strong and healthy broadcast muscle relaxes, letting the hand massage the face from the inside. When a child's broadcast muscle is snipped with a scissors, his words cannot leave his mouth, which becomes fat and overstuffed, leading to large, moist lips, and a slack, lazy face. He sits by the window and rocks in his chair, a suction tube dangling from his mouth. At night his mother digs into his mouth with a spoon, assisting him with the discharge. Sometimes she pretends to pat his head and read him a story.

The English language was first overheard in a wind that circled an old Ohio radio operated by a Jane Dark representative. Words from the language were carefully picked out of this clear wind over the next thirty years and inscribed on pieces of linen handed out at farmer's markets. When the entire vocabulary of words had been recovered from the old radio, it was destroyed, and the pieces of linen were sewn together into a long, thin flag that was then loaned out to various cities and towns, where it was mounted over houses. Once the fabric was hoisted on a flagpole, the language was easily taught to the people inside of their homes, who had only to tune into the call sign of the flag station, extract and aim their freshly-oiled antennas, and position their faces in the air steaming from the grill of their radios. When their faces became flushed and hot, they could retreat to other rooms and say entirely new things to the children who were sleeping there.

If you speed up a song or the sound of a man talking, and you broadcast this sound outside your house through speakers affixed to your roof, the trees will quiver as if bent by a western wind, and the birds of the yard will be grounded below the speech wires that connect the houses. By grounding birds, the air is kept clear of surveillance in case an important message is scheduled. Windows on the upper floors of houses are left open for language projection, and sometimes boys are seen scrambling from them, slipping down the roofs, falling to the ground, often reciting cries for help known as sentences.

The weather outside your house can be captured and preserved, then played back later through a simple AM radio. These radios can be taken on picnics to the lake, for customized weather and simple wind performances, benefiting the other families parked there to eat sandwiches and cast pebbles into the water. If several families stationed on blankets along the shore play their AM radios in a simulcast, calibrating the tilt of their antennas to focus their broadcast just over the water, the sky will appear stronger, the children's words will be clearly enunciated, and the currents in the water will ripple more realistically. Every family has a favorite weather style, and a radio that will play it back for them. Sometimes it sounds like the shortest words of the American language, in particular the first names that are used to summon people up from sleep, to groom their heads with a softly blowing oil, preparing them to be addressed by the largest person in the house, often the mother or father.

A radio was once referred to as a "weather bottle." People said, "Turn on the bottle, listen to this," and the bottle was shaken until air fizzed out of it and everyone laughed and enjoyed themselves. People bought bottles of old weather at farmer's markets and co-ops and poured them over their roofs, hoping to immunize their houses from special re-broadcasts of famous storms and Father's repetitive speech. Most storms could be had for a nickel, with a deposit on the bottle. Radios can't be turned off. They have four settings: man, woman, child, and low. Just like people, if too much happens, they fill up, burst, and die. A dead radio is treated similarly to a pet. It is burned, and the antenna is planted in a field. When children clutch a detached antenna, they are gathering strength to go home, when they are afraid to enter their rooms.

You can have a party and everyone will come to sit around your radio, which sometimes looks like an old, trampled flower. People pour water or milk on it and wait for something to happen, but the radio only gets older and produces a wind known as disappointment. At a party, people stand perfectly still and wring their hands, and the liquid is collected in a vial. In Ohio, when people meet, they smell each other's small radios, unscrew the cases, touch the tuning needle, shake the speakers next to their ears until the sound erodes into the words they most require to hear. Some people cry when they remember the first time they felt wind on their faces. Crying is a weakness of the face that can be corrected with a strong FM blast from a radio, tuned to a call sign in the high nineties. An emotion-prevention wind should occur in the home and last for some time after that. A family can then move freely from room to room, with only minor adjustments of the dial when their feelings grow too strong.

SHE
by
JASON BROWN

EVERYTHING NATALIE SAID SEEMED, TO HERSELF, TO HAVE BEEN SAID better by him. He was less fond of speaking, however, than he was of hitting people in the face, which seemed a more likely source of her love to those of us who were in speech class with him. It could be, we reasoned, she was in love with the kind of things he might say if he spoke more often.

It was easy for someone like David Dion to be casual about fate. He was still in junior high, but high school girls picked him up in their daddy's cars and had sex with him out at the pit. No one I spoke to on a regular basis had even been to the pit. He was not anyone's boyfriend, didn't need to be. It was hard to guess how old he was if you didn't already know, if he hadn't tumbled down into your grade from the grade above when he was held back. He couldn't be that smart, you could tell, from the way he grinned at himself, but he was smart enough to know he didn't have to be loyal to any one girl.

Dion fought high school boys all the time; that was nothing. Once he broke his fist against the face of a man in his twenties before getting his own nose smashed against the pavement. In school he sat two seats away from me in homeroom where he spilled over his desk, stroking his thin mustache and cracking his knuckles, one-handed, one finger at a time. In wood shop we were partners, making a gun rack. I made the rack, he kept it. He slouched back in his chair, his elbows on the sill, looking out the window from the corner of his eye like a prisoner. Not even the shop teacher said anything.

They were related, kids said. He was related all over, mostly in the next county, where every other ice fisherman was an uncle, every other woman behind the cash register an aunt, and the rest cousins. He could walk into any store out there and borrow ten bucks; he owed everyone, even me, at least that much. I loaned him one dollar at a time. He rolled the bills into joints and smoked them or sold them for two dollars, making a few bucks, he said, for later at the bar.

When Mr. Dawson of Dawson's Variety was told by one of his basketball players that Dion, their center, was in love with Natalie, he pictured the ridge of her muscle extending up from her knee into her track shorts. He had seen her the day before with Ron, the high school boy she went with, who was going to drop out to start in the air-conditioning business with his father so he and Natalie could get married as soon as possible. Her best friend Denise, whose information was no better than second-hand at this point, said, Well, it wasn't Love with Ron. Mr. Dawson overheard this. Denise was standing in his store with her friends Kristy and Francis waiting to buy a diet soda.

"I thought," Mr. Dawson said, "she was with that boy Ron."

"Well, she was," Denise said, secretly pleased at being the center of attention. "It just wasn't love," she said, her voice rising. "Anything but. Just a thing. This is Love."

My friend Andy's mother said, shaking her head sitting at their kitchen table with a half dozen of her friends, that Natalie had bloomed too early. That's why people thought she should stay with Ron, who was a good thing in the long run, even though he was homely with a protruding jaw and blemishes over his cheeks, and he was older. He was one of the Catholic boys, who would wait, and by the time they were ready and married she would have lost her looks, become heavy and distended, those legs thick as posts; just when no one else wanted her he would be there with enough desire stored up to blind his true sight for a lifetime.

One of the things she loved about him was that he always let the other guy have the first shot. He never in his life cold-cocked a guy.

He let them know first, sometimes days in advance. Someone would tell the guy, and they would meet. If the guy went down the fight was over. Dion walked away, or sometimes helped the guy on his feet. Once you get over the fear of getting hit, the same every time, he told me in wood shop, it doesn't matter what happens.

When Natalie's mother first heard that her daughter was in love with Dion, she said nothing, only stared at the wall. She was one of the last to know; people were afraid to tell her at first. Finally Mrs. Dawson called up to tell her while pretending she must already know. "You mean you don't know? Oh, my." Maybe, Mrs. Dawson was thinking, Natalie's mother will do something now.

Most of Natalie's clothes came directly from her mother's sewing machine, but they were not cheap-looking on her. Every article was made to fit every precocious curve. Her father, on disability from the Bath Iron Works, was rarely seen except at the Wharf having a few or driving around in his truck scratching his beard with his CAT hat low over his brow. He could only see out of one eye.

Before Dion, she and Ron would walk down the hill after school, passing my house, crossing the tracks, on their way to the public library, which was where a lot of us went, strange to say, when we had nothing else to do. They walked alone, holding hands, had been going out since she was in sixth grade, he in junior high. In sixth grade people kissed on the playground, Missy D and Kevin R yelling at each other across the lunch room, the curses from their lips exactly the opposite of the delight and fear on their faces, and there was even a story of David M., the short calm kid, getting a hand job at the movie theater. But no one went out, went steady, held hands in public at that age, except Ron and Natalie. Ms. Hegel, the librarian, had no worries when they sat down to hold hands across the top of the reading table. Others had to be watched and checked on, would be up to nasty business in the stacks among the geography books. Ron and Natalie would only kiss each other for half a minute on the grass in front of the library while waiting for his mother to pick him up for dinner, and then her mother would come pick her up. Later they would talk on the phone for thirty minutes, no longer, according to his mother's rules. His mother worried that her mother made no rules. A girl should have rules, his mother said.

Occasionally people saw them kissing in front of the library. Mr. Wally drove by and happened to stop at the corner and look in their direction. Mr. Dawson, on his way to practice, saw them once; her father saw them once, other kids saw them, I saw them, as I stepped out of the library door. They did not realize I was there. They sat on the steps two feet apart and strained their necks sideways to have their lips meet for this one moment, no more, before he checked to see if his mother was rounding the corner yet. Her mother was often late, and once did not arrive at all. Mr. Dawson, returning from practice, just before dusk, saw her sitting there, knees pulled up, and offered her a ride home.

My mother must have forgotten, she said, with her hands clamped between her knees, palms out. But Mr. Dawson suspected it was more than that—everyone suspected, and he asked her if everything, honestly, everything, was all right. Everyone knew everything was not what it should be in that vinyl-sided house at the edge of a field her grandfather had once owned but her father had sold off one piece at a time. Mr. Dawson said she could talk candidly, she could trust him, Ron's former coach, but not even Ron had ever been inside her house. When asked this time, by Mr. Dawson, she responded in the same way she always did: Everything is fine. I'm just tired is all.

At first it was hard to believe she and Dion were together at all. No one saw them together holding hands or even talking in the daylight. Denise reported seeing them kissing in the dark behind the school, and she was the first to confront Natalie about it, about Ron. Ron's over, she said. How? Denise wanted to know. How did this happen? Natalie shrugged her shoulders.

When she and Dion first got together, she insisted: not in the daylight, not on Central Street by Dawson's or Boynton's Pizza, not in his brother's car, which he drove only at night anyway because he didn't have a license, even if his father's brother was a cop and didn't care. People saw them, though, at the fringe of the bonfire's light out at the pit or down by the river at the landing on one of the benches far from the fluorescent lights.

At the same time Mr. Dawson heard that she was in love with Dion he heard that Dion had quit his basketball team. He went into the back room after Denise and her friends left and leaned his forehead into his hand. They are in love, Denise had said. Nothing from her mouth had ever interested him before this statement. He tried not to think of Natalie. She ran track; she had been into the store with her mother, with Ron. Ron with acne. When he closed his eyes he saw her tanned thigh last summer as she sat on the bench outside the store, blue shorts scrunched up above a pale line and the knob of her shoulder beneath her yellow sweater, and the curve at the corner of her mouth which would harden into a battered smirk, he knew, by the time she was his age—by the time she was half his age.

That afternoon the basketball team stood on the court in their practice gear, not bouncing the ball, staring off in different directions, in disbelief that Dion had quit for her. Mr. Dawson was late; he was never late. They couldn't believe Dion was with her right now. Maybe off in his brother's car or at his cousin's house, where both parents worked, or off in Vaughn Woods by the pond, or out by the pit waiting for it to get dark, or down by the river near the landing waiting for it to get dark. Any of them would have traded places with Dion. The game of basketball suddenly seemed pointless next to the thought of his hand on her hip, and she in her green slacks and yellow sweater burying her face in his flannel shirt, curling her fingers into his back, closing her eyes to hide, even from herself, how much she loved him.

When Mr. Dawson arrived, the team was sitting on their practice balls and on the bench, with their heads low. They hadn't noticed him come in, fingers splayed out in the air. The game of basketball seemed to him a cruel drama written to parody his frustration, and now he was forced to be its director.

They had only been together for a day, but it seemed to Natalie as if they had been together forever. There seemed no need to tell him anything; with one glance she knew he knew the years they had not been together were little more than preparation for this moment. She could tell from the turn of his hand hanging out the window of his brother's car what he was thinking about. He was thinking about her. When he looked at her she had to look away. When he thought about her, she was thinking about him. When he looked away, she looked at him; when she looked away, she could feel him looking at her. She realized now that she had always been looking for him, even though they had been in school together sitting just a few seats away, standing across the playground from each other, he with his friends at the corner of the school parking lot by the dumpsters, she with hers by the swing sets. She had seen him but not seen him. She had been alive but not alive, until now.

On the second day, she was not in school in her linen yellow shorts her mother had sewn together from Mrs. Nason's old drapes. I turned around and in my mind there they were, pulled tightly around her thigh by the angle of her leg.

Two days later there was a teacher's meeting after school to discuss the situation at which no one, least of all the principal, a tall man with Baptist visions, had anything to say. What can we do? Mr. Wally pleaded, his voice gruffer than usual. This was not, in other words, a passing thing. They could not just hold their breaths. The basketball team would not get to the championship, and every day, the men knew, glancing quickly at each other, they would have to see her leaving at the end of the day, as the days got warmer toward June, in her pink flannel shorts, or the blue satin ones, and the white silk shirt or the tank tops, the red bands holding her hair back from her cheeks, walking down the hill, not with Ron, but to be with him in all the dark crannies of the town wrapped in nothing but his old jacket, arcing her pale stomach toward the moon, her open mouth barely giving voice to her thought: Dion.

"What about your mother?" Dion asked as they were walking by the river. "She comes to pick you up outside the library."

She was surprised he knew this, that he had been paying attention to her long before today. Maybe she was right about the way love worked; it had been planned all along.

"My mother can wait," she said and pulled him forward, down toward the trees. She leaned into him with her hands flat against his chest. He couldn't breathe. Her lips tasted a little of spaghetti sauce. He pulled her closer and she let her body stand flat against his for a moment before pushing away. He reached for her pants, but she pushed his hand back, explaining to him that love has its natural course. She took both his hands in hers and stood very close to him without touching him. She explained that if they rushed love it would shatter like glass.

"Like glass," he repeated, amazed at the way she put it. She was like no one he had ever met. He closed his eyes as she touched his face, covered his lips with her fingers. When he opened his eyes again, she was running back up the trail.

"I'll see you tomorrow," she yelled and was gone.

The rotting smell of the riverbank came to him, and he noticed for the first time that it was cloudy and growing cool quickly. But everything seemed different, somehow luminescent, awash with mercurial light. He sat down on a rock and watched the water swirl in the current.

In the following days she formed a list of things she wanted to have and do and be without Ron. A boat, but not any boat, a giant motorsailor they could take all the way down the coast to Florida, so big there could be a storm and they wouldn't even notice down in their cabin below where there would be a fireplace and a television/VCR all in one. Who would be sailing the boat? Dion wanted to know. They would hire someone for that. But the rest of their life was imagined in modest proportions: dogs, golden collie mixes, not pure at all, three children, a house where everyone had a bedroom and there was one extra for a guest, and some land with a view of the hills around town. She didn't want to live down by the river or so close to a neighbor that you could see in their window at night. She had never thought of living somewhere else? He had thought of Montana. Montana—the word sounded chewed in her mouth. God, she said, shaking her head. Other places. Gardner? Farmingdale? Monmouth? Those places, the only other places she knew, were bad enough. Imagine what people were like even farther away. No, she wanted to go to Florida, though. Not to live, just to go there as the Nasons did every winter, taking their daughter Julie with them so that she came back with a tan, even if she did look like a squirrel. And no matter what time of year it was she would have fresh flowers in every room of the house. This idea from her mother, of how people really lived. And a horse for her daughter, in a red barn. And light blue carpeting in every room. Our room, she said, with a canopy bed, but he didn't know what one was. It has a kind of roof, like a tent. He didn't see the point but pictured it anyway, a bed with a tent in a room that already had a ceiling and above that a roof. He had pictured a cabin in Montana where you could look up and see the nails from the roof shingles coming through. And lavender, she said. No one would be allowed to smoke. Every room would smell of lavender. Like me, she said, and pressed her wrist to his nose. This was the smell of their future.

None of us had been in love, not really, until now. Anything we had called love came back to us as mockery in the face of this sudden flight from reason. Andy had said he was in love with Missy, and it was a shame Missy was not in love with him. A daily lament rose from him like the steam of the heat from the pipes at school. Andy's mother hit the counter with her fist. "They're too young," she said, talking about Natalie and Dion, and we knew she was talking about their tongues running along the inside of each other's teeth and the suddenly anxious too-tight grip of her hand between his legs, and the taste of each other's skin, and the smell of each other's bodies and the feel of him slipping inside her and her settling down over him, the shape of her mouth, the shape of his. She was talking about their bodies but thinking about the words they had used. Everyone knew. "Love," she finally growled, as if the creature itself had risen from her dreams to take over her kitchen. She gripped a package of spaghetti as if it were a club and stared at the wall, paralyzed by the idea of them out there.

They hadn't been going out for a week when she got in his brother's car and rode out to the next county. They ate at a mall at a Howard Johnson. She ordered an ice cream sundae and he ordered a grilled cheese sandwich to go in case she wanted to go all of a sudden. She ate her sundae and ordered a milk shake; he couldn't eat. He bought her a blue shirt in a fancy store, a boutique. It's a nice shirt, he said. It looks nice on you. It's a blouse, she said, turning for him in the parking lot with her eyes closed. A blouse, he repeated.

She made him drive faster, clinging to his arm, with her lips pecking gently against the nape of his neck. God, she said, God. Her breath smelled of chocolate. His eyes watered when she rested her hand on his knee and started to rub his thigh as if he were cold. She rubbed until his leg burned. Her stomach rose and sank over the gentle slopes as Dion pressed down harder on the pedal. The road to Monmouth was straight and rolling, the Firebird rising and falling as if with the swells of a heavy sea, the shocks rattling in a drum roll. Slow down, she said, but he didn't. What's in Monmouth? she wanted to know but didn't want to know. There was no reason to know, even though she had heard and did know. The bar everyone had heard about, the Chanticlear, which no one, at least no one from Bigelow JH, had been to. We heard it smelled of her cellar after a flood, the sweet twinge of wet walls and soaked carpets on a warm day.

It was a low windowless building tucked under a maple tree between the side of the road and a trickling stream, no light outside except the one Bud sign. This beer, golden from the tap, was sweeter than what Ron had given her, stolen from his father's icebox. She sat in the back of the room, far away from the others at the pool table, and stared down into her glass. She took a sip and put the mug down. He came over from the pool table and traced his finger along her lower lip, leaned over to kiss her. He loved her in that yellow sweater, her breasts weighted, pushing against the soft fabric, her yellow hair, each strand distinct, falling around her chin. She didn't want him to put on any music, she didn't want to play pool, she didn't want to have another beer, she didn't want to sit alone so many miles from home, she didn't want to be sitting under the bar light, dissected in its brightness at the end of this numberless dark road. So he took the keys to the car, the hell with the rest, and they drove all the way up to Monmouth over the Kennebec River and back again.

They held hands all the way; he said nothing and she loved the way he said it. She didn't want to go home, and so they kept going in another direction. All the roads looked the same at night. She said it clearly, to him, LOVE, just before dawn, and he was afraid as they parked by a river, farther away from home than she had ever been, of touching her. So she touched him as she had seen herself touch him in her mind, and just as she had imagined he held absolutely still. If he said anything, he said what she thought he would say, he said what she wanted him to say, what we all wanted to hear, things he had never said to anyone before, words he had never thought before, whose meaning he would not have been able to explain but felt as he said them as clearly as he felt her breath on his neck, as surely sweet as her hair was soft, as clearly as he felt he was not the same and would not ever want anything, anyone, as much as he wanted her.

The night she didn't come home, the first night ever, people thought of her bruised and bleeding in the corner of some motel room halfway between Hallowell and Mississippi, others thought of her in the Hyatt in Boston, the Marriott in Portsmouth. Or they were on a cruise, on the *Scotia Prince* headed for Halifax, gambling in black tie and satin dress. And still others said, shaking their heads: No, no, she was gone, long gone from us, lying somewhere by the railway tracks. The man in the caboose will find her the next time we hear the Boston & Maine. She's somewhere between Haymarket and Bangor, bleeding into the gravel, her linens smudged, silk torn, the blush of her cheeks chalk-white, and Dion halfway to Mexico. Andy was the only one who got it right, the more obvious answer: They lay side by side in the back of his brother's car parked by the side of a field in the next county. She pulled the blanket beneath her chin as he pulled her head against his chest and ran a single finger through her hair. When she tilted her head, only her bangs and her lips caught the moonlight.

Everywhere Andy and I went was in search of her, just as Mr. Dawson drove up and down Litchfield road and all the way across town to the quarry and back saying to himself he was on an errand when he was really hoping, just for a moment, to catch a glimpse of her. Her father was out looking for her now, too, in the truck, rifle at his side. Two of her uncles were on opposite sides of the town, covering all the roads leading in and out. Her mother told herself she had known the time would come; but not like this, she said to herself. Not with him. She had thought of Ron and her wedding, the white dress she would sew (had already spent hours, days, years, shaping in her mind). Even if they found her, she would not be the same now.

The members of the basketball team, sure now that they would lose the final game of the season and miss the playoffs, were home with their parents watching television or eating potato chips or talking on the phone or listening to their parents talking in the next room or lying on their backs thinking of Dion out there with her; they listened to the sound of crickets and cars passing and shouts from up the street and dogs barking and pots clinking in the sink and footsteps of sisters on stairways while they thought of him out there touching her neck with the tips of his fingers before looking away to drive the car or order another beer or wave to his brother, as if the practicalities of living could distract him, even for a second, from where he would touch her next.

"He took her, he took her," Natalie's mother moaned over and over to her husband and his brothers.

"He dragged her off. He threw her in his car and took her away." Natalie's father was on the phone, calling the police and everyone he knew, which was everyone, the fathers of all the basketball players, fathers of daughters who were Natalie's friends, younger brothers of fathers of Natalie's friends and basketball players, and of girls not yet old enough to be in junior high, though when they were another Dion would be waiting for them.

All over town parents of girls who would be like or wanted to be like her and boys who might think of doing what he had done lay in bed staring at the ceiling saying few words to each other: What do you think? We'll find them tomorrow. What will you do? Don't know. Do you think she's all right? I really don't know. They didn't mention what they were thinking, nor did their children, listening to them talk from the next room, give voice to their thoughts of what might be happening out there, what he might be doing to her. No image, no story, once started, would complete itself in their minds: she was tied in the back seat, the purple, no the pink silk shirt, ripped down the front and her pale breasts shivering in the moonlight with her nipples like cherries on cream pie. Where was he? Hovering above her. Just a hand comes into view; he was gentle now that he had what he wanted. Or she was running down the road in front of his headlights. They had pulled off the road, and she had gotten away, though just for a moment. Her blouse had been stripped off and was lying torn somewhere out of view, probably in the back seat or on the side of the road, and she ran just in her white panties with the cloth riding up between her cheeks above the tan line of her bikini, the point where everyone's eyes had previously been turned back briefly exposed now. Her head turned, her face flushed and mouth open, her eyes wide and wild, like a cat in high beams: He was catching up. And when he did catch up she would be in the back seat or on the side of the road, her back pressed against

the ground, her breath taken away by the weight of his body, all her
mother's clothing, so carefully sewn together, made well enough for
her daughter's daughter's children to wear as costumes of a previous
era, lying in shreds, and her face tied in a knot, biting her lower
lip, eyes pulled into her skull, as he lowered himself.

In our minds love had gone bad, but not in theirs. "No," she said,
pushing off his chest. "Not here. I want it to be perfect." He didn't
understand, though he obeyed her, and she pulled him back against
her on the seat where they lay together, her lips traveling over his
face. "Just hold still," she said. "I always knew," she said, "it would
be like this." He didn't know what *it* was or what *this* was, only that
he had been chosen. He closed his eyes as she pressed his face
against her sweater. All he could smell was her. "I love you," she
said again and again until the sound of her voice covered him like
a blanket. "I want to hear you say it." He said he had already said
it, but she wanted him to say it again, so he did, repeating it into
her sweater, into her breasts. "You do," she said, "Don't you."

She told him to hold his hands at his sides no matter what she
did. He smiled at her, as if she was kidding. You trust me, she said.
It was a question. He nodded in a way that made her love him even
more. He was her child. He asked her what was the matter. Her
eyes had watered. She told him nothing and ran her hand over his
eyelids, smoothing them closed. "Hold still." He nodded. "You nodded!" she scolded and he tried not to smile. She sat on his lap,
feeling her shorts ride up. She ran her finger along his forearm. His
fingers twitched. Abruptly she lay her palms flat against his chest
and pushed, angling her chin up. She took one shoulder in each
hand and ran her hands down his arms as if she were wringing out
wet clothes. He grinned. "Stop that!" she said. She undid her blouse
and bra then put one hand on his shoulder, one against the side of
his cheek, and lowered her chest against his face, wrapping her
arms around the back of his head. He raised his hands, she pushed
them back down; he raised them again, she took them and sat on

them. "There," she said. She leaned forward, pulling his nose between her breasts, his mustache tickling her skin, and found the edge of his knuckle between her legs.

They rocked together as if in an embrace of grief until her breaths came in quick, panicked bursts, as if she was short of breath, not him. She squeezed the back of his head so tightly he yelled into her chest. She rolled off him, backing against the far door, pulling her blouse over her chest. Her face was scrunched up, smeared.

"Don't tell anyone what happened," she mumbled.

His mind raced for something to say, not the wrong thing. "What?" he said. "What happened?"

She shook her head. "I don't know," she said. Whatever had happened it wasn't his fault. It was hers. She was cold. The windows had steamed up but were now frosted over. "It's all right," she said thinking of the movies, TV. It had all gone just like that until now. She tried to think of what would happen next. "I'm scared," she said, trying to follow the script. "Hold me." He moved over on the seat. Already, part of her didn't want him to touch her, but this couldn't be true.

She knew when she fell in love with him that she would be in love forever just as she knew when she woke up in the back seat the next morning, cramped and headachy, and looked at Dion sleeping with his mouth open that she was no longer in love with him and never would be. She opened the door and stepped out into the damp morning air. She began to think of Ron's long fingers resting on the steering wheel of his father's Mercury, his thin legs and gray slacks as they drove to the movies and held hands in the dark. She thought of his thin lips brushing against hers, his hand resting carefully on her shoulder, and of his parents reading in bed waiting for him to come home, his father's air-conditioning.

Dion stretched, scrunching his eyes, his limbs snaking around the corners of the seats up to the back dash. His T-shirt pulled up

to show his stomach. He opened his eyes and watched her standing
in the open doorway. He smiled.

"We should go," she said. "I'm afraid someone will find us here."
He shrugged. Obviously he cared nothing for what people thought.
How had she missed this before? He moved like an oaf, like her
father, slowly opening the door, as if there was no hurry. Digging
the keys out of his pocket. Finally he started the car and launched
them forward, speeding. At least they were moving; she rolled the
window down and stuck her face into the breeze as if into a splash
of water. Poor Ron. What was he doing now?

"I'm not feeling well," she said, making a show suddenly of holding her stomach.

He leaned forward over the wheel and shot her a glance. "What's
wrong?"

"I don't know," she said irritably, as if it were all his fault. He
recoiled a little against his door and leaned his elbow out the window, steering with one thumb.

As they neared her house, he started to get nervous, leaning
forward over the wheel.

"When am I going to see you again?"

She looked at the dashboard as if she hadn't heard. He pulled
over to the side of the road and turned to her, the words she had
been saying—his own name, and *I love you, I love you*—playing
through his head. He wasn't going to say them, they were her words,
and he didn't want to tell her to say them, but he needed her to
keep saying them.

She put her hand on the door. He watched it resting there. "I can
walk from here," she said and stepped out of the car.

"Where are you going?" He screamed so loudly she stumbled off
the road. She could see her house from here, across the road and
down the field.

"I don't love you anymore."

He was out of the car now with his hands on the roof, just looking
at her.

She repeated it. Her bellow drew out and continued as a groan as she bent over with her knees together and hands pulled around her stomach. Tears burst down her cheeks, her blonde strands sticking to her lips.

It seemed now that he must have known all along what would happen. He could have made a noise like the sudden roar of gravel pouring from a dump truck at the construction site where his father worked. This much force and more had built up in his chest. He could have crushed her words with his own. He could have screamed so loudly she would have ceased to exist, but he was silent.

She sensed him stumbling through the field after her. Her mother came to the window, saw her, and called her father who arrived at the window with his shotgun. Seeing him, she ran away from the house toward the woods. Her mother came out onto the front steps and screamed, "Natalie!" Natalie tripped and vanished into the blonde straw. By the time she stood, her father was on the phone, calling. Everyone left their phones hanging and ran for their trucks and cars, funneling from Central Street, Winthrop Road, and Water Street onto Litchfield Road. Dion tripped on a log, and twisted his ankle. She was out of sight. These were her woods; she had grown up playing here.

He stood with his arms apart, hunkered down, and screamed her name as loud as he could. She stopped running and looked up at the sky washing over the treetops. They could probably hear her name all the way in Bath, she thought. He loved her, he really did. She ran on, but stopped when her name sounded again and again, moaning through the trees like a foghorn, his voice seeming more desperate and distant. He was headed in the wrong direction. She almost called out to him.

Mr. Dawson opened his door and stepped out before putting his truck in park; it lurched forward slightly before he could hit the brake. No one was watching. His neighbor, Mr. Shumaker, ran across the lawn, taking long even strides while checking the chamber of his shotgun. Their boots crunched over the dried leaves and grass with the sound of falling water, all of them headed toward Natalie's father standing at the edge of the woods. "This way," he called and ran into the shadows. They all stopped running when Dion's voice called for Natalie. His voice, her name. They leaned over their knees, listening to their own heavy breathing. The smell of their own musty heat escaping from beneath their shirt collars.

They had guns. He stopped calling her name. She turned at the edge of Nason's field when she heard the silence. When she listened harder she heard the voices of her father, her uncles, their friends, and the fathers of her friends calling to one another. For a moment she wanted to take it all back. She did love him. Then she wanted to take it all the way back to never having loved him to begin with. She couldn't say now how it had started. Ron would never forgive her. No one would.

They caught up with him, all the men shouting at once, stumbling and waving. Dion couldn't hear what any one of them said, only fragments of words and phrases. Finally Natalie's father appeared and Dion could see the resemblance in the shape of his face, thin but sagging near the jowls. Her father was the only one not shouting as the rest formed a circle around him, the ends of their waving gun barrels like dark eyes. Dion raised his hands as the police had told him to one night in Monmouth. He closed his eyes and pictured the house he and Natalie were going to have, and the red barn with the horse, every room smelling of her wrist, the bed with the tent, the boat with the captain taking them down the coast to the sun. He could see it all so clearly it seemed as if these things had already happened and he was looking back now after a lifetime together.

"David Dion." It was her father's voice rising above the others. The father had a right to speak. He was the one wronged; anything he did might be excused later. Dion looked briefly at her father and the others. Her father's eyes darted around the woods, skipping off Dion's face every few seconds. Dion lowered his chin and closed his eyes again, holding his arms out so they would know he was unarmed. It seemed he had been waiting his entire short life to accept blame. "David Dion." His name again, and the picture Dion had formed on the backs of his closed lids of her father pointing a finger at him, eyes red with anger, almost with tears, was more accurate than the real thing. Dion waited for his name, imagining her father's mouth opening, his jagged teeth bared. Instead there was the deafening crack of a shotgun blast, and in the total silence that followed Dion found himself floating in the treetops, uncertain if he was dreaming or dying. The maple and oak leaves turned toward him and shivered. He saw the field beyond the woods where a burst of wind sliced a path through the grass like an invisible hand combing through hair. At the edge of the field near the road Natalie stood looking back. She made him so sad he had to look away, into the sun. When he looked back down it was too late: the image of the sun was burned into everything he saw.

I was outside our house throwing a tennis ball against the wall, pretending I was the star of a baseball game with scouts ready to sign me up, and was just winding up for another pitch when I heard the crack echo across town. My mother flew out the back door and grabbed hold of me, searching my arms and chest to see if I had been hit.

Mrs. Dawson dropped a sandwich roll at Dawson's Store, ran outside with the customers, and looked up at the sky. Natalie's mother fell to the floor in her kitchen. In her mind they were all dead: her husband, her daughter, and Dion. The police chief stood up from his desk and looked at the receptionist. He had been afraid of what might happen if people took the law into their own hands. This was the consummation of their relief.

When Dion opened his eyes he was still there, kneeling before his accusers, handfuls of dirt and pebbles sprinkled over his shoulders. All the men's eyes searched his body for wounds or blood, but there were none. Natalie's uncle had fired his shotgun by accident, blowing a hole in the ground and kicking up a cloud, nothing more.

Gazing back across the field to the woods where he lay dying, Natalie found it impossible to accept at first that they had shot him. But then it made sense, and she decided she would bear the mark of his death by never smiling again for the rest of her life. For her, the siren approaching from across town was the sound of an ambulance arriving too late, the second siren, which came a moment later, the sound of the police coming for her. She raised her chin and removed the strands of hair from her face to see over the tree-tops if Dion's soul was rising out of his body into the sky. In court, as in her prayers to him, she would beg for mercy, for pardon. She would admit everything, absolving everyone but herself. For a few moments this morning she had been a fool thinking love was not real, thinking she could live without him, and now she had lost everything.

KINDRED
by
KAREN MCKINNON

WE WERE ONE.

Our heads were down, fluff, fur, nuzzled, softest where our mothers kissed them. We dangled from their wrists which broke too easily. Their faces, young and full of pride and terror, proved that they were sisters.

I tuck the picture back inside the box it came in. The picture, the hunting knife from Grandpa for his twelfth birthday, its ivory grooves smoothed by being held by him, a rifled pack of Marlboros, and his heavy lighter with the wrong initials, my sonless father's. All his stuff fits in a box. Return address for once, but Soledad isn't what I meant by staying put.

I can smell the motel room, strangers leave a peculiar odor. I light a cigarette to extinguish their sourness and my fear. I don't smoke but he does. Wherever he is, whatever cell or lockdown, he must be breathing this deadness. He is in the pen. I'm doing time in a motel room.

I flick on the TV and turn off the sound to stop the talking heads from saying nothing that matters, or lies. I won't be like them. I will say what I have always wanted.

I lock the flimsy door to my motel room and get into my car. I drive about a mile through dust and gray before I find a drugstore. I walk past the gum and perfume and the makeup that might make me pretty. I find the biggest fattest red marking pen, buy twenty, drive my regret back to the motel.

We were each other's.

Our fathers hadn't left us yet and separated us after dark, like that would stop us. They were down the hall playing cards again and cracking ice out of trays and laughing and yelling at our mothers who were singing. I lay on a rough couch in the dark spare room and felt him fill the blackness. I'll stay until you fall asleep, ok? Ok. He raised the covers and lay down with me and breathed into my face. Then I heard yelling and it wasn't down the hall and he was being yanked and swatted and I said But I was afraid and they said Go to sleep young lady and slammed the door. His voice got dimmer and another door slammed and I heard nothing at all. In the morning he had a greening stripe around the little muscle he was proud of, he cocked his arm and showed me all the pullups he could do.

My hands are stained with red ink. I am trying to tell him what he wants to hear and what I swore to myself I'd never say to him and what we both know is disgusting in us. I started with I and that seemed wrong so I scratched it out with the marker and wrote We and that felt right. I had to sit down for a minute, to think of what comes next.

We were lost.

We were innertubing through the snow and found some animal tracks that we followed into the woods. The day was going and the trees were blackening and my heart was. We sank up to our knees and I wanted to stop but he said Come on, it'll be ok. I shivered and he put his stuffinged arm around me. Keep moving, it's the only way to stay alive. We sank up to our thighs and I felt heat and feeling and life drain from me. He rubbed his mittened hands up and down my parka to keep my blood from freezing, he held my mittened hand. It got dark and icy and our little bodies didn't sink so deep. We tried to slide but our Levis gripped the snow. Lie down he said. I was happy to. He lay on top of me and touched his wide nose to mine. I could've stayed like that. I could almost feel us touching. We're gonna pretend we're at Danger Hill, ok? Ok. We held each other's arms and started to roll down the mountain. I'm so dizzy. Can we just stop for a minute? We picked up speed. My face was scraped from tree branches and ice and his zipper which tinkled under his chin. Don't let go. I won't.

I hang the DO NOT DISTURB sign. I take a marker from the bag and then another and another and I pour my heart out on the walls of the motel room. My eyes are wet and my body is and I sprawl out on the bedsheets and relax from my exertions. There is no need to hurry, he's down the road doing two years for assault and I can live that long in the motel room on my cashed teacher's pension. I have all the time I need, for once he isn't going anywhere, he's already away.

We were in deep.

We were camping at a lake, Lost Lake, which was flooded. We swam past gas station signs and pine trees. Our parents grilled steaks, hot dogs for us. The long summer sun shone a light under the water and we spotted a drowned cyclone fence. He dove and I treaded water and watched the ripples he made. When they got still I looked back to shore and saw our fathers hunting firewood and our mothers mixing drinks and I knew they were too far away to save him. I pinched my nose and closed my eyes and let myself sink down. I felt around with my free hand and I couldn't find him and I thought he must be hung up on the spiky fence. I opened my eyes and I couldn't see him. I spun myself around and I couldn't see him and I let go of my nose and pushed myself quickly up. I poked my head above the surface and the water was perfectly still where I wasn't and I turned around and my heart was pounding and I was going to scream and he was climbing a gas station sign. I watched him use his skinny body to be strong.

We were hungry.

Our mothers made us pancakes hard as frisbees. We tossed them at each other till his father came and smacked him. Then he smacked his father and the juice bottles flew and their fists and their hate. His mother got a concussion. My mother got a cast. He drew a heart on it, cracked down the middle.

We were sick.

We had temperatures and we sat plumped up on stale pillows in his mother's bed. She'd been fired so she took care of us while my mother typed and mailed things in the city to support us. His mother brought us tomato soup and we burned our tongues. I tried to swallow a capsule but it swam into my grape juice. His mother ran out of patience and left us on our own. He fished the soggy pill out of my glass and put it on my tongue. Pretend it's not there and swallow, ok? I'll try. It went into my throat and stuck there. I tried to cough it up but gagged. He hit me on the back and the capsule rocketed out of my mouth and landed in a mushy lump on the bed and he cracked up and I thought his mother would hear us and get madder so I put my hand over his mouth and felt his warm wet lips against my fingers.

I swoon a little from the marker fumes and not eating and not leaving the motel room. I open windows in the main room and the bathroom and I cry. The fresh air hurts me, reminds me of our skin, our softness, our wronged intentions. The walls of the motel room reek

with all that we gave up.

We were in trouble.

We stained the man's white Caddy in the cherry war. The man
came door to door to find whose were juiciest. We ran to our tree in
his backyard and we climbed up to the highest fat limb and they
couldn't reach us and the man would wreck his suit if he tried. They
all stood on the ratty grass looking up at us and reddening. The
man's hands were on his hips and he examined the tree and our
mothers were too afraid to say anything and the man took off his
creamy coat. He was patient. He rolled his white cuffs into his blue
sleeves. He took off his shoes and his socks and his pants. Our
mothers looked surprised holding all the man's clothes and seeing
him in his underwear we scrambled. I followed him up to thinner
branches that held our carved initials and would hold us but not
the man who was resting at the first big fork of limbs and saying If
you come down now you won't be punished. We could tell when they
were lying. They'd said our father would be back. We climbed higher
and I was watching where I was going and I heard a crack above
me and looked up and flew down and hit with a thud and a crack
and all my wind was gone. My leg was broken under me and I
couldn't get up and run. The man said That's what happens to bad
kids and started to climb down, one foot safely on the ground, the
other about to push away from the tree and I heard Geronimo! and
the man and he landed next to me and he pummeled the man's head
and our mothers dripped clothes onto the grass and tried to pry him
off or hold his fists or pull his hair to stop him. The man balled up
and then the pounding stopped and I was alone with them. The man
got dressed and our mothers made him coffee and we sat at the
dining table waiting for him to come home and the man's clothes
and face were streaked with anger. My leg was killing me but I
didn't dare say anything. Then there was a siren coming closer, the
police were coming with him in handcuffs or they were coming to

have coffee and wait for him, to take him away. There was a knock at the door. It was an ambulance for me.

I drive to the laundromat, I drive to the store, I drive myself nuts between visiting hours, I drive to Soledad. We sit looking through wire mesh at the new lines on each other's faces. We press the phones to our ears, listening to each other breathe. You'll be out soon, everything will be ok. Ok he says. Don't leave me. I won't. I'm here.

We were too close.

We had climbed the metal ladder to the roof to see the fireworks and were standing near the trough that caught the rain. Our mothers had had too much to drink and were dancing, throbbing nearer, their dresses swiped our gangly arms when they slinked past. The strange men that night poured them wine not gin. We sat down, away from their saucy music, as far away from the grownups on the roof, at the edge, our feet hanging down. Promise we'll never be like them, ok? Ok. My thong came loose and we watched it fall in a hotpink hurry. The fireworks boomed and blazed and fizzled. We breathed smoke and fermentation and each other.

We were free.

We had run away, our lush mothers, our vanished fathers wouldn't come looking. The road was dirt and lake and it was still raining. I kept my arm around him inside his yellow slicker, felt his warmth, mine, his breathing as we walked, his new knife in a hilt stuck in his belt. He pushed my hood back on my drenched head when it slipped. We were going anywhere. I was happy. He was something else. I stopped him in the road and kissed him, searched his lips for yes. This is wrong, ok? he said, soon we'll hate ourselves. I had no reply. We stood there being rained on going nowhere. I let go of him and we went home.

We were going too far.

We had stolen the gin, replacing it with water. We drank it in my room and I pretended to pass out. I was sitting on the floor with my back against the wall and my head fallen back. I watched him through the slits in my mascaraed eyelashes. He was on his hands and knees crawling to me. He was so close I could smell him and he gently said my name. I didn't move. He sat on his heels and looked straight at me. Then he raised his hands slowly off his knees. I closed my eyes for real and hoped he'd do what I wanted. I felt the zigzagged laces of my shirt being pulled and opened. I tried to keep my lids from fluttering. I felt his breath on my cheek and it stayed there and I was spinning. And then he backed away from me. I heard him rustle in the corner where we'd left the bottle. I heard the screwtop turning.

We were careless.

We were sitting at the bar near the railroad station and he handed me a napkin and he left me. I stared at red pen words that spoke for him. Sometimes I feel like you're my long lost love.

He married my best friend. He did it for me, like he could free me. I wore a tacky dress of purple flowers to stand next to her not him. She felt certain she was the most beautiful. She told me about the sex and I didn't want to hear it but I did. She told me he didn't brush his teeth before bed, he didn't know when to stop drinking, he didn't come to the hospital after the kid was born but instead went to the bar to hand out cigars and strut, he wasn't paying his child support, he wouldn't answer the letters begging to let the kid be adopted by another man. The last time I saw her I met the kid. He was five. He didn't ask me questions, he knew I had something to do with his daddy even if I didn't know where he was either, he just watched me, to find out who he was. I did the same, wishing he were mine.

I watch TV and try to remember to eat. I unmake my bed, strip off the tattered gold flowers spread to cover sullied sheets, rinse my chalky glass which will never be clean, wash my dirty clothes in the sink, empty my ashtray. I pay the maid not to clean.

We were hopeless.

I didn't know what state he was in and I was afraid to go looking for him. What would happen if I found him? and what if I couldn't find him? and how would he ever find me if I left the one place he knew I was? I went to our elementary school every day for nine years, I taught reading and writing and waited for a letter. I got postcards with pictures of haystacks and ferris wheels. I turned them over and read the line or two in red signed Love Me and taped them to the walls of my kitchen and when they were full I taped them to the living room and the bathroom and the hallway to the door.

We were reconciled.

Our mothers were bloated and broke and he gave them refuge. They were inside his trailer simmering beans which was complicated, it required remembering to put down their highball glasses every so often to go to the stove and stir. Come on, I'll show you where the tornado hit. He always wanted to get me away from them. Do you think they'll burn the place down? I asked him. What if they do? he said as the screen door slammed behind him. We got into his open Jeep and tried to think of what to say. There was only one thing to say and it was up to me to say it. I watched him through the greening shade of my sunglasses. He wasn't wearing any, his eyes watched the road, looking for his destination not me. This is it he said and pulled off the dirt road aiming us at broken trees. We

sat there saying nothing. I leaned my head back on the seat cushion
watching clouds clump and split and drift away. You better go he
said. He imagined I had a life to return to, and I didn't want all
he'd done and all he'd become to protect me to be for nothing. He
drove me to the airport and he held me and stroked my hair and
said Shh, it'll be ok. I blubbered into his shirt I'm gonna write you.
You have to always tell me where you are, ok?

His face is guarded, his body is, but they can't stop his mind from
going where it wants. And we are used to that. I see his dark eyes
darken with worry and he says When I get out of here I want us to
really talk, ok? Ok. But first I have something to show you I say
smiling at my secret deposition. And I have something to show you
he says, rolling up his sleeve. In the trunk of his forearm are his
initials, sketchy and bluegreen under skin, with a plus sign below
them and below it blankness. Did it hurt? Yeah, it did.

I move the dresser away from the wall to get to the last place to
write. I have so much left to tell him that I should've said before,
so much left to show him we were wrong. I have two markers left
and I don't want to waste them. I uncap one and smell the harsh
cherry scent I like, see the word permanent, hesitate a little.

We were all wrong.
He had come to me, called my name, tapped on my window like
he used to, the habit long gone useless through force of will, his. I
parted my curtains with fumbling hands, saw through sleepy eyes
his changed face, felt his certainty gone, felt my life about to change,
myself about to be unloved for the first time. But he was there and
he was safe and I smiled through it, through my want, through my
window at him. Come in I said without voice. I plumped a pillow
behind my back, pulled the covers up, listened for his footsteps, his

breathing, his rejection, a confession or a lie to spare me. Something's happened he said. I can tell, tell me what. And then his face got even harder and his voice began to shake and it said I think I killed my father. I felt myself harden and I said He deserved it and I held him and I softened and I sheltered him until they came and took him away.

He has just shaved and his cheek looks new again. He says Do you miss your life? and I want to laugh and then I want to cry and all I can think to say is Do you?

I am afraid and the room is black and I flick on the bedlamp and see what I've done. And then I am afraid. He will see my insides raw and red, he will have no choice about me, he will pity me and placate me and then we'll be apart. I push my covers away and go to the wall near the door and rub delicately at the We. It doesn't smear, even when I wet my finger. And I can sleep.

Early release. His will be mine. I blot my lipstick, watch my lips float on tissue toward the trash, rearrange my stuff in the medicine chest to clear a place for his, rearrange the furniture in the motel room, put the small plastic TV in the closet, the dusty phone under the bed, the lampshades in the shower. Bare bulbs glare at my feelings like parents. I put a coat on over nothing, grab my purse, grab his box.

I drive slowly, deliberately so I won't crash and die and lose everything that matters. My bare foot pushes and pulls at the accelerator. Under my coat I am naked and misgiving, my stomach flat and nauseated from waiting so long, from wanting nothing but this. I wait at the gate and see him out in the open and walking toward me on the dirt road. I get out of the car and stand by the hood trying to hide my feet but then I don't care and I run to him, skipping stones with my soles. He smiles and I open my arms to take him away from the place that has held him for me and he holds me and

I take his roughened hand and walk him to my car. We sit in the

quiet of the front seat, looking out the window, saying nothing. I can't imagine taking him into the motel room, showing him what I've done, what I feel. I am stalling. I brought your box I say and push it toward him. He looks inside, holds the lighter, tries to spark it. You been using this? he asks. Yeah, do you mind? It should've been yours to begin with. He picks up Grandpa's knife and opens the blade. It looks dull in the weak light. He holds it to his face to inspect its blunt edge and I see Grandpa and his daughters and their husbands and myself in his frown, he holds it in his chapped sweet mouth and pushes up his sleeve, he holds it to his forearm, dips the knife tip into his skin, tenderly carves my initials below his. They bead and shimmer and begin to run like tears.

GETTING PAID
by
VICTOR LAVALLE

1.

COMING HOME FROM SCHOOL, I SAW A MOVING TRUCK IN FRONT OF my building. Big and yellow with the letters R-Y-D-E-R painted on the side in black. I was surprised because when people moved onto our block they used vans borrowed from some uncle's plumbing business; it was rare to see a moving truck that was only a moving truck. Someone had put their hands on money and couldn't wait to leave.

I stood by the thing, all locked up. Grandma would want to know who was leaving.

I leaned against a car parked on the street. The truck sat there like something left to rot; cars came up behind it and swerved around when the other lane was clear. I was about to toss rocks at the windshield from boredom when Tanya and Rich appeared, thinking they were dope because they'd been fucking at his apartment.

Rich put his fingers under my nose. This is the best kept secret in the world.

I pulled myself away from her smell because I had a crush on Tanya so bad.

She was fifteen years old, like Rich. He was handsome, had that Philip Michael Thomas look about his face, was going around with a du-rag on hoping his waves would come in.

—Who's moving? Rich asked.

I looked back at our building, tried to think of who could be getting out. There were only six floors but somehow it seemed taller and wider. To me it was more than big, it was limitless. A world.

Rich turned to Tanya, but she swatted his lips away.

—How long you been standing here? she asked me.

—Couple of minutes.

I could never stare into her face, she was like Medusa, but I mean it in a pretty way.

Tanya punched my arm; it hurt and I wanted to rub my shoulder but she was waiting for me to do that. Instead I said—Didn't hurt.

She burst into a smile. —Bullshit.

We were wearing our short summer shorts, it was almost that time of year; you couldn't have counted the scars across all our knees and shins unless you had an abacus.

—I bet it's Adrian's family, Rich whispered. He had to whisper, Adrian was Italian, one of the few white kids left on our block. To keep from getting beat up he told everyone his father was in jail, part of the Mafia. We'd all seen *Scarface* and knew what that meant.

—I bet they're moving to Howard Beach to be with the rest of the Mafia, Rich said. He fished a Jolly Rancher from his pocket; without offering either of us he stripped the plastic and popped it into his mouth.

Tanya said—All Italians ain't in the Mafia. It's Cubans too.

I nodded, she sounded so sure. I wanted to add something, but I was the kid with his head stuffed into comic books or martial arts magazines; I didn't have anything to contribute unless we were talking about the price of nun-chucks or a copy of *Power Man & Iron Fist*.

Rich grabbed Tanya's hand. —Let's go back to my crib, he said. —My dad won't be back till seven or eight.

She pulled away, smoothed her processed hair. —That's enough of you today.

Rich's shoulders dipped.

—And cut your fingernails, she added.

We went back to waiting and I would've gotten bored again if

Tanya hadn't sat down beside me on a car, rubbing her knees in a way that made me forget the movement of time.

My boy Marion came out holding a box fifteen minutes later. He walked to that goddamn truck and didn't see us until he'd rolled the back door up, tossed the box inside.

—Whassup? he said.

I walked up to the truck. The inside was stuffed up: couches, televisions, five nice dressers—shit I'd never seen in Marion's little-ass apartment.

Marion put his hand out and helped me climb in.

—So it's you who?

He smiled. —My dad's got businesses now.

—Your dad?

His father had been the kind of guy to try and be cool with me and our other friend Cyrus when we went over to visit, making jokes and talking to us about titties. Parents like that always struck me as stupid.

—Of course. My dad's been saving his money for years.

His pops had been getting drunk and buying Lotto tickets like everyone else who cashed paychecks on Thursday nights. Who did he think he was bullshitting?

—He wasn't saving up nothing, I said.

—Someone died, Marion whispered.

—Who?

—Some aunt who had a furniture store.

His father must have been the only heir, there was no other reason that knucklehead would get an inheritance. My asshole was smarter than Marion's pops.

Marion walked to the back of the truck, checking that the straps holding pieces in place were secure. It had only been a couple days but already he'd learned to keep an eye on his property.

—You and Cyrus are going to come over soon right? You should come see the house?

I climbed down, saying nothing; I wanted to get in and give my snooping grandma the scoop, she was at the window, watching.

2.

By the time I was fourteen Cyrus and I had been making the trip out to Marion's place in Long Island for a year.

All the places in this neighborhood were big, with lawns that needed lots of mowing. Every time we walked from the Long Island Rail Road station to Marion's house I watched those kids using lawn mowers to make everything even and clean and civil.

With Marion's family, cash was generating like electricity; when we got to the house they were having it renovated.

Again.

The place was draped in white drop cloth. Painters wandered around in uniforms with a company logo on their backs.

Marion's dad liked everything looking new, that was the one proof left that he'd come from our neighborhood. He was always replacing furniture, buying new art; every few months it seemed like they had moved into a brand-new spread. And always something brighter, more expensive and covered in a gold sheen.

We walked into the house and as soon as we did the painters shooed us out.

Marion asked if we wanted to see his school instead, we hadn't ever gone there before. Why would we, he had the best video games you ever saw.

When we got there me and Cyrus stood still, looking at it all like, What the fuck?

It was a royal French palace complete with the fucking fountains. The football field wasn't even a football field, it was for lacrosse and rugby.

—What the fuck is rugby? Cyrus asked. He was the tallest of us though that wasn't saying much.

—Rugby, Marion said like he'd been playing all his life. —It's British football. They don't use pads.

—Don't use pads? I said. —They must look all fucked up.

Marion shook his head like Cyrus and I had taken a piss on

Chardin's beloved grave, but I was forty-two times smarter than my old friend would ever be.

—So where do they play football? Cyrus asked, digging in his pocket for a piece of gum. He was always chewing gum in bunches, jamming them into the corner of his mouth so it looked like he was chewing tobacco. He thought he looked like Ricky Henderson, but as hard as he moved his jaw it just looked like that shit hurt.

—They play football here too. But it's not as popular as rugby or lacrosse.

—I don't even know what lacrosse is, I said, kicking up tufts of grass and dirt, playing dumb.

—You shouldn't do that Ant, Marion told me with his hand on my shoulder. —We like to keep the field in good shape.

—Man please, I said. —I'll take a shit on this field if I feel like it.

Cyrus laughed loud enough for the kids on the tennis courts to turn and notice. When they did, all at once, like automatons, Cyrus and me grabbed our dicks, gave a shake in their direction.

—Cut that shit out! Marion yelled.

I looked back at him with nothing to say.

The three of us made our way back to Marion's crib after about an hour of laughing like everything was still the same.

It didn't seem like Cyrus was thrown off by any of Marion's changes, but me, I was dizzy. Marion brought us into the kitchen and poured iced tea while the painters were on a break.

We went to the back and sat in their yard, listening to the grass grow. Cyrus did back flips while I sat there amazed that me and Marion weren't friends anymore. Marion's mother came out to us with more juice to drink. I thanked her, I wasn't rude.

When his mother found that the side door had shut and locked behind her (what kind of door on a house does that? how much would it cost?) she went and got the spare key from under a small rock next to the house.

I watched and nearly felt that bad that here, on a Saturday afternoon, she was showing a stranger their secrets.

3.

I waited six months and didn't visit Marion anymore. I didn't even speak to that kid.

Then I got very drunk on piss hard vodka. Ingested enough to think that going to Marion's house would finally be a good idea. Also, I called ahead and made sure they weren't there.

I didn't remember getting on the Long Island Rail Road and not walking, probably stumbling, toward the big fat home, but I got there.

I banged on the side door just to hear the sound, but also to make sure that no one had come back while I was making the trip. The driveway was empty and the lights were out. But soon I told myself to be quiet. I didn't want the neighbors turning on their lights, coming at me with bats and hockey sticks like the fucking Civilian Commandos.

I told myself—get the key, get the key—but my body wasn't making sense of the command so I forced the door open with my shoulder and a shove.

The kitchen had become something newer again, made me think I was in the wrong house until I turned on the lights and saw the pictures of Marion dressed like a gay clown or something, a store-bought outfit.

When the three of us lived in Flushing our friendship had been like coal, a thing so full of energy that mined properly it could fuel every light in Queens. But where was he? Out here now.

—Hello? I slurred more than once. I was loud and purposeful, but I was speaking only to myself and the empty architecture. The paintings on the living room wall were so minimal they had to be expensive. The television in the corner was as big as a bus. I turned it on.

I turned on everything: stereo, lamps, air conditioner.

I thought of exploring this house, but instead I sat on that black couch that came apart in eight sections, wondering what would happen if they returned to find me so full of something ugly that I was paralyzed.

I thought of nothing for a very long minute, then found myself and got up.

The television and the stereo were fighting for my attention; I turned them both off, all but one light. Unfortunately my head was starting to clear.

They kept their liquor in a glass case next to the TV, a smiling jar. My fingers were on the combination lock set in the door, the one with the scrape across the face. The one I'd watched Marion's father, long ago, move left, right, and left again. But my fingers were chaotic. I had to punch the glass. Ten, twelve times before my hand went through.

The rum. I took the rum because I'd never had any before. When I gulped I tasted nothing at all, but my eyes got loose in their sockets again and I knew I'd done the right thing. I moved like a fucking clod toward the stairs, dragged myself up to the second floor, taking a break again and again to pour some more liquor down my throat. I was so giggly by the time I reached the second floor that if someone had appeared I would have carried on a conversation like I'd been invited.

—Hello, I called out, but this time it was only to make myself laugh. I rose, opened the first door I found—his parent's room. It was a shitty room, small, very little furniture. The bed was so tiny I was sure Mr. Phillips was spending nights at the store or in the back of the furniture van.

The dresser had little inside; I went through every drawer, on a hunt for something to satisfy me.

I turned and opened the small closet. Mrs. Phillips's clothes smelled like stale perfume; I was struck momentarily by the fear that everyone had died and I was the only living thing in a house full of quiet spirits. But all my fears evaporated when I found the ugly little sock stuffed into a shoe.

I closed my eyes and unfurled the sock like a banner; when I looked again I saw the wonderful color of something I needed very badly. I could barely count when I was sober, but that night it came easily to me. The wad was all fifties and twenties. Twelve hundred dollars, that's what it was.

The house had lost its power for me; I descended the stairs, tripped and rolled to the floor. I lay there in a pile until I found I had control of my body again. A moment of clarity came across me like monsoons do in India, suddenly, full of anger—telling me to run.

I wanted to do more to them, make a greater impression on this family, on my friend. But I knew that any damage I did would be temporary. If I peed on the carpet or took a shit on their couch, eventually Marion's father would find a way to cover or remove it. Eventually they would forget me, while I would always remember them.

I stepped out into the night air to find it cooler than it had been hours before. I went back inside and took one of his father's coats.

I covered the distance to the Long Island Rail Road scared, unhappy. When I turned the corner and was hidden from the empty eye of Marion's house I felt no better. And no better when I reached the station where no one else was waiting for the 4:27 back to Queens.

I crouched on the cold concrete of the platform and took out the money again. I counted it once, twice. It was still twelve hundred, but each time I hoped there would be more. When I'd taken it, the cash had seemed like enough, but now the value was dwindling.

I folded the loot and put it away, lay on my back looking up into the black unfolding night. Electricity was buzzing dimly in the train tracks five feet away. I listened to it wishing there was a pattern, but sometimes the sound was high and whiny and a minute later it fell into a low, dull drone. I wanted it to make up its mind. I wanted to piss. For the way he started thinking he was better than me I wished Marion dead eleven thousand times, but if he had just moved back to our old neighborhood I was sure I could have forgiven him.

HOOK, LINE AND SINKER
by
JUDY BUDNITZ

———————

MY GRANDMOTHER CALLED. I FOUND A DOCTOR FOR YOU, SHE SAID,
Bev's grandson.

Bev was her best friend. They lived in the same white stucco
condominium complex. They played shuffleboard together. They
went to the swimming pool and did exercises without getting their
hair wet. They watched baseball games together, something they
used to do with their husbands and had always hated but now
couldn't get out of the habit of. The two of them had memorized all
the statistics; they'd learned all the catchers' crotch-signals.

Bev gave him your number, my grandmother said.

But I have a boyfriend.

Is he a doctor? she said.

No.

Is he a professional?

Not really.

Well then, she said and hung up in a huff.

I saved used condoms, labeled and dated and sealed in Ziploc bag-
gies in the freezer. I figured I might need them one day when I was
old and lonely and ugly, dried up between the legs but still wanting
kids.

I didn't trust sperm banks. What if there was a power outage?
What if they went bust? I was a paranoid housewife stuffing dollar
bills in my mattress.

I was dating a fisherman. I liked to go out with him in his boat early in the morning when he hauled in the nets.

The fish he caught had dreamy eyes and big, sensuous lips. Gazing out through the gauzy nets they looked like brides behind their veils waiting to be kissed. The bottom of the boat was always awash in fish blood.

He had a hammer that he used sometimes to bonk them on the head if they flopped around too much. He liked to stick his fingers in the slits of their gills as they breathed their last breaths. They can't even feel it, it's just a reflex, he'd say as juicy fish-flesh pulsed around his fingers, squeezing and fluttering.

He had an erection tenting his raincoat. I pretended I didn't see, but I wanted to bonk it on the head with his hammer.

The doctor rang the doorbell at seven. Without saying hello he sniffed my breath and felt my legs with his dry rubbery fingers. Then he scuttled to the corner and crouched there shrieking. There was nothing I could do to coax him out. Finally I went to bed and heard him tearing through the apartment searching for an open window. In the morning I saw that he had shed fur everywhere and urinated on my dishes.

He's shy, my grandmother said. Don't be making snap judgments.

Once, after sharing some moments of sticky intimacy with a man I didn't know too well, we both reached for the spent condom at the same time.

I'd like a memento to remember you by, I said, thinking: I'll put it in some ice, rush it home to the freezer to add to the collection, I'll take a cab, they say the sperm stay alive for at least fifteen minutes.

I'd like to keep it, to remember you by, he said and snatched it away.

But I couldn't let it drop, not this one, he was too good to pass up, six foot two with gorgeous thick hair and the kind of facial structure that comes from generations of careful breeding. I need genes like his to balance out my own. And I doubted I'd ever see him again. I had not given one of my best performances.

Oh, but you won't forget me, I said coquettishly.

No, the truth is you won't forget me. But I might need some help remembering you, he said.

This was unfortunately true, and not just because of my looks. His apartment was peppered with yellow Post-its reminding him of the names of things: "thermostat," "smoke detector," "VCR—insert tape before recording," "milk—check date—month day AND year."

He showed me a cruddy garbage bag in his closet. I've saved every single one since 1983, he said.

I let it go.

The doctor came again, this time bringing flowers, which was a nice gesture though he ate them all, petal by petal, in the first fifteen minutes. His fingers really were extraordinary, they must have had extra joints. He looked at me with love in his lemur-eyes.

Shy? He's something beyond shy, I told my grandmother.

He's a very bright boy, she snapped. He just doesn't rub it in people's faces.

I don't think it will work, I said.

Who are you to judge? she said. You, you're a terrible judge of character. I know what's good for you. What do you know? You were dating that man who went to court for being a child molester.

He went to traffic court. For parking tickets.

In a school zone, she said smugly. How can you be so naive?

I'm not naive. I just . . . I try to think the best of people, until proven otherwise.

Pish. So give the doctor another chance, Miss I'm-So-Open-minded.

I met a deaf man in my origami class. His cranes were impeccable, his creases sharp as blades. His name was Sheldon. We went on some dates. It was not as awkward as you might expect. We went bowling. He could feel the thunder of the ball, the crash of pins vibrating through the floor. He got the full experience, minus the headache.

We went to movies. He could generally infer what was going on, unless the acting was particularly wooden. Occasionally I wrote him little notes about plot points he would otherwise miss, pushed them onto his lap and lit them with a penlight.

Rereading the scrawled notes afterward was like looking at bad poetry:

She just said she's his mother.

I know all about you and him, he says.

She said: Those weren't vitamins

All the money was in that suitcase.

She left the baby behind.

I can't go on like this.

I brought the deaf man to Sunday dinner with my family.

Are you sure he's deaf? He doesn't look deaf, my mother said.

His ears look just fine to me, said my father.

Ask him if he likes the meat loaf, my mother said.

Do you like it? I said, but Sheldon was looking the other way.

But do you love him? my mother said. Can you make a life with this man?

Can he read lips? my sister asked and mouthed: Eat me.

He's nearsighted, I said.

My sister leaned across the table. Her hair fell in the soup. Eat me. Silently. Lasciviously.

Does he have one of those dogs? You know I'm allergic to dogs, my father said.

My god, Harold. He's deaf not blind, my mother hissed.

Stop talking about him like he's not here, I said. He's not invisible.

We all turned to look at him. By this point my sister was in his lap.

Well he certainly seems friendly, my mother said brightly. He seems to like people.

And he's even house-trained, my father said sarcastically. Stop talking about him like he's a pet.

We should never have come, I said.

Oh, they're just getting acquainted, my mother said. It must be his way of saying hello.

Sheldon was running his fingertips over my sister, he was reading her like Braille, he was skipping straight to the good parts. My sister had her lips to his ear. What could she possibly be telling him?

I'm sure he's a very nice man, my mother said desperately. She always turned into the optimist the minute a situation became hopeless.

We sat politely and watched them for a while.

He must be French, isn't he? Or Italian? You know how Italians are. They kiss everybody. Twice.

No mother, I said and stood up to leave. My chair skidded across the floor, a sound even Sheldon could feel.

He's just compensating, my mother said, you know, with his other senses, to make up for his hearing. I've read they do that. You know, like seeing, smelling . . . what else?

Touching, I said. Tasting. Yes, I know, I said. Sheldon, come, I called.

He didn't hear me.

I heard you went out with some deaf guy, the fisherman said. It was four A.M. He was spearing bait on hooks, dropping the nets in the water.

Oh?

That's what I heard, he said. Did you?

Yes, but I didn't mean it.

You mean it was a fake date?

I did it as a gesture, I guess. I wanted to show that I'm not prejudiced against people like that.

Well, that's very big of you. Have you ever dated a woman? Or, say, an Eskimo? A midget?

No.

Don't you think you should? Are you only dating me because I never went to college? Reverse-snobbism?

You never went to college?

I never finished. Look, it doesn't matter anyway, because he and my sister are getting married.

Married?

Well, that's what everybody thinks, and he hasn't said anything to the contrary.

Being deaf sounds nice, he said. I almost wish I was.

Why?

Well, you could avoid all of . . . this. Having these, these talks, you know? The serious talks. The do-I-look-fat questions. You know? Deaf people are just . . . excused. I'd like that.

You make noises like a deaf person sometimes, when we're making love.

What an ugly thing to say, he said.

What is that, anyway?

This? He reached into the bucket and pulled out another wet muscley lump. It bulged between his fingers, there were little strings hanging off it. This? It's bait.

What was it before it was bait?

He looked at it. It's always been bait. Some things are always bait. Even when they're walking around or swimming around or whatever, some things you can just look at and know. They're destined to be chopped up and stuck on hooks. Some things are just born to be used, their whole lives they're just waiting around asking for it.

The sky was mauving, it was turning the palest shade of pearly pink. The color of the pulpy stuff in his hands.

Your sister's really hot, he said. Where'd she get it, is she like adopted or something?

My grandmother came to town. I've got something special planned for your birthday, she told me.

My birthday's not for another nine months, I said.

I have to do your present now, she said. She did not look good, there were splotches of unusual colors—greens, purples—swimming under her skin. Her pupils were huge.

Are you high? I said.

I expected her usual squawk of incomprehension, but instead she said: Don't I wish.

She took me to Birnbaum's department store at five o'clock on a Sunday morning.

But it will be closed, I told her in the cab.

We need to get a good place in line, she said.

Sure enough there was already a crowd outside the doors. Birnbaum's annual wedding dress sale, she explained.

But I'm not getting married, I said.

But you will, won't you? she said. You'll need one eventually. Why not get a good deal now? Fifty percent off, sometimes more.

Why didn't you bring my sister? She's the one getting married.

Says she doesn't want a traditional wedding. You know your sister, she doesn't need any help.

By eight the crowd had grown sizably. Young women and not-so-young women, with mothers and sisters and teams of friends, lined up and panting at the doors which were due to open early for the sale.

What you do, my grandmother was saying, is grab as many as you can. Don't even look, just grab. Then later we can barter.

When the doors opened, everyone else had the same idea. We all poured inside, in seconds the racks were swept clean. Then women lugging sheaves of lace and white netting began the bickering and tug-of-war.

A tall thin man with a gorgeous scarf lifted a dress from my hands. I snatched it back.

Honey, this will never fit you, he said, it's a size six. He held it up against his own chest.

I've got time, I'll get there, I told him and snatched it back.

In your dreams, he said.

There were no changing rooms in the basement of Birnbaum's. All around us women were stripping down to leotards, spandex, underwear, and tugging up dresses. Bits of white fluff floated through the air like feathers in a henhouse.

I feel dizzy, a voice said and I turned and saw my grandmother falling. She fell forward slowly and landed softly, cushioned by the puffy tulle skirts she held. All I could see were her legs; she looked like a hoop-skirted Victorian lady upended. I saw the soles of her orthopedic shoes, spotless, as if they'd never touched ground.

Wedding dresses and grasping hands frothed on all sides, and as I leaned down to help her a woman with three-inch fingernails got one of them caught on my earring. It was a mess.

Later we learned that she had cracked both kneecaps and her chin-bone on the floor when she landed. Which is strange because I remember only softness and light, like those landscapes of clouds you see outside an airplane window, candy-floss or cotton balls or the fuzzy whiteness suspended in the center of ice cubes.

My grandmother called from the hospital.

Bev's grandson came to see me today, she said. The man's a genius.

What did he say?

He says they're worried about my bones getting brittle, she said. He says they're worried about my agnosticism.

Do you mean astigmatism?

You heard me.

I didn't know you were agnostic.

Well, it's a bit shaky. He says I need to either firm it up or else find a way to renew my faith, one or the other. Then I'll feel more at peace.

What does he know? He's only a doctor.

Would that we were all as perceptive as he is.

He said all this to you? He's never said a word to me, all the times I've seen him.

I told you he's shy. You're too hard on people.

I'm not. I'm open-minded . . .

Open-minded? In my day we called it loose.

That's different. Anyway, it's his fault. He's not normal. I could swear he has a tail.

And you think you're such a bargain yourself?

The doctor came over, bringing me one of those bottles of wine that come in a straw basket. Don't I look nice? I said and twirled around to show him just how nice I looked.

He sucked his fingers and sighed.

Say something, I told him, say anything.

He looked at me with limpid eyes. His small round nostrils were choked with hair.

What? I said. Are you mad at me? Is that it? Are you ignoring me? Fuck you.

But he would not be provoked. He hung upside-down over the back of a chair, chittering and moaning. His fingers skittered over my skin now and then, but in the same way that he touched the table, the walls, the floor. A pressing and a pinching, like searching for larvae under tree bark.

That's it, my patience is at an end, I said. But at the same time moving closer, positioning and angling, hoping the next time he touched me it might accidentally, miraculously be in the right place.

He must have a weakness somewhere, I thought. Guavas, pomegranates, papayas, persimmons. Kiwi. Breadfruit.

Sometimes the fisherman couldn't even wait to get back to the docks; he had to start slitting them open right there in the boat.

Look at that, he'd say and drape the two fish-halves over my lap. Isn't that the most beautiful thing?

And it was beautiful, in a way. It was the contrast: the metallic iridescence outside, the glistening bright slabs of muscle within. Human skin is not half as beautiful as fish scales; does that mean our insides are correspondingly ugly as well?

Sometimes we made love right there in the boat. He would have me lie down on the slippery piles of fish, scales and fins pricking right through my clothes, all those wide-open eyes pressing into the back of my neck. And he would rear up above me and then plunge down, again and again, making the boat rock crazily. If I looked up the sun seemed to leap from one end of the sky to the other.

You have such a beautiful body, he would say at these times, you do.

Which is always a lie, I know, it is something people say when they want something from you.

But sometimes it is nice to be wanted for a little while.

But I also knew that what he was really saying was: If only you had a tail like a mermaid. Is that too much to ask? After all I've done for you, the least you could do . . .

Sometimes when we were making love he missed my body entirely and plunged himself deep into the pile of fish. He always pretended it was an accident.

I'm so happy, my sister said. Her eyes were manic, forehead shiny. She was wearing the dress that my grandmother had fallen on.

I love you, she mouthed to Sheldon.

Sheldon smiled and said nothing. He'd bleached his teeth for the wedding, they were a slice of brilliant cadmium white on his otherwise unremarkable face.

What does she see in him, anyway? I said. Mom?

But my parents were pretending they'd never had children, they were waltzing round and round the room like a pair of wind-up dolls.

I wish my grandmother could have come, I told the doctor, she's big on weddings.

The doctor hummed quietly and made a steeple of his fingers. They were so long and skinny it was more of an Eiffel Tower.

Has she got her religion settled yet? Have her patellae healed?

He nodded wisely.

Patella's a pretty word, isn't it? Could you name one of your children that? Meet my daughters, Patella and Ulna. And my son Tarsal.

He still nodded but I saw sweat breaking out on the broad bare slope between nose and upper lip.

If you're supposed to end up with the person who understands you best, I ought to marry my grandmother, I said. Too bad that's not allowed.

He took my hand then between his cool, leathery palms. But they felt like cold dead things, there was no passion in them. I tried to pull him closer and he twisted away and ran scampering up and down the woodwork like a spider. He would not let me get near.

He reminded me of a nightmare I'd had once as a child, of all my pictures sprouting little black ant legs and running across my bedroom walls. Damn him for reminding me of that dream; now I'd have it again.

And would he be there in the middle of the night with his furry arms held open when I woke up screaming? Or course not.

I thought of a basket, upside-down, propped up on a stick tied to a long string, with bananas and papayas inside. Sometimes the only solutions are the simplest ones.

He started leaving flowers on my doorstep every day. And other things he thought I might like. Tanning cream, Florida water, halva.

A cinnamon roll that looked exactly like Mother Teresa.

My grandmother called from the hospital and said: He's not see-ing anyone else, you know. Only you. You're a lucky duck.

I lay in wait for him, the end of the string in my sweaty hand, but could never catch him. The fruit was green, then ripe, then overripe, then rotten. Rotten fruit smells the sweetest of all.

What's this I hear about you seeing a doctor? he said as soon as we were out on the water. Gulls were circling the boat. There were no fish in it, not yet. But they weren't stupid. They knew what was coming.

I did it for my grandmother, I said. She gets a charge out of playing matchmaker.

And I suppose it had nothing to do with the fact that he's a big fancy doctor?

Not at all, I said. All he did was bring flowers and make messes in my house, pull down curtains.

I liked the way he was looking at me, head-on and wide-awake in a way he usually only looked at a very large fish that refused to die.

Are you jealous? I said.

No, he said after a long pause. Not at all.

Why not?

Why? Because you'll always come back, that's why. Because I'm a hot thing in a cold world and you'll always come back like the proverbial moth to flame. Go run around with these deaf dumb and blind monkeys of yours. I don't give a damn. You'll always come back and you know it.

He understands me better than you do, I said. I can talk to him.

Oh, I understand you fine, he said. I understand just as much about you as I want to, I don't want to know any more. It would only disgust me.

How do you know?

And talk? Who needs talk? What's talk but a way of filling up the time between doing one thing and doing another? Might as well play solitaire.

Now was the time for the dramatic exit, some screaming and some slammed doors. But we were in a boat in the middle of the ocean. I longed for a helicopter, some waxen wings, a trapdoor in the sky.

You feel alive when you're with me, he said. The rest of the time you're just pretending. I know I'm talking in clichés, I do it on purpose. I don't want to waste brain-energy on conversation. I'm conserving it for more important things. I'm not as stupid as you think.

All morning I watched and he hauled in the fish, holding them flopping in his arms before clubbing them still.

The doctor's flowers stopped coming.

He must have finally given up, my grandmother said over the phone. Did you refuse him? You heartless girl. I haven't seen him for several days myself. I miss him.

Why are you still in the hospital?

Oh, complications. You know how they say. Cracked cuticles. Head, heart. Tired, tired. I have a boyfriend here, did you know? A nice young orderly named Phil. He says he admires my red, red hair.

We were out on the boat. The east was all gaudy zebra-striped purple and orange. I looked at it and thought, Miami, though I've never been to Miami.

I was wearing a raincoat of his, and his own favorite wool cap. He had given me his own pet knife to use, the one with the queerly shaped curving blade. We were baiting the nets.

This bait seems different today, I said. What is it?

It's the same as always, he said. Like I told you before, bait's just bait. It's bait from the minute it's born. You don't believe me? You ever look at a cow up close? You go look at a cow, you look up close in those big dumb sad cow eyes, and then try to tell me it ain't just Burger King killing time.

No, this bait is different, I said, where did you get it?

Big eyes like yours, he said. Sweetheart.

I knew I recognized something about it, a bit of cool smooth leathery hide, the bits of fur here and there, familiar.

Where did you get it?

You know where I got it, he said. Don't you play dumb. I ain't biting.

And now you might be thinking of the overturned basket, and the stick, and the string, and long fingers reaching out for the pomegranate seeds, the string tugging, stick jerking, basket falling, a sudden artificial night sky, chinks of light like stars in the wicker dome, stink of rotting fruit.

Which all translates into complicity, and baited hooks, and later a fresh fish mattress, two raincoats rubbing and squeaking on top of it. And so on and so on like this, day after day. Because to some people this moment together on the boat is the only real thing in life, and everything else is without value, is just filler. Foam packing. Polystyrene peanuts.

But you might also think I wasn't playing dumb, that I didn't know any more than you up to that point. And you might think of the many sharp objects in the boat, the hooks and knives, his own special very sharp knife with the curving blade. And there's the hammer, remember.

You might think of the nets, and a length of chain around one ankle, and the heavy three-pronged anchor. He is a big man, and cumbersome, but it is not inconceivable. You read those *Reader's Digest* stories about women (it's always women) who in extreme circumstances find the superhuman adrenalized strength to lift cars or wrestle bears to save their loved ones.

It is not inconceivable to imagine him suspended at the bottom of the ocean, fish eating away his flesh a nibble at a time, so that at first he looks pockmarked, then leprous, then he is like coral, full of tiny channels that the tiniest fish can swim through, and they nibble away until there is nothing left of him but the eyes, left flat and lidless as a fish's to witness what he has become.

Poetic justice, you might say. Perfect. Too neat to be believable. But then it's a fitting end, isn't it, for someone who went through life talking clichés.

It all depends on what you think of me, I suppose. I would hope you'd be willing to think the best of me, at least until proven otherwise. Don't be making snap judgments, as my grandmother says.

CITIES OF THE PLAIN
by
DALE PECK

SALT, BESIDES MELTING FROZEN WATER, ALSO ABSORBS THE COLOR of asphalt. Even though the snow and ice have disappeared now, last week's early snowstorm lingers on in variegated trails of gray salt lining the edges of the highway like the lace border of a scarf. The cold's gone, for now; the setting sun does its best to dry the ground. Still, it's impossible not to look at the glistening fields stretching out from both sides of the highway and think of the flood. But the more one looks at them the more that seems an impossibility as well: a world covered with water from horizon to horizon. What held it in, kept it from spilling over the edge?

It is the hour when headlights do little more than paint yellowish circles in the black tar in front of the car. In the passenger's seat, Marcus stares out his side window at clumpy plowed soil covering the earth like an angry scab. He clasps and unclasps his seat belt, then toes off his right shoe with his left foot and scratches his instep. Then he kicks off his left shoe. "Might as well leave them on," I say then. "We're almost there." Marcus starts at my voice, looks out the window again. "I don't see anything," he says. Fence posts and telephone poles whiz by, their connecting wires invisible in the falling light, borderlines and lines of communication nulled by nightfall. "Just a couple more miles, really." Marcus sighs heavily. He leans under the rental car's low dash, unties his shoes, puts them on, and then ties them again. He tightens the laces eyelet by eyelet, slowly, as if preparing to trek across these fields of sucking mud. Then: "Who's that?" he asks, as I pull into the drive. He points at a shadowed figure on the front porch, turning his head to get a closer look as the car speeds past the front of the house. "Wait here," is all I say. Marcus has already unbuckled his seat belt; sighing again, he clicks it shut. The squeak of his window seems incredibly loud in the dusky quiet. "Leave the keys," he calls. "It's getting cold."

The person on the porch turns out to be a man, thin, maybe fifty, brown and weatherbeaten. He wears overalls, a flannel shirt, a gray conductor's cap. He holds a knife in one hand, a stick in the other, and the pile of curled shavings on the porch's chipped floorboards suggest he's been waiting awhile for me. The shavings catch what's left of the light, taking on a golden cast. They remind me of the sprung links of a chain scattered around the man's feet, and as I stare at them a thought comes to me. A sentence really: everything is outside of me. Not just this farm and the history that shrouds it, but my emotions, my body even. I feel diffused beyond my skin, dissolved like a cube of bouillon in a pot of water. So much so that when the man whittles three more spirals off his stick I feel an ache in my own forearms, the tension as the blade pushes against the resisting wood, the sudden release when it cuts free at the end of the stroke, and I fall to the floor with the sliver of wood.

Then the man stands, folds the knife into a pocket, and with a dragging foot sweeps the shavings into the ragged hedge beside the porch. Coming back, he says, "Eliot Swope," and his hand in mine seems to squeeze me back into my body. "Real shame about your grandma," he says, looking down at two or three shavings still littering the floor, and then he heads inside. In the open door he turns suddenly and throws his whittled stick across the lawn; I have to duck so he doesn't catch me with his arm.

In the house all is brown and blue as always, the embroidery on the pillows only a little more faded than the last time I was here, the same afghan folded into the hollow of the ottoman's shot cushion. The air still smells of old people, but there, balanced atop the nestled ewer-and-washbowl set on the sideboard, is a basketball, its russet nubbled hide covered in illegible graffiti. Eliot stands in the center of the front room and gestures with a bent callused thumb. "Bedroom," he says, "dining room, kitchen, utilities, another bedroom, and the lavatory." I'm confused. Doesn't he know I lived here?

"Me and my wife and Laird"—he jerks his thumb at the basketball—"got the two bedrooms upstairs, so I suppose you'll be staying down here." He points again.

"You live here?" I ask then, even as I see the jigsaw puzzle set up on the end of the dining room table. For as long as I can remember my grandmother's two silver candelabra had sat there, their trios of white tapers always in place but never lit.

" 'Bout three years now," Eliot says. "Lost my own farm right about the time your grandma first took sick, so it kind of . . ." He casts his eyes around the old oval rag rug as if looking for the shavings he'd swept off the porch, and I just nod at the top of his head, look past it. It's too dark to see what the puzzle is though; it looks like a swirling watercolor, abstract, broken. "I suppose things work out for the best," Eliot says then. "I guess."

The back door's whine is as familiar as a toothache. It bangs closed and light floods the kitchen and then the dining room, and then a woman carrying a basket of orange and yellow squash appears in the doorway between the living and dining rooms. She is thicker than Eliot, not fat, not even plump really, but broad, boxy, solid, like a brick. "Wendell," she says, naming and placing me with a word as fixed as her smile. Not false, but finite, as if she is attempting to limit her knowledge of me to my name, my knowledge of her to her manners. In the new light I can see beyond her right hip that the puzzle is a view of mountains at sunset, the ochres and umbers of fall foliage echoing the squash in her basket.

"Please. Everyone calls me Win."

The woman's smile doesn't change for a moment and then she picks a squash out of her basket and holds it up to me. "That frost," she says. "I like to lost all my late vegetables. This is all I could salvage." Turning back toward the kitchen, she calls over her shoulder, "Dinner'll be ready lickety-split. I hope you like spaghetti squash. I'm Vera, by the way." Cutlery rustles when she opens a drawer and then there is a long silver knife in her hand. On the windowsill above the sink I see my grandmother's candelabra, their candles burned down to smoky gray nubbins.

"I think I'll eat out," I say. Behind me, Eliot says, "Nearly five. Café's closed." When I turn back to him he's leaning against the sideboard with his hand in his pocket fiddling with his knife.

In the kitchen, Vera's clunks methodically through squash on a cutting board. "Eliot's right. Hospital's all closed up too." I hear the wet sluice as she cuts through the squash's soft innards, the *clump* as she pushes through to solid wood, and though I know it's foolish I feel trapped between their two blades.

"I've got a sandwich in the car," I tell them then. "Don't wait up. I'll probably be out late."

On the way down the driveway the headlights glint off fresh gold letters on the mailbox. "What's that say?" I ask Marcus. He has to unroll his window, lean out into the cold. "It says 'Swope,' " he says, and I nod at this confirmation of my suspicions. "They want the farm."

Marcus doesn't reply immediately, but when I turn onto the main road he says, "Where are we going now?" There's an edge to his voice I can't identify: exasperation, boredom, maybe even fear, but when I reply, "To a pleasure palace," all he does is snort. The sun had set while I'd left him alone in the car, and the darkness, unilluminated by streetlamp or moon, is nearly total, relieved only by a few lighted clusters of farm buildings and an occasional animal blinking green or red eyes at the headlights. Even the brown-to-black fade of the horizon line is gone, and, strangely enough, so is the dislocation I felt in my grandparents' house. The darkness and silence of the prairie ease back to me with the familiarity of fog; the bright white lines on either side of the road, dimmed only here and there by a residue of salt, guide us straight to the future. I check the security of my seat belt and settle in for the ten-minute drive.

"Your pleasure palace?" Marcus asks as a red blur solidifies into neon letters announcing the Trail's End Motel.

I squeeze his leg. "Yours and mine."

The front parking lot has only one car, a Chrysler whose passengers, according to their license plate, hail from Nebraska, and who all, according to their bumper stickers, love Jesus and the Cornhuskers. In the back lot there are three more cars, Kansas plates on all of them, Harvey County stickers on two. Number 13, one of the motel's half-submerged rooms, was always my favorite. When I first came here it seemed cavelike, impregnable, but when Marcus descends the three steps and pushes open the door all I smell is basement mildew.

Marcus stands in the door with his nose wrinkled, but I push past him. "Wow. The same bedspread." Marcus puts a finger on the shiny acrylic spread as though it might shock him; it does, and he jerks his finger back.

"You remember the bedspread?" he says, grabbing it roughly and turning it back in a shower of sparks.

"Who could forget it?" I say. "A boy I knew called it Monet on acid."

Marcus looks at me skeptically. "You came here? With boys?"

I smile. "Actually, you're the second." Marcus looks at me a moment longer, then shrugs and smiles back at me. "I'm beat," he says, unbuttoning his shirt. And then: "You forgot your suitcase."

"Oh," I wave a hand. I move to him, help him off with his shirt, briefly take his nipple in my mouth. "I'll get it later." Right in the middle of things Marcus says, "Tell me his name," and, confused, I say, "Who?" "Monet on acid." "Oh. Blaine," I say, and Marcus smiles. "Blaine," he repeats, a touch of twang in his voice. "Don't that beat all?"

Marcus always falls asleep if we make love after six in the evening, and today's travels—five hours on two flights, four more in the car—have exhausted both of us. It's all I can do not to fall asleep beside him. He breathes quietly under the bedspread's electric blue and red petals, mouth open, hands under his cheek; one bare foot dangles over the edge of the bed and I stare at his curled toes until I realize they remind me of the whittled shavings Eliot had swept over the side of the porch. I ease his foot on the mattress then, cover it with the bedspread, and then I write a note telling him I'll stop by in the morning before I go to the hospital. Then I leave, locking the wooden door silently and catching the screen door as it swings shut. Soft light pushing through closed curtains on the second floor makes three glowing puddles in the pitch-black parking lot. I remember my headlights painting similar circles on the highway, and then, when I latch the screen door, its tiny click reminds me of something too: Marcus's seat belt, fastening in place. I open and close the door several times until a burst of adolescent laughter from the balcony nearly makes me jump out of my skin, and then, when I head for the car, I leave the door unlatched behind me.

Relic of the flood, acquired at an auction, the sofa in my grandparents' living room had been both pew and raft. For more than two decades it's filled one long wall of the living room, its darkly stained wooden seat softened only by a thin cushion covered with my grandmother's faded flowery embroidery. Well, Grandpa said the Sunday after it was installed, it's a damn sight easier walking six steps to this pew than driving all the way to Dighton to sit on the same thing in somebody else's church. Ed, Grandma had pleaded. She even went as far as invoking the preacher's—though not the Lord's—name, but Grandpa just flicked on the television. Nothing he can say, Grandpa said, I won't get from one-a these TV versions.

"Mr. Edmonds is not feeling right today," was all Grandma had to say to those who inquired after him, and by the time Wheaton had built a new church people had long since stopped asking. In the hastily erected tin-sided building, at seven, eight, nine, on a pew unsoftened by any cushion, I sat alone next to her rigid body, and when the preacher's voice grew particularly loud I would reach for her dress. That was the start of the hard weather—summers whose heat waves made scales on the surface of land and skin, winter winds that pricked your cheeks with snowflakes as tiny and mean as the heads of pins—but the start of it all had been the flood, the same flood that had destroyed the first First Methodist Church of Wheaton and taken Grandpa's crops and livestock and daughter and son-in-law. It's been years since I dreamed of it and I don't actually dream of it that night. Instead I dream of my grandmother's dress between my fingers, its material getting thinner, more faded, year after lean year. When the preacher's rants scared me, I always reached for that dress even though my grandmother always flicked my hand away. It's him you should be turning to, she'd say, nodding toward the front of the church. I was never sure if she meant the wild-haired blue-suited man who circled the lectern or the more somber unclothed man hanging from the cross behind him. Never again by water, the speaking man would say, as floods were a popular subject just then. But everyone, or at least Grandpa, knew that wasn't true.

Water, and Eliot's hand, awaken me in the morning. Outside there's not much light; inside, Eliot's clean-shaven chin seems pale with its own glow, and a second drop falls from his still-wet hair on my forehead. He's wearing what he had on yesterday but he carries his cap in his hands.

"Why'd you sleep here?" he says. "Could-a slept in one-a the bedrooms."

"The TV," I say. "I fell asleep watching it." In fact I had fallen asleep with the television on—it's off now—but the real reason I hadn't slept in a bed is that, of the two bedrooms on the first floor, one had belonged to my grandparents, the other to my mother.

"Should-a gone to the south bedroom," Eliot says. He makes a box with his hands, as in charades, only smaller. "There's one-a them little TVs in there." Before I can answer him he turns for the door. "Gotta get to the fields," he says. "Wheat won't plant itself."

I nod, close my eyes. When, after a moment, I haven't heard the door close, I open them again. Eliot is pushing his head into his cap as though it—his head—were a cork.

"Going to the hospital today?"

I nod my head slowly.

"Be sure to pay my respects to your grandma, would you?" Again I nod, the action, like an old-fashioned doll's, seeming to force my eyes closed. Behind them, Eliot says, "Laird got in late too. You really ought-a sleep in one-a the bedrooms." He closes the door silently then, as if trying not to wake me.

In what seems like seconds I smell the crisp tang of frying sausage, hear a moment later the faint sizzle of a skillet. I lay without moving on the pew, listening to grease popping, drawers opening and closing, china thumping on formica, until finally I open my eyes. The sun is high and hot and so bright it seems less to illuminate the room than burn the outlines of the windows on walls and floor. One square of light seems folded over the basketball on the sideboard like a cloth covering a communion chalice. Just then another drawer closes loudly in the kitchen, and Vera calls, "You awake in there?"

She appears in the doorway, a kerchief on her head, a narrow apron hanging between her wide hips like a loincloth. Both kerchief and apron are faded and clean, but there is dried earth on the knees of her jeans. "Wendell? It's almost noon."

In the kitchen a plate's already been filled for me. Three others, foil covered, sit on the counter. "Hope you don't mind," Vera says. "I've got to get the men their dinners before they get cold."

Dinner, I think. In Kansas the noon meal is called dinner—when it's not just called the noon meal—and during planting and harvest it's taken in the field. But then I remember it's October, and I say, "Shouldn't the wheat be in by now?" Vera barely sighs, packing the silvered plates into a shallow wicker basket. "Should-a been. Was actually. But that storm. Eliot and Laird had to start over." She speaks in a slight staccato as she packs napkins, cutlery, plastic cups in the basket. She laughs then. "That's Kansas for you. Last week snow, today nearly seventy."

I nod, forking a piece of sausage into my mouth. "Laird," I say after I've chewed, swallowed. "Is he tall?"

"Six-two," Vera says, hoisting a gallon mason jar of iced tea into the basket with one arm. Her thin biceps arches up, a loose flap of skin dangles underneath like its shadow. "Why do you ask?"

"Oh," I say, "I was just thinking. Those ceilings are pretty low upstairs."

"Oh," Vera echoes me, as if suddenly remembering I have a prior association with her home, a prior claim. She stares out the window through the branches of my grandmother's candelabra, and then she says, "Well, yes. He is tall. Tall and skinny. He played center on the basketball team."

She knots a white tablecloth over the basket deftly, sealing in her meal, and I nod as though she's confirming some notion of Laird I already had. " 'Bye," she says then, using her hip to open the door. I nod again, chewing slowly, imagining a tall, skinny, stooped-over boy moving around the slant-ceilinged room that had once been mine. But it's not Laird I'm imagining: it's Blaine. When Vera pops her head back in the door I blush as if she's caught me snooping. "Will we be seeing you for supper, Wendell?" she says, and all I can do is nod, pointing at my chewing jaw as an excuse for my speechlessness, even though my mouth is empty.

I finish breakfast, wash the dishes. Everything still goes in the same place and I still remember where everything goes, but scattered in with my grandmother's Blue Willow china are dishes I can only assume are Vera's, smaller plates with an all-but-evaporated gold rim around their edges. I shower, rushing a little, not quite aware of it until the hot water runs out like it always used to. I get dressed, taking the time to fit a piece or two into Vera's puzzle in between each item of clothing. What I'd taken for mountains last night are actually just a reflection in a glassy lake; the mountains themselves are still just a pile of scattered pieces.

I step out into the noon sun then, my shoes in one hand. Everything creaks: the screen door, the porch steps, my soul. The grass is dry underfoot but the dirt it grows from is damp and cold, the sun is hot but when a breeze stirs it's chilly enough to make me shiver. All I do is trace the perimeter of the yard. I resist the urge to explore the outbuildings, knowing I'll never get out of here if I do, and I also keep my eyes off the horizon, lest it lure me into the fields. I start my circuit at the place where I find the stick Eliot had thrown off the porch last night—not just one actually, but five, scattered like the bones of a wolf's meal. I gather them up and carry them to the rusted and warped wire fence that hems in the family plot. A cottonwood grows at the center; nine faded crosses ring it like saplings grown from fallen seeds. My grandfather's is the most recent, 1927–1981, the year I entered high school, and my parents' is next to it. To save room around the tree—room for my grandparents, I realize with a start, room for me—they'd been buried under one cross, and there's only one date on it as well, an end date, and, lacking real flowers, I lay Eliot's whittled sticks in its shade.

Then there's nothing to do but put my shoes on and go to the hospital.

Hospitals aren't the same everywhere. The one in which, too many years ago, my first boyfriend died—the first besides Blaine— was a tarnished version of a stereotypical citadel of healing. White walls had faded yellow or been dirtied brown, quiet solitude had given way to loud voices and an intercom alive with coded beeps and phrases. But the hospital here—meaning in Dighton, nearly twenty miles from Wheaton—is the real thing. Antiseptic to the point of being pristine, quiet as an empty church. The slight creak of a cart's wheels as an orderly walks by is the only sound I hear when I walk in, and only after she passes can I sort its odor from the ammoniac atmosphere. Sausage—soy, probably—for the patients' dinners.

It's hard to think of the young woman behind the desk as a triage nurse. She seems, despite her white uniform, just like a receptionist. "Edmonds, Edmonds," she says, scanning a dot-matrix printout. "Here we go. Two-one-two," she says, one digit at a time.

"Like the area code," I say, but the nurse only smiles at me blankly. "The area code? It's nine-one-three, sir."

Two hallways open off the lobby, but sunlight only fills the end of one of them. The nurse speaks one more time. "The west one, sir." The dark one.

At my grandmother's door I pause. I'm empty-handed, I realize, I should have brought something. But there are no corner delis for

flowers or chocolates, and so, wrapping my face in a smile, I push
open her door.

The dining car has been there ahead of me. My grandmother's
uneaten meal is on a wheeled table pushed to the side of the bed.
The long thick bones of her body seem laid in it like an archeolog-
ical reconstruction until I realize that the bulk of her is a cast that
inflates the blanket where just her legs should be.

The first word my grandmother says to me in twelve years is my
name. "Wendell," she says, and then she holds up one of her hands
and inspects her fingernails as if for dirt, then drops it to her lap.
There is a book open there, one I immediately recognize. An old
oversized gardener's tome whose color plates were paintings rather
than photographs. Over the years nearly all of its images had been
reproduced in my grandmother's embroidered pillows and slipcov-
ers, but, scanning the room, I don't see her knitting basket anywhere. Then, with a start, I realize that Vera had packed her
husband and son's dinners in that basket.

My grandmother's voice cuts into my thoughts. "You'll pardon me
if I don't get out of bed, I hope."

"No prob," I say, the false brightness of my voice flashing in the
room like a strobe. I pull a chair next to her bed, and after a moment
I take her right hand in mine and squeeze. I let go though, when
my fingers close around an IV tube taped to the back of her hand.
Cautiously, I retrieve it, as though it were an egg I'd dropped, but
she pulls it away.

"Still a little tender," she says, though whether she means the
IV's pinch or mine I don't know. She rubs the hand, her left, with
two bony fingers of her right, and when she's done I reach for her
right hand but she removes it to the other side of her body. "Your
mother was like that," she says, and I follow her eyes to a silent
television mounted above the door. "Always wanting to hold animals
when they were down, pet them, stroke them. You know what I told
her?" I shake my head. "I told her that the animals'd just as soon
she wasn't there at all, but if she had to be there they'd prefer it if
she kept her distance." I stare at my hand, still on the bed, then

pull it into my lap. "Always getting nipped by some sick dog or cat," my grandmother is still saying, the corners of her mouth as sharp as the edge of a field. "She had the most marked-up hands of any girl I ever saw." She breaks off then, looks down at her own hand: age spots, a short piece of tape, a dangling tube. "I was just saying it to save her," she says in a softer voice, "but she wouldn't never listen."

It's only then that I hear the fly in the room, a refugee from the changing seasons outside. It's annoyingly busy, flying and landing, flying and landing, but I don't see it anywhere. Instead I see a green dot jump on a monitor. It jumps again and again, and after half a dozen jumps the invisible fly's buzz resolves itself into a beep. The fly, I realize, is my grandmother's heart.

She uses both her hands to lift the remote control and change the channel, and as her arms move her heart speeds up, and only gradually does it resume its slower cadence after she lowers her hands to her lap. There is a thin line of sweat above her lip. Her hands are shaking.

She says, "You're sleeping at Eliot and Vera's?" as if she were already buried under the old cottonwood, the farm already theirs. I nod, unable to speak. "They're good people," she says then. "Thick and thin," she says, "they've stood by me."

Thick and thin: I think of Eliot's narrow waist and Vera's bulkier girth, Jack Sprat and his wife. "Are you leaving them the farm?" I say then, and my grandmother starts to nod her head, then stops it, her chin nearly resting on her breastbone. What I see then is that her hair, which had always been bound in a bun by the time I saw her each morning, has been combed down her spine in a thin gray-black thatch like the back strap of a priest's ceremonial mantle. For some reason I think of Vera then. How had she worn her hair, last night, before this morning's kerchief? Though I try, all I see is a cone of medium color, cut, and curl, but otherwise no more defined than a Magic Marker outline around an equally opaque oval of face.

"I was thinking to," my grandmother finishes then. "Unless you've finally decided to come back."

The sun is just starting to dip toward the western horizon by the time I start for the motel, but a thick layer of clouds hastens the darkness. When I flick my headlights on, it's yesterday, and then it's years ago. How many times have I driven this road? I look at its white-lined borders again. They don't lead to the future, I realize then, but to the past. By the time I pull into the parking lot, scattered fat drops of rain are falling on the windshield but I am awash in memory. I sit in the car until the drops on the glass start to coalesce, and then, with one pass of the wipers, they're gone.

"You son of a bitch."

This room, at once more and less familiar than any in my grandmother's house, or our apartment in New York for that matter. Its frenzied bedspread, the meek prairie print on the wall, the curtained window. It reminds me of my grandmother's hospital room. Not its white walls, but its sparse functional furnishings: bed, dresser, chair, horizontal poles with hangers, narrow door leading to equally utilitarian bathroom. Mounted TV, which you only look at to avoid looking at something else.

"You no-good lying sack of shit."

The boy who'd coined the phrase Monet on acid—Blaine, I remind myself, Blaine Gunderson—had worn his straw-colored hair in a shaggy whorl, and to heighten the effect he often ran his fingers through it in an arc that started over his left eye and ended over his right ear. He had clear eyes and if he was anything he wasn't afraid. He removed my clothes and his. He pulled all but the bottom sheet off the bed. When I shut the light off, he turned it on again. He said, I want to see you, and he would fix me with his clear blue gaze. When we first met, Marcus asked if it had been hard to come out in a small town in Kansas and I told him it had never been an issue. Blaine had outed me for himself.

Marcus's voice cuts into me like Blaine's eyes.

"Why didn't you just drug me? It would've been a hell of a lot nicer than spending nineteen hours and"—he glances at his watch—"thirty-seven, no, forty-seven minutes in this spoor-infested subterranean cell staring through a moth hole in a nylon curtain at the set of *Little House on the Prairie*—sans little house."

Blaine always said he was sorry we had to come and go separately. Sometimes I felt our most passionate moments happened in front of the door, either just after one of us had entered or just before one of us left. It's amazing how big some things can seem: With my back pressed against the door, my shirttails pushed up as high as my shoulder, I could feel the whole building through the small of my back. I felt the wood as a tree, felt its roots reaching into the ground and into the past, felt the whole prairie rumble as we shook that door on its cheap hinges.

"Goddammit, Win, are you even listening to me?"

I nod, but what I'm remembering is being the last to leave. In that room, with its tiny window, always closed, I could always smell our own sex. And that's what I would do: lie on the stripped bed and breathe in the wet air for twenty minutes until Blaine was long gone. I would stare at the white ceiling, run my hand over the mattress searching for his damp traces. One time I even thought of masturbating, but how could I? I was submerged in sex already. I was drowning in it.

Marcus's hands are on my shoulders, shaking me. "Goddammit, Win," he says again. "Why did you bother to bring me with you?"

It's all I can do to whisper then, "The house was supposed to be empty." Marcus's hands tighten their grip on my shoulders, and I only realize I'm swaying as his hands still me. "My grandmother was supposed to be in the hospital and we were supposed to have the place to ourselves."

"Damn it, Win," Marcus says, jerking me against his chest, squeezing my back. "Why'd you have to sneak out like that?"

"I thought she was leaving it to me," I say, "but she's leaving it to them." Marcus just holds me for a moment and then: "Did you think I'd tell them you were gay?" he says, right into my ear, and I shake my head and listen to the rasp of my stubble over his shirt. "I was afraid they'd tell my grandmother."

Marcus pushes me back to arm's length then. He seems about to let me go, then steers me to the bed and sits me down. "How is she?" he says, and I shrug. "Her bones are like straw. Her hip will never heal." Marcus bites his lip. "She raised you, right? After your parents died?" "Since I was seven." "They drowned? In a flood?" Marcus knows all this already, but I don't blame him for doubting it. Even I doubt it, though I spent two days huddled in the attic of my grandparents' house with my grandmother and grandfather, watching everything I'd thought was the world float by. Instead of answering Marcus I take him to the door, pull it open, walk out under the balcony and point. It's almost too dark to see, but not quite.

"What?" Marcus says. "The car, the fields? What?" But all I can do is point, farther away. Marcus squints. "Are those . . . hills?" he says, peering at the horizon. "They're called the bluffs," I say. "They weren't fooling that day." "Jesus Christ," Marcus says, and then he's quiet for a long time, and then he says, "Show me." "It's raining," I say, but Marcus takes my hand and squeezes it. "Show me," he says again, and then he looks around and lets go of my hands. I smile at him weakly and retrieve his hand. "You already know," I say, and pull him inside.

Later, the room surrounds us. Marcus sits on the bed. Marcus. Marcus had a normal Connecticut childhood; he has no hang-ups; until he let go of my hand I'd never seen him display even a hint of fear. I, on the other hand, am terrified of: sex, with anyone besides Marcus, wide-open spaces, snakes, guns, heights, and the past, by which I suppose I mean memory—not just what I remember, but what I've forgotten, what I've washed away like the flood washed away my town. In New York Marcus had been invisible to me: he was just my boyfriend. But in Kansas he's become the pillar around which the world spins like a ball tethered to a pole. I want to isolate him from all of this, New York and Kansas, his past and mine, so that I can see what I've tied myself to. Instead, it's Marcus who isolates me. He says, "I know you in a way these people never will," and what both frightens and comforts me is the certainty in his voice. That what he knows of me is all there is to know, that the past, like

Eliot's frost-bitten crop, can be plowed under, mulched, reseeded.

"Look," Marcus says, "if you need to go back, I understand." I try to kiss him but he puts a finger between our lips, smiles wryly, shakes his head. "Not tonight," he says, and I say, "Why do you put up with me?" "Because I've seen you when all this falls away," Marcus says. "When it recedes," Marcus says, and I know he's chosen the word just for me. "Now go, before you're late for dinner."

The first thing I notice when I enter my grandparents' house is that Vera has taken her half-finished puzzle apart. The box sits on the sideboard next to my grandmother's ewer and Laird's basketball, and in its place at the table there is a plate, a fork, a knife, a spoon. Eliot and Vera look up at my entrance, and a moment later the figure in the chair facing away from me turns and Laird looks at me as well, and then turns back to his plate.

Suddenly Vera is on her feet. "Please," she says, "sit, sit." She bustles into the kitchen, wiping her lips with the napkin that had covered her lap—a pointless gesture, as there is no food on the table, only clean dishes. "I just put everything back in the oven so it wouldn't get cold," Vera says. "Laird," she calls through the pass-through, "lend me a hand, will you?" Eliot and I stare at each other while Laird ferries dishes from his mother to the table, and then Eliot, like Vera, wipes his clean lips with his napkin. "Laird was supposed to play ball at Memphis State," he says without preamble, "but he wouldn't get on the plane."

"Aw, Dad, don't be telling him that," Laird says as he and his mother sit down.

"Now Laird," Vera says, "there's nothing to be ashamed of. Many people are afraid to fly. I'm not so sure I'd ever want to get in one of those things myself, should the occasion arise."

"You've never flown?" I say to Vera then, and her hands, which had been reaching for a spoon, drop back to her lap.

"Why, no," she says, her voice tight, her eyes focused on her plate, and only then do I notice that she's set the table with my grandmother's dishes.

"I never flew either," I say, "until I left." Vera's smile is pinched, but she's trying. "Well, then," she says, her voice soft again. "Shall we eat?"

Everyone starts with the closest dish: potatoes for Vera, carrots for Laird, bread for me, and butter too, the meat at the head of the table by Eliot. After we serve ourselves we pass our dish to the left. I find myself falling in love with this family's small kindnesses toward each other, the way etiquette replaces conversation. "Carrots, Ma?" "Thank you, Laird. Mashed for you, Eliot?" "I do believe I will, thanks. What can I get you, Wendell? White meat? Dark?" Everything is passed except the meat, which remains next to Eliot. Plates are held up to him, onto which he doles breasts, thighs, legs, wings. Their interaction reminds me of something, but the best I can come up with is the platitude "salt of the earth" until I take my first bite of fried chicken. The crisp peppery skin crackles in my mouth and all at once I realize they remind me of myself. They remind me of who I am, or who I used to be, before I got on that first flight.

The chicken sits on an oval platter with some kind of bled-ink picture, but it's only after seconds have been served that I see it's an etching of an old-time waterwheel. The harnessed water spins around the wheel's dial as quickly as it can, eager to circumnavigate and splash free; a man in a top hat and a lady with a parasol walk along a cobblestone path that runs adjacent to the painted river's course. They don't deign to look at the roiling water, and for a moment I am caught up in that—in the idea that every life, mine, Marcus's, this family gathered around me, has its unseen parallel in nature. Not a twin but an amplification, a revelation. A soul. This family's would be the hard knotted earth of the prairie, Marcus's a tree with roots like tentacles, holding him in place. What would mine be, I wonder, but the answer comes even before the question has formed itself: a crystal of salt, melting ice but dissolving in water.

It is at this point I am moved to say, "I don't want the farm."

Vera and Eliot and Laird all look up at me, but none of them says anything. "I make no claim," I continue, "you can stay here as long as you want." My words seem to fall on the table like bird droppings. I am thirty-three years old, but for the first time in my life I understand what it means to have power over another person. The power to give, the power to take away. "I'm not coming back," I say finally. "It's yours. It will all be yours." After another long moment Vera picks up her fork. "Well, thank you, Wendell," she says, and takes a bite of mashed potatoes.

After the meal Eliot and Laird and I retire to the living room for television while Vera does the dishes. "Don't even think about it," she says when I ask if I can help. "You've had a hard day, you just relax." Eliot takes a couple of my grandmother's embroidered cushions, puts one between his seat and the pew's, holds the other in his lap, but Laird doesn't sit down. Instead he paces the room. At one point he even picks up his basketball and bounces it on the floor, causing the ewer on the sideboard to jump inside its bowl. Eliot doesn't seem to notice but from the kitchen Vera calls, "Laird. Please." Laird spins the ball on his finger then, close up under the low ceiling, and I watch him and wonder if I should be sad that that's as high as he'll ever get, as far as he'll ever go. He goes to set the ball atop the ewer again, then sees me and grins sheepishly and sets it on the floor instead. "I think I'll head out," he says then, to no one in particular. "Bonnie?" Eliot says without taking his eyes off the television, and Laird nods. "I'll probably be in late."

He closes the door heavily, and the whole thin house shakes as it had when he'd bounced his basketball on the floor, and then the ball itself comes rolling toward me. It traces an edge of the rug as if in orbit, misses me by about a foot and comes to a stop under the pew. As it rolls toward me I notice again that it's covered in writing, and my stomach tightens when I suddenly realize it's covered in signatures. In names.

"Wendell?" Eliot says as I reach for the ball.

When they built the new library they put up a plaque with the

names of the twenty-seven men and women of Wheaton who died
in the flood. They say that those who died died in their sleep. That

the flood waters, in a torrent, mostly drowned those who, like my
parents, lived on Dry Creek Road. Farther away, as on the slight
elevation of my grandparents' farm, the water level rose quickly, but
not so fast that people couldn't take refuge in second stories, in
attics, on the roof. It was years before it even occurred to me to ask
why I'd been sleeping on the farm that night. "Your mother and
father always wanted another child," my grandmother told me, "and
that apartment only had the one room."

"Win?" Eliot says. The ball is in my lap and he is looking at me
strangely, and I realize I've started crying.

Before I left the motel that evening Marcus caught me at the door
like Blaine used to. He kissed me so hard my head knocked against
the wood and my mouth filled with a salty metallic tang, but when
he pulled back and looked at me he could tell I wasn't thinking of
him. Still holding me against the door, he looked around the room
as if Blaine might be hiding somewhere, and all at once he gasped.
"Did he die too? Blaine," he said, as if a name could measure loss.
"Is he dead?"

I nodded, checked my lip for blood; there wasn't any. "They're
all dead, Marcus. Every one but us."

Before I left the hospital my grandmother asked me one last time
to come back, and when I refused she didn't say anything, just
closed the book of flowers in her lap and let her folded hands be
cupped by the purple petals of the iris on its cover; now, across the
room, Eliot is kneading a pillow with that same flower embroidered
on its slipcover and I wonder if it's speaking for him or for her.

I look down at the autographed globe in my hands as though it
were the world of the dead, all the dead, past and present and future.
"Peter Lindman." "Josh Harder." "Bob Ross." "Jeff Goodenough,
State Champs '99." "Russell Ennis, love ya man!" There is no "Gunderson," no "Edmonds" either, but there, right under the branded
"Spalding," is the possessive "Laird Swope, #13." His name claims
this ball with all the ease that's eluded me in my own attempts to

claim this farm, Kansas, my past. It's as if the past is another country to the present, separated from it by an expanse of water, and all my efforts to consolidate my empire in order to protect it from future invasions has yielded is this ball. Though the names are less than a year old they've already started to fade, and I think that with one slip of the scribe's fickle pen they could have been written on a plaque in the Wheaton library or a quilt in a Washington museum. As my tears drip down on them they soften the ink, smudge the words, and begin the long slow process of washing them away.

THORAZINE JOHNNY FELSUN LOVES ME

(from his permanent cage of lifelong confinement)

by

THOM JONES

I USED TO KIND OF LIKE PEOPLE. THAT WAS BEFORE I WAS LIKE A teenager and stuff. I got pinkeye in Nepal and my mother, who is a doctor an all, paid no attention to me. My father is a psychiatrist. My parents don't give two shits about me. I was abused when I was little tho I can't remember all the details.

My father got me this kitten when I was six. She just recently died a horrific tragic death. Here's what happened: we moved into this swell new house out in the woods where danger is constantly afoot. Bobbie, see, didn't go out much because of her early life when they put her in with Ivan the Gorilla who has been celebrated in the newspapers, television, and magazines with no mention of Bobbie, who was just an obscure player in his ongoing saga of international fame. After Ivan she didn't want to go out ever never ever. See when she fell asleep Ivan would grab her and snatch her little cat body in his cell of lifelong confinement and bounce her on the walls like a Ping-Pong ball. Doomgirl told me that eight of nine lives were used up in Bobbie's tragic early life of peril, travail, hardship, and grievous loss. You see, Doomgirl's cat died, too. It had a tumor. Sometimes I think I have a tumor but I'm not a hypochondriac. My pinkeye was real and I didn't make a big deal out of it because we were in Nepal an all. I have a tumor deep in my guts and it doesn't know if it wants to grow or if it's just going to stay the same for a while and do nothing. When it hurts I think it is growing but weeks can go by and I don't think of it. I work part time at the state hospital where Thorazine Johnny Felsun passes me mash notes when I deliver his dinner tray to his cage of permanent confinement. I'm pretty well developed tho as I said I was abused when I was little and stuff and hate men. Sometimes Thorazine Johnny's hand touches mine through the slot when I am passing him his tray. His touch gives me a weird buzzing feeling that makes my head hum until I almost practically faint.

Once Doomgirl and I went down to Tacoma to see Ivan in his pen and he did something really gross. This is what he did: because so many people were staring at him he defecated and then he ate his own crap. Everyone got disgusted and left but I didn't walk away. I just watched him disdainfully with my cold dark eyes. What Ivan did to my sweet adorable an affectionate cat, Bobbie—what he did was completely totally wrong. I stared at him hard. He just ignored me like I wasn't nothing. I didn't go away or anything because I am something.

It was because Coco the Seattle gorilla had a catfriend that they put Bobbie in Ivan's cell of lifetime confinement, but they were not pals, not even for a single second.

Doomgirl says that the reason Bobbie was such a runt, so small an all, was that she didn't get any REM sleep during those horrific days of constant vigilance and starkest terror. Ivan was clumsy and couldn't catch my darlingest cat in a fair chase. She was my best trusted friend for ten years. When I came back from Nepal with pinkeye she was on my bed purring an all and it gave me emotional comfort. No matter how down in the dumps I got, Bobbie would cheer me up. She would hop on my lap and be my pal.

When Doomgirl's cat died we buried it in her yard in a Nordstrom's shoebox which we wrapped in waterproof bags. We put all her cat stuff in her coffin. All of her toys and a pillow so her eternal rest was comfortable.

Bobbie hated men, as I hate them. I think they reminded her of gorillas. Now Ivan is a big superstar. My mom saw a picture of him in *Time* and another one in *People*, which is a magazine she doesn't read, but it's in her office for her patients to read. I think her nurse is the one who saw Ivan's picture. Ivan doesn't look like other gorillas. His face is funny. He looks like an ugly despicable monster, a big thug. Doomgirl says Ivan looks like a Russian communist and she calls him Ivan Gregvonovich Gorilla.

So for all those years Bobbie wouldn't go outside because of her Ivan trauma. Then when we moved into the new and really swell house out in the woods, she sat in the window and watched the birds and stuff that come around here on an almost continual basis. Birds: pecking, bobbing around, singing melodies and doing bird stuff. Doomgirl says Bobbie's fear finally wore off due to the years of devoted loving care I nourished upon her. We would watch her go out in the back and stuff and roll on the concrete patio in the sun. Sometimes she would eat grass when she got a hairball. In the articles about Ivan it said that he was afraid to go outside to look at the sun, too. But then they said zoo professionals were hopeful he would marry one of the female gorillas, which is not going to happen, never ever never. I knew that just by looking at his ugly monster face.

Doomgirl is a lesbian and that is which I will be when I come of age sexually because I hate men so much. Doomie gives me haircuts and stuff. She is only seven months and four days older than I am. Together we do all of the wonderful and hilarious fun things two friends do. We go to the mall and shop and stuff.

When I was littler and Bobbie was hiding in the house because company was making noise and stuff, I would have panic attacks when I couldn't find her, and I would get hysterical and my mom would give me Xanax. My mother is a pediatrician but when we were in Nepal she ignored my pinkeye and I had pus and stuff coming out of both of my eyes. Doomgirl says the reason I got so panicked when Bobbie would go into hiding is that it's because I am a psychic and I was aware of Bobbie's tragic painful and horrifying last moments on earth, which had not yet come into being then but which I knew in some mysterious way was going to happen. She said I was seeing into the future with unrealized psychic powers. Doomgirl reads Taro and does Babylonian astrology which is superior to that crap that's in the paper every day. Pee-you that newspaper stuff is just junk and there isn't a hint of truth in any of it except sometimes Omar will hit a ringer. Doomie says that I am a natural and gifted psychic but I have not yet tapped my abilities and used them to the fullest potential.

What happened to Bobbie is tragic beyond belief so I didn't want to just come out with it or announce it without preparing the groundwork first. It saddens me to think that she was taken from her mother and stuff when she was so little. She was just a baby kitty an she was put in the confinement area with Ivan having to dodge him day after day trying to catch naps when the gorilla was asleep and stuff. I know this because I was there and the space was small even though Bobbie was a very fast kitten. I mean when we got her she was very fast and my dad called the guy that put the ad in the paper and said to him, Look mister, why isn't this cat settling in, is it very nervous? You see, this person was in the army and he worked at the store where Ivan was on display and his part-time job was to take care of the gorilla and he said that a bunch of animal activists were trying to have Ivan removed from the awful confinement area. Doomgirl says he didn't put that part in the ad because no one would adopt Bobbie if they had known about her gravely traumatic early days which used up eight cat lives in just under two weeks. I would have taken her.

"That's not the point." Doomgirl says, "most" people wouldn't have taken her. Her main feature was that she was "declawed" and that's why my father picked her out of the classified ads. He didn't want a cat that ripped up furniture. The man in the army agreed to take Bobbie back but I stood up for her and my father gave in and let me keep her anyhow even tho Bobbie knocked over his neon espresso sign and broke it and then she scratched him with her rear claws wrecking a shirt he liked when he tried to give her a pill.

When she was going out in the woods without claws to defend herself, I thought her rear claws only were good enough because I never saw much out there except for birds and squirrels and deer. Now, when I look at the circumstances of her gruesome murder I blame myself for not seeing what is as plain as the nose on your face. Here's what I should have known: that danger is afoot in the woods. I should have known this and should not have been such a stupid airhead. Like, duh, *hello*?

The first time she did an overnighter I had a fit and my mother had to give me Xanax but in the morning she came in wet with the rain. God. That was a close one. I was up all night smoking Parliament cigarettes with worry.

Once I tried to write a romantic novel but it was too hard and I gave up on it.

Ivan the gorilla liked it in the Atlanta zoo and would go outside and sit in the sun. His home of origin was the Congo in Africa. He was shipped to America as a little baby and the owners of the store in Tacoma fed him with a bottle and treated him like a baby until one day he went on a big rampage and wrecked the whole house an all. He was three and he was put in his cage of confinement at that time for he had proven himself to be the thug that he is. He lived on a diet of grapes and apples and when he got depressed the army guy would go to KFC and get him extra-crispy chicken wings. Or buffalo wings. I am a strict vegetarian and never eat meat and never have. I will never eat meat, ever, never, ever! Meat makes people into savages. I am also a vegetarian for ethical reasons. Two reasons actually: health and human decency.

Sometimes I used to think that when Bobbie went out into the night to explore the woods she was happier than at anytime in her short and tragic life. Doomgirl agrees with me. After high school Doomgirl wants to go to college and stuff and then become a doctor like my parents but instead of pediatrics and psychiatry she wants to become a plastic surgeon and operate on the rich and the famous. If Doomgirl was a plastic surgeon she should do Ivan first since his face is ugly and is the face of a thug-monster. The female gorillas at the Atlanta zoo attacked him when he was put in with them and they almost killed him. Now he never goes outside anymore. He's just in his back room.

My father got me my part-time job at the state hospital. Part of my duties is I deliver the dinner trays to the violent ward where

patients are kept in isolation cells. Boy! They have got some real
doozies in there. Like the Cyclops man with only one eye. He is a
true thug. There's Archie and Ignatz, the violent pinhead twins both
convicted of murder; and Angus Morgan, the Edinburgh Woodchop-
per who went on a senseless killing rampage but is legally insane.
It's them plus Scabdick Ray, Jamaica Kid, Walter and Rufas Doby,
retards that were connected at birth and did senseless crimes. Walter
isn't so bad, he just goes along with Rufas because they are connected at the liver through a six-inch horn. LeRoy and Nate—I don't
know their crimes. Thorazine Johnny Felsun is quite good-looking
and vain in spite of being exceedingly volatile so that every pre-
caution must be taken when he is moved here or there. Part of what
Thorazine Johnny had done was use psychopathic charm to seduce
girls and take them to his torture den and kill them on videotape,
all the while conducting a normal life as a charming dental products
salesman. I dump the government-grade meat from his tray and heap
on extra vegetables. On total vegetables I'm sure that Johnny would
get better an love me for saving him an stuff but since I don't deliver
his meals around the clock he gets meat in spite of my best efforts.

Because I'm "developed" I look like a grown-up nurse in my
white uniform. Johnny Felsun tells me how beautiful I am but I look
in the mirror and see myself and hate everything about me. Sometimes when the orderlies aren't around, I take off my bra to watch
his muscle get hard. I will smoke a Parliament and watch it get big.
He likes watching me smoke. Then he pokes it through the tray slot
and makes me stroke it for him until he *orgasts*.

When you have pinkeye you can still see though you have pus
and your eyes are sticky an all. My pinkeye is cured but I think I'm
going to die in a year. My dad says I am cognitively and intellec-
tually drained in every way.

I never told him about the mash notes that Thorazine Johnny
passes me or how sometimes I felt bad for teasing him so I let him
orgast at the back of my throat. Pee-you, it tasted awful!

Once Johnny bent my fingers back so hard two of them broke
and he made me cry. Other times he holds my hand tenderly and

kisses it and I get that buzzing feeling inside me. I will lift my skirt and push my bottom against the food slot but his muscle is too big to go inside me and for this reason he has to have sex between my thighs.

When Bobbie didn't come back on her fateful night Doomgirl came over to my place even though my mother is always rude to her and forbids us to hang out together when I'm grounded. Since Doomgirl has extraordinary psychic powers we were out and wandering in the field behind the house looking for her. There is a lake back there and this poor farmer owns it all and he has horses and stuff. I think the farmer hates us and thinks we are rich people or something. Both of my parents are members of the Wobblies as well as my grandmother on my father's side. Wobblies are okay but they like to get together and talk about the lumpen proletariat and the evils of a capitalist society.

Doomie and I combed that field and checked out the lake which looked so inviting from my beautiful bedroom upstairs but is actually filled with weeds and stumps: you wouldn't want to swim in it. Still the field is pretty and if you cross Park Road then you are right on the inlet and you can see the Sound and the saltwater. My mother can see the ocean from her bedroom. My father—he sleeps downstairs. The reason for this is because his crazy patients sometimes call him in the middle of the night and want to commit suicide. If he's red-eyed in the morning he might say to my mother: "I had to talk that stupid neurotic bitch, So-and-So, off the ledge last night!"

Thorazine Johnny got his hands on a cell phone smuggled in by one of his beautiful molls and called my dad and started telling him stuff about me. Johnny told my dad about the sexual stuff we did. I heard my dad tell this to my cold and heartless mother. My dad told her that beautiful women find Thorazine Johnny irresistible. My dad has to censor Johnny's mail because he is so dangerous. It makes my father furious. He says, "I'm not his goddamn 'secretary'!"

I waited for the hospital to change my duties after that cell phone call but it never happened. What happened is that they restricted Thorazine Johnny's library privileges. My father thought Johnny was making it all up when actually he didn't tell him the half of the stuff we do.

The second day of our search Doomgirl found a pile of fur in the clover field and stuff that looked like crop circles an all but was really nothing more than where the deer bed down for the night. What Doomie found was a pile of Bobbie's fur, so I took it back home. My dad said maybe Bobbie got into a wrangle with a raccoon or something and would come home when she calmed down.

I know Doomgirl is a psychic because on the third day of our frantic search she led me into this blackberry thicket near the side of the house. She said she "heard" birds in there, and there were birds, but just songbirds not crows or predatory birds that eat and live on the flesh of other creatures. We went in there and there was another pile of my beloved pet's fur and under that there was this moist bone that had pink tinges of blood on it.

My dad got mad when I led him to the scene of the crime. A blackberry bramble scratched him in the face. My mom, she refused to go out there at all. Once my father quit swearing, he pointed to the parts of the breastbone where the arteries pumped blood 'cause he said a bone is living tissue. First he says an owl ate Bobbie but later one of the neighbors said that on different occasions they saw a coyote on the lonely road that leads back to our house set in its idyllic spot in the woods—a house that you might read about in romantic novels. The summer of my sophomore year after I was fired from the button factory I tried to write the romantic novel but since I might want to be a lesbian an all I couldn't really think of anything that wasn't boring.

This neighbor says an owl eats an animal whole and you find the fur in its defecate, all in a tight packet that looks something like a little nest. The truth is that Bobbie was the victim of cutthroat coyotes which don't look very tough in pictures of them but in reality they are formidable killers.

When I thought of the time we buried Doomgirl's cat and had a nice ceremony an all I had to cry and my dad says I was going through Kubler-Ross stages of grief which involve denial, bargaining with God and finally, after much mourning, acceptance of the truth. He is always pointing out my negative personality traits but never gives me fatherly love or affection which is why I am going to die within one year's time.

Doomie says that's all plain nonsense and that my dad is a fool. I don't know why a coyote would eat a cat's head. I have seen our dog eat a rabbit and she just ate the best parts and left the rest. Doomie says maybe Bobbie was consumed by flesh-eating bacteria which are everywhere and just wait for your immune system to have a letdown and drop its guard and in a few hours you are totally consumed and they throw you in the boneyard.

Without my beloved cat I feel a deep loss, a hole in all of my being. See, Bobbie had the tragic beginning and the tragic end and in between she was just sort of nervous and stuff, like me. I am so afraid sometimes. My life is boring but I have violent action adventure nightmares and wake up more tired than when I went to bed. The days alone in my room are languorous empty centuries filled with dread and anguish. Or I will get real nervous and quake with fear. I think the tumor in my guts will go into a fast-growth stage and cause me agonizing pain ending in death. At night I feel better. I light up a Parliament on some nights and I look out into the night and wonder what it was that Thorazine Johnny Felsun *really* has done to end up in his backward chamber. I think if he knew me and we had regular talks he would love me and no longer have the urge to kill women. I get very wet when I imagine him putting his big muscle into my female part and orgast without even touching myself.

Sometimes on a clear night the firmament is filled with stars that are as beautiful as sapphires, diamonds, an all the jewels of the earth multiplied to the twelfth power of infinity. At times like this I am filled with hope and know that in spite of my failures as a romantic novelist I nonetheless will have a future life that is complete all in and of itself and that I will blaze a path of glory through the heavens and all mortals on this earth will know who I am and will recount my heroic and remarkable feats in great detail. People will fall at my feet and worship me. There will even be little bronze markers at the places I've been to, like Nepal where I suffered with pinkeye and complained not at all.

IN HIDING
by
JOYCE CAROL OATES

NOT THINKING *IS THIS A MISTAKE, TO BEGIN?* NOR *WILL I REGRET THIS?* Normally a guarded woman, she'd given in to impulse. Hadn't considered any future beyond the gesture of an hour. His name was Woodson Johnston, Jr.—"Woody." He signed this name with a thick-nubbed pen in black ink with a flair that suggested he wished to think well of himself.

Where'd he get her home address? A directory of poets and writers?

Please except my poetry as a gift. I love your poetry truly. Even if you dont have time to read my writings. Even if you dont have a feeling for it. I understand!

He was an inmate at Kansas State Penitentiary for Men in Fulham, Kansas. His number was AT33914. He'd sent her a packet of poems and a few pages of a prison diary. She was a poet, translator, part-time college teacher, and divorced mother of a fifteen-year-old son. For the past seven years, since the divorce, she'd lived in Olean, New York.

A snowswept November. Swirling funnels of snow like vaporous human figures dancing across the snow-crust, then turning ragged, blown apart. She'd opened the packet, quickly read Johnston's poems that had been published in a small smudgily printed magazine with a clever name—*In Pen.* The diary had been photocopied from a laboriously typed manuscript without margins. There were frequent misspellings and typographical errors and Johnston had written in corrections in a neat, crimped hand. Her heart was moved to pity, seeing these corrections. As if they mattered! But of course they mattered to the author.

Quickly she read the poems, and reread them. She read the prison diary excerpt. Johnston was talented, she thought. Her pity became sympathy. Impulsively she wrote back to him, just a card. *Thank you for your intriguing, original poetry. And your disturbing diary with its vivid details.* Mailing off the card, and that was that!

Except: "Woody" immediately wrote back. More poems, and more diary excerpts, and a snapshot of himself. A black man of about thirty-five, with faint Caucasian features, curly dark hair parted on the left side of his head and plastic-framed glasses with lenses so thick they distorted his eyes. "Woody" was smiling hopefully, but his forehead was deeply creased. He wore a shirt open at the throat, and a jacket. On the back of the snapshot he'd written *In happier times 6 Yrs. ago.*

She hesitated, this time. But only for a few minutes.

She sent Johnston a package of paperback books including one of her own and one by a young black poet from San Diego. (Though afterward wondering was that a condescending gesture? Perhaps even racist?) She didn't send him a snapshot of herself but there was one, blond-blurred and smiling, the poet at the age of thirty-nine, a few years back, on the back of her book of poems.

Sometimes, these long winters in upstate New York, she couldn't recall any previous life. Couldn't recall having been married, or before that. And her son Rick barely remembered a time before Olean. In her memory there'd been a young, wanly blond woman who might've been a next-door neighbor, a shyly smiling, self-conscious young wife secretly astonished that she was loved by any man, a man's wife, in time a young mother, all this blind-dazzling as winter sunshine on fresh-fallen snow and in truth in the deepest recesses of her heart (as she'd written in her frankest poems) she had never believed in such happiness; and so it had been revealed to her, in time, that her happiness was unmerited after all, the man who'd loved her had departed, withdrawing his love.

But leaving her with a son she adored.

A cheerful, good-natured boy. A natural athlete, a smart if inconsistent student. Rick had friends, he didn't mope. His good luck, his acne was all on his back; his face was smooth. What an acrobat on a skateboard! Though sometimes when his mother happened to see Rick and he didn't see her, she was troubled at his boyish face so melancholy in repose. His mouth worked, with unspoken words. She loved her son, and her son loved her, yet it was all she could do to keep from begging his forgiveness. *I'm to blame. I must be. I couldn't keep him, your father. Try not to hate me!* Yet she knew that Rick was embarrassed by her sentimental outbursts. He liked his mom droll, wisecracking like a high-minded Joan Rivers. In sheepskin jacket, jeans, and hiking boots in winter. Chunky dark glasses obscuring half her face. The admiration of his teachers when she visited the high school. For she was something of a local celebrity, to her embarrassment. A poet published with a respected New York press, translator of slender volumes of German verse, Rilke, Novalis. She was a popular teacher of poetry and translation workshops at the State University of New York at Olean.

Since the divorce she'd been involved with few men. Her romantic liaisons flattened quickly into friendships. It was as if her sexual life, her life as a woman, had ended.

Rick's thoughts on the subject of whether his mom should "see" men, or remarry, were ambiguous. On the sexual behavior of a parent, no adolescent can bear to speculate. If the subject came up, Rick winced, laughed nervously, rolled his eyes toward the ceiling. And blushed. "Hey, Mom. It's cool, OK?"

Meaning what? She had no idea.

She thought *Some illusions are too much strain to uphold, in any case.*

Olean was a community of married couples, many with young children. The divorced departed, or died. She was no threat to anyone's marriage. She was well-liked by both sexes equally.

Stalled in writing, she studied Woodson Johnston's snapshots.

234 · JOYCE CAROL OATES

(He'd sent her several by this time.) In one, she saw a small vertical scar like a fish hook just above his upper lip. In another, she saw a curious asymmetrical alignment of his eyes, and the left eye just perceptibly larger than the right. (A trick of the camera?) He spoke of himself as a *lone soul*. Even before prison he'd been, he said, *condemned to solitary confinement.*

She didn't query Johnston about his personal life, nor did she answer his polite but persistent queries about her personal life. If he'd read her poems (as he claimed to have done) he would know a good deal about her. More than she was comfortable with him knowing, in fact.

Never did she reply to his letters immediately. Always she put them aside on a windowsill or on an edge of her desk.

He'd been sentenced to life in prison. He'd sent her printed information about his case, his appeals, a photocopy of a letter from his attorney. She'd glanced quickly through these. She did not want to discover, and to be embarrassed by, Johnston's inevitable claim of *innocence. Mistaken identity. Police coercion. False testimony.*

Did Rick know about his mother's prison admirer, as she thought of him? She'd mentioned Johnston to Rick only that first time, and then not by name or very specifically; since then, not a word. Nor had Rick the slightest interest in the treasures on her cluttered desk, whether hard-won drafts of poems, translation projects, or poems and letters from others. Now that he was in high school, he rarely troubled to enter her study at the rear of the house, a winterized porch overlooking a shallow ravine. She'd glance around to see him leaning in the doorway—"Hey, Mom. I'm back." Or, "Hey Mom, I'm out of here." She smiled and waved him away, pushing her glasses against the bridge of her nose.

Oh, she adored her son! Now he'd become untouchable.

There were weeks, even months, when she forgot Woodson Johnston, Jr. Or would have forgotten him, except Johnston didn't give up, and continued to write to her. *I wish to live through you! I see so much through your eyes.* It was a rainy spring, a heat-paralyzed summer. She went away, and Rick went to visit his father. She returned to Johnston's letters, packets of new poems and prose pieces. She read his poems guiltily. Was he improving? Had the man any talent, really? (But what did "talent" mean, wasn't this a middle-class, possibly racist supposition?) Johnston asked her for honest criticism but she shrank from remarks more specific than "very good!" "excellent!"—"original image!"—"inspired!" Once, when she wrote "Unclear?" in the margin of a poem, Johnston fired back a two-page handwritten letter of defense and she thought, Never again. She had no right to interfere with the man's imagination, in any case. His use of black street talk, jazz and rap rhythms, obscenities, a zigzag-poetry she thought it, brash and childlike in its dramatic contrasts, innocent of poetic strategies.

She wondered if she was, unknowingly, a racist? Is this how a racist thinks?

She gathered Johnston's poems, some fifty new and printed, into a collection, and sent the manuscript to her New York publisher. She told Johnston nothing of this, but mailed to him, as if in parting, a popular paperback anthology, *These Voices: Black American Poetry & Prose.* She departed for three weeks in South America on a USIA reading tour, and when she returned letters from Johnston awaited her. She delayed opening them. Her publisher declined Johnston's manuscript with regret—"No market for this, I'm afraid"—and she sent it out to another publisher, a small press specializing in quality poetry. Weeks passed, and months. There came an early autumn, a fierce, dry winter. At her desk, she observed snow. When she won a literary prize, Johnston wrote to congratulate her. When she lost another, he sent condolences. *You are a beautiful woman. A beautiful poet-soul.* She laughed, and felt her face burn. What kind of fool does he take me for? This letter of Johnston's she tore into pieces and threw away. What a horror if Rick should discover it. He'd be shocked, worse yet he might tease her. *Hey Mom—beau-ti-ful? Cool!* She hadn't been beautiful as a smooth-faced girl in her early twenties, she wasn't beautiful as a mature, rather worn woman in her early forties. She thought *I should break this off with him. This isn't a wise thing.*

She ceased answering his letters. He continued writing to her, but at decreasing intervals. (Had he found another correspondent? Another sympathetic white-woman poet? She hoped so.) The small press declined Johnston's manuscript with regret, explaining they were cutting back on poetry by unknown poets, however talented. She made inquiries with other presses, hoping to send the manuscript out again, but weeks passed, no one was much interested, she began to grow tired of her own effort. She placed Johnston's papers in a closet in her study. That summer, she went to Ireland as a guest of Aran Islands Literary Festival, taking Rick with her, and when she returned there was a letter from the American Innocence Defense Fund in Washington, D.C. A lawyer representing Woodson Johnston, Jr. was asking her, in what appeared to be a form letter, for a contribution to help in the man's defense. She thought, *Am I surprised?* No. She did feel manipulated. But why, manipulated? After all, a man is fighting for his life. Of course, she was sympathetic. Possibly he was innocent. Mistaken identity? Police coercion? False testimony for the prosecution? She made out a check for $1,500, and sent this to the fund; and received a duplicate of the previous letter, thanking her for her generosity. But nothing from Johnston. She realized she hadn't heard from Johnston in some time. Was he too busy for her, now? Had something in her last, rather brief letter offended him?

She thought, relieved, *That's that.*

In May, in the sudden warmth of a glowing midmorning sun, she happened to glance out a front window of her house to see a car being driven slowly past. Out-of-state license plates. Was the driver looking toward her house? She watched as the car continued along the road, gathering speed, took a right turn and disappeared.

She lived, in Olean, in what was called a "development" at the edge of town, a suburban neighborhood now at least twenty years old, of medium-priced, attractive homes, split-level contemporaries, mock colonials, with identical acre lots and disfiguringly wide two-car garages and asphalt driveways. Her house was stucco and brick, somewhat shabbily overgrown with wisteria and English ivy. Forsythia bloomed in the front yard. Along the road were newly budded spruce trees planted at measured intervals. In the air was a heady fragrance of wet grass and sunshine.

She'd opened the front door, to look out. She closed it, and retreated to the living room, indecisively, watching through the plate glass "picture window" (as the realtor had called it) without knowing what she was watching for. She saw herself, a figure in a split-level American house on a suburban street she could not have identified. She saw herself, a woman both girlish and middle-aged, straggling shoulder-length blond hair faded to a smudged-looking gray-brown, her face plain, shiny, with puckers beside her mouth and lashless eyes, her quite fit, healthy body grown thick-waisted, and her upper thighs disconcertingly heavy. She wore a soiled white Orlon pullover sweater, her usual jeans and badly water-stained running shoes. She backed away from the window to observe, from a short distance, the out-of-state car, an economy Toyota, returning, this time parking at the curb. She saw a man climb out of the car, in a canvas jacket, a baseball cap, jeans, a lean dark-skinned man with glasses; his knees appeared to be stiff, he walked with a limp, self-consciously up the flagstone walk to the front door. His movements were deliberate and slow. He held his arms oddly, bent at the elbows, fingers slightly outspread. In the harsh sunshine, the lenses of his glasses shone. *See how I am being open about this? I am not dangerous. My hands are in full view. Unarmed.*

Quickly she retreated to the rear of the house, to her study. She shut the door. She was breathing with difficulty, a roaring in her ears. Morning light flooded the study; somehow she'd expected darkness, a refuge. On her computer, on her desk, a screen saver dreamily whirled pastel planets.

She heard Rick answer the door. Rick! She'd forgotten he was home, this was a Saturday. She heard no voices, only a murmur.

Then came Rick loping along the hall. "Mother? Mom?" Without hesitation he pushed the study door open. She was standing very still. Not by her desk, nor by one of the crammed floor-to-ceiling bookshelves, but in an alcove of the L-shaped room, on the far side of the closet, where cartons and excess books had long been gathering dust. Rick stared at her. She saw the shock in his smooth boy-face. "Mom? Why are you hiding?"

WHAT YOU KNOW
by
PETER HO DAVIES

———————

PEOPLE SUDDENLY WANT TO KNOW ALL ABOUT MY STUDENTS, WHAT they're like. What do I know, I want to say. I'm just a writer, a writer-in-the-schools. All I see is their writing.

So what are they like as writers?

They're shocking. Appalling, in fact. Indescribably awful (and when a writer, even one of my low self-esteem, says that, you know it's serious). The good ones are bad, and the bad ones are tragic.

When at the start of each class I ask them their favorite books their fifteen-year-old faces are as blank as paper. The better students struggle to offer a "right" answer: Catcher, Gatsby, The Bible (!). The honest ones, the stupid, arrogant honest ones, tell me, *For the Love of the Game* by Michael Jordan, or the latest Dean Koontz.

The most voracious readers among them are the science-fiction fans, the genre nerds, the heavy-duty book worms (all those sequels and prequels; trilogies and tetrologies), but none of them are de-terred for a nanosecond when I tell them that good science fiction is one of the hardest things to write. After all, they're thinking—I can see it in their eyes—it's just a matter of taste, isn't it?

As a matter of fact, no. I believe in the well-made story. Have your character want something, I tell them. Have a conflict. Have the character change. Learn these simple rules, and you can spend the rest of your life breaking them.

But most of the time I find myself telling them what not to write. All the narrative clichés. No stories about suicide. No flashbacks longer than a page. No narrators from beyond the grave. No, "And then I woke up," endings. No, "I woke up and then . . . ," beginnings. No psychedelic dream sequences. The list of boringly bad stories ("But it's supposed to be boring, life is boring") goes on and on.

"No suicides?" they say in their flat, whiny voices, as if there is nothing else, nothing better. "How can suicide be boring?"

Maybe not in life, I explain quickly, but in fiction? Sure. It's a cruel world of readers out there—callous, heartless, *commuting* readers, who've been there, seen that, read it all before. "I'm not saying you can't try to write about suicide," I console them. "I'm just saying it's hard to do well, that you owe it to the material to do it justice, to find a way of making it real and raw for readers again."

Writers aren't godlike, I tell them, readers are. Writers only create; readers judge.

They nod in complete incomprehension. Yes, they're saying. Yes, we see now that there is absolutely no chance we'll understand a word you say. We're just here for the extra credit. It's the nod you give a crazy man, a lunatic with a gun.

What redeems it? My love of teaching? I do love teaching, but for all the wrong reasons. I love the sound of my own voice. I love to pontificate about writing, get excited about it, argue about it (and usually win) with people who have to listen to me, more or less (unlike my parents, my friends, my wife). But always, behind their acquiescence, behind the fact that however bad my taste I'm still the coolest teacher they have (the competition is not stiff), lie the awful, numbing questions: "What have you published? Why haven't we heard of you?"

What really redeems it are the laughs. The laughable badness of their prose. The moose frozen like a *dear* in the headlights. The cop slapping on the *cuff-links*. The *viscous* criminal. The *escape* goat.

It's as if they're hard of hearing, snatching up half-heard, half-comprehended phrases, trusting blindly in their spell-checkers to save them. (Think! Think who designs spell-checkers for a moment. Were these people ever good spellers?)

I once had a heated argument with a student about the death knoll.

"Knell," I said.

"Knoll," he insisted with vehemence, until finally we determined that he was thinking of the *grassy* knoll. My way might be right, he conceded grudgingly, but his way made more sense. We took a vote in class (they love democracy) and the majority agreed. And perhaps this is the way that language, meaning, evolves before our very eyes and ears. "It's the death mole of literacy," I told them, but they didn't get it. Sometimes, I despair of language. If only there was some way for what I know to just appear, instantaneously, in their heads.

So *that*, if you really want to know, is what my students are like. Does any of it explain why one of them last week shot his father in the head across the breakfast nook, rode the bus to school with a pistol in his waistband, emptied it in his homeroom, killing two and wounding five, before putting the gun in his mouth and splashing his brains all over the whiteboard?

No stories about suicide? No viscous criminals?

In the moments after the crisis no one thinks to call me—as the other staff, the *full-time* staff are called—to warn me not to talk to the media. No one, in fact, thinks to call me *apart* from the media. "It's CNN," my wife says passing me the phone, then stepping back as if I hold a snake in my hands. But we're *watching* CNN, I want to say. I look at her and she mimes helplessness. It never occurs to me that all my fellow teachers have been asked to say nothing to the media, that this is why some bright spark in Atlanta after trying five or six names and getting the same response has slid his finger down the faxed list before him to "Other" and found me, not quite a teacher, but better than a janitor.

What he wants to know is if I had taught the killer, the dead boy, Clark, and when I admit, and it feels like an admission, nothing to be proud of, that yes I have, I have him—*had him* (watch those tense changes)—in a writing workshop, I can hear the reporter lean forward in his chair, cup his hand around the mouthpiece. I wonder for a second about him, this young journalist, probably around my age, looking for his big break. This could be it, I realize, and I feel an odd vertiginous jealousy, almost wanting to hold back. But later, listening to my voice over and over on national TV—a grainy photo from the latest yearbook and a caption identifying me as a writer, floating over a live shot of the blank school buildings—I'm glad I talked to him, glad I didn't say anything stupid, that I come across as dignified and responsible. I answer all his questions in the first person plural. "We're shocked and appalled. We'll all be doing our best to help our students through this awful period. Our hearts go out to the families in the tragedy." Later my mother will call from Arizona, then my colleagues, even the principal with a warning not to say anything else, but an off-the-record pat on the back for "our unofficial spokesman." "A way with words," my mother will say. "You always had a way with words." Even though she's never read a single one of my stories. I tell her it was easy and it was. It comes naturally. For months now I've been talking in the first person plural. We're pregnant, my wife and I. We're expecting. We're about to be parents ourselves.

"CNN," my wife says, touching her stomach. "Something to tell the kid." It's not often she's proud of me, and I'm pleased, even though I despise the network, its incompetent staff. I heard one anchor a couple of years back talking about a first in the "anals" of country music. Another time I caught a piece in which the President was described as being "salt and peppered" with questions at a news conference. Someone wrote that, was paid to. "I suppose I should be grateful," I tell my wife. "My caption could have read 'waiter,' not 'writer.' " And she smiles uncertainly, not sure who this particular joke is on.

What I tell no one, though, not even my wife, is the reporter's last question, off air, quietly into my ear after he has thanked me and double-checked the spelling of my name. Only the tone alerted me, otherwise this could have been the same as any of the previous questions—"Was he a good student? What was he like?" This final shot: "Do you have anything he wrote for you? A poem or a story?"

I said, "No," but something in my voice must have made him wonder because he added softly, "It could be worth a great deal." So I said, "No," again, more forcefully and then, "I'm sorry," and hung up.

Why was I sorry? Easier to explain why I said, "No," with that catch of hesitation. Because I couldn't remember, that's why. I had work upstairs, ungraded stories, the response to an exercise: "Write about a moment of extreme emotion: fear, hate, love, joy, laughter." The idea is to have them write about a true emotion and use this as a benchmark against which to compare the emotions of their fictional characters. Something by Clark might be there, if he'd done the assignment. They often didn't. And, indeed, when I look there's nothing, just a note—brief—he'd been sick, and below his own signature, another—larger, flowing. It takes me a second to realize; it's his father's.

So why was I sorry? Because I'm a writer-in-the-schools. I earn $8,000 a year ($6,000 less than my wife's bookstore job pays) and we are pregnant. I was sorry I hadn't had the nerve to say: "How much?" He might have even been bullshitting me, the reporter. CNN would never do business like that, right? But something in his voice, the shift of register, made me think he might have just slipped into freelance mode. The phone was hot where I was pressing it against my head, but for a second I could have sworn it was his warm breath in my ear. Now I wondered—$1,000, $5,000, $10,000? Who knew? I was only sure it would be more than anything I'd ever gotten for my own work. And out of this irony, of course, came this idea. *I could write a piece by Clark.* I could write it and sell it. I could. He was a loner, without friends. His father was dead. He was dead. Who would know?

No narrators from beyond the grave?

Have your character want something.

Ten thousand big ones.

————

As a plan it seemed so simple at first, at least if you separate it from the issue of morality. And separating from that issue is something I teach my students. Don't stop yourselves writing something because it might hurt someone; your family, your friends. Don't stop yourself writing it because you think it's too personal, sexual, violent. Don't censor yourselves, I tell them, at least not alone when it's just you and the paper.

Oddly, they're prudish. Reluctant to write about feelings, except in the safest most clichéd terms. Love, sex especially, makes them sneer with embarrassment, while violence is simply comic.

"But what's the point?" I remember one of them asking (I wish I could say it was Clark, but I can't picture him any more than I can bring to mind the faces of three or four other boys who sit in the back row with their baseball caps pulled low over their eyes), "what's the point writing it if you're not going to show it to someone?" And I have sympathy with this. I believe in writing for an audience. Writing fiction is an act of communication—not just facts or opinions like a newspaper, but emotions. I tell them this. And in truth once something is written, actually expressed, showing it to someone—the desire to do that—is hard to escape. It's the momentum of the act. So I tell myself that writing a piece as Clark isn't the same as passing it off to others as Clark's, but once you've got it—especially if it's good—what else is there to do with it? So perhaps the moral problem does lie behind this practical one: it should be easy to write this piece—it doesn't have to be *good* after all; it needs, in fact, to be bad to be good—yet, after all the mockery I've heaped on their work, I can't do it. I can't imitate my students.

God help me, I'm blocked.

Here's the trouble. If I'm to write this and overcome the lie of it I need it to mean something. I want to offer, coded, buried, subtly perhaps, an answer, a psychological, sociological subtext, that will explain these deaths, and in explaining offer some hope or comfort to us all. It may not be *the* meaning, but surely any meaning, even a sniff of meaning is what we want. It is the writer's instinct to offer these things and, beyond mere morality, I can't quite shrug off this duty to, of all things, art.

Which is why I find myself in my 1988 Subaru wagon, driving out to a gun range on the interstate called the Duke's Den. I have never fired a gun before and I decide that this—everything else not withstanding—is the problem. If I want to understand Clark, take on his voice, I should at least try to understand how he expressed himself.

And this, too, is what I teach them. Show don't tell. Write what you know. Did Clark's baseball cap bob at that one? Did he take notes? Some of them do and it still amazes me, makes me think they're making fun, when in truth they only set down what they don't understand. Show, they write carefully, and Tell.

Write what you know is even worse. They look at me as if I've asked them to raise the dead, as if they know nothing or everything. Some I have to persuade that their lives are important enough; others that they're not quite as important as they think. But either way what most of them know is deadly—not the stories themselves, nor their lives as such, but how they live them, think about them. The best ones, they know this already. Know it like an instinct. Write what they know? Not yet. Not until they know what they know. But the worst ones? They don't even want to know what they know.

"So is that why we can't write about suicide? Because if you know it, you're, like, dead?"

"Yeah, and there're no narrators from beyond the grave, right?"

They look at me, so pleased, so earnest, like they've figured it out and I feel my heart clench. I think about explaining that the rule really ought to be "Write whatever you know just a little more about than your reader." But truly what I want to tell them is that these rules aren't after all rules for writers; they're rules for people who are trying to be writers but won't ever make it.

So I don't get any suicide stories (although as one bright spark recently pointed out: "It's ironic, don't you think? Considering how many writers kill themselves"). Instead, I get first kiss stories, first joint stories, the death of pets, the death of grandparents, sad fat girls, thin sad girls. The tone is always the same—life is tragic; tragically small or epically tragic (the chasm, come to think of it, that suicide bridges).

Lighten up, I want to tell them. It's not the end of the world. You've got your whole lives before you. All the lines my father taught me when I was their age and deciding to become a writer, all the lines I've taught them to recognize as clichés. Except, as they like to remind me, that doesn't mean they can't still be true. Some people do have apple cheeks or strawberry hair or cherry lips (the fruit-salad style of physical description). Don't clichés, in fact, have to be true to become clichés? No, I tell them, we just have to want them to be true.

What else do I teach them? Certainly not how to be creative. I'm not into breathing exercises, or free writing, or journaling. Sucking up to the muse. Nor even how to write correctly—I'm no grammar maven. "How to tell stories," is what I told CNN, although the line never aired, and that's closer to the truth.

I teach them what Forster says: that there are stories and there are plots. That stories are simple sequences of events (this happened and then this and then that), but that plots are about causes, motivation (this happened because of this, on account of that). Plots are what stories mean. And the truth is that life is all stories and fiction is all plots, and what we're looking for in Clark's story is the plot that makes sense of it. Which is why it has to be someone's fault—his, his father's, the NRA, Nintendo, Hollywood, all the escape goats—doesn't it? This happened because of that or that or that. Or all of them.

So I teach them how to tell stories, or (since we're all storytellers every time we open our mouths) how to tell them better, which is to say I try to teach them to make sense of their stories, to figure out what they mean if they mean anything. Because the way we tell stories explains them.

Write what they know? Mostly, I just try to help them know what they write.

So that's what I teach them; how to plot.

And if that's beyond them, what I try to leave them with is this: when in doubt, when stuck, blocked, or fucked, to always ask themselves, "What if?" (Even if their instinct is to ask, "So what?")

What if I pick up a gun and fire it?

The range is quiet. It's the weekend after the shooting, we're still in shock. I show my driver's license and join for $25, which entitles me to rent guns from behind the counter for $5 an hour. It seems so cheap—what can you get for five bucks—but as I buy ammunition for my choice, a .38 caliber revolver (I just pointed to the first gun I recognized from TV), I realize that this is what costs. Guns are just game consoles, VCRs—it's what you put in them that costs. The man behind the counter is unfailingly polite and helpful. He reminds me of a hardware salesman, the kind of guy in a brown apron who'll show you how to use a tool, dig out exactly the right size of wrench or washer for your job. The kind of guy who loves what he does and who'll tell you all about it if you're not careful. His name is Vern, and above his head, hanging up like so many hammers and saws on a workshop wall, are all manner of guns, not just pistols but rifles, even a replica Tommy gun, the kind of thing Al Capone might have used. There's an air of fancy dress about the display; an air of the toy store, the magic trick. On a ledge at the very top of the display is a line of model railway rolling stock. Vern is a train enthusiast, a hobbyist.

After the gun and the shells—they come in a plastic rack, not the waxed paper box I expect—he hands over a pair of ear defenders and then asks, "Target?" I must look puzzled, because he repeats himself. "What kind of target?"

"What kinds do you have?"

He grins, glad I asked, and starts to show me. There's a simple roundel, each ring marked with a score, the "classic" silhouette, a

sheet covered in playing cards for "shooting poker," a double silhouette of a gunman and a woman, his hostage, and finally a set of
caricature targets of everyone from Saddam Hussein to Barney. I
take the classic silhouette and Vern rolls it for me and secures it
with a rubber band. He hands me the lot—gun, shells, target, ear
defenders in an EZ-carry plastic tray—and points me back toward
the range, which is separated from the shop by double-glazing.
Through the glass I can see one man, broad shouldered, graying,
balding, firing. "You put your headset on in the booth," Vern tells
me, indicating the double set of doors between the shop and the
range. "Take lane three."

Inside, with the ear defenders pinching my skull, the shots from
the other man in the range sound like a distant hammering pulse. I
set up in the lane beside him. Place the gun on the counter and the
shells beside it, work the toggle switch that brings the target toward
me on a wire. All this is familiar from the movies. When the target
board arrives I'm momentarily at a loss as to how to fix the silhouette
to it. I look around and there's Vern on the other side of the glass
pointing and when I look again I see a tape dispenser mounted to
the wall.

I run the target back about halfway to the rear concrete wall. It's
ridged, corrugated, and it takes me a slow moment to realize that
this is to prevent ricochets. The concrete makes the range cooler
than the shop, like a bunker and it smells, but only faintly, of the
Fourth of July, fireworks. And this creeping nostalgia, the insulation
of the ear defenders, the odd underground cool, give the experience
an air of unreality.

The target jumps about on the wire for a few seconds like a
puppet and I wait until it's still before turning to the gun. Vern has
taught me how to load it, flipping out the cylinder and dropping in
the shells. It's a six-shooter, but he warned me to put five shots in
and leave the chamber under the hammer empty, "to save your toes."
The bullets go in very easily and quickly—the whole thing feels
well made in a way that very few things do these days—and I slide
the cylinder back into the gun. I hold it away from me and down

and then slowly raise it. Vern has shown me how to cock the hammer and fire or how to pull the trigger all the way back. He has advised me to keep my trigger finger outside the guard until I'm ready to shoot. I'm frightened of it going off before I'm ready, of seeming dangerous. But once I have it in position, cocking it is simple and when I fire my first shot I'm surprised how easy it comes. (Vern is a good teacher.) There's a crack and a small flash from the gun, but the recoil is almost playful in the way it bats my hand up. I've hit serves that jarred worse. I look last at the target and see a small neat puncture in the shoulder of my silhouette. Almost too neat, but for the slight tearing of the paper. I fire again. And again and again and again. Because after all, what else is there to do? By my fifth shot I'm not cocking, but experimenting with pulling the trigger back. Two of my shots score tens in the target's chest. With my next set I take aim at the head and put all five on target. I feel like Dirty Harry, or Steve McGarrett. Just not Clark.

Beside me as I'm loading again, the other shooter reels in his target, unrolls another and tapes it up. He's old, grandfatherly, dressed in polyester, metallic blue sansabelt pants and a teal polo shirt. He nods and I nod back. He looks like a bowler and I realize that's exactly what this experience is reminding me of, bowling. I'd laugh at him rather than nod back, that slightly too portentous nod, except that he has a loaded weapon on the counter before him, a tool with which he could kill me. It occurs to me that if he took that into his head the only thing stopping him would be the fact that I might shoot back.

I try to ask myself what this might have meant to Clark, but I can't guess. The experience isn't inspiring, just deadening, mechanical. I feel the panic rising again, the greed. We need the money. I think of my own son, my unborn son (I wanted to know the sex; not for me the surprise ending), for whom I'm doing this, and I wonder what might possibly ever drive him to kill me. I know I thought about killing him. We talked about it, about a termination, an abortion. We hadn't planned on this. I kept thinking something would come up; a new job, a major publication. I had a story with one of the slick magazines and they had held it for weeks, months, so long my hopes were rising day by day. A score like that—thousands of dollars—could change our lives. I found myself putting my imaginative energy not into new work, but into visualizing that moment, the letter in the mail, not in my own self-addressed envelope, but the magazine's embossed one, telling me blah, blah, blah, *delighted*. I didn't say so, but I think I'd decided we'd keep the baby if I sold the story. When the rejection letter ("too familiar") finally came with that sudden rushing inevitability they all have, I couldn't stop shaking. My wife, used to rages or resignation, was speechless. But later, lying in bed I realized, *how insane*. In the morning, we talked it through again and I told my wife I thought we should go ahead and she cried and held me and I felt saved.

So the thought that one day in some world this child might kill me, might shoot me in the face, who wants to imagine that? And yet, and yet, when I think of my own father, there have been . . . moments. If I had a gun, knew how to use one. Oh, yes. But petty reasons, anger over a grounding, over using the car, disappointing him. Not worth killing for. Not worth going out and buying a gun and lying in ambush for. But if the gun were to hand? Not worth running upstairs for, perhaps, not worth crossing the hall for, but if it were on the counter (what the fuck would it be doing on the counter? but just suppose), on the table, in my hand. I did punch my father once. I'd come in late and he waited up, barred the door to my room. We yelled at each other and I raised a fist. There was a moment when I could have lowered it, merely threatened, but having made it I couldn't stop. I hit him and he took a step back, out of surprise, I think. "Do that again," he told me when he'd recovered himself, and I did—bowing to that curious complicit male desire to make a bad thing worse, to transform an accident, a mistake, into a tragedy, to render ourselves not hapless, not foolish and vain, but heroic, grand, awesome. And he took the next shot too, and then he beat me unconscious (in fact, he only raised his own fist and I took a step back, fell down the stairs and knocked myself cold—so close is tragedy to farce—but the first version makes a better story). Except if it hadn't been a fist, if it had been a gun I'd raised, he wouldn't have had the chance, would he? And all over nothing.

He's dead now, my father, and as I empty the gun I'm thinking of naming my son after him.

Shooting is actually duller than bowling, I'm finding, duller and easier. I can daydream while doing it. There's something effortless and magical in the seemingly instantaneous bang and the appearance yards away of a small hole. I fire another twenty rounds. I move the target back, forward. I shoot to kill, I shoot to wound, I shoot from the hip. I suddenly understand why someone might rent a machine gun. What I want most in the world I realize is a moving target, a more interesting target. The idea on the range is marksmanship, but there's no real challenge here. I look down the barrel of my gun, but watch the shots of the man next to me. He doesn't seem much better, and I've only been shooting for twenty minutes. I watch him cluster his shots in the high scoring body of the target, one, two, three, four. Nothing. And something about the rhythm, my focus on his target, makes me swing my gun over and put a fifth shot into the face of his target. Perhaps because of the angle I'm firing from, the bullet makes a ragged hole, tearing loose a strip of paper that curls slighty, flaps like a tongue. I hold my breath, horrified. I keep the gun raised, keep sighting down it. I can't hear anything from my neighbor behind his screen. Perhaps he's reloading, hasn't noticed. The pause goes on and eventually, I empty my revolver, slowly and methodically into my target. When I'm done and my gun is down and I'm pushing out the shells, I feel a heavy tap on my shoulder. It's him. He's waited for me to empty.

Have some conflict.

He mouths something, and I shake my head, lift an ear cup.

"What the hell was that back there?" he asks again, gesturing toward the target, without taking his eyes off me. His hand is huge and mottled red and white where he's been gripping his gun. His other hand is out of sight.

"Sorry," I tell him, and it sounds as if I'm speaking in slow motion. "A. Mis. Fire?"

He looks at me for a long moment, waits for my eyes to meet his, the dark muzzles of his pupils behind their yellow protective goggles. It occurs to me that they are the exact same shade as my computer screen, and I imagine my precious last words drifting across them, the letters springing into existence under the beating cursor: "like a dear in the headlights." Finally, he nods and says, "All right, then," vanishes back behind his booth.

I reload, pressing the shells home, letting their snug fit steady me, and wait for him to start firing again. And wait and wait and wait until my hand begins to tremble, and finally I can't not fire. The gap between thought and action is so fine. It's like standing on a cliff, the way the fear of falling makes you want to end the tension, take control, jump before you fall. I felt the death mole, if you like. I felt it burrowing forward, undermining me.

Only when I'm empty, do I see my neighbor's target beside me jerk finally. He puts five rounds into the head of his target in a tight fist, then draws it toward him, packs up and leaves. I still have ammo left. Unfinished business, like a chore. I pick the gun back up and fire round after round after round like hammering nails.

Sometime in there—after the fear wears off and then the elation, and the boredom sets in—I realize there's nothing to learn here. This won't tell me anything about Clark. And the thought of the continuing failure fills me with sudden despair. I put the gun down for a moment, afraid of it. I have about one suicidal thought a year, but this isn't a good time to be having it. And then the moment passes, because I know with an adrenaline fueled clarity that killing myself won't make any kind of difference. I know my wife will go on, my son will be born. My work won't suddenly be discovered. There's no point. And it's a crushing feeling. Knowing that the ultimate gesture, the very worst thing you can do is nothing special, a failure of imagination.

I fire five more times, reel in my target, roll it up in a tight tube. When I return my gun and pay, Vern gives my credit card a long look.

"I thought I knew you. You're the teacher from that school. You were on TV." He shakes his head sadly, and for a second I think it's a moment of contrition, and then he says, "What are you teaching those kids, anyway?"

Have your character change.

I pass behind school on my way home and I have to stop, I'm shaking so much. It's in my bones now, the distant ringing shudder of the gun. My hands smell of powder, my hair, my shirt, and I clamber out of the car before I gag. There's an old pack of Marlboro Lights in the glove compartment from before my wife got pregnant, and I fumble for a cigarette, suck on it until all I can taste is tobacco smoke. The storm fence here has been festooned with tokens; flowers, cards, soft toys hang from the wire. Damp from the dew, a little faded already, they ripple in the breeze, fluttering and twisting against the chain-link as if caught in a net. I lean on my hood, watching the twilight seep up out of the earth toward the still bright sky.

What do I teach them? I teach them that telling stories is the easiest and hardest thing in the world, and among the looks of disbelief and confusion there's always one who nods, who gets it, like the teenage fatalist who asked me once, "Because there are only so many stories, right? Like seven or something." Seven, or ten, or a dozen, although no one can agree what they are and there are countless ways of telling them wrong. But the theory feels right. A finite number of stories, which writers try to tell over and over again. So suicide is boring? Then how do you make it not boring? How do you make it exciting? How do you make it new? So original, so vital, that it speaks to an audience?

Before the light fades completely, I step up to the fence to read the messages. The first moves me close to tears, and I sag against the wire. It's such a relief. I read another and another, hungrily, but by the time I've read a dozen, my eyes are dry as stone. I snatch at them, plucking them down, the ribbon and colored wool they dangle from gouging through the soft card. Taken together they're clichéd, mawkish, misspelled. There are hundreds of them stretching forty, fifty yards in each direction, as far as I can see in the gloom, like so much litter swept here by the wind. And I want to tear them all down, I want to rip them to shreds. Every awful word.

GEORGE LASSOS MOON
by
DAVID GATES

AUNT LISSA'S SAYING SOMETHING VERY SERIOUS, AND BAD CARL'S playing with the metal creamer thing. He thumbs the lid up, lets it drop. Tiny *clank*. Aunt Lissa says, "Are you following?"

"Absolutely."

"Give me strength." Big sigh. "All right, enough said. What'll it be? I don't imagine you've been eating."

"Coffee," he says, which makes him sound blown away (like he's *not*) because he's got a cup right in front of him. He just means he's fine.

"You've got to eat a *little* something."

"Let me look in the Book of Life." He lifts the menu from the metal rack. "Pray *Jee*-zus that mah name be written thar." Inside they've got a color picture of a hot dog with gleaming highlights. "This is incredible," he says.

"Why am I doing this?" Aunt Lissa says.

"You're an enabler," he says. "That's a joke." He'd better start marking them as such.

"Carl. You do understand what's going *on*, yes? Could you look at me?"

He sees in Aunt Lissa's eyeglasses a tiny thing of his own face. Boy he is *never* taking drugs again, except down drugs. "You mean do I know I got arrested?" he says. He rubs his fingers back and forth across the stubble on his jaw and it sounds exactly, *exactly*, like sawing wood. He's even going to get off the Paxil, which makes like an empty space underneath your consciousness. Gives the other shit a boost too.

"Thank heaven for little mercies." She looks at her watch. Man's watch. "I still don't quite—you were visiting somebody here?"

"Long story." He thumbs up the lid of the creamer thing again. Lets it down without a sound.

"I don't want to know, do I?" She checks the watch again. "Now what about your job? Do you need to call them? I assume this is a working day."

"Hey, it works for me," he says. "Joke."

"All right. I've done my duty," she says. "I guess I should tell you, I called Elaine. I had no idea you were . . ."

"Right," he says. "Actually, you know what I actually want? I actually want waffles." He holds his palms six inches apart to show her the squareness.

"Is there anything you *would* like to talk about?"

He picks up his fork and drags the tines across the paper napkin. "Okay, what movie?"

"What movie *what?*"

He nods. "Think about it."

Sigh. "You know, since your thing isn't until Friday? Why don't we go down to the farm for a couple of days. I'm sure Henry would like to see you."

"What are you, on the pipe?" Actually he wouldn't mind just staying right here. He looks down at his feet under the table: wet running shoes in a puddle of snowmelt. He'd patched them with Shoe Goo where the soles were separating from the uppers: so much for this, what's the word, this *canard* that he doesn't take care of himself. This duck.

"He *is* your brother," Aunt Lissa says.

The waffles arrive, and Carl mooshes the ball of butter with his fork. "You never guessed my movie."

"I'm afraid I'm not following," she says.

He sucks the fork clean, drags the tines across his napkin again and holds it up so she can see the marks.

"Wait," she says. "This *is* ringing a bell."

"Should." He puts the napkin in his lap. "You took me to see it. Film series they used to have?"

She claps her hands. "Of course." Shakes her head. "What could I have been thinking of? You were all of what?" She watches him pour syrup. "If I could have just a bite," she says, "I'd be your friend for life."

When they get to the car, Aunt Lissa paws in her purse, then looks in the window. "I *knew* I left the keys in the switch," she says. "Is your side locked?"

"You don't have a spare?"

"Actually, I—oh. *Damn* it. It's under the hood, and of course you can't—oh. This is *so* exasperating. Well, there's a gas station." He looks where she's looking. Sunoco: sky blue, sun yellow. "Maybe they have a Slim Jim."

He looks at her. "How do you know about Slim Jims?"

"I've done this before," she says. "Don't ever get old."

"Yeah, I wouldn't worry."

"Oh, pooh. Just because—oh, I don't know. We don't have time for this discussion now."

"Thank heaven for little mercies," he says. "You want me to go over?"

She looks at him. "It's nice of you, dear. But I think I'd better."

Aunt Lissa's driving him down the Thruway into the snow country. It's the pea-soup Volvo Uncle Martin bought the year he died, and she still steers strong-handed, chin jutting. She'd looked older when she showed up at the jail, but now she's settled back into Aunt Lissa. Drunk driving. Which is the most incredible joke in the world because he was just drinking to try to ease down off the other shit.

In fact wasn't it right along here somewhere, near the exit for Coxsackie? He had Hot Country Radio going because the Best of the Sixties Seventies and Eighties started playing Here come old flattop, which was *not* a helpful song when you just wanted words that hooked up to something. Once he caught himself watching for the place where the Big Bang happened, except that was actually on the Connecticut Turnpike, near Exit 63. Meanwhile he was working on a theory that if he could make it as far as Kingston he'd be okay. He had a bottle of Old Crow between his thighs, sticking up like a peepee, or a tepee—you know, as in "sticking up like a tent pole"—which he put there precisely *because* it was a joke. Here, he'll spell it out: being drunk fucks up your sexual performance. When the cop pulled him over, he turned the radio off, but decided that hiding the bottle would look furtive. The cop said, *And do you know how fast you were going, Carl?* And Carl said, *I think I got carried away by the radio,* which was *not* a surreal saying but just the very, very traditional association of uptempos with driving fast. He pointed at the radio as evidence. The cop said, *You were going thirty miles an hour.*

Black trees stick up out of the white hillsides. Sky seems white, too. He closes one eye and looks from hills to sky, then back again. Maybe what it is, the sky is a darker white? Aunt Lissa's telling him, again, the story of how she and Uncle Martin came to buy the place in Germantown. The house just *spoke to her,* that's her formulation, so they stopped and an old woman came to the door. *We were admiring your house and just decided to stop and tell you so.* And the old woman said, *Well it happens to be for sale, and my son is coming tomorrow to put a sign up.* They bought the house, Henry bought the hill.

Carl thinks Aunt Lissa might actually have turned *into* that old woman, but actually that might be just to scare himself. As a kid, he used to scare himself thinking that his mother, to keep from dying, had quick turned herself into Aunt Lissa when she saw that his father was steering them across the divider. Since his mother and Aunt Lissa were sisters, it looked believable. He used to watch Aunt Lissa's face and see his mother in there, coming and going.

They take the exit for Catskill and Cairo, and pass an abandoned cinderblock store with plywood in the windows and a Henry Craig

Realty sign. "Hammerin' Hank," Carl says. "Now that has to make you proud." Zero reaction.

Aunt Lissa stops at Price Chopper, then takes him into Ames, where he picks out a three-pack of Fruit of the Loom briefs, three black Fruit of the Loom pocket tees, a gray hooded sweatshirt, 90–10 cotton-polyester, which is incredible for just some mystery brand, a package of white socks and a pair of Wrangler blue jeans, the darker blue to last him longer. Aunt Lissa says she'll treat him, but he says No, no he has money, like flipping away his cigarette before the firing squad.

Coming around the last corner he tries to see if he can tell independently what it was about the house that *spoke to her.* It'll be a way to test his—let's say this exactly—his *congruence.* He squints and says in his mind, *Okay now what exactly is the charming thing here?* Like, *There are x number of bunnies hidden in this picture, can you find them?* Could it be the wooden gingerbread along the porch? No, because "form follows function" is a major thing in world esthetics, and Aunt Lissa takes the train down for shows at the Modern. Yet olden fanciness is also a thing; she gardens with heirloom varieties. See, this is the kind of shit he needs to be able to sort out again.

She parks by the kitchen door, then reaches under and yanks the hood release. "Fool me twice, shame on me. Could you get the groceries?" She gets the hood up and pulls a magnetic hide-a-key box off the engine block. "Voilà." Closes the hood and tucks the hide-a-key up under the front bumper. "There. You don't think anybody would look there, do you?"

"*I* wouldn't," he says.

Up the hill behind Aunt Lissa's house, Henry's lights are on, and white smoke snake-charms out of his metal chimney. Can you actually own a *hill?* Half a hill, really, but it's like the moon in that no one sees the side that's turned away. Down low in the sky, there's a thing of orange that tints the whole snow. He takes the bags, follows Aunt Lissa onto the screened-in porch and stands shivering while she rattles a key in the storm door. "We never used to lock up," she says. If this were a movie scene, you'd cut right there.

He closes the door behind him and rubs his feet on the hairy brown mat. That old-refrigerator smell of an empty house in winter. Aunt Lissa clomps in her flopping rubber boots to the thermostat and the house goes bump; then she clomps into the kitchen. Carl hears water running. The *foomp* of a lighted burner.

She comes back in, rubbing the knuckles of one hand, then the other. "It should warm up soon," she says. "I keep the downstairs at fifty." She pulls a chair over to the register. "I put water on for tea."

"You have coffee?"

"Instant."

He makes a cross with his index fingers.

"It's terrible for you anyway." She sits down, still wearing her coat. "Supposed to be a full moon tonight. I hope it doesn't cloud over again."

"When the moon is in the sky, tell me what am I," he sings, *"to do?"*

"Wait, I *know* that song," she says.

"So what movie?" He thinks he hears a car, gets up and goes to the window. A Grand Cherokee's pulling up behind the Volvo, headlights beaming, grille a toothy smile. "Huh. Looks like a small businessman."

"Be nice."

The headlights go out, the car door opens. "Yep," he says. "Big as life and twice as natural."

Aunt Lissa turns on the porch light. There's Henry wiping his feet.

"I saw you drive in, so I thought I'd stop down," Henry says. "Carl?" Quick look at Carl.

"Yo, mah buvva," Carl says. "You keepin' it real, yo?" Henry cocks his head. "You know," Carl says. "Like real estate."

"I'm not up on my jive talk." Henry turns to Aunt Lissa. "Why don't you come on up to the house while it's getting warm in here? Connie's making soup."

"Yum," Aunt Lissa says. "We might stop up later. How about some tea? I just put water on."

Henry twists the sleeve of his leather jacket. "So how'd it go?"

"Well, I suppose it was fine," Aunt Lissa says. "I don't have a lot in my experience to compare it to."

"Hell, I should have done this."

"But you had your closing. It was perfectly fine."

Henry looks at Carl. "So what were *you* doing up this way?"

Carl looks at the tabletop. Honey oak with flamelike grain. "I don't know, long story."

"Aren't they all. Hell happened to your face?"

Carl shakes his head

"Christ," Henry says. "Shouldn't he be back in detox?"

"I hate to do it," Aunt Lissa says.

"He goes up in front of a judge in this kind of shape, they'll do it *for* you."

"I think what Carl needs most is just to get some rest," she says.

"*I* think what Carl needs most," Carl says, "is a good old pop of Demerol. Speaking as Carl."

The way he knows Henry heard this, something jumps in that fat throat. "Well they're probably going to want him in some kind of a program."

"Hey, *Teletubbies,*" Carl says. "That's actually an incredibly cool show."

Now Henry looks at him. "I'm glad this amuses you, Carl."

Aunt Lissa gets up, so the thing that's been going on for a while now must be the whistling teakettle. Good that it's *something*. "Now what's anybody's pleasure?" she says. "We have Earl Grey, plain old Lipton's, camomile . . . Green tea?" Sad: Back when she used to read him *The Tale of Peter Rabbit,* she said camo-*myle*.

"Actually, I better hit it back up the hill." Henry looks out the window. "Looks like it's starting again."

"Sorry, this is kind of getting to me," Carl says and goes into the kitchen, where steam's whistling out of the little pisshole. He takes the kettle off the burner and the noise stops.

"Lissa," he hears Henry say, "are you sure you're up to this?" Or maybe he said "listen."

"Oh, for heaven's sake," she says.

He hears the door close, and Aunt Lissa comes into the kitchen. "You had to show off for him."

"He's a dick. Pardon the expression." Carl hears the Cherokee start up, and he looks out the window: snowflakes fluttering through headlight beams.

"I know the expression," she says. "Now help me put this stuff away."

"Is that a denial?" he says.

"You," she says, "are wicked."

The way all this current shit started, he'd gotten involved with a person who was also from Albany—actually Schenectady—and when they'd been together a couple of days, she'd thought up this idea. Rent a car, both get as much cash as possible from their cash machines (this was like a Saturday night), buy whatever they could, drive up to her parents' house, her parents being in Florida, and sell it at a major markup to all these people she still knew. This was a very young person: cigarette smoker, chopped-off hair bleached white. Tiny stud in her left nostril that looked like a blackhead and seven gold rings around her left ear; nothing in her right. So when she went on modeling jobs she could give them two different looks.

She was temping, filling in for somebody's assistant. Carl at this point was sort of not living at home anymore, staying with people, carrying his laptop and a duffel bag with clothes and DVDs: *42nd Street*, *Spellbound*, *The Maltese Falcon*, *It's a Wonderful Life*—you know, the Western Canon. What was weird, he didn't feel weird. This was thanks to the Paxil, which he was now getting through two

doctors at two drugstores, because the Oxford doctor had said 40 63
milligrams was "rather a lot." And he was using again on top of it,
but not big-time, and mostly to help him write: he'd been posting
stuff about *42nd Street* on this actually really very serious Web site.

any dickhead can see that dorothy brock (bebe daniels) is the
same person as peggy sawyer (ruby keeler), but the scrim of
gender may prevent said dickhead from discerning that julian
marsh (warner baxter) is also mutatis mutandis a projection of
the "sweet" sawyer's nut-cutting inner self, the very name sug-
gesting she'd "saw off" your "peg" to get "a leg up," it being
no accident that brock's "broken" (note further pun) leg is
sawyer's big "break."

He told the temp with the things in her ear that there were all
too few outlaws on the seventeenth floor, and he said Albany was
their shared shame. Then she was bold enough to show up at the
Christmas party when she'd only worked there a week. He said could
he get her a drink—he was on like number three—and she said,
"So how much of an outlaw *are* you?" He held up his left hand,
worked his ring off and said, "Observe me closely." He pinched the
ring between thumb and forefinger, showed her both sides, put it in
his mouth and swallowed. It scraped going down, but no worse than
swallowing, say, a hard candy. And it would, in theory, be recover-
able. He chased it with a last swallow, put his glass down and pulled
his cheeks open with his forefingers. She ignored this, looked in his
glass, then looked at him. "How did you do that? Let me see your
hands."

Anyhow, you'll never guess what happened: They ended up using
most of the shit themselves. They pretty much stayed in her parents'
bed, watching cable, DVDs on Carl's laptop, and a video called
Barely 18 that her father kept duct-taped up inside his radial saw.
And *Monday Night Football*, which is how they figured out it was
now Monday, or had been Monday. Carl called his supervisor's voice
mail and said he had the flu. This Kerri—he'd briefly thought the

i was a turn-on—called whoever's voice mail it was and said she had food poisoning. Carl pointed out how stupid this was: She'd have to come up with something else tomorrow. And she said, Well it would've been nice if he'd said that before.

They'd gotten like two of their eight hundred dollars back when they had this fight—*literally* a fight, where she was hitting him and he hurt her wrists trying to hold her and she told him, *Get the fuck out, just get the fuck out.* She'd dug it that it took him forever to come—the Paxil plus the other shit made an orgasm just too high to climb up to—and then she stopped digging it. *I don't like you, I don't know you.* She hit first, remember that. He grabbed her wrists with both hands, found he didn't have a third hand to hit her with, then tried to get both her wrists in one hand so he'd have a hand free, and she broke loose and hit again, *Get out get out,* in the middle of the night, middle of the afternoon actually.

So he got in his car and made it onto the main drag, just barely, where he pulled into some non–Dunkin' Donut place, like an indie donut place, guided the car between yellow lines and closed his eyes: it looked like when they score a touchdown and the flash cameras go off. No way he could drive all the way back to New York like this. Had to get something to take the edge off, and he had no idea where you went in Albany anymore. Actually, Aunt Lissa would put him up, but he was in no shape to deal with her: she was in the sort of space where she'd be "hurt" if he'd "come to town and didn't call." He had an incredibly scary thought that it was actually her in the car next to him, but he nerved himself to look and it was just one of those Winnie-the-Pooh things.

He went in and bought a fat old sugar donut, which he thought might weight him down, take him earthward, but the shit he'd been snorting made it taste nasty and he spit the mouthful into a napkin. Though in all fairness, maybe it really did taste nasty. At least there must be a liquor store open, unless it was already Sunday again.

Morning sun on snow. Clean blue sky.

Carl's sitting at the kitchen table looking out the window. Aunt

Lissa's gone to town for the paper and left him with what she biblically called "tea with milk and honey," though it's hard to trust its dimensionality: it appears to be a flat khaki disc fitted into the cup. Halfway up the hill, Henry's house hangs off like the house in *North by Northwest.* Snow clings along the tops of the tree branches in simplifed versions of their shapes, and dead apples, like dog-toy balls, hang from the leafless apple tree. Some have a curve of snow on top, like a phase of the moon.

When he hears Aunt Lissa's car, he gets up and turns her radio back on. The *diddle-diddle-dum* morning baroque had been sounding too much like thoughts racing. What we've got now is some sprightly guitar piece. Almost certainly not a harp.

She sets the *Times* before him, like the dainty dish before the king. "Voilà," she says. "Glorious morning out." She drapes her coat over the back of a chair. "Now what would you like? I can fix pancakes, we have oatmeal . . ."

He shakes his head, holds up a hand.

"Toast? You can't not eat."

"Let me guess. Is breakfast the most important meal, do you think?"

"Stop."

"What about the importance of dietary fiber?" That was when he remembered about the ring. Long gone. Must be.

"You're welcome to sit here and make witticisms to yourself," she says. "I've got to work on my presentation." Aunt Lissa's reading group is doing *To the Lighthouse* next week.

"Don't we all," he says.

He manages to hold back from retching until he hears her on the stairs, then gags up nothing, and feels sweat popping out of his face. After a while, he stands up and sees how that feels. He scrunches up a slice of bread in his fist to make a bolus and eats it just for something solid. Then pops his Paxil and puts his mouth under the faucet. The cops got a hard-on when they found the Paxil, of course—*And what's this, Carl?*—but they had to give it back. Actually, he really needs just to get off of absolutely everything and just purify, purify, purify. On the other hand, don't the laws of physics suggest that all this not-unhappiness will have to be paid for by an equal and opposite period of negative happiness, an equal distance below the baseline? Lately he's big on that thing about being nice to the right people on the way up because you're going to meet them again on the way down, "people" meaning entities in your mind.

He goes back up to the guest room to lie down again. For a nightstand she's put a lamp on a small mission bookshelf that she's stocked with light reading. He picks out *Try and Stop Me*, by Bennett Cerf, and stacks the two pillows against the headboard. The idea is what, that Bennett Cerf has so many stories you better not try to stop him? Carl's studying a cartoon of Dorothy Parker hurling a giant pen like a javelin when Aunt Lissa knocks on his open door.

"I was going through some pictures the last time I came down here." She holds up an envelope. "I pulled these out to have them copied for you and then of course I forgot all about them. Don't ever get old."

"Yeah, you warned me about that." He claps hands, then holds them out, meaning *throw it*. She comes over and hands it to him.

He flips through with Aunt Lissa in his peripheral vision. The one of him as a baby, held by his mother wearing a black dress and pearl necklace, his father in a tuxedo, grinning a Mr. Skeleton grin, his fingers making a V behind her head. The one of Uncle Martin pitching to him in the backyard in Albany, when he was like eleven and had Henry's old Hank Aaron bat, with *Hank* in quotes. The one of him at six, in that red flannel cowboy shirt with the white pinstripes and slant pockets. Chubby cheeks. Little heartbreaker.

"*These* cover the waterfront," he says, still looking at that last one. "Incredible."

"Now you can't have them until I make copies."

"I don't know where I'd even keep them at this point."

"Well, they'll be here. You know, it's *such* a glorious day. You really should go out and get some fresh air."

Outside, the cold makes his face sting, but he can feel no dif-

ference to his body thanks to Uncle Martin's old Eddie Bauer coat.
Maybe she'll give it to him: That thing where you have a hoodie
under a denim jacket doesn't really cut it. He walks as far as the
corner, to the house with the sign on the lawn that says STOP THE
DREDGING. It's about the Hudson River.

Walking back to Aunt Lissa's he now sees something else that
could have spoken to her: that vine that—losing the word here—
ornates? that ornates the porch in summertime and is now this brown
wirelike arrangement clinging to the chalky posts. Does green somehow seep back up into it, or could a whole new vine grow quickly
enough to replace it every year? Both seem impossible, yet one must
be true. But he remembers the name: Dutchman's pipe. Now that's
something that hangs together: when Carl was a kid, Uncle Martin
used to have this expression for a hopeful patch of blue among the
clouds, *enough to make a Dutchman a pair of britches.* It gave you
the idea of big people living in the sky.

When the phone rings, he's back looking at *Try and Stop Me.* He
can't really follow the anecdotes, but he's into the cartoons. In one,
captioned "Mankiewicz en riposte," a smirking man removes a cigarette from his mouth and blows a cloud of smoke with an arrow in
it at a quailing man. The anecdote presumably would make clear
whether we're talking Joe or Herman. See? Carl cold *knows* this shit.

Aunt Lissa calls, "Carl? For you." He gets up off the bed, pads
out into the hall with socks sliding on the glossy floor and looks
down the stairs at her looking up. "Elaine."

The wall phone in the kitchen is still the only phone in the house.
Aunt Lissa's going to break her neck some night coming down those
stairs. Because of the socks, he's extra careful himself.

"Carl. Hi. I just wanted to make sure you were okay."

"Oh. Yeah. You know, thanks."

"Lissa called me yesterday. Apparently she didn't know that, you
know . . ."

"Right," he says.

"I hope you didn't mind that I told her."

"No, no. God no." He picks up Aunt Lissa's egg timer. Such an amazing touch, giving the Wicked Witch red sand. "So," he says. Like, *To what do we owe the pleasure?*

"I really didn't call because I want anything," she says.

"Right." He sees something move out the side window and puts the egg timer down. Just a gray squirrel across the snow.

"So are you using again? Or just drinking?"

"Neither one. You know, to any degree." He picks it up again.

"Well, so how come they busted you?"

"Oh, you know. Just a stupid thing. Open container."

"I heard it was a little more than that."

"Well, you know. They throw in the kitchen sink to make it sound really dire."

"Right," she says. He would actually like to steal this egg timer. Whip it out at parties. "Did I tell you somebody called about the guitar?"

"And?"

"He wanted to know if you'd take less."

"Like how much?" He puts the egg timer back, sand side down, like a good boy.

"He didn't really say. I've got his number here."

"Look, why don't you just call him, get whatever you can get and keep the money, you know? I mean I owe you for this month and last month, plus the—"

"Okay, look," she says, "let's not worry about the money for now."

"Right." But Carl heard that *for now,* don't think he didn't.

When he wakes up, out of a dream involving King Tut's tomb, he smells something yummy. It's like a famous smell, but he can't come up with the name. Not coriander—much more household. He goes down to the kitchen.

"You must have needed that nap," Aunt Lissa says. Something's louder. "I thought I'd make a quiche to take up."

"Oh. So."

"Connie asked us for around seven."

"Cool."

"I know it's not the most comfortable thing for you."

"You figured that out," he says.

"I must say, they *have* been wonderful."

"In all fairness," he says.

She pokes a fingernail through the plastic that covers a—like a bouquet—of parsley on a styrofoam tray, and plows it open. *Nosegay?* "You know, I've often thought we made a mistake keeping Henry at Mount Hermon after the accident. If we'd brought him back to Albany to finish high school, maybe you two would've had a better chance at . . ." She takes the parsley over to the sink.

"Bonding?" he says.

"It's easy to make light of it."

"Yeah, I guess I'm just a merry-andrew," he says. "Like a merry widow."

She turns the water on and begins washing the parsley.

"Shit, I'm sorry," he says. "I didn't mean anything by that."

"I do all right," she says.

He watches her dry the parsley in a dish towel.

"So when I get this in the oven," she says, "what do you say we try on that suit? You'll want to look as respectable as we both know you really are."

"Now that hurt," he says.

She laughs, a girl-laugh. "What are we going to do with you?"

Up in her bedroom, she opens the closet door and pushes jingling hangers to the side. "I gave his suits to Goodwill, but he kept this one down here just in case." She holds up a gray suit with fat lapels.

"I hear these are coming back," Carl says.

"Never you mind. Let's see the jacket on you."

Carl puts the jacket on. Tight in his armpits and across the shoulders, sleeves too short. She lifts the pants up to his front. "Well," she says.

"They've obviously mistaken me for a much shorter man," Carl says.

"Maybe I can let the cuffs down," she says. "We'll make this work."

By seven o'clock it's already down in the zeros, but Aunt Lissa insists they walk up the hill. Carl puts on the Eddie Bauer, Aunt Lissa hands him the quiche to carry and they step out into the cold. She doesn't know he found that vodka under the kitchen sink, so he keeps his distance from her. Sky's so incredibly clear there looks to be nothing between you and the stars, as if "the atmosphere" were an exploded theory like phlogiston.

"Jim!" he says when Henry opens the door. "They didn't tell me *you* were here. It was *grand* of you to come."

Henry says, "Let's not let the cold in, shall we?"

"Where can I put this?" Carl says.

"What is it?"

"I thought I'd make a quiche," Aunt Lissa says.

"Christ, you didn't have to do that." Henry holds out his hands. "Should it go in the oven?"

"Wouldn't hurt just to warm it up," Aunt Lissa says.

Aunt Lissa takes one end of the couch, Carl takes the other. Over on the sideboard, cut-glass decanters with silver tags like good doggies: SCOTCH, RYE, BRANDY. At different levels, but all the same amber.

Connie comes in from the kitchen, wearing black leggings as if she were a slim person, and a big sweater that comes way down. "Lissa, that was so nice of you. Carl? Good to see you too?" She bends down to give Lissa a kiss and Carl can't help but see her movieolas swing forward.

"Now what can I get anybody? Tea? Hot chocolate?"

"I wouldn't mind just a touch of that port you had the other night," Aunt Lissa says. "But I bet Carl would take you up on the hot chocolate."

"Yeah, let's go crazy," Carl says. That vodka could use a booster, but he can bide his time. Shit, if he gets a second alone in here, he can tip up a decanter.

"Carl, you haven't changed a bit," Connie says.

"Me either," Carl says. She gets a look on her face like, *What?*

They eat while watching *Who Wants to Be a Millionaire*; Connie says she's *totally hooked on it.* It's a new one on Carl, but he likes the thing where the host guy and the person are sitting across from each other in the middle of space, and the damned-soul voices are going *Ah ah ah.* There's a question where, was Mata Hari a spy during (a) World War I, (b) World War II, (c) the Vietnam War, or (d) the Gulf War? The person says (b) World War II, and Aunt Lissa says it amazes her what people don't know. Henry says it amazes him what people *do* know, like when they get onto those questions about rock bands. Talking Heads, that was his last new band. And that's got to be how many years ago? Connie wants to know, what exactly *is* trivia? Because to one person it may be trivial, but. When the show's over, Henry gets out the cards for gin rummy and asks what would anybody like. A touch more of that port for Aunt Lissa, Diet Coke for Connie, same for Carl. Henry gets himself a glassful of ice and pours in SCOTCH. Carl is absolutely fine with this. If nothing else, he'll eventually get another crack at that vodka. He fans his cards out and holds them up to his face for a sneaky smell of them.

At ten o'clock Henry puts on the news. Big fire in Albany, hoses arching icy roostertails in the dark and a young woman talking into a microphone and blowing out white breath. "The apparent cause?" she says. "A faulty heating unit."

"A faulty crack pipe," Henry says.

"Now, you don't know that," Connie says.

"I know that part of *town.*"

She gets up. "I better put that stuff in the dishwasher."

Aunt Lissa gets up, too. "Let me give you a hand."

Now there's a thing about the dredging, people in parkas outside some building holding signs. "Those G.E. fuckers have got the ya-hoos stirred up," Henry says. "The money they spent buying ads, they could've cleaned *up* the fucking PCBs."

"Wait, so you think they *should* dig up the river?" Carl had assumed Henry was a Republican.

"What do you do, just let sleeping dogs lie? That philosophy hasn't gotten *you* too far. Your thing is tomorrow, right?"

"Ten A.M."

"Well I guess if you manage not to lose your shit in front of the judge, they'll let you off with a fine. Yank your license, of course."

"I don't plan to lose my shit," Carl says.

"They're going to want cash probably. How much you have with you?"

"Couple hundred." That was before the clothes.

"Got to be more than that," Henry says. "So you were planning what? To hit *her* up?" Tosses his head in the direction of the kitchen. "Look, call my office. Here." Lifts a hip as if to fart, digs out his wallet, hands Carl a card. "Or call my cell. I'll probably be out showing. That's got all my numbers. Let me know how much to bring, and I'll drive up myself."

"You're kidding. Well. Thanks." Carl looks at the card, then reaches up under his sweatshirt and puts it in his T-shirt pocket.

"Yeah. So I'm assuming that you don't need to be here past to-morrow. Correct?"

"I honestly haven't been thinking."

"Well why don't you honestly get cracking and *do* a little think-ing. I mean, I know you're the one damaged soul in God's green universe."

Carl gives him the finger, but Aunt Lissa's coming in from the kitchen and he converts it to scratching his nose. "We should think about getting down the hill," she says to Henry. "We need to be there by ten."

Henry gets up. "Let me run you down."

"The air'll do us good. Do *me* good, anyway. That last glass of port was the bridge too far."

"Then you should definitely let me drive you."

"Oh pooh," she says. She crooks her elbow at Carl. "I've got my protector here."

When they get outside, the moon's up: big, round, alarming. Carl says, "George Lassos Moon. You remember she draws the picture?"

Aunt Lissa stops walking. "This looks a little slippery through here," she says. "Could I have your arm till we get past this part?"

Carl raises his right elbow and feels her hands clamp around the puffy sleeve. He takes a couple of baby steps: Now she's got *him* worried. "So what movie?" he says. "Easy one."

"Carl, I'm sorry," she says. "I've had enough for one night."

The sun's on their right as they head up to Albany. Carl's pulled the visor over, but he can't face too far left because he had a couple of pulls at that bottle of vodka when Aunt Lissa went up to brush her teeth; he's opened his window a crack to let out fumes. He also thought to pour his Paxils into an envelope and fill up the vial; only a shot, but it could come in handy. Another blinding-sunny day. Too warm to wear the Eddie Bauer; it's draped over his seat back. The pavement's wet and Aunt Lissa has to keep squirting fluid and using the wipers to clear salt-spatter.

"I wonder," she says. "Do you remember when you first came to live with us?"

"Yeah, I remember thinking it was weird that all my stuff was there but it was the wrong room," he says, at the windshield. "And that incredible wallpaper. The bucking broncos."

"Now that," she says, "was Martin's idea," and he knows the whole rest word for word. *I remember he came* "I remember he came back from the store with the rolls under his arm, and he said" *Now this is what* "Now this is what a six-year-old boy would like."

"Right." Aunt Lissa's spin on the whole thing has always been that she and Martin just picked up where his parents left off, as if it deeply made no difference who anybody was.

She does another wiper thing.

"You know," Carl says, "I don't think in all these years I've ever even said I appreciated what you guys did?"

She takes her eyes off the road long enough to stare at him. "You can't be serious. I still have that lovely letter you wrote the day you graduated from high school."

"That," he says. "Yeah. Well, I guess the point is, here I am again."

"This too shall pass," she says. "I'm only glad that I'm still able to help."

"What, the son you never had?" He says this by way of experiment, to see how it would feel to go just the opposite way and be a total shit.

"I imagine there's something of that." Aunt Lissa smiles, shakes her head. "Do you want to *really* talk?"

"Probably not," he says.

Sign for the New Baltimore Service Area.

"I need to use the rest room," she says. "Shall we get you some coffee? They have a Starbucks now."

"I thought it was bad for you."

"You *told* me I was an enabler," she says. "You know, you still make the mistake of thinking you can see everyone and no one can ever see you. It was cute when you were six."

He shades his eyes and looks out his window below the visor. A farmhouse with a cinderblock chimney goes by.

"Have you thought what you're going to do?" she says.

"I guess take a bus back to the city." Make some calls to see who he might be able to stay with.

"I mean in the longer term."

"Oh that. Yeah, I thought I'd run for Congress. Mah fellamericans . . ."

"Give me strength," she says. "You and Elaine have been married what, two years?"

"Give or take."

"Well, isn't there a chance that . . . ? I don't know. I've hardly met Elaine." She swings left to pass an ass-dragging station wagon, black Lab pacing in the wayback behind a dog gate, then into the right lane.

"Well, I *would* say, come up and stay with me until things get straightened out." Shakes her head no. "It's not that you're not welcome."

"But what would Henry say?"

"Henry can say whatever he damn well pleases." She sighs. "He'd be right."

In the service area, she parks next to a Sidekick with four cross-country skis on the roof rack. A leg sticks out the driver's window: sheathed in metallic blue, foot wearing some robot sneaker. It's a pretty woman with iridescent blue sunglasses and big blonde kinky hair, tipping a flat silver flask into her mouth. She sees him looking and lifts the flask by way of a toast. Carl can't read this. Outlaw recognition? Or to scandalize, mistaking him for what he must look like? Light blue oxford shirt, maroon tie, gray suit.

Aunt Lissa, getting out of the car, misses the whole transaction. "Aren't you coming in?"

"I'll just hang."

He watches her go inside, then gets out of the car. "Cheers," he says. He takes the pill vial out of his pocket, pries the cap off, and drains the fucker. The woman draws in her leg, and up goes her window. He walks around to the front of Aunt Lissa's car, squats, feels behind the bumper and plucks away the little metal box. Then goes over to the Sidekick and circles his fist counterclockwise. The woman puts the window halfway down.

"How about I race you to New York?" he says. "Loser buys the first round."

"I'm waiting for my friend," she says. "Plus, you're going the wrong way."

"So I'll race you to what? Lake Placid."

She rolls up her window.

"Bitch," he says. But again just experimentally, like pretending to be somebody who'd hit on a woman and then call her bitch.

He gets into the driver's seat, his bottom warmed by leftover heat from Aunt Lissa's bottom, and sticks the key in the switch. If he really does this, all she actually needs to do is go back inside and call Henry. Henry of course will make her call the police, call the police himself, so you'd want to get off at the next exit and take back roads down. Be a good joe and leave her car at the train station in Poughkeepsie.

Experimentally, he backs out of the parking space. Puts it in drive, turns left, toward the entrance ramp, stops, puts it in park and races the engine, playing with how it would feel. Feels incredible.

CONTRIBUTORS

Aimee Bender is the author of *The Girl in the Flammable Skirt,* a collection of stories, and *An Invisible Sign of My Own,* a novel. Her short fiction has been published in *Harper's, The Paris Review, Granta, GQ, Story,* and many other journals, and has been read on NPR's "This American Life." She lives in Los Angeles.

Jason Brown was a Wallace Stegner Fellow at Stanford and is now teaching in the MFA program at the University of Arizona. He is the author of the story collection *Driving the Heart and Other Stories.* He is at work on a novel.

Judy Budnitz is the author of the story collection *Flying Leap, If I Told You Once,* and a forthcoming collection of stories. Her short fiction has appeared in *Story, The Paris Review, Glimmer Train,* and other journals. She has taught fiction writing at Brown and Columbia Universities.

Peter Ho Davies is the author of two collections of stories, *The Ugliest House in the World* and *Equal Love.* He is a member of the MFA faculty at the University of Michigan.

Sylvia Foley's collection of linked short stories, *Life in the Air Ocean,* was chosen by the *Los Angeles Times* as one of the Best Books of 1999; the title story won *GQ*'s 1997 Frederick Exley Fiction Competition. Her fiction has also appeared in *Story, Open City, Zoetrope, LIT,* and *The Antioch Review.* "y's story" is from a series of stories she is compiling tentatively titled *The Alphabet of Desire.* She lives in Brooklyn, New York.

Mary Gaitskill is the author of the novel *Two Girls, Fat and Thin* as well as two collections of stories, *Bad Behavior* and *Because They Wanted To.*

David Gates is the author of the novels *Jernigan* and *Preston Falls,* and a collection of short stories, *The Wonders of the Invisible World.* He writes about books and music for *Newsweek,* and lives in Brooklyn and Washington County, New York.

Philip Gourevitch is a staff writer at *The New Yorker.* His most recent book is *A Cold Case.* His first book, *We Wish To Inform You That Tomorrow We Will Be Killed With Our Families: stories from Rwanda,* won the National Book Critics Circle Award and the *Los Angeles Times* Book Prize. His short fiction has appeared in such magazines as *Story, Southwest Review,* and *Zoetrope.*

Thom Jones is a National Book Award finalist. His stories have been anthologized in *The O. Henry Awards, Best American Short Stories,* and *The Best Short Stories of the Twentieth Century Anthology,* edited by John Updike. His fourth book, a novel, is forthcoming from Little, Brown, Inc. He lives in Olympia, WA.

Victor LaValle is the author of the story collection *Slapboxing With Jesus* and a forthcoming novel titled *Homunculus*. His work has been published in *Transition, Tin House, Bomb,* and others. He is an assistant professor at Columbia University.

Jonathan Lethem is the author of *Girl in Landscape, Motherless Brooklyn,* and five other books of long and short fiction. He is also the editor of *The Vintage Book of Amnesia.* He lives in New York City and Toronto.

Max Ludington's stories have appeared in *Tin House, Nerve,* and *Outerbridge.* His first novel is forthcoming from Doubleday. He lives in Santa Fe, New Mexico.

Ben Marcus is the author of *Notable American Women, The Age of Wire and String,* and *The Father Costume.* His short fiction has appeared in *Harper's, McSweeney's, Tin House,* and *Conjunctions.* He is the fiction editor of *Fence* magazine and lives in New York and Maine.

Karen McKinnon was selected by Francine Prose to receive the New Voice Fiction Award. "Kindred," her first published story, originally appeared in *Global City Review.* Her first novel, *Narcissus Ascending,* is forthcoming from Picador.

Joyce Carol Oates's novels include *Blonde, We Were the Mulvaneys, Broke Heart Blues, Black Water,* and *Because It Is Bitter, and Because It Is My Heart, them* (for which she received a National Book Award), as well as the forthcoming *The Barrens* (under her pseudonym Rosamund Smith), and *Middle Age: A Romance.* Her stories have appeared in such publications as *Harper's, Playboy, Granta,* and *The Paris Review,* and have been anthologized in *The O. Henry Awards, The Pushcart Prize, The Best American Short Stories of the 20th Century,* and *The Best American Mystery Stories of the 20th Century.*

Dale Peck is the author of *Martin and John, The Law of Enclosures,* and *Now It's Time To Say Goodbye,* as well as numerous shorter pieces published in *Granta, The Nation, Village Voice, Out,* and other publications. He lives in New York City.

Francine Prose is the author of ten novels, most recently, *Blue Angel,* which was nominated for a 2000 National Book Award. Her other books include *Hunters and Gatherers, Bigfoot Dreams and Primitive People,* two story collections, and a collection of novellas titled *Guided Tours of Hell.* Her stories, reviews, and essays have appeared in *The Atlantic Monthly, Harper's, Best American Short Stories, The New Yorker,* the *New York Times,* the *New York Observer, Art News, The Yale Review, The New Republic,* and numerous other publications. She is the winner of a Guggenheim fellowship, a 1989 Fulbright fellowship, two NEA grants, and a PEN translation prize.

Victoria Redel, a poet and fiction writer, is the author of the novel *Loverboy,* a collection of short fiction titled *The Road Bottoms Out,* and *Already the World,* a collection of poems. Her work has been published in numerous journals, including *BOMB, Antioch Review, Missouri Review, StoryQuarterly,* and *The Ohio Review.* She is the recipient of a poetry fellowship from the NEA and the Fine Arts Work Center and teaches at Sarah Lawrence

College, Columbia University, and in the MFA Program in Creative Writing at Vermont College.

Dani Shapiro is a novelist whose books include *Playing with Fire, Fugitive Blue, Picturing the Wreck,* and most recently a memoir, *Slow Motion.* Her work has appeared in *The New Yorker, Granta, Ploughshares,* and other magazines.

Elizabeth Tippens is the author of the novel *Winging It.* Her short stories have appeared in *Harper's, Ploughshares, Mademoiselle,* among other publications; nonfiction in *Rolling Stone* and *Playboy.* She lives in New York City.

PERMISSIONS